THE CULT OF TRULAND

A TALE OF FAME, MURDER AND MAN'S QUEST FOR THE PERFECT TALK SHOW GUEST

KEVIN BRASS

cover design: John Patterson/ShakeWell Creative
interior design: Timothy W. Brittain

Book I

1

Sy Walcott woke up pissed off that morning, which was not unusual. He considered anger a right of old age, sort of like the good parking space at Whole Foods. As he stood in his kitchen mulching oranges with his six-speed juicer, wrapped in the fluffy robe he stole from the Ritz in Bora Bora, he couldn't control the bubbling irritation.

The morning had started with some vagrant pounding on his neighbor's door at 6:30 a.m. Why the hell was some asshole banging on his neighbor's door at *6-fuckin'-30-a.m.?* In this neighborhood? He'd paid $6.5 million for a beach house that looked like a Swiss chalet to get away from that shit. Going back to sleep wasn't going to happen. And then Theresa balked at a little nookie, like she couldn't be bothered. Maybe she'd be a little more accommodating if she was back working as a temp making ten bucks an hour, that's what Sy was thinking.

Taking Theresa's runt dog for a walk on the beach was an option, but the mutt might take a dump on the sand and then the beach Nazis would throw a fit. He was too old to be picking up dog poop. And he couldn't handle one more conversation with that fuckin' lifeguard,

Lieutenant Danny, who never wore a shirt and kept reminding Sy he was a "lieutenant," like maybe that meant he was in hand-to-hand combat in Da Nang.

All in all, it was turning into a fuckin' lousy morning.

Pulverizing the fifth pure navel orange imported from Valencia, extra high in calcium, he was startled by a loud crash. Sy grabbed the remote and turned down the radio, thinking it was another stunt on that dumbass *Kid Mike and Bob* show.

Another crash, more of a clanging sound, metal on metal.

"What now?" he said, the half-squished orange dripping in his hand.

He walked into the living room, the room Theresa had decorated with a collection of Indonesian antiques.

A shadow crossed the side window. Sy froze, his bare feet slapping on the Balinese wood floors.

Somebody was definitely out there. Sy slid behind the wicker couch, which offered little protection. *Damn, Theresa and her bentwood.*

Another crash, followed by a muttered curse. The idiot couldn't seem to navigate the damn trash cans. Sy peered over the couch just in time to see a blur of movement, somebody in a gray sweatshirt running through the alley. Sy stood, half-squished orange at the ready, but the intruder in the hoodie was already through the gate to the beach.

"Fuck me," Sy muttered. "I might as well be in Compton."

Now he'd have to call the beach patrol *again* and warn them that if they didn't corral these hoodlums, he was going to file a federal lawsuit. Shit. He'd probably have to talk to that damn Lieutenant Danny.

Yes, Sy thought, it was definitely turning into one shithouse of a lousy morning.

2

Jake Truland sat next to a hovering microphone in the sealed quiet of the radio studio, bathed in the Ty-D-Bol-blue glow of a neon sign, eerie and cool. Imitation pinewood paneling covered the walls, accented by patches of frayed duct tape and acoustic foam. The maze of simmering neon tubes hanging over the door was shaped in the form of what appeared to be an extremely agitated frog wearing a horned Viking helmet.

"We're the Pagan Gods of Rock," the sound engineer announced, his disembodied voice echoing in the studio's tinny speakers. "You know, hard-rockin' frogs."

The engineer had introduced himself as "Stuart, never Stu." His round Lennon glasses and Day-Glo green scarf were a blur behind the studio's smoky Plexiglas.

"Think, like, really deranged Viking frogs. Maybe you could try it, you know, with a little zip?" A sharp click indicated the discussion was over.

Alone in the studio, bathed in the blue light of the Viking frog,

Jake took a long sip of his triple-dip hazelnut latte. A son of SoCal, he wore a tattered yellow Hawaiian shirts, jeans and sandals. His eyelids were heavy, but every brown hair was neatly in place, giving him the perpetually boyish look that drew comparisons to Bobby Kennedy or Zac Efron, depending on the magazine. He was not a morning person, a story line that Stuart-never-Stu had apparently missed. Jake was hurt, a bit. His morning grumpiness was legendary in the industry, thanks to his appearances on the much-YouTubed "Morning Jerks" three-show arc on *Bobby Jane Talks!* At the end of the first segment, a 300-pound Korean woman had charged the stage, her motives unclear. Bobby Jane's stage crew of ex-SEALs Tasered her into submission. The episode was popular in reruns, especially in Bulgaria, where Bobby Jane was enjoying new life.

This day had started at 6:30 a.m., too early. Vince had sent his nephew, Elgin, to pick Jake up, knowing he would need some encouragement to do a morning radio show in Tijuana. Vince insisted he show up in studio; he said he owed a favor to the station's general manager. "*Kid Mike and Bob* are hot. Tops in 35-to-45 disgruntled housewives," Vince had said. And so Elgin, Vince's nephew, had announced himself by loudly banging on the door of the Del Mar beach house at 6:30, wearing a tattered black KoЯn T-shirt and jeans the color of dirty bathwater.

"Radio history awaits," Elgin proclaimed, pulling his arm over his shoulder like Patton ordering the tanks on to Germany. He led Jake to a vintage canary-yellow PT Cruiser with mag wheels. The door panels featured an artfully painted image of an Amazon warrior queen wielding an ax and sword, her breasts bursting through a leather-studded bra.

In general, Jake tended to avoid drivers. They were typically mindless gossips, uncontrollable, eager to sell any story for a buck. A few years ago, in the Obama years, a driver told *Sizzler* that Jake had spent 36 hours driving around Fresno doing lines of cocaine off Jackie

Conrad's ass, which was only partially true. Ordinarily Jake would have enjoyed the resulting headlines: "A Cheeky Encounter for Jake!" "Blizzard on Mt. Jackie!" But the story broke the same week Vince was pushing a story line about Jake working with blind kids in Ecuador, which made it a case of bad timing.

For as long as he could remember, Jake had jonesed for that kind of attention—the buzz of news coverage, the tingle of a media happening. When he was a kid he'd paged himself in department stores just to hear his name announced over the speakers. He grew up jealous of Baby Jessica, the girl who fell down the well. He looked on with amazement and wonder as the media gathered from all over the world to focus their cameras on the old well, fighting each other for the possibility of a glimpse of the little blonde girl. Baby Jessica could pull a thirty share tomorrow on *Hollywood Now!* if she wanted. You had to respect that.

Jake had never fallen into a well, so he had to work at it. In his early days as a writer, when he was happy for the occasional magazine assignment, Jake eagerly worked the gossip columns and tabloids, mining for that one-line mention, the well-placed photo. In the process, he developed his skills at the well-managed media flurry. No publicist for Jake. After the release of his second book, *Sodom's Niece,* every morning he bought copies of all the New York tabloids. If he wasn't in at least one a week, then his goal was to be in two the next week. He scored his first major coup when he orchestrated an *Exposé* cover story after a weekend spent nude tobogganing in Zermatt with the daughter of Libyan strongman Muammar Qaddafi.

He pursued fame the way an entrepreneur stalks venture capitalists. He worked long hours, never deviating from his goal. Writing was a craft to Jake, a means to an end, a chance to get on the talk shows. His best-selling titles like *The Sequel: Sodom's Nephew,* and *Reagan, My Sweetie* were almost universally savaged by the critics. But they were always discussed, always controversial. His *Book of Truisms* hung at number one on the best-seller list for seventeen weeks. At one point, a *Maxim* poll found more of the magazine's readers knew Jake than knew the vice president of the United States. But only thirteen percent said they had actually read one of his books. To Jake, it didn't really matter.

"Can we try a take now?" Stuart-never-Stu was getting snippy behind the tinted Plexiglas.

Jake positioned himself in front of the hovering microphone. Stuart held his index aloft for a second, threw his scarf over his shoulder, and brought his arm down with a flourish. The neon Viking frog began to blink.

"This is Jake Truland. Remember brain cells die at an extraordinary rate in the morning. I think this station is called X-KUL. Don't know why."

Jake pushed back from the microphone.

"The frog, man. You forgot the frog!" Stuart-Never-Stu's Lennon glasses almost fell off, he was shaking his head so hard.

"The frog?"

"The frog. Ya gotta mention the frog."

"There's a frog rule?" Jake laughed.

"Forget the frog and all sorts of frog shit rains down. Please, please say something about the frog... And I need three seconds more." Click.

Stuart-Never-Stu raised his arm and paused before shooting his finger at Jake, this time with a touch of menace.

"This is Jake Truland, and I don't know about you, but I think X-KUL should stand for X-Sucks. A virus-ridden bot chooses the music. The disc jockeys are losers. And I think the frog has herpes."

"Perfect! Dead on." Stuart-Never-Stu punched a button with the flourish of Othello. "It be digits."

The instant the frog stopped blinking, the studio door burst open and a middle-aged man with a thinning man-fro hustled into the room like a lawyer late for court. A black leather jacket hugged his shoulders; a baby blue dress shirt was open at the neck, revealing a slight whiff of chest hair. A Rotary Club pin twinkled on the narrow leather lapel. He was followed by a short man dressed in black jeans and a black T-shirt, clutching a laptop.

"Stewie, coffee," the man in the black leather jacket snapped as he settled onto the stool across from Jake. "And none of that Kona crap."

Stuart-never-Stu looked like he was about to reply but decided against it. Instead he wheeled and stomped out a back door, the scarf catching air.

The man in the jacket—Kid Mike, leader of the top-rated *Kid Mike and Bob Show*, Jake assumed—was trying hard not to look at Jake, really working at it. No hello. No handshake. He hunched over a stack of papers, urgently shuffling through the pile like maybe he lost his coupon for a free Del Taco combo platter. Jake sipped his coffee. Kid Mike said nothing. His partner, Bob, sat at the far end of the table, intently staring into his laptop.

"So you're Truland?" Kid Mike said finally, without looking up from the papers. "Did Elgin bring your bio?"

Kid Mike looked up and glared at him. If they were on the basketball court, Jake would have slugged him for that look. The guy was screwing with him. A bio? Jake recognized the attitude. Kid Mike was working either the *I'm-tired-of-you-pampered-stars* line or the always-popular *Truland-is-sacrilegious-scum* angle.

Schmooze was worth a try. "Look, Mike, I'm a fan. I was really impressed with your unemployed white women numbers. Really strong. You should be proud."

He gave Kid Mike the big smile, the one *People* magazine mentioned when he was third runner-up for "Sexiest Man Alive" in 2010. "His smile could freeze a yoga class in mid–downward dog!!!" the magazine proclaimed, earning Jake the coveted three exclamation marks.

"Quit the crap. And it's *Kid* Mike. Don't call me Mike. OK? I had it legally changed. Not Kid. Not Mike. *Kid Mike.*"

Kid Mike gave him the glare again. Bob sat silently, hunched over his laptop.

"I'm the assistant program manager here, not some piss-ant DJ, OK? My boss wanted you. You're here. But I don't give—"

"Maybe, we—"

"—diddly-squat. You may be some big shot, but what you wrote about the King was just plain wrong."

Ah, so it was *Truland is sacrilegious scum*. Bummer. There was no bantering with the sacrilegious-scum crowd. Kid Mike was apparently part of the large and vocal contingent who believed Jake's latest book, the semibiographical historical novel *Blue Suede Pimp*, was a tad insulting to the Elvis legend.

"Ten seconds," Stuart-Never-Stu said through the speaker, apparently ignoring Kid Mike's coffee request.

Jake considered his responses. This could go a lot of ways. Dead cat mode was always an option. He could answer the snippy questions, offer a few vaguely controversial sound bites, and maybe spark a couple of Babblecock stir-ups. But Kid Mike was easy prey. And Wednesday was traditionally a slow news day....

Stuart twirled behind the tinted glass and shot his finger at Kid Mike. Ted Nugent's "Cat Scratch Fever" welled up in the speakers. Bob's finger danced across his laptop. The neon frog started flashing.

3

Later, Trulandniks would carefully dissect and examine the events of that morning, often finding profound significance in the exchange at the radio station. Some contributors to *The Blurb* said that without a doubt, Truland knew what was to come, that he'd had a premonition. Much was made of a helicopter seen in the area around the time Truland left the station.

For Roger Talbot it started the same as any other Wednesday, his favorite day of the week. The *Del Mar Gazette* came out on Wednesday, and there were no deadlines for two days. Beyond fielding calls from a few irate readers and accepting congratulations for his latest column, he didn't have to do crap on Wednesday. And on this sunny Wednesday he was choosing not to do crap. Maybe he'd go for a jog on the beach, he thought as he settled into his Office Depot desk chair with the *Los Angeles Times* sports section arrayed in front of him. Or maybe he'd pull on the wet suit and splash in the waves for a while; maybe smoke a joint under the lifeguard stand.

A knock interrupted his planning. A tall blonde woman waved

at him through the office window. An old friend from Seaside High, Sandy ran a one-stool hair salon next door. Her salon, like his office, featured a wide window fronting the Coast Highway. While Roger usually hid in his office, Sandy waved to people walking down the street, a staple of Del Mar's social scene.

Roger tried to ignore her. She tapped on the window again. He raised the *Times*. A beat later she stuck her head through the front door, which he had forgotten to lock.

"Hi cutie," she said. "Did you hear about the fire?"

"Yeah, of course," he said, lying.

Damn. Sandy always scooped him. He was supposed to be the man in the know, the clued-in newspaper guy. The Web site promised "Del Mar's latest." How the hell would she know about a fire?

He looked out the window. Traffic did seem a bit heavy. He waved at Sandy. "On it," he said, moving papers around his desk.

He turned on the scanner, which produced a range of squawks and gibberish—lots of dialogue for a Wednesday morning, excited voices. Something was going on.

"Sounds like a house going up in the valley," Sandy said.

"Yeah, that sounds about right." He feigned interest in the scanner traffic, punching the volume button, stalling for time.

Roger weighed his options. It might be news. He could call up Miles, the fire department flack, maybe head down the highway to check it out. But it was Wednesday. And the front page of the *Times* sports section beckoned with two features and a column on the Lakers' new point guard from Mongolia.

"I think I'm going to send out Jane," he said. Jane was the *Gazette*'s newest reporter. She was still more housewife than journalist, but she was eager to get back into the swing of things now that her three kids were off to college. Hell, Jane would probably be excited about a house fire.

4

Jake and Elgin saw the smoke as they crested Del Mar Heights, revealing a 180-degree view of the Pacific over the crowns of the eucalyptus and pine trees. At the bottom of the hill they hit a traffic jam, a long line of cars on the Coast Highway, barely moving, clogging the intersection. Elgin rolled down the window of the PT Cruiser and clasped his hands together, begging an old lady in a Cadillac to let him into line. She ignored him.

A coastal breeze was blowing the smoke inland, spreading it out like a black flamenco fan. Through the Cruiser's sunroof, Jake could smell the ash, the odor of burning wood. Elgin nervously cranked the sunroof closed.

The Coast Highway was a parking lot. All around, drivers were dealing with the situation in the singular style employed by Southern Californians when faced with a commuting disaster. The initial anger of horns and shouted ethnic slurs was dissolving into a communal calm. To his left, Jake saw a woman flat-ironing her hair in front of a drop-down cosmetic mirror, using her knees to steer. Ahead, a pair of college-age men in shorts and tank tops abandoned their pickup and set up lawn chairs on the grass along the side of the road. Stretching out in their lawn chairs, they pulled beers from a plastic cooler. Two news helicopters hovered overhead, circling around the edges of the dark cloud of smoke.

"We need some tunes," Elgin said as he plopped back on to his sheepskin seat cover. The stereo burst on. An announcer's hurried voice screamed major breaking news.

"—origins are unknown, but the inferno is threatening several homes in the Del Mar area, caring not a whit for the valiant efforts of firefighters who—"

"Dude, we need tunes," Elgin repeated, punching a button and calling up the thumping bass of early Linkin Park.

Jake punched it back to the news station. Elgin winced and tightened his grip on the wheel, years of requests to turn down the music boiling inside him.

"We go now to Mark McLemore at the scene of the Del Mar inferno," said the announcer, the "care not a whit" voice. "Mark, what can you tell us?"

"At least one house has been partially destroyed, Ken. Fire department officials are refusing to estimate the economic impact of the inferno, but damages are thought to be in the thousands. That's an exclusive quote, Ken. He definitely said damages *in the thousands.*"

His voice wavering a bit, Mark said the smoke had grown so intense he was forced to back off to the safety of Bully's, a local restaurant and bar, which he described as "a community relief center."

"Mark, you take care of yourself," Ken said, striking a fatherly tone.

"Ken, I'm only doing my job."

The base of the smoke funnel rose from the valley north of town, where a side road led to a strip of beachfront houses. A lagoon and railroad tracks separated the stretch of homes from the Del Mar race-track, "Where the Turf Meets the Surf."

Jake's house was in the center of that coastal strip, a few doors down from Burt Bacharach's old place.

Jake looked at Elgin. Elgin nervously looked at the cars boxing them in. Then they both looked at the bike lane.

"Just get me close," Jake said.

"Dude, no way."

"Elgin, I just want closer."

"I can't..."

"Elgin, don't be a wimp."

"But, dude, there are cops everywhere. And, you know, it's no big deal, but, I, you know, I've had some trouble...."

"Elgin, closer. That's all I'm asking." Jake tried to calibrate the epi-center of the smoke cloud. "You can do this. No big deal. Just get me *closer.*"

Elgin straightened up, gripping the steering wheel at ten and two. After a quick glance over his shoulder, he eased the Cruiser into the empty lane and nudged the gas. Several drivers cursed at him. The guys in the lawn chairs raised their beers in a toast. After a block, two cars pulled out and followed.

Elgin was leading a parade now and his confidence grew.

"Go for it, Elgin," Jake said.

A parked Ford jutted out into the bike lane. Jake saw it first. Elgin didn't waver. He moved the wheel a fraction of an inch, his arms extended straight out, an F1 driver navigating a tricky chicane. They missed the Ford's bumper by no more than an inch.

"Dude, I'm Dale-fuckin'-Earnhardt," Elgin said.

Jake heard the sound of a skidding car behind them, the screech of brakes locking up.

Elgin sped up. Jake looked at the speedometer.

"Maybe we should slow—"

Elgin twisted the wheel to his left, making a sweeping turn onto the beach road, ignoring a red light and the blaring whistle of an angry traffic cop. And then the bike lane ended, blocked by parked cars. Elgin jerked the wheel to the right, sending the Cruiser, tires straining, onto a steep driveway leading to a parking garage.

"End of the line, dude," Elgin said, yanking up the emergency brake.

As Jake jumped out, the traffic cop ran up, panting, his belly bobbing against his gun belt.

"You two are in big trouble," he said, gasping for air. He appeared to be reaching for his gun.

"Officer, do you know who I am?" Jake said, flinching as the words came out. He never used those words, the tackiest line in the business. Truism #18: *If you have to tell someone you're famous, you're not.* But he was mesmerized by the black plume of smoke.

"Hey, wait a minute…" The moment of recognition.

"I live down there. Call your boss. I'm sure it will be OK." Jake hurried past the cop without waiting for a reply.

"Yeah, chill out," Elgin yelled.

Jake ducked under a ribbon of yellow tape and moved down the hill. The smoke blocked the morning sun and made his eyes water. A light flurry of ash created a ghostly winter scene. He heard the helicopters overhead but couldn't see them. Waves of heat and thin mist from the water hoses splashed across his face. Every few steps he tripped over the thick hoses that covered the road.

Parts of the house were still on fire. Slivers of orange and yellow flickered at the base of a wide black tornado rising from what was once his kitchen. The north side of the house was a blanket of flame. Three streams of water pummeled the flames; firemen fought to hold on to the thick hoses. The twin thirty-foot palm trees that framed his patio were ablaze, the flames shooting into the sky.

Through the smoke he saw Sy Walcott's house, the one that

looked like a Swiss chalet. Walcott, dressed in a silver Nike sweat suit, was frantically hurling a blanket across a burning wood sculpture of a dolphin. He was screaming at a group of firemen, pleading with them to redirect their hoses at the sculpture. The firemen ignored him.

The north side of Jake's house was completely engulfed, but the south face appeared almost untouched. A bay window, a strange rustic touch in the stark modern design, floated in the midst of the flames. *Architectural Digest* had blurbed about the bay window in a feature, praising its "humanness." The photographer on that shoot had also liked the media room, especially the wall devoted to tapes of Jake's talk show appearances, including what were always referred to as "the rare Maury Povich tapes." The media room looked surprisingly intact, a colorful island surrounded by a black shell of ash and burnt wood.

A fireman in a bright orange jacket and yellow helmet stuck out his arm and blocked Jake's path. "Whoa, you stop here," he said.

Jake pushed forward. "It's my house."

"I know, I know," the fireman said, walking backward but keeping his arm locked in front of Jake.

"Do you know who—"

"I know exactly who you are," the fireman said, stopping suddenly, his arm a fence rail. "And you stop, now! There is nothing you can do. You and I are going to walk back fifteen yards. Right now."

Jake obeyed but kept his gaze on the house. As he watched, the south wall collapsed, sending up an explosion of sparks and flame. Ash and debris filled the sky.

"There go the Povich tapes," he said out loud to no one in particular.

5

Eric Branson was cooking breakfast in the fire station when the call came in. Most firefighters maneuver to avoid cooking chores. Some play possum, cranking out burned hamburgers and dry chicken, just to get out of the duty. But Eric liked the job. To him, it was a way to bond with the crew, an opportunity for a green kid with a college pedigree to win friends. In his second week at North City 222, Eric whipped up a chicken Parmesan that earned him weeks of respect from his station mates.

This morning he was working on eggs Benedict, always a challenge. He was whisking egg yolks when his radio crackled.

"Hope you aren't setting out the china," the chief said, his bullhorn voice blasting from the two-way radio.

"Somehow I knew my hollandaise was ruined," Eric replied. He was, in fact, disappointed.

"Better get out here soon. It's got weird written all over it."

"Weird? Good weird?"

"I'd say bad weird," the chief said.

By the time Eric worked his way through traffic, there was little remaining of the house. Light smoke billowed from piles of black rubble. Firefighters sat on the curb looking bored, while probies rolled up the hoses. Some wandered through the wreckage, occasionally swatting at something with an ax. This was how things usually stood when he arrived. Nothing remained except a mystery.

A man wearing a red bombardier jacket and a bright yellow helmet approached, not smiling. "Eric, it's about time you made it."

"Sorry, Chief."

"I'm fairly PO'ed I missed out on your eggs Benedict." The chief jabbed a finger at him. "Tomorrow. Make sure you use a little of that, ya know, Chinese mustard. And no candy-ass excuses." Chief Ron Donatello liked his eggs Benedict with a kick.

"I think this is a good one for you, Eric," the chief said. "I don't see no kids playing with matches around here. No signs of electrical problems. Flared up real quick. We never had a chance."

Eric took out his notebook.

"The guy over there, the old guy in the silver sweat suit shouting at Tank?" The chief pointed at a short balding man gesturing wildly at a burly fireman. "He says he saw a guy in a hoodie in the alley a few minutes before all hell broke loose."

The man was pointing over and over again at the fire damage to his house, which Eric thought resembled a Swiss chalet.

"He seems to think it was rogue gang activity," the chief said. "I don't think he's going to be much help."

"I'll eagerly await Tank's report," Eric said. "Anyone inside?"

"Nope. But get this. The owner is Jake-fuckin'-Truland."

Eric followed the chief's gaze to a tall man with wavy brown hair in a Hawaiian shirt and jeans moving across the street, holding a phone to his ear. An overweight woman in her 40s ducked under the yellow police tape and scurried over to the man, a pen and magazine in her hands. The man maintained the cell phone under his ear and signed an autograph with his off hand without breaking stride, a feat of impressive fluidity.

"Who?" Eric asked.

"Jake Truland. Come on, man, even Mr. Ivy League must have heard of Jake Truland?"

Eric winced. He was tired of explaining to the crew that San Jose State wasn't Ivy League. "Yeah, right, Truland, sure." The name did sound kind of familiar. Eric wrote the name in his notebook. The chief rolled his eyes. And then Eric's attention turned to the smoldering house.

The house looked like a giant derrick had scooped out the interior, leaving only a blackened frame. Piles of ash, burnt wood, and gelatinous heaps of smoldering materials covered the area where the house had collapsed on itself. Anything that couldn't burn, like the refrigerator and washing machine, stood as partially melted statues, covered in black soot.

Eric walked slowly through the site, examining each pile of ash, starting from the outside and working in. Pools of water covered the area, and the burned wood let off slivers of steam. Occasionally he stopped and used a Swiss Army knife to pry off small pieces of wood or prick at a pile of ash, depositing each sample in a little plastic bag.

After completing a circle of the house, he found Truland sitting in the courtyard of a small Mediterranean bungalow across the street from the beach. He was talking to a hyper kid in a KoЯn T-shirt.

Eric walked up and flashed his badge.

"I gotta go," the KoЯn fan said, wheeling and heading for the street.

Eric turned to Truland. "I'm with the fire department."

"Do you know who has been contacted?" Truland said.

"Contacted?"

"I don't do Fox."

Eric was confused.

"And I'm not going to do any one-on-ones, be clear about that."

"I'm not media relations, Mr. Truland." Eric pulled out his badge again. "I'm the investigator on the case."

"There's a case?"

"I need to ask a few questions."

As they moved toward a stone table, Truland suddenly stopped, grabbed Eric's right shoulder, and momentarily lowered his head a few inches. For a split second he didn't move. Eric thought he might be having a seizure. Then Truland's head bounced back up.

"Sorry, photo op," Truland said. "That guy over my shoulder in the alley dressed like a lizard? He strings for *Sizzler*."

Eric saw a man in a long leather jacket and a scraggly beard with three cameras dangling from his neck. He was holding one camera high above his head, trying to get around the outstretched arms of a uniformed cop, who was fending him off like a basketball forward guarding the hoop.

Eric wasn't sure he understood what had just happened.

"Couldn't resist," Truland said. "Habit."

They sat at the stone table. "Mr. Truland, tell me about your whereabouts this morning."

"I didn't burn down my own house," Truland said with a wry grin, which made Eric smile, too, like he couldn't help it.

"It's routine," Eric said. In fact, it was routine—establishing a timeline, going through the basics. "Did anybody else have access to the house?"

"No, no one."

"Not even a maid, someone like that?"

"You can't have a maid in my line of work."

"Excuse me?"

"Maids."

"No maids?"

"You can't control maids," Truland said. "They sell stories to the tabs. And they steal. Suddenly your home movies are on TV, and you don't even have a distribution deal."

Eric wrote in his notebook, "No maids."

Something about Truland looked odd to Eric. He was strangely emotionless, seemingly unaffected by the fire. Truland efficiently detailed his morning schedule, describing some sort of confrontation with a DJ in Tijuana like it was a meeting with his banker.

"Anybody else have a key? A friend? Relative?"

"No...yes, well...Becky, of course."

"Becky?"

"Becky Hooks. My friend." The way he said it made Eric think she was more than a friend. He wrote down, "Becky Hooks?"

"Does she live here?"

"No."

"Was she here today?"

"No, she's not here. She's never here. She lives in Texas. Austin."

"Bitter girlfriend? Angry boyfriend?" Eric wrote in his notebook. "Any reason to believe someone may have wanted to burn down your house?"

That made Truland stop. For the first time he seemed to be calculating his response.

"Sure, lots of people," Truland said. "Too many to name."

"But recently? Now? A new threat?"

"None that I can think of."

"But you're thinking of old threats, maybe?" Eric caught a slight waver in Truland's attitude.

"I get threats all the time. Most I don't take seriously. Right now the Prince of Wales is really angry with me. So is a biker gang in El Cajon. Look, I'll have my associate send over some names. Most of it is online."

Eric could tell the interview was winding up. Truland was reaching for his phone.

"How long have you lived here?" Eric asked.

"Six years." Truland was moving into his phone.

"It's a great spot," Eric said, nodding toward the water. "I surf Fifteenth Street. Still my favorite break."

Truland turned to look at him, perhaps sizing him up for the first time. "I haven't seen you...yeah, I guess I *have* seen you in the water."

"I'm usually out pretty early," Eric said.

"More of a sunset guy myself." Truland's demeanor shifted. "You longboard, right? Old school."

"I like the slow breaks off Fifteenth."

"Yeah, I bodysurf. So I end up at Grandview and—"

Truland paused. "Eric, is it? Look, Eric, I know you're just doing your job, but I really don't think this is arson. I probably just left my iron on."

Eric left Truland in the courtyard. As he crossed the street he detected an audible murmur from the crowd, only to sense it subside when they realized Truland wasn't with him. The crowd covered the street and the opposite sidewalk, penned in by yellow tape and a phalanx of bored-looking cops. A photographer working for the sheriff's department roamed the tape line shooting faces in the crowd—standard procedure, in case the perp returned to the scene of the crime.

Eric's report to the chief was brief. "Something's up," he said.

"Great, just what we need. Cum-plex-a-tees," the chief said. "What is it?"

"You were right about the gas traces."

"Gas traces. Yeah, that's kinda relevant."

"There are several flash points. And as far as I can tell, seems like a wide variety of suspects. Do you know anything about a friend, a..." Eric flipped through his pad. "Becky Hooks?"

"Sure, Rebecca Hooks. Ya really gotta pick up a *Sizzler* from time to time, kid."

"What about her?"

"You'd know if you ever went out and mingled with the real world. She's a lawyer. And a real looker, considering she's a lawyer and all."

"Are they...an item?"

"Item? What kind of word is that? You mean are they doing the dirty deed?"

Eric winced.

"Who knows?" the chief said. "That's part of the deal. No one really knows for sure. Personally, I think he's banging her. I mean, if I—"

"Chief."

"Yeah, right." The chief pointed at the smoldering house. "So what do ya think? You ready to say somebody torched the house of our fine, upstanding Mr. Celebrity?"

Eric hesitated. "Don't know. I need to wait for the lab."

"But you think something's up, and for that you're going to make my life miserable for a while. Ain't that right?"

"Maybe." Eric liked it when the chief went into his battered old cop routine. "Either way, I think you might want to be careful about what you tell the horde," Eric said, nodding at the reporters, who were crowding around the short balding man in the silver sweat suit.

"Right, careful. You know me. I'm always careful."

The chief walked toward the mob of reporters with his arms out, calling out to them in his booming voice, which could shake the rafters of the firehouse. "OK, you jackals," he yelled, "line up for your feeding."

Not far away, a gangly, pot-bellied man in an oil-stained gray sweatshirt moved through the crowd. He avoided the line of photographers, sliding along the back of the crush of people straining to glimpse the remains of the flames. Even on his tiptoes, he couldn't see anything. So he jostled and pushed through the crowd, ignoring the protests.

Soon he was on the sidewalk that ran along the beach side of the street, standing next to a bored-looking policeman who was leaning against a palm tree. Nearby a Happy 8 news van worked through the mass of people. The crowd surged toward the van, hoping to catch a glimpse of one of the Happy 8 news team. Several cops waded into the crowd, urging people to move back.

The man quickly looked around. No one was paying attention to him. In the crowd, a woman was screaming and hopping up and down, yelling that the Happy 8 news van had run over her foot. "*I'm going to sue! I'm going to sue!*" Firefighters carrying medical equipment hurried to her aid.

When he was sure no one was watching, the man in the gray hoodie jogged to an alley between the house that looked like King Arthur's castle and the one that looked like a Swiss chalet. He quickly unlatched a gate and moved down the narrow cobblestone path. When he reached the gate that led to the beach he paused, listening, breathing heavily. He looked back. No one was following.

That night Roger Talbot left Bully's early so he could catch the evening news shows. He guessed Jane had caught the basics of the fire for her online story, but it was Jake's house, and he knew that changed everything.

Hollywood Now! opened with the sound of electronic drums pulsating over aerial footage of flames consuming the beach house. A sultry woman's voice rose above the music. "Hades' fire reached for mysterious hunk Jake Truland today." The music surged. "The flames spared Truland's soul, but not his lavish Del Mar beach mansion." A fanfare worthy of Nero's entrance to Rome filled the speakers. "I'm Tammy Bandita and this is *Hollywood Now!*"

Images of celebrities on red carpet and probing searchlights swirled across the screen. "You're here, *now*," a deep male voice proclaimed, "behind the scenes of the most glamorous place on Earth,

Culver City, California, just a stone's throw and a martini swirl from Hollywood...."

The camera swished from a view of a palm tree to a tight shot of Tammy Bandita at the anchor desk, her hair blown slightly by unseen winds, a hint of cleavage glowing.

"Jake Truland is alive this morning—but just barely. A fire that started under...sas-spi-shuss circumstances"—she drew out the word "suspicious," a slight lisp adding an alluring tone—"devastated Truland's beautiful beachfront mansion." She paused, a moment's breath. "The same beautiful mansion *Hollywood Now!* showed you *exclusively* six months ago."

Cut to video of Truland's patio six months ago, with the Swedish deck chairs and the Philippe Starck–designed suntan lotion table.

"Now it is nothing more than a burning mass of broken dreams." Cut to video of the patio in flames.

Another swish and the camera was back on Tammy in the studio. Pausing, she turned her left shoulder toward the camera, letting her blouse dip a millimeter. "*Hollywood Now!* has learned San Diego County officials believe something is very weird about this case." Like magic, a graphic appeared over her right shoulder, superimposing an old promo picture of Truland over a blurry shot of the smoldering fire, with the headline in dripping red letters, "Truland's Hell." She paused and raised her left eyebrow. "Stay tuned to *Hollywood Now!* for *exclusive* details on Truland's hot tragedy."

Roger was enthralled. She made "exclusive details" sound like a whispered invitation in a dark bar moments after last call.

6

Q: *What did you want to be when you grew up?*

Jake Truland: *Older.*

Q: *Come on, no grand plan?*

JT: *Do you remember those nude photos of Madonna that mysteriously showed up in Playboy, right around when her albums started to tank?*

Q: *Sure, I loved those photos. Black and whites. Lots of torn wifebeaters.*

JT: *Right. I always wondered about her armpit hair.*

Q: *Excuse me?*

JT: *Think about it. She was about to strip down for a guy with a camera. Why didn't she shave her armpit hair?*

Q: *Maybe she was going Euro.*

JT: *Maybe, but this is Madonna. She was probably making publicity decisions in the crib.*

Q: *I guess... I never...*

JT: *So was she thinking that armpit fur would help her vibe*

*in the bohemian demo? Or was she forecasting a change in
personal hygiene politics?*
Q: *Or maybe she just was, you know, kinda gross.*
JT: *Exactly.*

— From "The Lost Interview"

At 6:45 a.m. the *Hollywood Now!* studio was a buzz of activity centered around a long narrow room lined with small cubicles. Segment producers scurried from edit bay to edit bay, looking at tape, exhorting editors to hurry, pleading with others to insert or delete clips. The room zipped and burped with the sound of a dozen different music tracks and narrations starting, stopping, rewinding, and fast forwarding, mixing with the harried screeches of over-stressed reporters and producers working the phones with their already caffeinated counterparts on the East Coast.

Jessie Dunbar sat in front of a wall of monitors on the raised round platform known as the bridge, intently watching the previous night's show, oblivious to the bedlam around her. Every morning she scanned the show for mistakes and potential problems as she ate her breakfast of fruit bowl, protein bar, and Red Bull in preparation for her morning meeting with her boss, Sharon Jones-Jones.

It was always a meeting fraught with danger. After Sharon Jones-Jones's three decades in the trenches, no one doubted her Hollywood savvy and ruthlessness. And no one made fun of her name. She was born Sharon Jones and married Abraham Jones, a party-loving movie producer with a cozy Malibu bungalow. When they divorced after 13 months, citing "mutual emotional duress," she kept the dual names, under the theory that Jones-Jones was "historically accurate," although it's doubtful anyone ever thought of Sharon as much of a history buff. Through two subsequent marriages she adamantly refused to add the names of her spouses, although she occasionally signed documents

"Sharon Jones-Jones-Rodriquez-Qi," the last reflecting her short but tumultuous alliance with a Korean media magnate.

Every morning for the past year Jessie and Sharon had met at 7:00 a.m. to review the previous night's show. It had been their daily ritual ever since Sharon plucked Jessie from the Bunny Patch, the pool of eager segment producers, anointing her at a youngish-looking 31 as the show's senior broadcast producer. Jessie always cringed at the idea of returning to the Bunny Patch—fighting and clawing for choice assignments, sabotaging a friend for a chance at a Justin Bieber baby scandal story. Even worse, she feared going back to local TV news, the TV wasteland. That would never happen—*never happen*—and she often swore to do whatever it took to make sure she never again spent her days bantering with prima donna weathermen and American Legion bake sale organizers. Jessie approached each morning meeting with Sharon Jones-Jones warily, ready for the land mines.

Huddled on the bridge, her sweater pulled tight against the air conditioning, set low to cool the video equipment, Jessie was feeling good about last night's show. No fireworks, nothing to upset Sharon's conference call with Farmore corporate. Truland was a no-brainer, consistently popular with the core audience, according to internal Farmore studies. She scanned the overnights. All the numbers were up from last week, typically between 1.3 to 2.7 percent, with the biggest bounces in the 43 markets where Farmore owned stations. Moving into Sharon's office at exactly 7:00, Jessie felt she was on firm footing.

Sharon was talking on the phone. She pointed to the black-and-chrome chair in front of her black-and-chrome desk. Sharon liked the ruthless bitch look, which Jessie respected. Sharon had succeeded in an era when every ex-cheerleader and failed porn star wanted to work in TV news.

On Sharon's vanity wall Jessie noted a picture of Truland and Sharon huddled over a table at the Casa de Guac. Truland had set it up, Sharon explained during Jessie's first visit to the office. He tipped a photographer from the *Hollywood Tattler* about the dinner date as a little gift for Sharon. The *Tattler* was thrilled to get a photo of Truland, but the editors were enraged to find him sitting next to the executive producer of a competitor. Ultimately, they ran the photo anyway, with a headline referring to Truland's companion only as an "unidentified Hollywood party girl."

Sharon wasn't saying much on the phone. She nodded over and over again. "Right. Uh huh. Right." When Sharon hung up, Jessie could tell she wasn't in gal pal mood. Sharon's face was so red, the tinted wave of hair cascading across her forehead seemed to light up. Jessie raced through the rundown from last night's show in her mind, trying to figure out what may have stirred corporate. The report on Stan Bean's affair with his costar? Speculation about the Prince of Earl's new girlfriend?

"You know what it was." Sharon said, flashing her ability to shoot info-digesting laser beams into Jessie's head.

Jessie hesitated. "No, not specifically…"

"Bambi? Bambi doesn't ring a bell?"

Bambi rang a bell. Last night's show included a 20-second voice over on Bambi Lambard's lawsuit against Prodorp Productions, charging the company with firing her for refusing to get a boob job in preparation for her role in its latest remake of Chekov's "The Seagull." The *New York Times* called it Titgate. Yesterday's report was a simple court update, after a judge refused her lawyer's request to subpoena a porn actress to testify as an expert witness on the physiological implications of fake breasts. "Bambi vows to fight on, even though she knows the odds are against her," Tammy read as the cameras zeroed in on Bambi's sad eyes, before cutting to a shot of her looking despondent in a Suzy Wong thong bikini.

"Bambi?" Jessie couldn't think of anything to say. "You didn't like the bikini shot?"

"Don't be an ass." Sharon glared at her, a puma ready to pounce.

Jessie tried to remember the script. It was a fairly standard VO/SOT. And it was a D-block story, practically a throwaway.

"That girl's a tramp," Sharon said. "A two-bit slut. It should have played as a stripper looking for an easy buck." Sharon turned to her computer, clearly not interested in discussing the topic. "She's trying to gouge Prodorp, and you made her into a hero."

"But that's how the story played." Jessie didn't get out of the Bunny Patch without showing some backbone. "Did you see those tears? Those were real."

Sharon whipped around and slapped her palm on the desk, loud and sharp. Jessie winced. "Let me make this clear. You missed the story. We're done with Bambi. No more Bambi. Bambi is toast."

Sharon put on her reading glasses with cold precision and began to scan the script from the show. The topic was closed.

"Where did this bit about something weird in Del Mar come from?"

"That was me," Jessie said.

"Who was the source?"

"A contact who works for the county in San Diego. He was listening to the scanner and heard a fireman refer to it as weird."

"Weird in what way?"

"He didn't know...just that it was weird."

"Your source, he works for the fire department?"

"No, waste management."

"What the hell does someone in waste management know about a fire?"

"Nothing. But he is a San Diego County official, and he heard them say on the scanner it sounded weird. That's all we said. It's clean."

Sharon seemed satisfied. "OK. Now, who the hell made Tammy say 'suspicious'? One of the writers fucking with her again?"

Jessie had known this was coming. Everyone knew Tammy had

problems with multisyllabic S-words. "It was just a mistake. It slipped through. Tom wrote it. He's new."

"How 'bout 'mysterious' next time?" Sharon said, giving Jessie a slight wink over her glasses. The linguistic challenges of the anchor represented their shared burden. Once Tammy had gone over their heads and sent a personal complaint to Ralph Farmore himself, after a script made two references to Sarah Stanislaw, an actress making news for a sex tape. Tammy thought it was a deliberate attempt to make fun of her speech impediment. Her agent threatened to sue under the Disabilities Act.

Jessie quickly moved through the list of possible stories for that night's show. There was a behind-the-scenes report on the new Farmore Studios release starring Reese Witherspoon as an enterprising lawyer who poses for *Hustler*. Witherspoon wouldn't talk, but *HN!* had an exclusive interview with her 14-year-old costar, who was recently captured by a cell phone camera doing tequila shots in a Santa Monica dive bar. And they were ready to run an exclusive interview with Betty Aquilar, the star of a new hit hospital show, who was accused of calling a costar the n-word during a network party.

But Jessie knew there was only one story. Truland. Fire. Possibly arson? Everything else was simply filler. Sure, it was only a house fire. Back in Phoenix, a house fire wouldn't make the 5:00 p.m. news. And she realized this house was owned by a legend of the cheap attention-getting stunt. But that didn't matter. It was Truland...and fire. And they needed a lead, preferably a story they could arc over the next few days. Heck, she might get a month out of it. The holidays were coming up. They could only do so many celebrity turkey giveaways.

"Was it arson?" Sharon asked.

"The official fire department statement calls it a 'fire under investigation.' But it looks pretty damn ominous."

"One of those Elvis wackos?"

"Who knows?"

"But you think there's something more there?"

"Yes, definitely." Jessie had prepared for this moment. She had already decided to commit to Truland, all in. "This could be a big one. I feel it."

"Spidey sense?"

"Yes, definitely Spidey sense."

"OK, let's not screw around then. Full court press. Everybody is going to want a piece of this one."

Jessie knew the score. They spent ten minutes working the angles and potential headlines.

"I don't want to be seeing any exclusives on *Inside News*," Sharon said. "Do whatever it takes. Tell Vince he's got to play ball on this one."

Jessie gathered up her pads and started to leave, her marching orders clear. This was DEFCON 4.

"Oh, and Jessie?" Sharon stopped her in her tracks. She used her Commander-in-Chief voice. "Do what you have to do, but no helicopters, OK? Corporate is going apeshit over the helicopter budget."

7

"What's this about a fight at a radio station?" Vince bent over the *Herald,* shoveling Canter's famous matzo brei into his mouth.

"It was nothing," Jake said. They were in a corner booth, hogging a red vinyl half-circle designed for eight. Canter's, located a couple of blocks from the CBS Studios and open 24 hours, was a legendary haunt of old Hollywood, once the place to see a trashed Ava Gardner or Warren Beatty on a late-night prowl. Then it was overrun in the '70s with bingeing rock stars and Benzedrine hounds who sat in the booths at 3:00 a.m. and poured sugar into their water. This morning, the customers were a trio of black-clad rockers, a couple of old writers from *M*A*S*H,* and a swivel-headed family of six from Tucson.

"Says here you were in a fight with a DJ," Vince said.

"It was no big deal."

"This is not bad. Listen to this."

Vince read out loud:

"Just hours earlier, Truland was in an on-air confrontation with a rock 'n' roll disc jockey in Tijuana.

Truland was defending his latest work on XKUL-FM, the "Pagan Gods of Rock," when a conflict arose with disc jockey Kid Mike, a.k.a. Leonard Blackman.

The altercation began during a discussion of Truland's book, Blue Suede Pimp, *a quasi-fictional account of Elvis Presley's life. A group called the Society for Elvis' Living Trust recently encouraged people to burn copies of the book and staged a demonstration outside the New York offices of Farmore Media, the book's publisher.*

Professional acoustic specialist Stu Radcliffe said a fight broke out during one of the commercial breaks, soon after Truland made a remark about the color of the disc jockey's leisure suit..."

Vince stopped reading. "He was wearing a leisure suit?"

Jake felt the need to refocus the conversation. "Vince, my house just burned down."

"I love that they mentioned the book."

"Everything I own is gone."

"This is great. This is perfect," Vince said. "We can leak that the police are interviewing the DJ. Every time they mention the investigation, they'll have to mention the book."

"I was talking to the DJ on the air when the fire broke out. There are recordings. I doubt he'll be much of a suspect."

A thick-thighed waitress wearing a hairnet and a faded yellow uniform appeared before them, pad in hand. Jake ordered the matzo ball soup. Without looking up from her pad, she turned and left.

"Soup is appetizer food, Jake, you really should take better care of yourself." Vince spent forty-five minutes at the gym every morning and subscribed to *Men's Health*, making him a fitness expert.

"Vince..."

"OK, OK, I'm sorry." Vince reached across the table and put a hand lock on his forearm, using the grip formed with regular stops at the Gripilizer machine. "I know, it's tough. Everything was destroyed?"

"Everything."

"Even the Maury Povich tapes, you said?"

"Everything."

"That's tough. This must be a very hard time for you." Vince was using his best consoling voice. Then he broke into a broad smile. "There. Happy? Now, do you want to do *Cathy!* or *Wolf*? Your choice."

"You know, Vince. You're a dick."

"There's no reason to mope, that's all I'm saying. But I got it. You had a rough night." Vince was serious again. "You know you could have come by the house, right? Crashed at my place for one night."

Jake sighed. This was a recurring sore point between the two of them. For 20 years Vince had served as his agent, booker, mouthpiece, and occasional spy. But Jake traveled alone—no entourage, no personal assistant, no handler—and he never told Vince where he stayed, never. Vince always offered to let him stay at his place when he was in LA; Jake always refused.

Vince's irritation level increased after Jake pulled his Salinger, disappearing for two years. Though one stretch, *Where Is Truland?* was a minor cable sensation. His Q rating skyrocketed. Occasional sightings of Jake eating chicken-fried steak in a Phoenix diner or playing craps at a Macau casino fueled the mystery. He won an Emmy in absentia for Best Performance in an Extended News Cycle (Six Months or Longer). *Bartlett's Mobile* routinely listed him as one of the world's most-quoted celebrities, despite his going more than three years without giving an interview.

During his Salinger, Jake occasionally sent cryptic messages to Vince hinting of shark fishing in Polynesia or goat farming in West Texas but never told him his real location. Vince always answered questions about Jake's whereabouts with a wink, implying knowledge he didn't actually possess.

After Jake dramatically reappeared, popping up on the final episode of *Survivor: Des Moines,* he continued to hide his movements from Vince, more out of habit than strategy. It was part of the game. Vince never knew when Jake might appear unannounced at his office or his favorite restaurant, and Vince never ceased to be annoyed by Jake's mysterious travels.

Last night, after renting a BMW in San Diego, Jake checked into the Sallie Mae Motel, where he often stayed when he was in Los Angeles. The Sallie Mae was a vintage California motor lodge, with a yellow neon sign proclaiming "Our rooms are clean." A deposit was required for use of a TV remote control.

To Jake, the Sallie Mae was the perfect hotel, far removed from the celebrity-infested boutiques of nearby Beverly Hills. A few blocks from Canter's, the Sallie Mae was in the heart of LA's largest Orthodox Jewish neighborhood, surrounded by old synagogues, delis, and, in the random mix of LA, several tasty Ethiopian restaurants. No one who recognized him in this neighborhood gave a rat's ass, as long as he didn't take the last good table at Dupar's. And in LA that's all the attention he wanted. LA made his toenails curl.

"Hey, again, I'm sorry," Vince said. "You know I'm just kidding." Vince was fidgeting, playing with a napkin. "Come on, it's just a house. You always said houses are just hotels with bad maid service. Wasn't that, like, Truism 943, something like that?"

"That was five years ago. I liked that house."

In fact, Jake was feeling unexpected pain. He'd saved to buy the house, spending extra on lawyers to carefully keep his name far removed from the ownership documents. He was famous, not rich. The house was his biggest purchase ever. He didn't buy expensive cars; he rented. He preferred Tommy Bahama to Armani. His watch was Timex. On the road his hotels, restaurants, and bar tabs were all deductible under the tax code's special "celebrity exemption" section, installed by the eager-to-please post-Obama Republican Congress. The house was it, in terms of extravagant expenditures.

The soup arrived, the waitress sliding the bowl across the table, the ball of mush sloshing in Canter's famous thin broth.

There was silence as Jake started on his soup.

"Do you think, maybe, Urbina had something to do with this?" Vince asked tentatively.

Jake didn't answer. He never really talked to Vince about Urbina, nothing about the details, and he wasn't going to start now. It was complicated. Three days earlier he had revealed to Vince that he was not renewing his personal services contract with Teddy Urbina's company, Klutch.

Vince wouldn't let it go. "Come on, the guy's a thug. It must have occurred to you."

"Or maybe it was Elvis's ghost." Jake worked on his soup. "Tell me what you got going," he said, changing the subject.

"Right, you can't dwell." Vince pulled out a wafer-thin electronic device, which began to glow in his palm. "You have to move on. Time to get back to work. Think of the possibilities."

Vince paused for effect. "Personally, I think you probably can get a whole week out of *Inside News*."

Vince began poking at his device.

"Part one can be something like 'Jake Truland's Hidden Pain,'" Vince said. "And then maybe we'll find one of your old maids for part two, maybe talk about all the wild parties at the house. It'll kick the rock 'n' roll demo."

"I never had a maid."

"Doesn't matter."

"I never threw any parties there."

"You're getting off track here." Vince was on a roll, using his thumbs to type notes. "Maybe have the maid...*a housekeeper*...drop a hint that a few of the babes were underage. That'll be good for part three—'Truland Teen Sex Shocker.' Nice, right? *Sizzler* will probably have to do a follow."

Jake didn't add anything to Vince's laundry list, but he didn't stop him. "Did you talk to Becky?"

"Last night," Vince said. "She's checking into the Modernaire." Becky always stayed at the Modernaire, where the parking attendants were discreet. It was on a side street just off Sunset, within walking distance of the Whiskey, behind the Viper Room, where River Phoenix had died.

Jake began to focus on Vince's list.

"OK, tone down the 'Truland's pain' angle," Jake said. "Nobody likes a whiner." Jake flashed on an image of his charred home. "Let's go easy on this."

"Easy?" Vince's voice cracked a bit.

"Just take it down a notch."

"No teen sex shocker?"

"No teen sex shocker."

"But we have to give them something."

"OK, call *Power News*, tell them to have a photog at the Modernaire tomorrow morning, early. Be vague. Tell them to give it to *Inside News*. Nothing to *Hollywood Now!*"

"Nothing?"

"Stiff 'em. Don't return calls."

"You are a vengeful mo-fo. Sharon Jones-Jones will shit."

"Too bad. She'll get the message."

Vince smiled and feverishly thumbed. "After the arc, I probably can get $10,000 for an interview," he said hesitantly. "And I bet your appearance fee is going up. I could get 25K for a club opening in Miami."

Jake thought about it. "No, no personal stuff. Not yet," he said.

Vince released a hint of disappointment but nodded vigorously.

"Right. Smart. No problem. What about the VOPs? You're still on for the Voice of the People awards, right?"

"Yes. But tell the *Post* I'm going to cancel. That'll spark some Babblecock chatter. And find the phone video from people who were at the house. Make sure the right people get it. We don't want it ending up premiering on some local news show."

"What about the bloggers?"

"Fuck the bloggers." Jake counted more than 13.5 million "associates" in his Babblecock closet. He had attracted more than 4.5 million Twitter followers, even though he'd tweeted only once: "The beans are cold." He didn't need bloggers.

For the next ten minutes Vince thumbed vigorously while Jake ran through a list of instructions, his mind working efficiently through the issues.

"That's it," Jake said, completing his list and his soup. He gave Vince a pat on the shoulder and got up to leave. Jake always left first and Vince followed ten minutes later, after paying the check. Check paying was a dead zone for Jake, an awkward space where movement stopped and people were forced to stand together, mingle, and occasionally chat.

As Vince walked out the door, the waitress with the hairnet headed for the pay phone in the hallway, next to the men's room. She pulled a crumpled napkin out of her pocket and dialed the number written on it. The reporter from the *National Gossip* Web site had said he'd give her $20 every time she called in, whether he used the tip or not.

8

Eric Branson drove the bright-red Del Mar Fire minivan north on I-5, engrossed in a wave of nostalgia. When he was a kid, after his parents divorced, once a year his mother loaded him into the car for this same 45-minute drive north to Orange County to buy cheap furniture from Scandinavia. They'd rush back home to assemble the bookcases and chairs, their version of mother and son quality time. For years Eric thought of Orange County as the "place with Ikea," never knowing or caring that Disneyland was only twenty minutes up the road.

Today was one of those perfect SoCal mornings, when the dark blue sky is only occasionally blocked by a meandering white cloud, pushed along by an unseen ocean breeze. And there was basically no traffic, something that happened as often as a solar eclipse. Eric rolled down the window and soaked in the rush, thinking that moments like these make SoCal a perfect place.

The drive north was a pleasant diversion from the daily life at the fire station. There were few fires to investigate in Del Mar. Most of his days were spent overseeing station chores and bureaucracy, from the nonstop cleaning process to community events. He was regularly chosen as the station representative at fairs and bake sales and church socials—the duties his colleagues were more than happy to dump in the lap of the college grad.

Eric didn't mind the extra tasks. His life was simple these days. He didn't have a girlfriend. Most of his social life revolved around his former teammates from high school. They surfed in the morning, worked out in the afternoon, and watched the Chargers on Sunday. Every Friday night he met his mom for dinner. Vacation days were spent on road trips down the Baja coast with his buddies, looking for the best breaks to surf. Winter was snowboarding trips to Mammoth.

The Truland case was a welcome diversion, a chance to conduct a real investigation. There were many unanswered questions. Hopefully this trip to Orange County would answer at least some of them.

When he exited I-5, he hit a long line of barely moving cars that snaked toward the parking lot of the Orange County Convention Center. Eric maneuvered the fire department's minivan into an emergency lane and parked in an "officials only" spot.

A large crowd blocked the sidewalk. Several broad-shouldered women in matching red sweat pants with white stripes eyed Eric warily. Nearby a 40ish woman dressed as Princess Leia, in a white linen robe and ear muff hairdo, sat on a bench breastfeeding a baby who looked too old for breastfeeding. Next to her four women in matching yellow vests and pink tights stood in a half-circle, smoking cigarettes. Eric recognized their costumes from *Super Mom*, the new TV show about a mother who tends the kids during the day and fights crime at night. While he stared, three women in black cocktail dresses stomped past, their high heels clacking on the sidewalk. Each carried a placard saying, "We Love You Lindsay!"

Eric followed the Lindsay-loving girls to a check-in table in the Convention Center's grand entrance hall, positioned under a massive glittering-silver sign, proclaiming *"Welcome to GirrlllCon!!"* He identified himself to an elderly woman wearing a large badge, who directed him to the northeast corner, level two of Main Hall Two C, "next to the Gossip Lounge."

Main Hall Two C, Eric discovered, resembled a hanger big enough to park a few of Boeing's new 797 Skyliners. He was assaulted with a blast of noise. Ahead of him rivers of women splashed through an endless grid of booths, stages, and various installations, each blaring their own music and announcements. As far as he could tell, he was the only man in attendance. Many of the women wore costumes, but not all. Some wore business suits. Others pushed elaborate baby carriages—the biggest baby carriages he'd ever seen, the luxury Winnebagos of baby carriages, fully equipped with turn signals, strange antennas, and minifridges.

Trying to avoid the surge of humanity, Eric was pinned against a massive eight-story video wall displaying a pulsating image of the face of radio talk show host Lindsay Bowman, the former child star who was appearing in TV ads endorsing a chain of rehab clinics. In the distance, whirling mini-searchlights wildly danced across the side of a huge Egyptian pyramid.

Eric's head was on a swivel. He took copious mental notes. No doubt about it, this story would score him a few points at the next firehouse dinner. Overhead balloons and various radio-controlled spaceships floated above the show floor. An imitation dirigible painted bright red pulled a banner advertising "BethAnn Baily's Red Meat Facial Cream." *What the heck was that?* The blimp navigated around wide pink banners dangling from the ceiling rafters, each featuring the image of a woman who looked remarkably like Eric's mother, except this woman was dressed in some sort of metallic suit and was posed in a fighting stance holding a long spear, apparently anticipating the imminent attack of an unseen space bear. Each banner touted a different message under the figure: *You are that Girrlll, Let's Be Girrllls!!!*

Eric struggled to push through the narrow aisles; he always seemed to be going against the flow, no matter which way he turned. His noticeably non-girl status drew more than a few smirks. Many of the women seemed angry. Very angry. A fight broke out in the line to get a picture taken next to a statue of Tyra Banks. Not far away, next to a booth advertising *The Jane Austen Book Club*, a cluster of women dressed as Renaissance wenches squared off against what looked like a gang of really pissed-off sixties pop singers, with tight skirts and pageboy hairdos.

"Thou art out of thy league," spat a wench in a leather tie-string bustier.

"Back off, chickie," replied a Twiggy look-alike in yellow Day-Glo knee boots.

The crowd swept Eric past the commotion before he could see how the confrontation was resolved. In the next section Eric saw the kid from that old TV show, he forgot which one. The kid was probably 50 now, but Eric still recognized him. He sat behind a desk signing copies of his book, *I'm Still Cute.*

An announcement came over the hall speakers, drowning out all the other speaker systems. "Reminder Girrlllss, Johnny Greco will be signing autographs and discussing his new book, *Perfect Party Decorations, the Greco Way,* at booth 243 in fifteen minutes." A rumble went through the hall. Eric sensed a sudden shift in the tide. An opening appeared. He strode forward, narrowly missing a squadron of four women pushing identical baby strollers aligned in a V attack formation.

Eric found Vince Trello sitting behind a folding table near the restrooms, cell phone to his ear. The agent waved him to a metal chair. Eric thought it was strange that Trello wanted to meet here, but he went along. "It will be educational," Trello had said on the phone. "You know, for the case." The Convention Center was also halfway between Los Angeles and Del Mar, saving Eric a trip into the traffic zoo of central Los Angeles. And Trello assured him he had "important information" for the investigation.

"What is this?" Eric asked, looking around the bustling hall.

"This? This is the largest fan event in the southwestern United States."

"I always thought these things were for comic book geeks." Eric had to shout to be heard over the Harry Connick Jr. song blaring from the PA system.

Trello laughed. "Look around you, kid. This is the largest collection of free-spending consumers in the known world."

"It looks like a bunch of housewives."

"Who do you think is running the world? They got money. And they've got a lot of time on their hands, now that the nannies are raising the kids."

"But where are the men?"

"Hah, who cares? These women are gold. And they're tired of using their money to buy Botox treatments."

Two women in business suits scurried past, heading toward a long line around a booth promoting the new Catharine Longo movie, the one where she plays a Thai kickboxer who goes undercover to find love and tragedy with an Australian transvestite. A 30-foot poster showed Longo lashing out with her kicking foot, her face a mask of rage.

Eric felt the need to refocus the conversation. He pulled out a small notebook. "What does this have to do with Jake Truland's house fire?"

"If Jake Truland walked in here right now, there would be a riot," Trello said. "Even today, no doubt."

Eric wrote down "riot." "Know of any people here who want to burn down his house?"

"I don't know, maybe half."

"You seem to think Mr. Truland has angered quite a few people."

"Yeah, he is very good." Trello seemed to be bragging.

"Good?"

"Jake can stir things up. He is a genius, never forget that." Trello leaned forward, a conspirator sharing a secret. "Most people these days, they freak out pretty easy. Mr. Anchorman gets caught with his pants down and he immediately starts with the mea culpas and turns to Jesus. Jake, he embraces the opportunity."

Eric wasn't sure he understood. "How does that explain why someone would want to burn down his house?" Overhead, a loud-speaker announced that David Hasselhoff would be signing auto-graphs in the Xena Pavilion in fifteen minutes. Eric heard shrieks in the distance.

"I wanted you to have these," Trello said, sliding a manila envelope stuffed with papers across the table. "These might help. They're from the last six months. I had my girl separate out only those with a direct threat."

There were so many papers jammed into the envelope, the flap wouldn't close. Eric pulled out the wad of paper and started thumbing through the stack, amazed at the bulk of people who wanted to do Truland harm. Most of the missives seemed well thought out, grammatically correct. Many used quotations from old literary works. There was none of the crazed scrawling of most threatening letters.

"Now don't be giving any of those to *Hollywood Now!* Those are for your investigation only."

"Of course not." Eric was offended. Sharing materials pertinent to an ongoing investigation with the media would be in violation of at least three department regulations.

"No, right, of course not," Trello said.

Eric went back to the papers. Trello studied him. "You ever been on TV?"

"Couple of times," Eric said, focusing on the letters.

"What kind of shows? News?"

"Yeah, that kind of thing..."

"Perfect. You should do *Cathy!*"

"What?" Eric looked up from the stack of papers. "Why would I want to do that?"

"*Cathy!* has a twenty-eight share. That would be a good reason."

"All communication on the case needs to go through the public information office."

"Right." Trello laughed.

Eric returned his attention to the papers. He was mesmerized by the creative level of hate directed at Truland. "Who are all these people?"

"I will tell you that for every one of those wackos, there are a dozen more who love the guy, who would give their left tit for a chance to get his autograph. The *Book of Truisms* has been downloaded 3.3 million times. Don't forget that." Trello paused for effect, and then added, "It's really helped people."

"These people seem to have given quite a bit of thought to ways to hurt Mr. Truland." Eric held up one of the letters and started to read. "*Although you once brought light to my TV, I feel it is the duty of all women to silence your black cloud of doom....*" Eric put the letter down and looked at Trello. "Black cloud of doom?"

"If I recall, I believe that particular scribe was upset at Mr. Truland's failed relationship with Jackie Conrad."

"She seems pretty upset about it."

"Look, if you want to get a clue, go talk to that wacko from SELT."

"SELT?"

"The Society for Elvis's Living Trust. Look, write this down—Cassandra Moorehead. She's the head wacko. She'll give you an idea of what you're up against."

"Where can I find Ms. Moorehead?"

"Mrs.! Don't ever give her that Ms. shit."

"OK, but where—"

"Try booth 414."

"She's here?"

"I think she lives here."

Ten minutes later, fighting through the flowing masses, Eric found booth 414. It was almost deserted. A rotund woman in a brown pantsuit sat in front of a large banner of Elvis, circa White Vegas Jumpsuit Era, looking skyward toward a shining star.

"Are you Cassandra Moorehead?"

The rotund woman turned on like an incandescent lightbulb. "Why, yes, I am," she said, her smile beaming. "The one and only."

"I understand you're the head of SELT."

"CEO, sweetie. And director of innovation solutions."

Eric introduced himself.

"But I haven't seen you on TV," she said suspiciously. "If you're the investigator on the case, why haven't I seen you on TV?"

Eric described department policy and the chain of command, but the woman seemed only partially swayed.

"Why, that's just *mucho está bien*. Don't you worry, honey. I'm sure your day will come and you'll be on TV right soon. Don't you worry."

Eric was unclear why he was supposed to worry, but Cassandra gave him little chance to interrupt. She was a butterball of energy.

"Is this your first time at GirrlllCon? Isn't it absolutely *maravilloso*? Do you speak Spanish, Inspector? *Lo siento, mi Español.* I'm trying to learn. Don't you think it's so important to appreciate the language of our Spanish brothers and sisters? After all, they now are something like 150 percent of the population, if you know what I mean. Isn't it incredible? Why, 15.2 percent of our members are non-white. Most people don't know that."

"Ms., er...Mrs. Moorehead, do you know anybody who might want to burn down Jake Truland's house?"

"Why, sure." Moorehead beamed. "Lots of people."

He was going to have to rework his question. "Anybody from

your group, maybe? Anybody you think might have acted out?" Eric was looking for a reaction.

"I guess it's possible," she said, her smile bright enough to guide ships at sea.

"Anybody in particular?"

"Oh, don't be silly. I don't know anybody who burned down his house. Heck, if I knew something I'd be on *Cathy!* tomorrow."

Eric made a mental note to record the next *Cathy!*

"Sweetie, I know lots of people who might like to burn down that man's house," she continued. "But I don't know anything about anybody actually doing something about it."

"Why do people in your group hate Mr. Truland so much?"

"We don't hate him. Oh no, no, that's all wrong. We just want him to burn in the fires of Hades for all eternity. We are definitely not haters, Mr. Branson."

"But, why do you want to see him burn in the, uh, fires of Hades?"

"Because he has defiled the saint," she said, peeking over her shoulder at the giant Elvis. Eric noticed for the first time she wore a necklace with a guitar-shaped locket. "Dear, he chose to take the Saint's name through the mud for his own vile and disgusting gains. It's his own dang fault. It was a sin and wrong and I think many of our members are quite right to feel the pull of vengeance."

Eric wrote down "pull of vengeance."

"That. And a lot of the gals are upset over the way he treated Jackie Conrad. She seems like such a nice girl."

Eric wrote that down, too.

"How many members are in your group?" Eric asked.

"Well, we just got a strong influx from Utah and northwest Georgia, so I'm not quite sure."

"Take a guess."

"Well, it's hard to say, after our last meeting."

"A guess."

"Well, if I were guessing, I'd say we're up to 1.2 million, give or take a hundred thousand. Two-point-two million, if you count Babblecock closets."

Eric's jaw dropped, apparently noticeably.

"Isn't it *fabuloso*? Many people are very moved by the story of Elvis and his personal connection to scripture," she said. "Many find comfort in the group. It offers a deeper meaning." She reached for a colorful brochure on the table and handed it to him. "And we offer a very substantial discount on tickets to Graceland and Dairy Queen and all sorts of places. That is a very popular perk of membership." Her smile beamed at 600 watts. "Everybody loves perks."

That evening, Eric was changing in front of his locker when the chief appeared behind him, carrying a pile of pink message slips.

"I got 37 calls from reporters today," the chief said. "Who the hell are these people?"

Eric waved his own stack of pink slips. "I got eight calls alone from something called *Digger*. One guy offered me ten grand to talk."

The chief perked up. "Ten grand? Really?"

Eric gave him a rundown of his trip to Orange County. "Lots of suspects, no leads," he said.

"Anything from the lab?"

"Not much. It looks like three obvious flash points. They're guessing it was just garden-variety lighter fluid."

"Christ. That's all we need."

"I'm going to start following up on some of the obvious stuff tomorrow, see if we can't get some traction."

"Yeah, well, don't kill yourself. The sheriff is going to Bigfoot on this one. ICIC is taking over. Let them handle it."

That didn't surprise Eric. Two years earlier, shortly after a local TV sports reporter was charged with running a brothel out of a downtown condo, the newly elected sheriff set up the Important

Crimes Involving Celebrities unit, commonly referred to as ICIC. The Truland fire had ICIC written all over it, but that didn't mean Eric liked losing the case to the hotshot detectives.

"I've still got to cover the basics," Eric said. "I need to clear a couple of things."

"Do what ya gotta do, then let ICIC have it," the chief said. "I don't want one damn call from that prick sheriff, right?"

The chief paused. "You know that blonde muffin on Channel 2?"

"The one with the dimples?"

"Yeah, she called me last night. At home. Jiminy Cricket, she's cute. Damn nice little butt."

There was a silence, the chief lost in his imagination. Then he snapped out of it and turned back to Eric. "Make this go away, pup. Make it go away fast."

9

The pot-bellied man, still wearing his stained gray sweatshirt, sat on a worn plaid couch staring at a rolled-up Macy's bag positioned atop the wooden cable spool that served as his coffee table. It was like a pile of jewels or a statue to be admired, he thought. It was treasure, like the stuff you'd find at the bottom of the ocean.

His toe tapped the stain on the rug where he'd dropped a plate of spaghetti a few months ago. When the light came in through the brown curtains he'd bought at Goodwill and hit the stain just right, it made him think of two lions mating. The TV was on, showing a new reality show called *Khloé Kardashian's Celebrity Kickboxing*. But he wasn't paying attention.

All he could do was stare at his prize, his found treasure.

He needed to work through this. Play it right. Play it smart.

But, oh boy, Elaine was going to shit. They hadn't really spoken in weeks, not counting the time at the post office when she was in such a big hurry. Maybe she really did have a hair appointment, maybe not. It didn't matter. When she heard about this, heard what he'd done down in Del Mar, she wouldn't be able to say he's a guy "with nothing going on" anymore, that's for sure.

That was all going to change. All those guys in high school who voted him "the guy most likely to get a job at Denny's," they'd show a little respect. He'd work a deal, maybe go on TV. Hell, those SELT toads in Atlanta would be begging for his insights, eager to know what he knew. No more insults, no more nasty notes telling him to quit posting messages on Babblecock or "face prosecution."

Elaine was going to shit.

He just had to think it through. Play it right. Work the angles. Get the word out. Maybe alert the media. That's all. Make a few bucks. Play it smart.

10

Jessie woke up promptly at 5:00 a.m., jolted awake by Lindsay Bowman's voice on the clock radio. She quickly showered and threw on jeans and a loose blouse, moving from bed to the apartment complex's underground garage in twelve minutes. Not long ago she might have stayed in bed for an extra fifteen minutes, cuddling under the blankets with Jeff, her last boyfriend. A chef at a swanky French restaurant, he hated the early morning alarm...and her work. But that was, what, a year ago? He was just a distraction, she'd said after he left, an anchor holding her back.

This morning, even before her eyes were fully open, she was thinking about Truland, looking for angles. The *HN!* coverage wasn't cutting it and she knew it. Last night's show was weak. "Standard day two crap," Sharon called it. She was right. The only new video was fifteen seconds of Truland and Becky Hooks walking out of a damn hotel. And *Power News* had hit her up for $5,000 for that clip, nonexclusive, a full-on rip-off. The rest of the coverage was primarily reactions from celebs walking the red carpet for the premiere of the movie *Seven Blades of Death*. Always a crapshoot, the red carpet yielded precious little, beyond the notoriously crack-addicted country singer who offered a big thumbs-up to the camera and urged Truland to "Stand tall, dude, don't let them beat you down." The country singer ended up in the second slot, right after a Tom Cruise blip. Tammy teased the clip of the singer with, "You'll never guess who is offering a shout-out to troubled Jake Truland."

It was pretty slim. To make it worse, nothing else was going on; the city was in the midst of a disturbing slowdown for celebrity mayhem. Under normal conditions, the Truland fire should be able to carry a week of stories. Driving down Ventura at sunrise, the streetlights still blinking orange along the corridor, she speed-dialed the office, just to make sure her Truland Task Force was on the case.

Brenda answered the phone on the first ring, the way Jessie knew she would. Brenda was a diligent, hardworking former newspaper reporter. But she was new to TV and needed handling.

"Anything?" Jessie asked.

"Nothing new," Brenda said.

Jessie wasn't surprised. "Gather up Freddie and let's do a three-way," she said, navigating through a four-way stop.

Freddie was her Obligatory Gay. Every crew in Hollywood needed at least one. Freddie was an ambitious six-foot-two swish, clued into every secret network in town, primarily the receptionists and hairdressers and personal assistants who made Hollywood tick.

"*Jesssssiiiiee,* when are you going to get *heeeere?*" Freddie squealed into the phone.

"Ten minutes and I want ideas when I get there. Good ideas."

Freddie chimed in. "Did you get through to Trello?"

Clever Freddie. "Don't you worry about Vince," Jessie said.

"*Welllll,* I'm afraid I have some bad news for you," Freddie cooed, in his best secret sister tone. "You're not going to like it."

He was right. An *HN!* engineer had intercepted an *Inside News* satellite feed. The rival show was doing ten minutes on Truland tonight, kicking off a week-long series titled *Truland's Hidden Pain.*

"Girl, those bitches are promising six exclusives this week," Freddie said. "Can you believe their testies? Six!?"

Fifteen minutes later Jessie was in Sharon Jones-Jones's office.

"Fuckin' Tom Cruise?" Sharon barked. "They're doing exclusives on Truland's fire and we've got Tom Cruise at the fuckin' dog wash?"

"Damn Vince," Jessie muttered under her breath.

"What the hell is going on, Jessie?"

"Vince is screwing us." She regretted it the second she said it.

"Since when do we rely on an agent to cover a story? The biggest celeb whore in recent memory gets his house burned down and we're getting beat by *Inside News*?" Sharon yelled it loud enough for most of Culver City to hear. Jessie felt a brick pounding on the top of her head.

Five minutes later she sat alone on the bridge, a leper, dead meat. No one made eye contact. Tammy Bandita stopped by to console her, the ultimate humiliation. "Don't worry, sexy sport," she said, taking an opportunity to work on her enunciation. "You'll get 'em tomorrow."

Brenda and Freddie gathered around, looking forlorn.

"I'm still getting nothing from the cops," Brenda said.

"Screw the cops," Jessie snapped. "You're not going to get anything out of the cops. Stop thinking like a print geek." Jessie didn't like to snap at her, especially in front of Freddie. Brenda was five years older than Jessie, and that complicated things. But she was still fresh meat in this game.

"We're making TV," Jessie said. "Think story lines. Think names. We need video, any video. I want an exclusive by the 1:00 p.m. taping."

Jessie composed herself. She grabbed a protein bar, took a swig of Red Bull, and started handing out assignments. Two interns were directed to beat checks—calling all the law enforcement agencies, bureaucracies, news services, and assorted sources for updates. They would be logging tapes for the Fox affiliate in Baton Rouge if they didn't make ten calls an hour, Jessie assured them. Another intern was assigned to use the reverse phone directory to call Truland's neighbors, looking for any nugget of information. Brenda would follow up with relatives and friends, anybody who even remotely knew Truland and might offer up some sort of tidbit. Freddie would troll for celebs, anyone with a connection and a good name for a tease.

After they scurried off, Jessie sank down in her seat, frustrated and tense. She didn't have much faith the efforts would produce any results. In this game, exclusives were usually the result of negotiations, a phone call and a deal, a little quid pro quo. But Vince wasn't calling her back. Something was up. She was out of the loop, and she didn't know why. *Why wasn't Vince calling her back?*

She picked up the phone and dialed the *Power News* office. The desk editor yawned when he picked up. He was coming off the night shift, ready to go home. "I got video of Jackie Conrad going into Jambo's," he said. "I got Sid Bateman coming out of Jambo's. I got Tiffany Minor going into Walgreen's. Nothing on Truland. Nada. I felt lucky to get that shot for you at the hotel."

Jessie checked out the row of clocks along the walls, telling her the time in Beverly Hills, Dubai, Ibiza, and six other global capitals. One hour to go before her follow-up meeting with Sharon, a tête-à-tête she was dreading.

She grabbed her protein bar and retreated to the quiet of an edit bay, hoping to find something interesting in the piles of Truland tapes. That was her old trick from the days in the Bunny Patch. Work the video. Look for stories missed by the other producers, who were too lazy to do anything but read the tape logs.

The three hours of raw video from the Truland fire were already logged, carefully annotated by a 22-year-old former beauty queen who was leaving next week for a weekend anchor job with the FNN affiliate in Buffalo. Jessie plunked in a tape and started thumbing through the logs, written with annoyingly perfect penmanship.

The pictures were a blur of smoke and shaky camera shots. She saw nothing unusual in the commotion of firefighters and onlookers. Footage of a blond ten-year-old boy with some sort of bright yellow Asian cartoon character on his backpack made her stop. She recognized him from the network coverage. Teary-eyed, he said, "The fire was so hot and smoky. It was the most amazing thing I've seen in my whole life." Two cable channels used the bite in their ads after the fire, she recalled. In the raw footage after the "hot and smoky" line, the little boy cracked a wide smile and asked, "Was that good?" Jessie made a note to assign a PA to follow up with the kid. There might be a good "instant stardom" angle. The kid was cute. Maybe the headline would be something like, "Youngster Shines Through Truland Tragedy."

She fast-forwarded to video of Truland. A producer once told her that Truland always—*always*—knew when he was on camera. She described it as "his gift." The scenes from the fire certainly contained a hint of staged drama as Truland sat slumped on the curb, phone to his ear.

She whizzed through the video. There had to be something.

Freddie stuck his head into the booth. "Looking for inspiration?"

On-screen, the camera quick-panned to a young man in fire department-issue dark blue pants and a light blue shirt. The photographer stayed on the man striding across the street toward Truland.

"Who's this?" Jessie said, tapping the screen.

"Oh, he's darling," Freddie said.

Brenda appeared behind him. Jessie tapped the screen again.

"That's, uh, I don't know his name, Eric something," Brenda said. "He's the fire guy, the investigator."

Jessie studied his face. He was soap opera actor handsome. His face leaped off the screen.

"What do you know about him?"

"Not much. He's not talking. Everything is routed through the flack."

"Is he the lead investigator?" Brenda wasn't getting it.

"Yeah, but like I said, he's not talking."

Jessie toggled to fast forward. Images swirled past. Camera rolling, the photographer walked up to the investigator, microphone extended. "Excuse me, can I ask you your name?" The young man looked momentarily surprised but appeared too polite to keep on walking when someone was talking to him.

"You need to talk to that guy up there in the yellow hat," he said. "OK?"

Jessie replayed the segment three times. Fast forwarding, she caught glimpses of the investigator in the background, examining the charred walls of the house, talking to other firefighters. The camera really liked him. Even in the debris, he came across clean and scrubbed, with the type of boyish good looks that filled up the screen. The housewives in Iowa would love him.

Jessie pulled her laptop closer and did a quick search. She found the investigator's name and bio on the Del Mar Fire site. She switched to a media database. Branson's name didn't appear in any of the print coverage. But both NBC and *Inside News* had used his name, noting he refused to comment. Damn. That meant he was already in play.

Jessie tapped the screen. "Let's run a background on this guy. Tell me something more."

Brenda made a note on her yellow pad but didn't leave. She looked nervous, uncertain.

"Something else?" Jessie asked.

"I don't know if I should even mention it..."

"O.K."

"I mean, it's almost certainly nothing—"

Jessie didn't have time for this crap. "Just speak."

Brenda moved into the edit bay and slid into a seat next to Jessie, uncomfortably close. She slid Jessie's laptop closer. "I found this on a search this morning. You know, I was just looking for stuff and I had taken that class on online research and—"

"Please, please, please just *tell* me."

Brenda turned the screen toward Jessie.

Jessie was confused. "EBay?"

"Check it out." Brenda said, pointing at the screen. "It's a Truland manuscript. *Blue Suede Pimp*. Supposedly an original."

"So?"

"Those are rare. They never come up on the market."

"I really don't have time for memorabilia—"

"But look at this." She pointed to the user name, the person who'd posted the manuscript. "EscondidoDude."

"Again, so?"

"Last two days the front desk has received..." Brenda quickly checked her notes. "Five...five calls from a guy who said he had..."—again she thumbed through the notepad—"inside information from the scene of the fire. Terry on the desk said the guy always emphasized that he had 'inside information from the scene of the fire.' It was like, you know, his mantra."

"Sounds like another crank."

"Exactly. And he never left his name. But get this. He told Terry he lived in Escondido, in case we wanted to talk to him. And I checked and his number is in Escondido."

"You think phone guy is EscondidoDude? You think he'd use his own hometown like that?"

"It seems like an awful strange coincidence."

"That's pretty damn thin." Jessie was losing her patience.

"No, look, I know it's a long shot, but how did EscondidoDude suddenly come up with an original Truland manuscript?"

"I don't know, how?"

"Look at these messages." She pulled a rumpled stack of pink messages from her pocket. "Every one hints that he knows something about the fire. That he has inside information. Jessie, he's talking like he was *there*."

Jessie ran through the information. Brenda might be a fish, but she possessed strong reporter instincts. It *was* odd. How did the schmo get a manuscript?

"You think maybe it's a robbery gone bad?"

"Or maybe a deranged fan gone bad. Either way, I'm thinking that it's a wild coincidence."

"OK, leave me EscondidoDude's phone number," Jessie said, turning back to the monitor. "But focus on our fire hunk. Let's see if there is a story with our young investigator."

As Brenda jogged off, Jessie contemplated the image of the handsome fireman. *Inside News* and *Dish* were probably already camped out at the fire station, hoping Branson would come out and talk. But they would get bored. Once he refused to cooperate, he'd be labeled as a stuffy prick and the crews would move on.

But Jessie didn't think he looked stuffy. He had a wholesome quality. Audiences loved wholesome and, most importantly, she knew Sharon Jones-Jones loved wholesome.

But that didn't help her today, not with Sharon Jones-Jones waiting. Shit. She looked at the screen. Then she looked at the row of clocks. Time was ticking away in Dubai. Shit. She still didn't have a substantial lead. Damn, Vince. She needed a strategy, a plan.

She looked back at the screen. She looked at her notes. She looked at the clocks. And then she looked at the pile of pink messages—Brenda's eBay guy—EscondidoDude. The guy left his name as Buddy Landau. What the hell, she thought. She dialed the number. On the fifth ring, just as she was about to hang up, a hoarse voice answered. He sounded a bit disoriented. When she introduced herself, she heard a sudden crash in the background, like maybe he had tripped over something.

"Seriously?" he said. "This ain't some kind of prank?"

"You called here several times, Mr. Landau. What did you want to say?"

"Well...I...see...I just wanna let you know, I might have, you know, information that may be important to the case."

"Have you gone to the police?"

"I don't like cops," he said, in a way that made Jessie believe him.

"What do you want, Mr. Landau? You know we don't pay for stories."

"That's not what I hear. I hear you pay big bucks for all sorts of things."

In fact, he was right. They didn't pay for stories, but they did pay for video and access, often funneling the money through a service like *Power News*. Sometimes they hired sources as consultants, if they were valuable. But Landau didn't need to know that.

"Mr. Landau, did you attempt to sell a Truland original manuscript on eBay?"

Jessie heard him say, "Shit." Then another crashing sound. "Maybe," he said. "And maybe there is more where that came from."

"Like what, Mr. Landau?" She was starting to get interested. Brenda had a point. How did this guy get an original manuscript?

"I can't say that. But let's just say there's a lot more. Stuff Truland may not want out in public."

"And this is connected to the fire."

"Uh, maybe, you know, I—"

"You're going to have to give me some idea of what you're talking about, Mr. Landau, or I'm going to have to go."

"No, wait. What if I tell you I was there?"

"Where?"

"You know, *there*. The house. That day."

"You were at the fire?"

"I cannot confirm or deny that. I think if you want anything more, maybe we should meet and I'll give you a little taste of what I got and then maybe you'll be interested."

"Are you saying you want to be interviewed, Mr. Landau?"

"You mean on TV?"

"Yes, Mr. Landau, on TV. Is that what you want?"

"Well, no, I mean...maybe, sure....But, no, no cameras. Not now. I just want to meet. Show you what I got. And, you know, maybe, you'll...you'll see some value in what I got."

Jessie weighed her options. There was something in the man's voice that suggested he wasn't a typical crackpot. And what did he mean? He was "there?" Her Spidey sense was in overdrive. What the hell, she thought. She should meet Mr. Landau, that's what her instincts told her.

She would go to Del Mar; that would be the plan for Sharon. It was time to get on the ground in Truland World. Work the story. Go back to her reporter roots. She could take a stab at the fire hunk, while she was it. Maybe he was raising an orphan kid. Or maybe he went to high school with a future supermodel. It was worth a shot. At least she'd have a plan. She'd have something to feed Sharon.

11

Two lean figures jogged down the Del Mar beach at low tide, loping across the hard-packed sand. Baseball caps pulled low, dressed in colorful sweat attire, they ran past the imitation King Arthur castle and the fake Swiss chalet and stopped in front of the hulking remains of the burned-down house.

Jake Truland tugged on the bill of his cap and scanned the beach. He always preached that jogging was the most effective disguise. Truism #57: *Hiding in the open is always the best camouflage, unless you're a deer.* No one looks twice at joggers. Besides, it was good cardio.

Becky Hooks pulled up beside him, her brown ponytail bouncing out the back of her cap. At the sight of his ruined house, she stopped short.

"Holy shit," she said. "What a friggin' disaster."

With three long strides, she crossed the ice plant and ducked under the yellow tape that surrounded the site. She moved briskly through the piles of rubble, ignoring the soot covering her running shoes.

"Jake, I'm so sorry," she shouted, running her hand across a blackened tube that once served as the banister for the stairs.

"It's just a house," he yelled back. Conversations with Becky often took place at shouting decibels.

"Did they save anything?"

"*Nothing!* Not even the *Povich* tapes."

"Who the fuck cares about the *Povich* tapes?" she yelled back.

Jake moved into the debris, stepping carefully to avoid the shattered glass and steel. He finally caught up with Becky, who was inspecting the area that was once the library. "Vince thinks we can get at least a five-day arc out of it," he said. "Did you see *Inside News* last night?"

Becky turned and gave him a half smile, half smirk—of course she didn't watch *Inside News*. Without warning, she crashed through the wreckage and wrapped her arms around him in a bear hug, squeezing hard.

After what seemed like several minutes, she pushed him back. "You must be devastated," she said.

"You're supposed to say that you miss the photos the most," Jake said.

"No, Jake. Look at me." She held him at arm's length. "Don't be a prick. This was your home. You had a connection here. It's OK to admit it."

He knew she was right. That sense of loss had been burbling inside him for days, a strange feeling.

"This place was your haven," she said. "Your escape from that other world of yours."

"I'm dealing with it."

"Maybe you should try dealing with it, you know, like a human." She punched him in the arm, hard.

Again, she was right. Del Mar was his escape hatch. It was a two-hour drive south from Los Angeles but technically out of the Hollywood sphere of influence. Several Hollywood types had homes scattered along the coastline. For years Ravi Shankar owned a house a few miles up the road, which is how Jake found himself discussing Mongolian meditation techniques with George Harrison one night, long ago.

But there was more to it. The lifestyle was part of him now—the beach, the early morning volleyball games in the cold mist, body surfing at sunset. It had changed him, altered his focus, his rhythm of life. There was always a single fin tossed in the trunk of his car, just in case the waves were up. He had a special app to track surf reports.

"Nothing personal, but you were kinda an asshole before you moved down here," Becky shouted back at him, as she strode back into the wreckage. "Maybe you should rent down here for a while. Suck up some mellow vibes."

Jake laughed. Becky always displayed an uncanny ability to cut through his crap. Emotion flowed out of her, unfiltered and unvarnished. She never tried to soften her gut reactions, never held back on a snap judgment. She walked with a gangly open style, all swaying arms and rolling shoulders, leaving the impression that she was about to stride over and slap you on the back at any given moment. One of her Texas friends described her "as a gulper, not a sipper," and that always seemed about right.

At first, he was skeptical of Becky's total lack of cynicism. They met at his publisher's office—her firm represented the book company, which was exceptionally concerned about certain passages in the *Gidget Manifesto* that seemed to imply that Frankie Avalon "enjoyed anal sex."

The publishers were eager to find a way to rephrase the passages.

"Grow some balls," Becky told them.

When Jake started to find success, he urged her to come along for the ride. Instead she set up her life on a wooded street in Austin, raising a son and daughter with her boyfriend, now husband, Bob, who worked for the local bank. Most of her family lived within 20 miles; holidays were huge affairs of bacchanalia and good cheer, amid her dozens of relatives and a tight-knit group of friends, many of whom she'd known since elementary school. Jake never attended.

For Jake, Becky was a connection to an alien world. And to him, the most amazing part—the part he had the most trouble grasping—was her slavish devotion to their relationship. There was never a judgment; never a hidden agenda. When Jake grew increasingly remote, even when he disappeared, she never wavered. "Just call me every once in a while, asshole," she said.

Together they moved through the charred remains like two generals inspecting the battlefield, silent and respectful. There was little to see in the ashes, except for the occasional burned corner of a videocassette or a sliver of glass or furniture that managed to avoid the flames.

"They don't think it's an accident," he said. "They called Vince."

That stopped her. "Who called?"

"The fire department."

"Have there been other arsons?"

"No. I mean, I don't know." Jake paused for a second. "There's something else."

"Spill it."

"Vegas."

"What about Vegas?"

"That might have had something to do with—"

"You think that cockroach Urbina has something to do with this?"

She never liked the Urbina deal. She was always pushing him to get out of the "personal service" contract with the Vegas casino. She knew Urbina was a wild card. His holding company controlled a variety of interests, in addition to the casino, including a line of fashion accessories, several major market radio and TV stations, and a chain of massage parlors in Milwaukee.

"He was a little irritated last time I saw him."

"Why?" she said, sounding more like a lawyer.

"I told him I was quitting. He wanted me to sign a new deal. I said no."

"Jake, that's wonderful." She tried to dive hug him, but he agilely stepped aside.

"Well, I don't know how wonderful it is, all things considered," he said, looking at the remains of his house.

"Why did you quit? I thought you liked the idea of turning the Harlot into the celebrity sleaze capital of the world?"

"It wasn't fun anymore. And I read a report from a Maryland research firm. It turns out the likability factor of anyone seen in Vegas actually decreases by a factor of seven."

"Seven?"

"Seven. They did focus groups."

Jake found it hard to explain why he decided to ditch the contract. He'd stewed on the decision for months. In some ways, he still wasn't sure why he was now so adamantly against the arrangement.

"Teddy upped the bonuses. I still said no."

"Fuck 'em."

"He offered options."

"Jake, you're not Vegas. You're a lot of things, but not Vegas."

"Maybe that was it."

"You really think Urbina did this?" she repeated as they stepped through the ashes. "I mean, the guy is a balls-out nutcase, but this is a little extreme, even for him."

"He was fairly angry."

"But why would he burn down your house?"

"Send a message. He calls them Remind-o-Grams. He bought the URL."

"Quitting pissed him off that much?"

"Well, there was more."

"Like what?"

"I might have called him a douche bag. In fact, the actual phrase was probably 'douche bag gangster.'"

She laughed. "He is a douche bag gangster. Did you tell the cops?"

"No, no way. There's no point. Either way, it's just business. It wasn't a bad deal."

"Fuck 'em," she said again. "Forget the deal. You don't need it."

"That's what I thought." He knew Becky would back him. Vince scoffed when he said he was walking away from the deal. He said Jake was pissing on the money tree. But Becky understood.

"Still, maybe you should tone it down on this one," Becky said, kicking at a pile of blackened debris. "Play it low key."

"Yeah, low key."

"Maybe don't make it into an international sensation."

"You know Vince," Jake said, as he picked at the metal carcass of his Konacka 6X-Y, the world's best equalizer. "He smells opportunity. You don't pass up a natural."

"That reminds me," she said. "*Hollywood Now!* is calling more than usual. How should I handle it?"

Jake thought about it for a second. "Stiff them."

"Nothing?"

"Don't even send them a statement," he said.

"How should I explain that?"

"Don't."

"Ouch," she said. "Not the bitch slap. That's cold."

"Sharon didn't give us good play on the Elvis ghost rumor," he said. Two weeks before his book hit stores, several major newspapers had covered a report that Elvis's ghost was seen at a Taco Bell in Nebraska. It was a nifty cross-promotion and led to a series of articles and a *20/20* exposé, "The Resurrection of Elvis." All the stories mentioned Jake's book. Vince wanted a feature on *Hollywood Now!* but Sharon had vetoed it.

Becky paused, knowing the next question wouldn't go over well. "What about Urbina?"

"Don't worry about Teddy," he said. "I'll take care of Teddy."

After Jake dropped her off at the Modernaire, Becky hurried to her room and dumped her purse and keys on the king-sized bed. She plucked out her phone and called Janice, the nanny watching Ben and Jessica, her kids. Janice was a fifty-eight-year-old spinster and queen of the local knitting society. Ben, her twelve-year-old, hated her and hated the idea that he still needed somebody to watch over him. Jessica, on the other hand, was learning to knit and had developed a fascination for English comedies on PBS.

Janice picked up on the fourth ring. She sounded annoyed by the interruption. At times she seemed to barely tolerate Becky, even though Becky was her employer and a partner at a downtown law firm. Janice didn't approve of Becky's travels and she barely held back her contempt for her lenient parenting.

"There has been a change in plan," Becky said.

"Oh, I see," Janice said.

"I'll be staying in LA for a couple more days. Can you handle the extra duty?"

"I suppose so. Of course, your children will miss you."

Becky sighed. In reality, Ben was at the age when any day without a parent around was a good day. "It'll just be a couple of days."

"Well, you just stay as long as you want," Janice said with the voice of the martyr-to-be.

"Thanks, Janice, love ya." Becky quickly hung up. Bob was playing golf; she'd have to wait to call him. Instead she called her secretary, Bonnie, and told her to cancel her appointments for the next three days.

12

Jake never spent any time correcting media reports, which is why many people believe he met Teddy Urbina on a mysterious snorkeling expedition in Belize, as reported by two well-respected investigative journalism sites. In fact, Jake's relationship with Teddy Urbina was the result of a drunken craps binge in Vegas.

In the celebrity game, Vegas is like Dog Beach, an open trade zone, where all the dogs are free to romp and play without fear of territorial conflict. In Vegas, amateurs mix with the pros, the God-fearing with the heathens. The outrageous is easily ignored in Vegas; no one cares. A man wearing a banana suit blends into the crowd in Vegas.

Normally, Jake didn't drink much. He was more of a joint-at-sunset kind of guy. Two of his three well-publicized trips to rehab were simply plants, stories to fill slow news days. He made the cover of *Sizzler* when he voluntarily committed himself to a ten-day "freshener" after throwing a trash can through the living room window of Jackie Conrad's beach house. The third trip to rehab was legit. And it was bad timing, coming right after he started work as a pundit—a "voice for independent America"—on the highly rated *Attack Zone*. But rehab was really about replacing three days of jail time on a disorderly conduct charge with thirty days at Clapton's oceanfront recovery center on Antigua, which he'd always wanted to check out.

However, in Vegas he drank. It just seemed like the right thing to do. On this trip he was drinking Scotch and hoovering up fair amounts of cocaine, in a style reminiscent of Mick and Bianca in the bathroom of Studio Fifty-Four, circa 1978. Something about cocaine and Vegas went together, and he didn't fight it.

By 11:00 p.m., he was losing big at craps at the Harlot, a slightly off-strip tower that displayed the car Tupac was in when he was shot. The black 750 BMW sedan with the shattered windows was positioned in the lobby as a way to attract visitors. The Harlot was a favorite of serious players. No one asked Jake for an autograph at the Harlot.

Down twenty-five grand at craps, he switched to blackjack at about 3:00 a.m., hoping to shift the karmic flow, a sound and proven strategy. Blackjack was the valium of the casino, a way to take the edge off. Blackjack was closer to bingo than craps. There was time to chat. Call for a drink. Let the dealer bust a few times.

And then there was the weather girl. He'd always had a thing for weather girls. This one was from Des Moines or Little Rock or someplace like that. She was blonde and drinking gin and tonics. She recognized him. He recognized her. She liked dogs. He liked dogs. He laughed. She won. She hit on sixteen and won again and everybody at the table cheered. Then she hit on seventeen and won and a small crowd started to form.

It went on like that for a while. The more she hit on fifteen and sixteen, the more she won. Each time she beat the dealer and won four dollars, she squealed like she had just won the Miss Des Moines competition, bouncing up and down in her chair and clapping her hands together. Jake thought he might be in love.

The weather girl's strategy grew looser and her bets increased to six dollars and she kept on winning. She hit on fifteen with the dealer showing a three and won again. The crowd cheered. Jake clinked glasses with her mid-squeal and everyone was having a good time—everybody except the guy sitting between Jake and the weather girl.

He was fortyish and wore a Boss sport jacket and a finely tailored Ralph Lauren baby blue dress shirt—most likely a midlevel Wall Street analyst who had watched too many videos by the Artist Formerly Known as Sean Combs. For every hand the weather girl won, he lost. She hit on fifteen and won; he hit on twelve and busted. The blonde cutie stayed on thirteen with the dealer showing a king; he hit and busted. Hand after hand. She bet $6 and won; he was losing $100 to $150 on every hand.

"Your girlfriend is playing like a moron," the analyst type said, loud enough for everyone to hear.

"I think maybe she has been blessed by a Balinese goddess," Jake said, looking deep into her blue eyes.

The weather girl blushed.

"Fuckin' gibberish," the man said.

The dealer, a pockmarked man in his thirties in a fake leather Western vest, quickly dealt out the next hand. The weather girl showed a fourteen. She hit. The dealer looked to the pit boss. The weather girl bounded up and down and clapped her hands. "Gimmme, gimmeee, gimmeee," she squealed.

The pit boss, a hulk with a buzz cut, silently nodded. The dealer nodded back and dealt the weather girl another card. It was a seven. She squealed. The crowd cheered.

The analyst showed a twelve and hit. The dealer slapped a king on the table; a bust. Jake had blackjack.

"This is fuckin' ridiculous," the man in the Boss jacket said. "Mary Sunshine is playing like a retard and I'm getting pounded."

"Please keep your voice down," the dealer said, nervously glancing at the pit boss.

"New shuffle," the man said. "I want a new deck."

"There is a full shoe," the dealer said.

Jake could have stayed out of the exchange, but that was unlikely, given the combination of Scotch, cocaine, and weather girl. And the guy was a prick. Jake leaned in close, flashed the *People* magazine grin, and whispered in his ear. "Play the cards and shut the fuck up."

"Why don't you go fuck yourself," the analyst said.

The hulking pit boss appeared in a puff of cheap cologne. "That's uncalled for, sir."

"What? I gotta put up with this crap just because pretty boy here is trying to get laid?"

Jake looked right at the man. This time he wasn't smiling. "Maybe you should find another table."

"Go fuck yourself. You really think she is going to fuck you?"

At this point, Jake could have easily let the casino handle the situation. But the Scotch was a pool of mud blocking the veto message from his brain, while the cocaine urgently texted him instructions.

Jake put his right arm around the analyst's shoulders and gave him a quick, straight punch to the solar plexus, fast and hard. The man lurched forward, gasping for air.

Later Jake would argue that this was a perfectly defensible response to the situation, but even in the moment he realized he was crossing several lines in the Vegas VIP etiquette manual. As soon as brain reception was restored, he decided that, all in all, it was a good time to switch tables. Without waiting for a response from the pit boss, Jake scooped up his chips, winked at the shocked weather girl, and twirled off the stool.

Normally a move so well executed might draw a nice murmur of approval from the crowd, but the analyst recovered enough to lunge back at him, popping up straight into the tray carried by a Harlot waitress, sending a dozen drinks flying. And maybe disaster would have been averted, even at that point. But the waitress reacted badly, screeching in the manner of a Tasered steer, dislodging not one but both of the pasties of her official Harlot waitress costume.

Even then, it could have gone down as nothing more than another amusing casino floor incident, except one of the drinks, a black Russian, landed on the right shoulder of Juan Renteria Morales, aka the Serpent. Mr. Morales, allegedly the assistant kingpin of the Sonora drug trade, was shooting craps with three of his compatriots, who were positioned around the room, looking nervous. When the black Russian hit Morales, he, too, reacted badly. Screaming at an octave that seemed to surprise even his compatriots, he leaped forward, spilling chips across the table.

At that point, all hell broke loose. Hearing their patriarch's screams, Mr. Morales's associates pulled automatic weapons with the grace of Lido magicians. Security guards reached for their own weapons and barked orders into unseen microphones. Some women fainted; others screamed. Men grabbed for chips. Fights broke out. A pit boss used pepper spray to keep crazed patrons away from his chip trays. Three rodeo cowboys from Texas yelled, "Let's roll!" and dove for Mr. Morales's colleagues. Gunfire erupted, sending bullets flying around the casino floor, ricocheting off slot machines.

Jake saw none of it. Seconds after he collided with the waitress, he was knocked over by an unidentified Samoan tourist, who leaped at the sound of Mr. Morales's first screech. Falling over backward, Jake's head bounced off the side of a roulette table, knocking him cold.

When he woke up, Jake was sitting on a metal chair in a dank, windowless room filled with gray filing cabinets and boxes of office supplies. Two fit-looking, unsmiling young men in Brooks Brothers suits guarded the door.

His head ached and he was still a little groggy. He didn't try to make conversation with the Brooks Brothers kids.

After fifteen minutes, a short man in Armani walked in, nodded to the Brook Brothers duo, and silently took up a fashionable position in front of Jake. Leaning against an old metal desk, he folded his arms across his chest, striking a pose, his black curly hair shiny from doses of what appeared to be top-of-the-line products. In his haze, Jake wondered if maybe he had accidentally wandered into a photo shoot for a midlevel men's magazine.

"By my account, you owe us $115,000, give or take a few cocktails," the Armani man said, skipping the small talk.

Jake acted like he was calculating the numbers in his head, scrunching his brow. "Give or take a few cocktails," he said.

"I note you have decided that credit cards are no longer convenient for you. That you prefer the Harlot Club, our very special concierge service."

"It is a very nice service," Jake offered. In fact, he liked it quite a bit. There was always a plate of fresh chocolate chip cookies waiting in his suite when he arrived.

"You clearly enjoy its liberal lending criteria for craps players."

"I also like the complimentary buffet breakfast. Although your sausage weenies are not the best."

The man with the curly black hair gave a little laugh. "True." And then he stopped smiling. "You're in trouble, you know. I don't think you realize two people caught bullets tonight."

Jake paused for a moment and tried to figure out how that might have happened, based on his memory of the event. "OK, I'm willing to defend myself on the charges I bumped into a waitress. I'm guessing the cops will be merciful."

"We're not calling the cops."

That was a surprise. Jake was already looking forward to the photo op. Maybe he'd develop a new look. He never understood why celebrities didn't take more time to consider their mug shots. They'd employ a team of eighteen makeup artists for a passport photo, but when it came time to pose for the cops, they offered nothing but a dumb, caught-in-the-headlights look, even though everyone knew it was going to be on *Digger* in two hours. He was thinking this occasion called for a look of calm defiance, with the wisp of a sneer. But it apparently wasn't going to happen.

"Then this is the new Harlot Club lounge?" Jake said, looking around the storage room. "That's nice of you. I appreciate the extra mile."

"I just couldn't let you leave without a little chat."

Jake eyed the unsmiling security guards, who looked like they were on their way to a Princeton frat social, in their matching blazers and earpieces.

"What, you're going to break my legs? I thought the mob was out of Vegas?"

"I'm not the mob. I'm vice president of marketing and catering." The man held out his hand. "Teddy Urbina."

"You're going to take away my buffet privileges?"

"I work for a multinational company, wiseass. Oil production. Pork futures. Bolivian copper mines. And fashion accessories. Klutch? Maybe you've seen the commercials?"

"The one with the duck?"

The man didn't smile. He gave Jake a practiced stare. "Don't you think we can hurt you?"

That sure sounded like the mob. "Breaking my legs would hurt me. Banning me from the casino doesn't hurt me. So either call the cops or let me go."

"OK, I'll ignore that," Urbina said, his irritation showing. "Don't try to play me. I know your game. You probably want to be arrested. Your Q will get a boost. Look at you. You're enjoying this."

Jake was, in fact, enjoying it, just a bit.

"Sweeps is coming up. You're probably already working on your denial press release. Getting that day two hit, right? You bastard. I know you, you bastard."

Jake was impressed. This guy knew his stuff.

"Fuck you," Urbina said. "I'm not even going to mention you in the press release. Nothing, *nada*. Anybody calls, we've never seen you. Fuck you, asshole."

Urbina paced for a few minutes and then sat down behind the gray metal desk. He stared at Jake for a good forty-five seconds, rolling a cigar in his fingers, a gesture Jake thought was a little over the top.

"So what are we going to do about this situation?"

Jake knew the line was from a movie but couldn't place it.

"Not only do we have this ugly incident, for which you are clearly responsible, we have the issue of the money, which we would like, now."

"Now?"

"Yes, now. Or perhaps you didn't read the fine print of the Harlot Club Membership Agreement. Wait, I'm sure I can find you a copy." He made a show of trying to find the agreement on the storeroom shelves. After a few beats he said, "Sorry, you'll just have to take my word for it."

"I'm famous, not rich," Jake said.

"What about your house? Your cars? I see your picture in the magazines. You live like a king."

"Leased. Posed. Come on, you must have run a credit report. What's this about?"

Urbina smiled. "Let's return to the issue of whether or not you believe we can hurt you," he said, with a smug expression.

Jake considered that for a moment. He didn't know Urbina, but he knew enough about the various corporate interests involved in the Harlot to understand the complexities. Just two months earlier the *Globe* had reported on three union contractors employed on construction of the Harlot's new parking garage who were found dead, floating in the pool of Babylon, the Harlot's arch competitor.

Jake nodded his head. "Yeah, I believe that you can hurt me."

"Good," Urbina said. "Then we know where we stand. We can talk like businessmen. No bullshit."

Urbina offered a proposal. And although still groggy, Jake could see that it wasn't a bad deal, in a lot of ways. Or at least, that's what he thought at first. There were clear benefits. Things were slow. Urbina was kind of funny, in his own way. Later, when Jake told Vince about the deal, he enthusiastically agreed, saying it was a "win-win."

Technically, Jake signed an open-ended personal service contract with Klutch Enterprises, a conglomerate that controlled the casino, oil, and mineral interests and the "relaxation" facilities in Milwaukee, as well as Klutch, the leading provider of fashion accessories to the northeast United States, France, and several provinces in Romania. Despite his pedestrian title, Urbina was on the board of directors of the conglomerate, which also had a vague reciprocal promotional agreement with Tangent Enterprises, a company controlled by Urbina, according to Klutch's notoriously vague proxy statements.

In exchange for "payment to be determined," Jake operated as something of a freelance marketing operative for Klutch and the Harlot, using his unique gifts. From time to time, Jake would let it leak that he was ensconced in the Harlot's Royal Palace suite with his latest girlfriend—news sure to attract a hive of photographers, who were always graciously allowed on the grounds to shoot pictures of the Royal Palace suite and its "world famous cascading hot tubs."

More often Jake arranged for a young starlet or the latest hunk to spend a weekend of decadence at the Harlot, and then tipped off one of the tabs. Or he'd arrange for *Sizzler* to learn a married actor was spotted in one of the Harlot's extra-private poolside cabanas with his costar. And maybe the costar would be wearing the latest Klutch sweats when the photog appeared. Those were easy hits. But, at Urbina's urging, Jake became more creative. He arranged for the $20-million-a-movie actress to run into her ex-husband and his new bikini-model wife on the tennis courts. The resulting catfight made the cover of *Tattler*. When incidents needed fleshing out, Urbina supplied bellboys or valets to unofficially corroborate stories. In one of his larger successes, the *Globe* ran a story about a supposedly gay boy band singer's rendezvous with a hooker in the Harlot's ginger-tinted steam bath, "part of the recent $33 million Klutch Kool Spa expansion," the stories noted.

All in all, Jake didn't think it was a bad deal. The Harlot created cash flow. And it kept him in the game during slow times. For celebs on the make, the Harlot became the hot spot, a place to be seen. Soon it joined the pantheon of Vegas's profitable landmarks to sleaze, along with the Hard Rock pool and the strip club where porn-star Jenna Jameson started out giving lap dances. According to industry analysts, the Harlot's market share jumped 6.5 points in eighteen months, a move management attributed to the Tupac death car exhibit.

13

"Buddy! Get the hell over here!"

Buddy Landau hated when the cocksucker assistant manager yelled like that. The shop was loud enough, with all the air guns and falling wrenches and Lynyrd Skynyrd blasting on the boom box. It wouldn't kill the guy to walk over and talk to him like a civilized human being. In his off time, Brian, the assistant manager, worked as an assistant coach for the junior varsity football team at Mt. Carmel High. He acted like that meant he was diagramming plays for the Chargers, the way he lorded it over the staff at the Quikie Tune.

"Move the cars in bays two and three," Brian yelled at him.

Buddy slowly wiped off his hands with a rag. Fuck that. "Rick and Al can move their own cars," he yelled back. *Fuck Rick and fuck Al.*

In two flashes Brian was right next to him, in his face, so close Buddy could feel the ripple of his cheap Mt. Carmel High windbreaker.

"Don't give me grief, Buddy. They're mechanics. You know the drill."

"There ain't no fuckin' drill, Brian." He couldn't believe Brian was pulling this shit. "They change oil, just like me."

"Look, son, my players talk back, they run laps till their feet bleed. Just move the damn cars."

Buddy couldn't believe it. *My players*, like Brian was fuckin' Bill Parcells. And he called him "son," even though Brian was just two years ahead of him at Mt. Carmel. Hell, Buddy used to beat up Brian's little brother.

Buddy clenched the rag and fought for control. Soon, he would be able to tell Brian where to stick his game whistle. But right now he didn't want to make waves. The manager, Big Ed, was still pissed off at him about last week, when he forgot to put the drain plug back in that Mercedes.

So Buddy threw down the rag and shook his head, making it clear he wasn't buying Brian's crap. But he moved the cars. He just had to be patient. Things were working out. He'd made a few calls, worked a few angles. The eBay deal hadn't panned out. One guy sent him an e-mail saying, "No feedback, no shit." Buddy wasn't sure exactly what that meant. But now the producer from *Hollywood Now!* was coming over. That would get the ball rolling.

He'd already made a list of things to do, just to make sure everything went well. Number one was to take the bag and hide it. He didn't want to slip up and give her too much. Number three on his list was "Don't masturbate." He wanted to stay sharp.

This was the big time, and Buddy was ready for it. It was smart telling the producer no cameras. Let her work for it. Maybe she would pay him for an interview. She sounded cute on the phone. Maybe he'd invite her to The Food Hut for a burger, if things worked out. Either way, he'd probably make a fortune on eBay alone, once word spread and he figured out that feedback thing.

Last night he called Tony, Elaine's brother, just to chat and let him know something big was going on; not really saying anything, just hinting. To help Tony get the picture, he even mentioned Truland and said a TV producer was stopping by. Whatever you do, don't tell Elaine, he told Tony. But Tony just grunted, apparently not understanding the seriousness of the situation.

14

Through the front office window of the *Del Mar Gazette*, Roger Talbot spotted Sy Walcott in his silver sweat suit working his way across Camino del Mar, heading in his direction. Roger's heart sank. One of the few downsides of his job as editor of the one and only local paper in Del Mar was dealing with Sy Walcott and his fellow Grays, who vigorously opposed any attempt by the Greens to impede their parking privileges or choice of architecture. Roger looked for an escape route. If he had to listen to one more rant about dog poop politics or Nazi volleyball players, he swore he'd vomit on his desk.

Roger rolled his chair back and ducked his head under the desk, reaching for something on the floor that wasn't there. Maybe Walcott wouldn't see him and keep on walking. He searched the floor, afraid to raise his head. The little bell on the front door jingled. *Dammit.*

He poked his head up, defeated. But it wasn't Walcott. Becky Hooks stood in the doorway.

"You look like a jackass," she said.

"I was looking for something."

"Yeah, right."

They hugged like old friends, even though they had met only once. Eight years earlier Jake had arranged a meeting in New York, in a dark bar called the Casket. When she sat down, Roger remembered thinking Becky was the prettiest girl he had ever seen. Her eyes were lime green marbles; she wore a red scarf. That night she had controlled the dinner conversation like a conductor. For the first time, he saw Truland upstaged.

Roger closed the office, looking in both directions for Walcott as he locked the door. They headed to the beachfront patio of one of his favorite local bars, the Fire Pit. For fifteen minutes they drank Coronas and talked easily. Roger told stories about Del Mar politics; she talked about her kids and her volunteer work opposing a Walmart in the neighborhood.

Becky picked up a copy of the *Gazette* left on a table. "No fire coverage?"

"It's in there. Page eleven."

"Page eleven? Jake Truland isn't big news for the *Gazette*?"

"Trust me, *Gazette* readers are far more interested in the new sewage plant." In fact, Jane was upset that he buried her coverage. But the *Gazette* wasn't the place for Truland news, not on Roger's watch. He took a long slurp of Corona. "Besides, I think I'd explode if I touched that world."

"*I'm* here. You going to explode?" She said it with a smile.

"I kind of feel like it's possible. I expect an army of *Cathy!* producers to parachute in at any moment."

She laughed. "Jake has that effect." She took a gulp of beer. "You're not like him. You don't have the gene."

"What gene?"

"The gene that makes you fuckin' crave *Cathy!* producers

parachuting into your backyard. Hell, you might as well call it the Truland Gene."

"He does have a clear focus."

"That's him. Big-ass focused." Becky slid into her Texan when it suited her.

"That makes him sound like one of those guys who paints his face blue and holds up a sign at baseball games. He's not like that."

"Don't bullshit me. You get it. You maybe have a sliver of the gene. But you're way out of Jake's league."

Roger understood. Sure, he liked seeing his byline, got a little buzz when a reader approached him at Bully's. But he didn't yearn for the attention, not the same way as Truland. He didn't need it, not anymore.

"There are certain things Jake won't do." Roger was enjoying this banter with the woman who knew Jake better than anybody. He never talked about Jake.

"Hell, there aren't many." Becky laughed.

"Jake never did a sex tape."

"That's right."

"He just said no."

Becky raised her Corona in a toast. "The man does have lines he will not cross."

They both took long drags off their beers. The sun moved closer to the dark blue horizon.

"You know, he never told me how you candy-asses met," Becky said. "You don't exactly run in the same social circles."

Roger laughed. "I was at the *Gidget* junket," he said.

Becky rolled her eyes. "Oh *gawd*, not another *Gidget* story. I didn't know you were part of that mess."

"I had a front row seat."

The saga of the movie version of *The Gidget Manifesto* was one of the tent posts of Truland's fame timeline. For artistic reasons that remain vague, Bob Starkman, director of a popular series of action movies featuring a rogue Denver policeman, *Mile High Cop*, optioned *Manifesto*, Truland's first best seller. The script called for a very nonlinear retelling of the book's central story of a bikini model gone bad. Farmore Studios paid $1.2 million to secure the rights for Starkman, who saw it as a surreal parable about man's struggle with feminine morals and bad hairdos. Accomplishing his artistic vision would require construction of a $76 million fully operational quarter-mile-long beach set in a water tank in Ensenada, Mexico, as well as vast amounts of full frontal nudity. (In exchange for the studio's willingness to finance the project, Starkman agreed to direct *Mile High Cop IV*, which a reviewer later called "a slice of excrement piled on top of an altar of untarnished ego and greed.")

Truland rumors swirled around the production. This was long before his hermit days, yet he was already seen as an elusive figure. One column reported that he was on safari in Kenya and extremely miffed at the film adaptation of his book. Another suggested that the film's leading man had threatened Truland, after stories spread that Truland was engaged in an affair with the actor's wife during filming.

When it was time for the press junket to promote the release, Roger was working the entertainment/politics/high school sports beat for a small daily in Oceanside. The invitation for the *Gidget* press junket arrived the same day his editor told him to cut down on long-distance phone calls, as part of a "budget reevaluation." That seemed like a pretty piss-poor way of rewarding Roger for a series of witty columns on the demise of the TV sitcom, not to mention his two second-place awards at the recent North County Press Club. So Roger decided to fly to New York on the studio's dime to provide his readers with coverage of *The Gidget Manifesto*.

Midway through the first day of the junket, Roger fled the roundtable discussions of the film's costume design and audio engineering. Fast-walking through the garage of the Hyatt Regency, he almost knocked over a couple locked in a passionate embrace, their arms wrapped around each other like Burt Lancaster and Deborah Kerr on the beach in *From Here to Eternity*.

It was Jake. And the woman was the 23-year-old costar of *Gidget*, who was at the time engaged to a big-name actor, a Ben Affleck look-alike. Roger quickly moved past the couple without saying a word.

That night, after confirming the studio was still picking up his tab, Roger was back in the hotel bar, drinking Scotch and hoping to avoid the other junketeers. Without a sound, Truland appeared beside him, smiling.

"Let's talk about what you saw this afternoon," he said.

"Why?" It wasn't Roger's first Scotch.

"I'm interested in how you're going to play it. Maybe I can help."

Roger held up his hand. "Don't worry, I'm not going to write about it." He was probably more than a little drunk. "Frankly, I really don't give a damn."

"There might be angles you're missing."

"Seriously, I don't care. I'm going to write my little story about the fascinating behind-the-scenes details on the making of the movie, sprinkled lightly with your views on avant-garde French cinema. It will be witty and insightful and everyone will be happy."

Truland paused for a moment and then ordered a Scotch. "Funny, I didn't sense you were that interested in my insights into Godard's perversity," he said. They spent the next three hours talking about the Lakers and the relative merits of North County surf breaks.

Finishing the story, Roger said, "From then on, every once in a while, he would just call, out of the blue."

Becky raised her Corona in toast, once again. "He does like his out-of-the-blue calls."

"I don't really know why he kept calling me. At first I guess I was flattered. But then, you know..."

"You never wanted anything from him. I think pretty much

everybody he meets wants something from him. Or he wants something from them."

They watched the waves. The bubble of conversation on the deck mingled with the occasional squawk of a seagull.

"I'm going to hire a private detective," Becky said, breaking the mood.

"Why?"

"Something is going on. It's serious and he won't do anything about it." She quickly brought him up to date on her opinions about Urbina's role in the fire. "He thinks it's all part of the fuckin' game. If he won't do something about it, I will."

"That's why you came to see me?"

"I wanted you to know. If you talk to him, don't let him cruise through this one. It's not just another photo op."

"You really think he needs his own private investigator?"

"It's Hollywood. Everyone needs their own private investigator."

"But what about the cops?"

"The cops don't know Hollywood. And they don't know Urbina."

"So you think a PI can get evidence on Urbina?"

"He can at least find out if Urbina is involved. And maybe let Urbina know that Jake still has some mojo in town. Let him know somebody is watching."

"Are you going to tell Jake?"

"No. He would be pissed. And I don't give a damn."

Roger drank his beer. The seagulls squawked. And Roger thought how lucky Jake was to have this woman by his side, not giving a damn.

15

As she approached the wrought-iron gate of Casa del Rey del Mar, Jessie Dunbar tapped her blouse twice and looked over at the white van parked across the street. "Testing. Testing. You getting me?" she said. The microphone was taped to her bra. A hand emerged from the passenger window of the van with a thumb up.

Technically, recording someone without their permission was illegal in California and assorted other states. But she knew it was sometimes better to have the tape and worry about the consequences later. The courts were vague these days. Tapes could always be destroyed. But they might be a valuable trump card, in case somebody accused you of something. She learned that in her first year out of J-school.

Casa del Rey del Mar looked like a thousand other two-story courtyard apartment complexes with Mexican names, she noted, checking her jacket pocket to make sure she remembered her notebook. She'd spent the last hour interviewing the sheriff, who assured her that the county's finest were using the latest technology to solve the Truland case, thanks to the "safety-first commitment of the people of San Diego County." He offered her a ride on the helicopter, but she turned it down. Hell, she had her own helicopter. None of that stuff would make air. She spent the next hour staking out the fire substation, hoping to convince the cute investigator to talk, but he didn't come out and he wouldn't pick up the phone.

It was shaping up as a wasted day, unless something panned out with EscondidoDude. Research came up with very little on Buddy Landau, except for an aggravated assault charge that had been bumped to a misdemeanor three years ago and a restraining order from an ex-girlfriend, which looked like pretty standard relationship bullshit.

Jessie looked around the deserted courtyard. As far as she could tell, Escondido was all empty beer cans and trailer parks. Next to Casa del Rey del Mar, weeds and overturned shopping carts covered a vacant lot.

When Jessie knocked on the door of apartment 212, she heard a sharp thud, followed by a cry of pain. "Dammit," she heard a man say.

The door jerked open. "Hey, you're right on time," said the man who opened the door. He was probably 25 to 27, dressed in jeans and a brown T-shirt. He was big, maybe six-two, with a beer gut and skinny arms and a complexion that had clearly created a challenge during puberty.

"Come on in," he said, pulling back the cracked door.

Jessie nervously looked back at the van across the street. She didn't take a step forward. "I'm Jessie Dunbar from *Hollywood Now!*," she said, taking a side step and holding out her hand. She needed to make sure the camera guy in the van got some video of the guy. This might be their only chance.

Buddy took the bait. He turned back into the door frame, making himself visible to the street, and reached out a hand. "OK, all right, no problem, I know who you are."

Jessie dropped his hand and didn't say anything for a beat, milking it for the guys in the van. "Thank you for agreeing to see me, Mr. Landau," she said, still not moving.

"Hell, everybody calls me Buddy. Go ahead and call me Buddy. And aren't you going to come in? This ain't the kind of conversation I want to have out on my front stoop, if you know what I mean."

Jessie didn't budge. She counted to ten in her head, letting the guys in the van squeeze out a few more seconds of video. Finally she said, "I can only stay for a second. I'm on deadline. I'm sure you understand."

Buddy seemed shifty, agitated. He was rubbing his nose a lot. *Is he a meth-head?* This was a mistake, she thought. She nervously looked back at the van. The crew was ten seconds from the door, hearing every word.

"Well, come on in. No reason to be scared or nothing," Landau said, urging her inside.

Buddy's apartment was decorated with what looked like the residue of a bad frat party. The only furniture was a plaid couch and an old wood telephone spool serving as a coffee table. This was a really, really bad idea, Jessie was thinking. And then she spotted a tattered poster in the hallway, a classic cover shot from one of Truland's books, *Amazon Lore*, featuring a stunning six-foot blonde, a character closely modeled, it was reported, after a well-known Scandinavian Olympian javelin thrower.

"Like a Coke?" Buddy said. "I got some juice, too. Orange juice. Or maybe some water?"

Jessie tried to size him up. He seemed friendly enough and he was smiling. But the smile was fake, insincere. He looked like a guy with a mean streak. And he was so jumpy.

"Water will be fine."

Buddy bounded into the linoleum kitchen. From an open shelf, he grabbed a glass with a restaurant logo and filled it from the kitchen tap.

Jessie wandered over to a folding table holding a bulky computer and piles of papers. She noticed the familiar SELT logo on some of the papers. A snow globe sat on a small shelf behind the desk. Looking closer, Jessie saw it depicted a character who resembled Elvis slumped face-down across a bed of gold velvet. It was a favorite among Truland collectors.

Before she could read any of the papers, Buddy interrupted her with the glass of water. He eyed the papers on the desk. "Maybe we oughta get down to business," he said.

"What business exactly is that?" Jessie asked.

"First, I got a couple of ground rules," Buddy said.

"Ground rules?"

"Ground rules. You know, provisions."

"OK, provisions. What provisions?"

"I don't want to talk about that day."

"That day? You mean the day of—"

"That's right. That day. The day in question."

"Then what are we going to talk about?"

"Anything except that day."

They were still standing, facing each other, each holding a glass of water but not drinking. Jessie looked at the plaid couch. Buddy looked at the couch. Jessie decided she'd rather stand. Buddy seemed unsure how to proceed. Finally Jessie leaned on the arm of the recliner and Buddy leaned against the arm of the couch.

"I have some...let's call it...stuff," he said. "Stuff that might be of interest to you."

"What kind of stuff, Mr. Landau?" He seemed to be working from some sort of rehearsed script. "I think you need to tell me what we're talking about."

"Wait right here." Buddy twirled and practically jogged down the hall.

Jessie jumped up and headed back toward the desk. "This is

weird, guys," she whispered into the microphone taped to her bra. "Lots of SELT stuff." Before she could go any further, she heard Buddy bounding back down the hall and she scurried back to the arm of the recliner.

"Take a look at this." Buddy threw a bound stack of papers onto the wood spool, seeming satisfied by the heavy plop.

Jessie picked it up. It looked like a manuscript of *Blue Suede Pimp*. She noted the publisher's stamp and the routing numbers. Thumbing through, she could see hundreds of deletions, insertions, and scribbles in the margins, practically on every page.

"Is this what you posted on eBay?"

Buddy seemed taken aback. "Yeah...but, hey, how did you know that? I didn't use my name or anything. Did eBay give me up?"

"Let's just say we have our sources. Mr. Landau, I think I told you, I'm not really in the memorabilia business."

"But, wait, there's more." He loped back down the hall and returned with another pile of papers, which he handed to Jessie.

Thumbing through the stack, Jessie saw several contracts, all bearing Truland's name. Deal memos. E-mail copies. Some involved personal appearances and show deals. Several carried the Klutch corporate logo. There didn't seem to be any organization to the stack, but there must have been at least fifty different contracts, covering several years. It was a treasure trove of Truland story lines. Several of the sheets appeared burned on the edges.

"Mr. Landau, where did you get these?"

Buddy stiffened. "I can't talk about that. Are you interested or what?"

"You understand, if these were stolen—"

"Stolen, hell, no, I didn't steal them. Let's just say I acquired them."

"OK, OK. Just so you understand, we can't knowingly be involved in a crime."

Jessie looked through the stack of contracts again. Many were dirty and smeared, like they had been picked out of the trash. The papers weren't the story; the fire was the story, she reminded herself. She had to get him back to the fire.

She decided to change direction, see what happened. "Mr. Landau, are you involved with SELT?"

Buddy looked at the computer table and smirked. "SELT? I've got nothing to do with those wackos. I'm just trying to set 'em straight, get 'em to talk sense."

"Set them straight about what?"

"Elvis is no saint. That's not what Truland is about. Truland is all about freedom and partying. It has nothing to do with no Saint Elvis."

"So would you call yourself a Truland fan?"

"A fan?" Buddy seemed taken aback. "A fan? Hell, no. It's not like that. I read the books. Hell, everybody read the books. But it was really about the way he flipped off the man, you know. I mean, the way he, you know, blew off the wannabes. My girlfriend Elaine—I mean, my kinda girlfriend—she could quote lines from his books. But, you know, I'm off that. I'm done with him."

Buddy was angry. She considered bolting for the door. She remembered the restraining order and his *kinda girlfriend*.

Jessie studied the charred and torn stack of documents. She wanted the papers, wanted them badly. But the months of quickie headlines would pale compared with breaking news about a new suspect in the Truland fire. A new suspect could draw a twenty-four share, no problem.

She decided to roll the dice. "Mr. Landau, did you set the fire?"

"Wait, no, I said—"

"I'm not the police, Mr. Landau—"

"Yeah, I know, but—"

"We have video, Mr. Landau. I know you were there." That wasn't true. But it was a familiar reporter gambit.

"Shit." Buddy appeared close to panic. "OK, but what if I was? Big deal. You said so yourself."

"But if you were at the fire, maybe"—she chose her words carefully—"then people might assume you were involved."

"Huh? I...But that's not true. Maybe we outta end—"

"OK, I had to ask. But you have these documents. People are going to ask questions."

"What kind of questions?" Buddy looked confused, agitated. His foot tapped out a steady beat.

"Best way to clear this up would be to go on camera. Tell your side of the story." She caught herself. "You know, share your reactions to the scene, that sort of thing."

"On TV?" Buddy perked up. Jessie had seen the look a million times. You could almost see their ears twitching whenever she mentioned going on camera.

"Would you pay for that?"

"I think I told you we don't pay for news," she said.

"But this isn't news. It's papers. I've been reading up. You guys pay for papers and photos all the time. I heard you paid $3 million for a picture of Rihanna's baby. This is a helluva lot better, *a lot better*, than Rihanna's fuckin' baby."

"Buddy, if the papers are so important, maybe you need to take this material directly to the police."

"No, no cops," he snapped. "I told you, no cops."

Bingo. "OK, so you'd rather tell your story to us?"

"Yeah, I mean, I guess—"

"And if we take the papers, then you would talk on camera? That would be the deal."

"No! That's not what we're talking about. I mean, maybe later." Buddy was visibly trying to control his anger, wrestling with it. He jumped off the plaid couch and grabbed the stack of papers. "I've got something you want, and I'm guessing there might be others who want it."

Maybe this guy is smarter than I think, Jessie thought.

"How much do you think they're worth?" she asked.

That got Buddy's attention. He sat back down on the couch. Finally he said, "Ten thousand."

That impressed Jessie. He didn't go too high or too low. "Maybe if you let me take a few—"

He cut her off. "No, these ain't going nowhere...and the rest of the documents aren't here either," he added quickly. "They're some-place safe." The way he said it, she doubted that was true. The docu-ments were probably stacked up in a box in the closet. But she liked the sound of "more documents."

"And if we do that, will you go on camera?"

"Let's just say I'm not predisposed to do that at this moment."

"So you won't go on TV?"

"Well, let me amend that." He said it with a long *a, ay-mend*. "I might consider going on TV, if the price is right. First we take care of one thing, and then maybe we can talk about the other. And maybe that can be part of the, you know, the deal. But we'd still have to fol-low some ground rules."

Again with the ground rules. Jessie decided it was time to get the hell out of there. "OK. But I can't approve that kind of money. I'm going to have to talk to my boss. In the meantime, I don't think you should be talking to any other reporters."

"Fine, great," he said, maybe a little too eagerly. "But don't, you know, dawdle about it. Lots of people are going to be interested in this stuff, if you know what I mean."

Five minutes later, Jessie was in the passenger seat of the white van, heading up I-15, exchanging high fives with the crew. "That was bigtime creepy," the audio guy said, leaning between the driver and passenger seats.

Behind the wheel, the photographer said, "We got maybe twenty seconds at the door. Clean. When he starts looking around, that's great stuff. He looks like a serial killer."

Jessie was still riding the adrenaline rush. She felt the camaraderie of battle, swapping stories with the team. "You wouldn't believe his apartment," she said. "It was like John Wayne Gacy was the decorator." They all laughed. "And get this. He had a huge Truland poster on the wall. You know the cover shot from *Amazon Lore*? The one with the blonde?"

"Oh yeah, I love that poster," the sound guy said.

"So what do you think?" said the photographer, a well-muscled 35-year-old veteran of TV news.

"I think that was one strange dude," she said. "And I'll tell you, I was damn happy to get out of there when I did. I was ready to call you in."

"We were ready to go," the photographer said, slapping the back of her chair. "When he got all upset about the cops, I was going for the door."

The sound guy chimed in. "I couldn't believe you asked him straight up about the fire. That took balls."

Jessie felt the blood rush to her face. "I know, what was I thinking? But I felt like I had to do it. And, boy, there was something there. The way he reacted? I wish we had a camera on his face. It definitely threw him."

"And he didn't exactly deny it," the photographer said, keeping his eyes on the road.

"Damn right, he didn't deny it. And I was thinking he wasn't surprised by the question. He was ready for it."

The photographer gave her a look. "So, seriously, what do you think?"

"I'm thinking that video is going to be big," she said. "It better be in focus."

She sat back in the van's commander seat. In fact, she wasn't sure what to think. She clicked through the evidence. It sure seemed like the guy was hiding something. And the charred papers looked like they were pulled straight from the scene. If he got the papers from the fire, that meant he was there, and if he was there that might mean he could have set the fire and found the material in the remains. And if he set the fire, what else could the guy be into? SELT? Hired by a scorned lover? She began to tingle at the possibilities.

Jessie pulled out her phone and speed-dialed Brenda. The producer picked up on the first ring, as always.

"What we got?" Brenda said.

Jessie ran through the highlights.

"And he wouldn't go on camera?" Brenda said. "That's a drag."

It was a drag, Jessie thought.

"And I guess the papers don't really say anything," Brenda said. "He could have gotten them anywhere. He could have bought them off somebody."

Jessie felt the excitement draining away. Brenda was such a buzz kill. *Dammit*. She was right. What did they really have? The guy was pretty damn creepy, that was for sure. And the charred documents sure seemed to connect him to the fire. There was definitely something there. But deep down she realized they didn't have a story, not yet. They'd have to buy the documents and that meant time with the Farmore attorneys, and who knew how long that would take?

"What should I tell Sharon?" Brenda said.

Ah, that was the question. What to tell Sharon? Sharon wouldn't want some half-baked hunch. She'd shoot it down in a flash. Without some cool video or the cops confirming that the guy was a suspect, they didn't have squat. Maybe Farmore would pay for the documents, but only if she could prove there was something more to the story. She needed to prepare her case.

"Tell her I got some good sound from the sheriff. Exclusive," she said.

"Nothing about our Mr. Creepy?"

"No, leave it alone for now. Let's see what happens."

She snapped the end button and cursed to herself. They were so close. She could feel it. It was like she had just sat in the living room and chatted with Ted Bundy or Jeffrey Dahmer before they were arrested. She knew the guy was a bad dude; she could feel it in her gut.

16

Twenty miles from Glendale, the offices of Aleksei "Dick" Borovsky spread across the 30th floor of a gleaming glass and steel tower in Century City. A receptionist pretty enough for the cover of *Vogue* took Becky's thumbprint—"standard procedure," the unsmiling receptionist-model said—and showed Becky into a plush office of dark leather and mahogany. "Would you like something to drink?" the receptionist asked. "Soda? Vitamin water? A banana daiquiri?"

Borovsky was known as the private investigator to the stars, although he primarily worked for the studios and the agents, the string pullers. To Becky, he seemed like the right man for the job. He knew the lay of the land, understood the nuances.

Borovsky's office was a windowless cave, covered in bookshelves and the usual array of vanity photos and weighty tomes. A row of six TV monitors glowed silently across the top of one wall. Aside from that, it looked like an old-world lawyer's office, except for what appeared to be a Russian Kalashnikov automatic rifle mounted on hooks behind the desk.

Borovsky entered through an unseen side door. He was tall and thin with a sharp hook nose and deep-set eyes. He didn't waste time with small talk. "Is this about the fire?" he said.

"Yes and no."

"You must be a lawyer," he said.

Becky walked him through the basics. Then she cut to the chase. "There's one other thing." She chose her words carefully. "Jake has a long-standing business relationship with Klutch Enterprises in Vegas. The relationship soured recently."

"You mean he works for Teddy Urbina?"

Becky knew she had come to the right guy. "Three years now. Personal service contract with Klutch, recently expired."

Borovsky rocked back in his high-backed leather chair. "That changes things," he said. "Fashion accessories can be a very complicated business."

Borovsky appeared lost in some deep computation. "I acknowledge that, on first review, it is relevant to speculate that Mr. Urbina may be involved in some way in Mr. Truland's problems. But to prove that, and to...*engage* Mr. Urbina in this query, will take an extra layer of time and...subtlety."

"I understand. Should we bump to a two-man team and say, twenty percent overtime?"

Borovsky smiled. "Yes, I think that should negate the extra commitment necessary. But that's not what I mean. I need some assurance that you understand the situation. You're asking questions, but I'm not sure you really want the answer. What good will an answer do you?"

Becky understood the question. "Mr. Truland is looking for a career shift. He's not going to be able to get anywhere if he can't accurately address the situation."

"I understand." Borovsky leaped up and extended his hand. "And, who knows, maybe it will be as the TV shows say, and this is all the result of Elvis's pesky ghost. Or perhaps an overeager fan. It's quite possible that Mr. Urbina has nothing to do with this. Fire is often the passion of deviant personalities."

As she drove back to the hotel, the phrase "deviant personalities" stuck in her mind. Truland's world was full of deviant personalities. Inflaming passions was one of his skills, a specialty. She often wondered about the mind-set of the obsessed housewives and bored shut-ins who gravitated toward Truland, the fan base that fueled the ratings and filled the talk show audiences. The idea that one might have gone over the edge sent a shiver down her spine. It wasn't a new thought.

Three blocks from the hotel she noticed a black SUV following her down Sunset. It stayed three or four cars behind, never closer, never further. She turned south on King, cutting across two lanes of Sunset traffic, a life-threatening maneuver. The black SUV followed.

Could be paparazzi, she thought, glancing at the rearview mirror. If it was a crew; that would piss her off. They should know better. She was a civilian. Everyone knew it. Sure, every once in a while her name would pop up. A few years ago the crews tracked her for a few days after *Sizzler* published a story with the headline "Truland Gal Likes the Gals." That had the members of her book club cracking jokes for months. But these days they generally left her alone. They knew they weren't going to get anything, beyond video of Bob picking up the newspaper in his boxer shorts. She didn't hide, so there really was no value in her picture.

She tracked the black SUV for a few more blocks. The person behind the wheel wasn't driving like a meth-head tabloid photographer. He was purposely staying back, watching, waiting. Becky's Texas blood started to boil. She wasn't going to put up with this shit, not from some rogue cameraman.

She gunned the engine of the BMW, bolting down the narrow street. The SUV stayed with her. She navigated a few quick turns; the

SUV followed. One more quick right and the BMW bounced into the driveway of the Modernaire and came to a screeching halt. She yanked up the emergency brake, hopped out of the car, and strode to the sidewalk, ready to kick some paparazzi ass. Modernaire parking attendants rushed to her aid. But it was too late. The SUV accelerated past the driveway. All she caught was a glimpse of the black van's tinted rear window as it turned back onto Sunset.

17

The chief was waiting in the station kitchen holding a stack of message slips when Eric Branson returned from the grocery store. "Hey, Mr. Popular, where you been?"

"I was having trouble finding dill weed." Eric was working on a grilled fish recipe. He started putting away the groceries.

"Why are these guys still on you?" The chief was clearly irritated. "I thought this puppy was all sheriff now? Why are they calling you?"

"I don't know. I've been telling them to call the sheriff."

"Then what the hell is this?" he said, waving the phone messages. "What the hell is going on?"

That was a good question. But Eric hadn't heard from anyone in the sheriff's department since the day after the fire. They were supposed to coordinate and keep him in the loop. Instead, he got nothing more than the periodic all-hands e-mail update, not a single call. In his short investigation he had picked up a lot of information about SELT and the vast network of people annoyed by Jake Truland, not to mention the physical evidence at the scene. He sent over his detailed reports; not a word back from the detectives.

Eric made up a plan, on the spot. "I'm going over to talk to the ICIC boys this afternoon," Eric said. "See if I can't get some answers. Make sure we're out of it."

"Good plan," the chief said. "Take these." He pushed the phones messages at him. "Do it before the dill fish."

Eric drove the back road to the sheriff substation, avoiding the I-5. When he was in high school he rode his bike on this hilly, winding road, which, at the time, ran through two miles of empty farmland. He was always embarrassed to show up at school sweaty and out of breath from the ride and then have to ride home after football practice. Most of his friends lived in Rancho Santa Fe and drove their own cars; some drove Mercedes and BMWs.

Today the reconfigured, widened, and restriped road with advanced digital sensors to monitor traffic cut through a landscape of endless tract developments with names like Hacienda del Mar la Vista, with four-way stoplights and Italianate strip malls every quarter mile. The sheriff's headquarters was part of a six-story municipal complex in the heart of Rancho Con Sierra Vista. When Eric checked in at the front desk, the duty sergeant said Detective Brown wasn't available.

"I can see him," Eric said. "He's right there." Eric pointed to a Plexiglas window; Brown was clearly visible at a computer terminal.

"So you know the detective?" the desk sergeant said, apparently unconcerned that he was just caught in a lie. Eric identified himself. The desk sergeant remained unfazed.

"And what is the nature of your business with the detective?"

Before Eric could answer, Brown rapped his knuckles against the Plexiglas and waved him back.

"I was just thinking of you," the detective said, gesturing him toward a Herman Miller desk chair. The word around the fire station was that the sheriff had managed to work an extra $3.4 million for office furniture into last year's antiterrorism budget amendment. The sheriff, a former county supervisor, had also managed to buy a new helicopter in the deal.

"I just got off the phone with Randolph Manor," Brown said. "Randolph Manor himself, you know, from TV?" Brown's round face glowed red. He was in his early thirties but had already lost most of his hair. Everyone in law enforcement knew Brown's story. Two weeks before the fire he had transferred into ICIC after stumbling on ten tons of marijuana during a liquor store robbery investigation, earning him a promotion.

"I told Randolph no, of course. But you know, at a certain point we have a responsibility to talk to these guys. It's our public duty. Did you catch me on ABC last night?"

Eric had missed it. But he had watched the sheriff on the local news. The sheriff stood in front of the new helicopter, dressed in full dress uniform, cradling his custom flight helmet with "Top Cop" boldly lettered above the face shield. The case, the sheriff had said, was moving in "new and exciting directions," which surprised Eric.

"Look, I'm just checking in," Eric said. "Did the lab guys come up with anything on the physical evidence?"

"There is no physical evidence," the detective said. "The lab guys found nothing. No fingerprints. No clothing traces."

"I sent over the physical evidence. There was—"

"Oh, yeah, well, there was physical evidence, but nothing we could use. No suspicious half-burned ID cards lying around." Brown laughed heartily at his own joke.

"What about the accelerant swabs?" Eric was getting annoyed. The detective was treating him like a rube.

"The accelerant was..." The detective shuffled through papers on his desk, finally finding the paper he wanted. "'Garden variety lighter fluid.' Look, the mook even wrote 'garden variety.' Can you believe those science geeks? They all think they're auditioning for *CSI*."

"What about SELT? Anything coming of that?"

"Yeah, SELT..." Brown looked momentarily confused.

"I sent over a report on SELT."

"Of course, yeah, SELT. Very interesting stuff." The detective seemed bored. "What a bunch of wing nuts."

Eric was moving past annoyed. The detective's attitude was unprofessional. Eric didn't expect an invitation to review the case file, but he was a fellow detective. He was here to help.

"What was all that about 'new and exciting information' last night?" Eric asked.

"You know, the investigation is ongoing, and—"

"I worked the scene, Detective."

"Yeah, and you did some mighty fine work, er...what do they call you guys, 'Fireman'? 'Inspector'?"

"Inspector."

"Right, Inspector. The sheriff wants this case to carry on for a few more days. So the investigation continues, and it's going in new and exciting directions. That's the way it is. Who knows, maybe something will pop up."

Pop up?!? That was the ICIC idea of an investigation?

The detective turned back to his computer monitor. The screen displayed an eBay page.

Eric had promised the chief, but this was ridiculous. "So you don't mind if I continue to poke around a little bit?" he asked.

"Yeah, sure, Inspector. You poke around. But make sure you keep us apprised of your investigation."

"Of course."

"And give us a call before you contact witnesses. You wouldn't want to be bumping heads with a sheriff's investigation."

"Right." Eric got it. Investigate, but don't talk to witnesses. Eric was being dismissed. "What about these?" Eric pulled out the stack of messages and tossed them on the desk.

"What are these?"

"Media calls. What should I tell them?"

Detective Brown turned back to Eric, and his eyes narrowed. "You tell them to call the sheriff's department ICIC spokesman. That's what you tell them."

"I have. They don't seem that interested."

"Then you say nothing," Brown said, in the tone of a marshal in an old Western telling the town drunk to get out of town. He gave Eric a hard look.

"Inspector, no media interviews. That straight?"

"Straight."

"The sheriff wants to keep a tight lid on this."

Eric nodded. A tight lid. Right.

Two nights later Jessie was living her nightmare. Except instead of sitting in social studies class naked, she was listening to an *Inside News* reporter saying, with the type of hyperbole usually reserved for presidential assassinations, that the "*I-N* I-team" had "new, exclusive, tantalizing details" about the fire at Jake Truland's house.

The former Dallas Cowboys cheerleader was the anchor: "In this exclusive report that you will only see on *I-N*, our investigative strike team reveals inside information never before reported. Only on *I-N*. Seen nowhere else. Exclusively."

Those *I-N* assholes really loved their exclusives.

"Tonight, the connection between the fire that ravaged Jake Truland's home and his mysterious ties to a Las Vegas fashion accessory company." On-screen, a helicopter buzzed over the Las Vegas Strip at night, providing breathtaking shots of the glimmering hotels.

"Damn," Jessie muttered, "they're even bringing out the helicopters."

The former cheerleader laid out the story. Truland was working for a notorious fashion accessory company. Reports of a dispute. Police investigating Vegas involvement in the fire. For accent, a tearful model turned Vegas stripper shared tales of fashion accessory brutality. There was even rumor of a possible congressional investigation of the fashion accessory industry. *A congressional investigation?! The mother lode!* Every reporter dreams of a story that prompts a congressional investigation.

She couldn't believe they'd missed it. This was going to explode. Vegas fashion accessory executives out to get Truland?! A fashion angle?! Where in hell did *I-N* get it? This sure didn't come from Vince. It might have leaked from the sheriff's department. But the sheriff PR reps were scrambling and very nervous, not acting at all like gloating media leakers. After talking to the main flack for five minutes, Jessie was convinced he didn't know anything about Vegas.

The wrath of Sharon Jones-Jones was her immediate concern. In minutes, Sharon's bugle voice would ring out, summoning Jessie to her lair. And there was no way the meeting would end well.

Jessie was already clicking through the possibilities for future employment. The other entertainment news shows were out. She'd be seen as damaged goods. What publicist would return a call from a producer on Sharon Jones-Jones's shit list? The network news magazines would laugh at her. They wouldn't give a damn about her degree in journalism or that piece she did on the homeless when she was an intern at the Yuma station. God, she'd probably have to go back to local TV news. She'd be lucky to find a job stacking a show in a midmarket, like Portland or Detroit.

"Jessie! Now!" Sharon's voice was louder than a bugle. And everybody in the newsroom heard it. Jessie couldn't face the pity stares as she made the long walk through the newsroom.

Sitting in front of Sharon's chrome throne, Jessie tried to psych herself up. She knew Sharon had no respect for the bunnies who cowered in front of her. But Sharon screeched for five minutes without a break.

"I was expecting better of you. I thought you could handle a big story. But you've been getting your ass kicked from day one."

Jessie knew she was right. She deserved this. But she couldn't just sit and take it. Her mind was racing. She'd be toast in another five minutes. She had to come up with a plan, an alternative. She had to give Sharon something, *anything*.

But Sharon didn't let up. "And now we're going to spend a cycle chasing an *Inside News* story. And it's *fashion accessories?!* This has Showtime movie written all over it. What are you going to do about it? How the hell are you going to follow this?"

"I'm not." Jessie just blurted it out.

"What do you mean?"

"I think they blew it." She was letting the words come out, hoping they would lead somewhere. "The story is wrong."

Sharon looked at her like a leopard eying a wildebeest. "Why are you so sure about that?"

"Because...well, I'm not sure if it's wrong, they may have a source... but I've talked to the real suspect." She was committed now. No way out. "Ask me, I think he did it. This Klutch story is just smoke."

"Why haven't you told me about this suspect before?"

Jessie ran down the general details about Buddy Landau. "I didn't think we had it yet. But it's almost ready to go. I was thinking of pitching it for tonight, actually. I'm going to get the cops on record about it. Confirming he's a suspect. Then we'll be good to go."

Sharon looked suspicious.

"I'm telling you, this guy is the real deal. There's just too much evidence. If he didn't do it, he was involved." Jessie couldn't stop herself. "The cops are taking this guy seriously." That was just a straight-out lie. But she was grasping, desperate to prove to Sharon that this was a real story.

"Then why don't we have the cops on the record?" Sharon wasn't convinced.

"I've been working it. But now I think they're—"

"No cops, no story. Legal will never go for it. What's the video?"

Jessie ran down the meeting at the door, not mentioning that she was miked. She'd save that detail for later, in case she needed it.

"And no one else has this guy?" Sharon asked.

"No one. Just us."

"You need the cops. Suspect, person of interest, something," Sharon said.

"That's no problem." Jessie was improvising now, dancing on a pin. But Sharon seemed ready to go.

"The cops have to say he is the subject of the investigation," Sharon said. "A person of interest. Something."

"No problem. I'm going down there this afternoon. I was going to tell you once, you know, I got it nailed down."

"We need an exclusive." Sharon was on board. Her tone went from scolding to collaborator. Jessie jotted notes. "Don't screw this up," Sharon said as parting words.

Jessie practically ran out of the office, flush with the energy of the death row puppy adopted on the way to get the needle.

Ten minutes later Jessie was on the road with the same crew from Escondido in the same white van. On the drive south she phoned the sheriff's department every fifteen minutes. She tried the flack, the detectives, the sheriff's personal secretary. But she couldn't get a return call. On a hunch, she told the photog to head toward the Del Mar fire station. She left a message on the investigator's machine, imploring him to call her back, assuring him that she had "very important information related to the Truland investigation."

When they pulled up forty-five minutes later, a snippy fireman said Branson wasn't around, sending Jessie's heart plummeting through her large intestine. They sat in the van for fifteen minutes, waiting. Just when she was about to give up hope, the wavy-haired investigator jogged up to the garage, shirtless, in red shorts, covered in sweat and gasping for air.

She jumped out of the van and raced over to him. "You're a hard man to get hold of," she said, out of breath. She introduced herself, huffing and puffing after the run from the van.

"You're the one who left those messages on my answering machine," he said, bent over at the waist, looking like he might puke. "Something about important information?"

"It is important," she said.

"Then you should take it to the sheriff's detectives." His voice was a wheeze.

"Those guys? You have got to be kidding. They're not going to listen to anything I say. Those guys are useless."

"Hah, you got that right." Branson was getting his breath back. When he straightened up, Jessie's head was in line with his glistening bare chest.

"This is way too important for those ICIC guys," she said. "They'll just bury it."

He still looked suspicious. But he nodded his head in agreement. "OK, what do you have?"

"This is awkward." She hesitated for effect. She had spent the drive down from LA thinking of how to approach this conversation. "I need to tell you some things. But I can't tell you too much. You know, journalism ethics."

Branson nodded his head in a noncommittal way. He seemed to be going along. She gave him a big smile. "First off, I have to ask if you mind if I get the camera out here. We are TV."

"No, no way. I'm not authorized—"

"OK, no problem, no problem. I have to ask. But you know, just between you and me, unauthorized people go on TV all the time. It might do you some good."

"You're the second person who has said that. What kind of—"

"It might, you know, raise your public profile. Maybe lead to other opportunities."

"Ma'am, I'm a firefighter. I'm not really sure what you mean by other opportunities."

Jessie blushed. Nobody called her "ma'am." They were probably the same age. At most she was a year or two older. But he was so polite, so sincere. She decided to let it drop.

She couldn't stall any longer. "I have to ask another question. Off the record. And I mean it, off the record. I'm not even taking notes. But I have to know something before we can talk." He didn't object, so she charged on. "Are you guys really investigating the fashion accessory connection?"

Branson contemplated that for a second. "I have to be honest, the sheriff guys aren't exactly keeping me in the loop. But just a hunch. Just between you and me? I doubt it."

She caught a wisp of frustration in his tone. Her hopes soared. "What about a guy in Escondido? Anybody bring up a guy in Escondido?"

"Again, I'm not sure. But, no, I don't think so."

Jessie's heart sank. No investigation; no story. "Maybe you're investigating a bitter fan?"

"I've been looking into some of the SELT people, but nobody who really leaps out."

Jessie laughed. "SELT? Come on. You're looking at SELT?"

The investigator seemed offended. "There appear to be some obvious suspects in the organization."

Jessie had to smile at his innocence. It was like he lived on a different planet. But she needed to keep him talking. Make him feel relaxed. "Geez, Eric. Can I call you, Eric?"

He nodded.

"I hate to burst your bubble. But SELT is a front."

"A front?"

"A patsy. A sham."

"What do you mean?" The guy seemed genuinely baffled. "What kind of sham?"

"Maybe not a sham. It's a creation."

"Creation? Who created it? You mean that woman? Mrs. Moorehead?"

"Cassandra? She was a VP at a marketing agency in Nashville before she took the gig. That woman is smart."

"But then who—"

"Vince. Vince Trello. Come on, you must have known that? It's Scandal Management 101. If a story is going to have legs, you've got to have an angry mob, bitter opposition. And sometimes, if there is no angry mob, you have to create your own."

The investigator appeared to be processing the information. "That doesn't rule them out as suspects," he said. "There are some people in there who definitely need checking out."

"That's true," she said. He was softening up.

"You said you have some vital information?"

She took a deep breath. She'd experimented with different ways to play it. If she gave him the soft sell, he might just ignore her or "take it under advisement" or some other mealy-mouthed legal term employed by detectives. She had to convince him this was important.

"I think I know the guy who did it."

He frowned. "What makes you so sure this guy did it?"

She had him hooked. She tried not to sound too excited. "Look, I have to be careful. This is dicey territory. As a reporter I can't be seen as aiding law enforcement."

"Anything you say will be protected. It's still an ongoing investigation."

"I've been in his apartment," she said. "I've seen some things."

"Is this the Escondido man you mentioned?"

She nodded. He was hooked. "I feel like I have this important information. But the sheriff doesn't know anything about it, and this guy may be getting away."

Eric nodded. "I understand. I appreciate your journalism ethics. But you need to tell somebody."

She gave him a piece of paper with Buddy's name and address. "This stays between you and me, OK? But I think this guy may have started the fire at Truland's house."

"Why do you think that?"

She gave him a brief synopsis, leaving out most of the details. "He showed me some things. I can't be more specific than that."

He took the slip of paper. "OK, thanks for bringing it to my attention. I'll make sure the detectives get it."

Jessie squirmed. That wasn't enough.

"But the sheriff's detectives will just blow it off. You know those guys."

Eric smirked. "I'll make sure they see this one," he said.

Jessie was ready to burst. That wasn't enough. She needed him to say it. She needed to hear the words.

"You promise me you'll investigate it? You, personally. You'll make sure there is an investigation?"

"Sure, definitely."

Jessie could scream. *Just say the words!*

"No, really, it's, you know, fair to say somebody will look into him, right? Not just sweep it under the rug?"

"Don't worry, there is going to be an investigation on this one, I promise."

That's it! Jessie practically leaped in the air. *An investigation!* That's what she needed.

As soon as Jessie hopped back into the van she called Sharon. "We got it," she said. "Nailed."

"Did he go on camera?"

"No, but he confirmed. We can say police...no, *authorities* are investigating the guy. Definite."

By the time she was back in the office, the entire shop was in full motion. Jessie felt the buzz of activity, the crush of excitement of the big story, *her story*. The editors already had a rough cut, working off a script written by Brenda, relying heavily on the dark video of Buddy hovering in the doorway of his apartment.

"The lawyers have signed off," Brenda said proudly, as they took seats in the cramped edit room. The editor was still laying down music, a spooky electronic beat vaguely similar to the theme from *The Exorcist*. "Once they heard the guy had a record and restraining order, they relaxed. You know, it's tough to ruin the reputation of a guy with a record."

Jessie was taking notes as the rough edit played on a ten-inch monitor, when she realized Sharon was standing behind her, holding a copy of the script.

"Good work on this," Sharon said. "Let's give it the full court press."

"I already have three crews heading to Escondido, and we're working react at the *Wonder Duck* premiere tonight."

"Good. And let's try for Becky again. This might be one she'll want to comment on. Maybe get some Texas indignation."

Jessie punched a note into her iPhone.

"I think the key may be this Elaine girl, the ex-girlfriend," Sharon said. "We get her, we get the motive. We get the motive, we get the case." Jessie smiled. Sharon loved *Law & Order*.

Sharon slid back into the chaos of the newsroom. Her head was about to explode. This was her chaos. *Her story*. This was going to be big, no doubt about it. Everyone would pick it up. Hell, maybe even the wires would go with it. *Those I-N assholes are going to shit in their pants!* Soon everyone in the country would know the name Buddy Landau.

Book II

19

Q: *Some people think you're a philosopher. Do you think of yourself that way?*
A: *Everybody is a philosopher. Rodney Dangerfield was Aristotle.*
Q: *But do you think people should look into your words for wisdom?*
A: *It depends on your goal. If your goal is to be on TV, I highly recommend it.*
                                    —Interview with Esquire, *July 2009*

Buddy Landau slept late on Tuesday morning. He wasn't due at the Quikie Tune until 1:00 p.m., so what the hell, he thought. He didn't notice his answering machine light flashing wildly. He had turned off the phone so Brian couldn't call him in for a double shift, like he knew the prick would.

In his wifebeater and boxer shorts, he went out to pick up the mail, part of his morning routine. He was hoping maybe the *Hollywood Now!* producer had decided to simply mail him a check, in order to get things rolling. He hadn't heard from her since their meeting, but he felt like things had gone well. Any day now he'd be rolling in it.

Still groggy, he stepped out on to the second floor landing.

"Get back in there, you asshole!" someone yelled. Buddy saw the manager of Casa del Rey del Mar, a nasty biker dude from Florida, standing next to the communal barbecue in the courtyard. He was frantically waving his arms. "Get the hell back in your apartment, dumbass!" he shouted.

Buddy turned to look down at the landing. Ten feet away, in front of his neighbor's door, a woman in a brown business suit crouched low, commando-style, spider-walking toward him, holding a microphone in front of her like a bayonet. Behind her a scraggly guy with a ponytail struggled to hold a video camera steady, trying to avoid tripping over the crouching woman with the microphone.

"Can I get a statement?" the woman screamed at the top of her lungs, even though she was just a few feet away.

Buddy looked around. She sure seemed to be talking to him. He looked down at his wifebeater, which had a small stain on it from last night's chili feast. Maybe the biker dude manager was giving him some good advice.

"Just one question," the woman with the microphone shouted, practically bursting one of his eardrums.

Buddy jumped back into his apartment and slammed the door. What the hell was going on? He moved over to the window and pulled back the corner of the curtain and almost leaped out his skin. The woman had her face pressed up against the glass, looking right at him. He screamed. She screamed.

"Get the hell off the property," the biker manager shouted at the woman. She and the photographer scurried down the walkway.

Buddy saw a row of antennas sticking up above the courtyard

wall behind them. Each was attached to a panel van painted with various logos and catchy slogans. There must be at least a dozen, he figured. At least twenty photographers and reporters huddled around the entrance to Casa del Rey del Mar, below the wrought-iron arch with a crown on top. All the photographers were aiming their cameras at his window.

Buddy jumped back. He pulled the curtain shut. But when he covered one end, an inch gap appeared on the other side. He pulled the curtain to the left, and then there was a gap to the right.

What the hell was going on? Could it be that the other TV shows had followed *Hollywood Now!* out here? He turned on the TV and quickly flipped through the channels, past the nature shit, past the chick channels, and...*there was his apartment.* It was a shot of his front door, tight enough that he could see the crack in the middle, the result of some altercation involving a previous tenant. He flipped the channel, and there was his apartment again, this time a close-up of his window.

He hit the floor, chest down on the baby-shit brown carpet. He crawled on his belly to the window and peeked out the corner. The photographers were still huddled around the gate, cameras on their shoulders. He looked back at the TV. He looked down at the photographers. That was them! They were live! They were taking pictures of his window, and there it was on his TV.

He laughed out loud. He couldn't believe it. There was Casa del Rey del Mar, right there. People all over the world were watching his apartment, right now. He crawled back to the remote and raced through the channels. At least a dozen showed his apartment.

And then he turned up the sound.

"The suspect is known to have a history of violence..."

Another channel.

"...as first reported by *Hollywood Now!*, a syndicated entertainment news program..."

Another channel.

"...evidence suggesting involvement in a radical anti-Truland organization..."

Another channel, and there was Elaine. *Elaine!* And she looked kind of hot, in a pouty kind of way.

"I always thought he was kind of peculiar," she was saying. "And he always had this kind of thing about Truland. It used to make him kind of upset every time I brought him up."

What the fuck? "Peculiar?" Fuckin' Elaine was calling him "peculiar" on TV?

He flipped the channel again.

"Evidence reviewed by our sources confirms that Landau may have been at the scene of the fire that morning," said a stern blonde in a bright blue suit. Video from the day of the fire appeared in a box over her shoulder. "Exclusive FNN video appears to place Buddy Landau at the scene of the crime."

With a whoosh the video went full screen and froze on a long shot of the crowd on the street. A small white circle appeared, and damn, that was him! With a white circle around his face!

"We've also confirmed *Hollywood Now!*'s report that authorities are, indeed, investigating this man and his potential connection to the fire."

Connection to the fire? They were investigating him in connection with the fire?

Then they cut to video of the San Diego County sheriff walking through a parking lot, looking frazzled. "Hell, yes, we're looking into it. Of course we're looking into it," he said without slowing his pace.

Looking into it? What the hell?! Looking into what?

The TV went back to the stern blonde in the three-piece suit. "Go online now to learn more about this new suspect in the Truland case, Randolph Martin Landau."

Randolph Martin Landau? Holy crap! I'm a three-name dude!

Three-name dudes are always guilty! What the hell? How did I get to be a three-name dude?!

Buddy was frozen, staring at the TV. Now they were showing the Quikie Tune, and the announcer was talking about "alleged prior conflicts with the law." Buddy turned down the sound. The image shifted back to his apartment, another close-up of the window and then a shot of his truck. Buddy jumped up and ran into the bedroom to make sure all the blinds were closed.

20

Sitting on the bridge, surrounded by television monitors tuned to Landau coverage, Jessie wallowed in her success. No patronizing looks today, no way. She was the star again, the hero, the go-to gal. She felt the rush of hitting a game-winning home run in the bottom of the ninth, the winning basket in overtime. *She shoots, she scores!! The crowd goes wild!!!*

Her magic moment came twenty minutes after the story ran, when the wire services picked up the report, giving Landau the formal stamp of a legitimate news story. Ratings for that night's exclusive report were up 6.7 percent from the same day a week earlier. The next morning Landau was mentioned in *New York Times* and *Washington Post* online reports. Some reporters hedged, crediting the report to *Hollywood News!* in case it wasn't true, but that made the scoop all that much sweeter. When the sheriff confirmed that an investigation was under way, all the news outlets were on Landau, including *Inside News: Morning Edition*. The ex-cheerleader anchor looked visibly distraught as she reported, "A new suspect is emerging in the strange tale of the disastrous inferno that has engulfed Jake Truland." Their "exclusive" was an interview with a woman who said she once worked at Truland's Del Mar house as a maid.

That afternoon, Sharon Jones-Jones made a show of parading across the newsroom to the bridge. She grabbed the unsuspecting Jessie from behind and gave her a big hug.

"Way to go, girl, I knew you had it in you," Sharon said loudly enough for everyone in the room to hear.

"Thanks, boss," Jessie said, flustered at the unusual public display of affection.

Sharon rolled up a chair and adopted a conspiratorial tone. "This is one helluva story. This guy feels like a character out of *In Cold Blood*. I just wish Truman was still alive to write it."

"Yes, that is too bad." Jessie didn't know what else to say about Truman.

"You really pulled a big one out of the hat, young lady. I just love the way the story resonates. I knew that girl, what's her name? The girlfriend? I knew she would be the key to the story."

"You called it. That really made the whole story play." Jessie couldn't believe Sharon was gushing this way in front of the entire newsroom.

"So what's next?" Sharon asked.

21

Eric found everyone on duty in the fire station's break room, watching yet another round of live reports from the Escondido apartment complex. A roar went up when Channel 9 cut to a tall blonde reporter in a loose green blouse. She was standing on the sand in front of the remains of Truland's house. The wind tugged at the buttons of her blouse, exposing a hint of belly button. The firefighters cheered. Channel 9 was a favorite in the squad room.

Eric flipped the channel. There were groans and shouts of protest. Somebody threw a water bottle at him, just missing his head. "Business," he said, ignoring the protests.

Eric wasn't surprised when *Hollywood Now!* ran the story on Landau. The frazzled producer probably already knew they were going to air the report when she came to see him. She obviously cared about her work. It was important to her. She was kind of cute, the way she wrestled to get the words out, clearly trying to say everything just right. She seemed desperate to do the right thing and tell the authorities about the suspect before the story aired. Her passion and eagerness for her work was impressive, something he rarely found in his fellow firefighters.

"Turn back to the belly button, you degree-lovin' cocksucker," Tank shouted from the couch.

Eric flipped through the channels. On Channel 4 he caught the tail end of an interview with a woman identified as the suspect's ex-girlfriend, who appeared to be doing interviews in the parking lot of a Walmart. On FNN, a scowling ex-prosecutor was decrying the sheriff for not arresting Landau. "Why, there might be a known murderer and rapist sitting in there plotting new crimes," she said in her exaggerated Southern accent. "It defies logic and common sense to think that the sheriff in San Diego County is twiddling his thumbs while ordinary people in Escondido have to worry if a sadistic fiend is living in their community—"

All hell was breaking loose. Detective Brown sounded frazzled and irritable when Eric called to offer help. Eric had never mentioned Landau's name to the detective. He figured it was better to investigate on his own, at least at first. Eric didn't feel any need to share his prior knowledge with the hyper detective, but he felt guilty enough to want to assist, if he could. According to Brown, the detectives were having trouble getting a search warrant; a judge was refusing to sign. "Some problem with probable cause," Brown said. But the sheriff was using a few clauses of the Patriot Act to search through computer and phone records, he said.

"So don't worry, the investigation is on track," Brown mumbled hurriedly before hanging up.

In the break room the squad was loudly debating the relative merits of Channel 4's new weather girl and the station's brunette investigative reporter, who was on-screen in a sheer white blouse and skintight pants, reporting live from the Escondido apartment complex. "Camel toe, definite camel toe," Larry the ladder man shouted.

Eric turned up the volume. "The News Action Investigative Team has learned exclusively that the suspect has ties to SELT, the radical anti-Truland organization. We've also learned that the suspect, seen here trying to avoid our cameras"—Landau was shown for a split second in his boxer shorts jumping back into his apartment—"has connections to groups known to advocate violent and subversive activities." As she spoke, the camera zoomed in on a second story window. The shot was freeze-framed for effect. Clearly visible in the bottom left corner was a bumper sticker for the Clash.

22

Jake spent that evening in the water off Venice, thrashing around in washed-out two-to-three-footers as the sun went down. He only caught a couple of waves. Most of the session was spent splashing around in white water. It didn't matter.

When he pulled into the Sallie Mae parking lot it was dark, darker than usual. One of the bands in residence must have shot out the lights again, Jake thought as he locked up the rented BMW. As he approached the elevator, he saw a man in a Brooks Brothers suit loitering near the entrance—a muscular guy in a blue blazer standing in a parking garage trying to look inconspicuous.

Jake wasn't completely surprised when he opened the door to his room and found Teddy Urbina sitting at the tiny desk provided by the Sallie Mae.

"Nice digs," the fashion accessory executive said, looking uncomfortable in the plastic straight-back chair. The other Brooks Brothers twin was sitting on the bed, eyeing Jake with a clear look of annoyance.

"I see you brought the marketing department," Jake said.

"Yeah, it's a kind of an off-site," Urbina said with a chuckle.

"Make yourself at home. But, sorry, no room service. And no minibar."

"We won't be long," Urbina said. "Shut the door." Urbina gestured for him to sit in the orange overstuffed chair. "So this is where you escape to? This is where you hide out?" Urbina made two-finger quote marks when he said "hide out." "You didn't think we could find you?"

"I wasn't hiding from you."

"I know...I know. You're Truland the Mysterioso. A fucking ghost. All image."

"Teddy, you're not sounding like much of a marketing executive."

"I'm not feeling like much of a marketing executive right now," he said. The Brooks Brothers dude perked up at Urbina's anger. "I don't like seeing Klutch on the TV news."

"You love being on the news. That's why you paid me."

"Don't play the ass. They're talking about a congressional investigation, Jake. Nobody likes congressional investigations."

"Except congressmen."

"You're pissing people off. Even more than usual. This isn't like you."

"This is really all about my contract, right?"

"Let's start with your contract. Are you back? Because if you're not back, I've got very little to say on that topic."

"Teddy, I made up my mind. I'm moving on. What's the big deal?"

Urbina laughed, a harsh cackle. "Are you kidding? The Harlot brought in $143 million in free cash flow for Klutch last year, as you probably damn well know." Urbina was bragging. That must have really pleased the boys in New York. "You want to fuck with that? You think the board of directors is going to let you just walk away?"

"And that's why you burned down my house?" Jake decided it was best to lay the cards on the table.

"Is that what you think? Really? Good, you think that." Urbina started to rock back in the plastic chair but momentarily lost his balance. He quickly regained control. "I remember you once acknowledged that we could hurt you. You said that. But I don't think you really believed it."

"What do you want, Teddy? You're not here about the contract."

"You're damn right. I'm here because Lindsay Bowman did two hours of her show on Klutch yesterday, and I had a goddamn private investigator banging on my door asking about you. I had to stop and think for a while about how damn stupid you might be. And after thinking about it for a while, I couldn't decide how stupid you really are. So I'm here."

"I don't know what you're talking about. I haven't talked to anybody about you. Not once. I certainly don't know anything about a private investigator."

Urbina eyed Jake for at least thirty seconds, sizing him up. Urbina considered himself one of the better poker players in Vegas, thanks to his 235th-place finish at a World Series satellite tournament in Laughlin.

"OK, let's say I believe you," he said. "We still have the problem of your ongoing relationship with Klutch and this increasing friction between us. We used to be partners, Jake. What happened? You don't love us anymore?"

"I don't love the game anymore. I don't love the idea of someone burning down my house."

"Come on, you still feel the buzz. Admit it."

"I earned my keep, Teddy. I'm changing the strategy. Reconfiguring. It's time."

"Time? You think you're the fuckin' timekeeper? This is the fashion accessory business. I have people to answer to in China. You get me? China?"

"Let's get something straight." Jake was angry now. He leaned forward in the orange chair, which smelled vaguely of vodka. "You can't touch me, and you know it. So let's stop all this tough guy shit."

Urbina appeared amused. "My tough guy shit? Jake, I'm offended. But please, why exactly can't I, as you say, touch you?"

"You come anywhere near me. You try to screw with me again. I will go public. One phone call and you'll be on the cover of *Sizzler*. And it won't be some kiss-ass *Marketing Monthly* profile."

"Jake, you're being rash."

"Don't fuck with me, Teddy. You know I can do it with one phone call. Hell, I can guarantee a full week on *Tattler*. Your *board of directors*"—he said it with a smirk—"are sure as hell not going to like a *60 Minutes* exposé on Klutch's business practices."

Urbina glared at him, using the look he practiced in the mirror.

Jake didn't waver. "Teddy, come on. You know the story can be you and a gerbil up your ass, no problem. How do you think that would play?"

Urbina strained not to blink.

Jake ignored the glare. "You know what I'm talking about. It could get ugly real quick. You'd be the headline, not me."

"OK, Jake. Don't get riled up." Urbina was still trying not blink, but the muscles on the sides of his eyelids were twitching. "Let's just say we're at an impasse. A tense point in the negotiation. Maybe you need a day or two to rethink your position."

"I don't need to rethink anything, Teddy. We had a good run. Let's just let it go."

Urbina stood up, rising to Truland's chin. He gave Jake the stare, but then thought better of it. He walked to the door, Brooks Brothers assistant in tow. "Nothing is that easy in Vegas, Jake. You of all people should know that."

23

Dick Borovsky wiped his hand across the finely polished surface of his mahogany desk, the one JFK used when he was in Hyannis Port. Supposedly JFK made love to Marilyn Monroe on this desk, or at least that's what the agent from the auction house said. Borovsky paid $250,000, but he didn't necessarily believe the story. He didn't believe many of the stories he was told.

Borovsky had been busy since his visit from Becky Hooks. First off, he called two executives at Farmore Studios to update them on Truland's activities. Calling the studio might be interpreted as ethically questionable, but both executives were clients, due to an unfortunate incident involving an underage Romanian girl. He had a fiduciary responsibility to them, too, he reasoned. Neither sounded surprised by Teddy Urbina's potential involvement in Truland's problems, Borovsky noted.

Next Borovsky called a producer he knew at *Inside News*. Borovsky owed him a favor. The producer had helped bury a story about his heiress client who was picked up by police in a routine sweep of a

Long Beach crack house. When she was arrested wearing a gold-trim Versace original, she indicated to the officers that she was merely an acquaintance of the toothless crack dealer, known locally as Spike. It was merely a social visit, she told the officers, who noted that her version of events differed from the story told by Mr. Barlow, aka Spike. "The ho' say she blow me for a dime bag," he said. "I say, shit yeah."

Inside News caught wind of the story, but fortunately for the heiress Borovsky was able to convince the producer to kill the "unsubstantiated smear campaign," in exchange for an exclusive on an actor facing charges for beating his wife and three comped nights in the Princess Scarlett suite at the Harlot. Calling the *Inside News* producer with a Truland tip was one more payment on the old debt.

Dealing with Teddy Urbina was a tad trickier. Finding him wasn't the issue. Borovsky and Urbina both played in a twice-monthly private poker game hosted by the mayor of Las Vegas in an off-Strip apartment. Sending out surveillance teams to follow Urbina and dig into his records didn't seem like a wise move. It was unlikely to produce any answers and it would very likely piss off Urbina, which was also pointless.

Yet, he did feel a certain obligation to his client, who he assumed was actually Jake Truland. And Truland was an unknown variable. Truland floated outside the system, a wild card. Even with his lengthy list of contacts, Borovsky wasn't sure who Truland talked to, who he played, who he had dirt on. There was always the chance that Urbina was not involved, which only increased the necessity for extra tact.

Eventually Borovsky called an old friend, a former homicide detective in Vegas. He told him where to find Urbina.

"Am I jacking him up? Should I bring a buddy?"

"No, definitely not. Be polite. This is an informational interview."

"A what? I'm giving, whadda ya call it? An informational interview with Teddy Urbina?"

"Yes, exactly. Very polite."

"What the hell will that accomplish?"

"I want you to judge how he reacts. Get a sense of the lay of the land."

"Yeah, OK. Sure. Good plan. I'll get the lay of the land." The detective hung up without a good-bye.

Two days later, Borovsky accepted the detective's report. "How did he seem?" Borovsky asked.

"He seemed kinda pissed. That's how he seemed."

"How did he react when you asked him about the fire? Did he seem surprised?"

"Yeah, he seemed real fuckin' surprised that I had asked him such a dumbass question."

That wasn't a whole lot of information, but Borovsky considered it $20,000 well spent—or at least $20,000 his client spent well. He'd write a report making it clear that his investigation extended directly into the subject's office.

Now, sitting at his desk admiring the shine once buffed by Marilyn's butt cheeks, he knew it was time to take the investigation to the next level. The case had taken some interesting and unexpected twists. Truland had a gift for fireworks, he thought, and sometimes those fireworks rained money. This Landau character certainly changed the story line. But Dick Borovsky still couldn't determine who that story line would benefit and, more importantly, how it might benefit him and his clients. It was time to get proactive, he decided. He picked up the phone and dialed back one of the Farmore studio execs, the younger one, the one with a special weakness for Eastern European prostitutes. He was the favorite to get the CEO job, which made him the perfect candidate to supply a few answers to Borovsky's many questions.

24

For two days Buddy Landau didn't leave his apartment, subsisting primarily on Top Ramen, microwave popcorn, and tap water. He stayed near the center of the living room, sunk down on the couch, afraid to go near the windows.

The day after the camera crews showed up, Brian called to tell him not to come into work. "The corporate guys think it will be for the best."

"For how long?"

"No need to rush, sport. You just take care of what you need to take care of."

"But Brian, I need to work. No work. No money. *Comprende?*"

"This comes from corporate, big guy. They hired specialists to consult on this...you know, situation."

"But for how long?"

"Until further notice."

"Further notice? How long is that?"

"It's a time to be determined."

"Determined by who?"

"We'll notify you."

"Brian, come on, man. No work, I starve."

"It's corporate, big guy. We'll notify you."

"This just doesn't seem right. You can't just fire me. I have rights."

"If you have any questions, I encourage you to call the Buddy Landau Crisis Hotline. Wait, I'll get the number."

"You got a crisis hotline with my name on it?"

"These corporate guys, they don't mess around."

Buddy didn't bother to write down the number. He tried to call his sister in Idaho, but she didn't answer the phone. Elaine's brother-in-law picked up, but all he said was, "Get a lawyer, Buddy, a good one."

Three or four camera crews continued to hover by the court-yard gate of Casa del Rey del Mar. A tall dude wearing camo fatigues appeared to be living in a beat-up Toyota parked across the street. When Buddy made a dash for the mailbox, hoping for some good news, he saw the man lift one of those small handheld video cameras and track him the way a hunter tracks a deer through a scope.

Buddy was going crazy locked up in the apartment. Every time he turned on the TV, there was somebody talkin' about him as if they knew everything about him. One reporter girl, who looked like his favorite Chargers cheerleader, the Mexican girl with the cleavage that resembled the Grand Canyon, talked about his DUI arrest, making him sound like John Dillinger. It took him two minutes to realize it *was* his favorite Chargers cheerleader. But that didn't make him feel any better, since she was basically calling him a demented lunatic.

The final straw was seeing Elaine on *Cathy!* It looked like maybe she had spent ten hours in a beauty salon. Her hair was arranged in some sort of beehive with a gold pin. She sat next to Cathy on the white couch, sitting up straight with her ankles crossed, a lace hanky in her hand. Periodically she dabbed at her eyes with the hanky as she told Cathy what an asshole Buddy was during their "long, sordid relationship." At one point Cathy hugged her, gave a real deep squeeze. The camera moved in close and Buddy saw a little bitty tear in Cathy's eye.

That's when he knew it was time to make a run for it. Supplies were running low. He was down to two packets of Top Ramen. He'd sell the documents and go someplace, maybe Fiji or Seattle. Right now he didn't know where, he just had to go.

There wasn't much to pack. Looking around the apartment, the sum accumulation of his life wasn't worth fifty bucks. He didn't want any of it. Even the old banged-up computer that took ten minutes to turn on wouldn't fetch five bucks from Goodwill. He gathered the pictures of Elaine and his important papers—his birth certificate, the car registration, his tattered old Social Security card—and slid them into his Chargers backpack, the one he got for free on Fan Appreciation Day. Two pairs of jeans, five T-shirts, his crumpled gray hoodie, and a few pairs of underwear went into an old duffel bag. At the last minute, he decided to take his old .22 hunting rifle, the one his dad gave him before he got sick. If things got tough, maybe he'd hole up in some mountain cabin for a while, live off the land.

Before he left, he carefully removed the loose tile in the bathroom next to the sink and pulled out the stack of documents. He took half the papers and stuffed them into the backpack and replaced the tile. He figured they were safe here. He didn't want to get pulled over and have some dumbass cop heist his whole stash. Besides, he figured he'd only be gone a few days, a couple of weeks, tops.

He waited until after dark to make his move. At 9:00 p.m., he couldn't wait any longer. He tossed the backpack over his shoulder and grabbed the duffel bag. He turned off all the lights and slowly opened the door, trying to make it not squeak. For once he was happy that the stupid hick manager had refused to replace the lightbulbs on the landing.

He padded down the back stairs like a cat burglar, watching for any activity by the gate. The Toyota was still parked across the street, but the camo guy looked like he was asleep. At the bottom of the stairs, he peered into the garage. He didn't see any reporters in the shadows.

"Hey, asshole!" The voice echoed through the covered garage. "Where the hell do you think you're going?"

It was Steve, the biker-manager, holding a broom, obviously engaged in important managerial duties.

"Keep it down, will ya?" Buddy whispered.

"I don't have to keep it down, asshole. You've made life around here a real pain in the ass lately, you know that? I caught some asshole reporter pissing on the back wall yesterday."

"Dan, I can't talk now, I'm kinda busy."

"You trying to skip out on the rent? Because if you are, I'll call the cops right now."

"My rent's paid up and you know it."

"You sure look like you're skipping out."

He kept on walking, not really interested in Steve's analysis. He was elated when the truck started, first try. One of the advantages of working in a tune-up shop, he thought. When he hit the street, he turned left because the camo guy was parked to his right. He got on the freeway and headed north—south led to Mexico and he didn't speak any Mexican. Twenty minutes later his gas tank was nearly empty and he was losing radio reception, so he looked for a place to turn off. The brightly lit sign for the Ramona Motor Lodge advertised rooms for nineteen dollars and ninety-nine cents a night and free HBO, which sounded like a good deal.

25

J ake needed to get out of Los Angeles. The story was spinning out of control. He knew it. The Klutch report was bad. He still wasn't sure how *Inside News* had linked the Vegas deal to the fire. Then there was the Escondido character, a wild card, a variable completely outside the lines. Jake understood he wasn't pulling the strings anymore; he was simply another character in the show.

"Do you want to float something?" Vince asked. "Maybe give it a new spin?" Presenting an alternative story was an easy way to shift the tide, to regain control. *Truism #327: When you lose control of the game, start a new game.* But the idea of working a counter-story didn't seem right in this case; there were too many unknown elements. The players were not responding as expected.

"Let's lay low," he told Vince. "Run silent, run deep."

"*Sizzler* offered twenty grand for an interview. Guaranteed cover tease. Full edit approval."

"No way." Jake caught a flash of disappointment. He didn't want Vince to pout, so he added, "If they are willing to go to twenty now, they'll go to thirty in a week." That seemed to perk up Vince, but it did little to suppress Jake's burbling unease, the feeling that there wasn't a good course of action here. After the surprise visit from Urbina, he fled to Del Mar, as he usually did when Los Angeles became too oppressive. But now his beach house was gone.

At 9:00 p.m. Thursday night, Jake showed up unannounced at Roger Talbot's house in the Del Mar Hills.

"Want company?" he said when the groggy newspaper editor opened the door.

Roger was OK with Jake's sudden appearance. Jake was a fairly low-maintenance houseguest. That night he joined Roger on the couch for a *Sopranos* marathon. Conversation centered around the relative legacies of Kobe Bryant and Jerry West. Jake was always unusually interested in the latest battles between the Gray and Green parties in Del Mar.

Over the next two days Truland, wearing a surf shop sweatshirt, shorts, and flip-flops, was a familiar sight in the area. For several hours a day he huddled in the corner of the local coffee shop, a converted 1940s train station. He wrote in peace, ignored by the beach town customers. If anyone noticed him, they didn't care.

Roger didn't ask about recent events, and Jake didn't offer any clues. But after 48 hours of dissecting the Lakers' defensive rotations and the decline of modern cinema, Roger could no longer hold back his journalistic curiosity.

"What's happening with the guy in Escondido?" Roger asked as they ate rolled tacos piled high with guacamole and cheese on the patio of Bobbyberto's, their favorite taco stand. They were sitting on the cement benches on Bobbyberto's outdoor patio along the Coast Highway; it was high noon.

"I talked to the detective," Jake said, a chunk of guacamole spilling out of his mouth. "He seems to think the SELT connection was a big breakthrough."

"That's it? A SELT connection? I'm not sure some SELT members know to use a spoon with soup."

"There is some sort of hang-up on the search warrant. The judge thinks there are probable cause issues. And he hates the sheriff."

"Do you know Landau?"

"Never heard of him."

"Not even a nasty letter?"

"Seriously. Nothing."

"But you—"

"As far as I can tell, he was completely off the radar. Not even a request for a digital autograph."

"You still think Urbina did it?"

"He's my leading suspect." Jake gave him the CliffsNotes version of the meeting at the Sallie Mae. "He practically confirmed it. But something is still not right. Klutch would never let this leak."

That surprised Roger. Jake always seemed to know who was pulling the strings. It was one of his gifts. Roger unwrapped another serving of rolled tacos.

"What are you—"

Roger's question was interrupted by a short snapping sound. Roger's *horchata* exploded in a spray of white foam and ice cubes. Roger looked at Jake, perplexed.

There was another sharp snap, and a spray of concrete chips erupted from the far end of the table.

Jake grabbed Roger by the collar and pulled him down.

There was another snap and another splash of stone table top. A concrete sliver sliced into the arm of a blonde surfer girl sitting at the next table. "Oh shit," she screamed, grabbing her bleeding arm and falling back.

Another crack and a pile of guacamole and white cheese sprayed across the patio.

"This guy really hates Mexican food," Jake said. He was ripping off a line from *The Jerk*. But Roger wasn't about to chastise him, as he huddled under the stone table splattered with guacamole.

26

News of the taco stand shooting kicked the Truland story into the stratosphere. From Babblecock to *Meet the Press*, the apparent attempt on Truland's life was the topic that was trending, percolating, and being shared. All six network news programs led with Truland. A *New Yorker* reporter posted a 10,000-word online think piece examining the decline of celebrity culture, "post-Kardashian." Four bills were introduced in Congress focused on banning sniper rifles. Several cable talk shows shifted into full lockdown, giving Truland the twenty-four-hour treatment.

Hollywood Now! played the story pretty much like every news outlet in the Western Hemisphere. Jessie used the conservative headline "Truland Target of Sniper Attack." Simple. Newsy. No need to sensationalize this one, she told Sharon Jones-Jones. It was now an attempted murder investigation. And there were still too many unknowns.

At this point, there was no definitive evidence of what happened at the taco stand, according to the sheriff, who was personally holding daily briefings. There were alternate theories. The *Los Angeles Times* quoted Roger Talbot, the local newspaper editor who also was at the taco stand. "For the record, why the hell isn't anybody considering that I might have been the target?" he said. "Have you ever been to Del Mar?"

By Jessie's count, media outlets appeared evenly split. Some backed the Lone Wacko theory. Others focused on the Revenge of the Fashion Industry. A certain portion of the population believed the shooting was part of a government plot to eliminate subversive celebrities. A congressional investigation of the fashion accessory business was now certain, FNN reported. A congressman named Titweiller, a Constitutionalist out of South Carolina, was already convening a special fashion accessory industry subcommittee.

This wasn't a Truland story anymore. It was a celebrity murder investigation. Homicidal corruption in the fashion accessory business! Rogue gunmen loose in the "idyllic coastal enclaves" of Southern California! Mad stalker after Truland!

As the producer who broke the Buddy Landau story, Jessie was suddenly in demand. Competitors who would slice a poodle's throat rather than lose a scoop to *Hollywood Now!* called to request sit-down interviews. A decision was made to allow her to do an exclusive sit-down interview with Farmore News Network's most prestigious talk show, *Buzzsaw*. Jessie was nervous but held up. She offered host Bobbi Mann two official, never-before-released tidbits—mention of the Truland movie poster in Randolph Martin Landau's living room and confirmation of the SELT papers on the desk, something she had only told to the police. Both items were picked up by the wires the next day.

That morning, an FNN reporter, Templeton Smith, the network's lead investigative reporter, phoned asking for help with sources. "Maybe we can collaborate," he said. Jessie's jaw almost fell off her face. This was big time, the rare crossover, a network news correspondent "collaborating" with *Hollywood Now!*

Truland had morphed into a strict nuts-and-bolts crime drama, in terms of coverage. Jessie pushed Brenda to work the sheriff's department and all the official agencies. The Hollywood network of busboys, hotel maids, and concierges was fully mobilized and informed of hefty bonuses for actionable intelligence. A flash went out to agencies, private investigators, and publicists who might be tracking likely interview targets. A special bounty was offered. Jessie twice left messages for Eric Branson, the fire investigator, but he didn't return her calls.

There was little else she could do, beyond work the usual sources and follow the string of official announcements and developments as the story unfolded. Attempted celebrity murder investigations took their own course.

At this point, there was only one prize—Truland. She knew it. Everything else was confetti. Whoever got Jake first would rule. He was the one missing element, the one man who could put a bow on the story. But Truland had vanished, off the radar. No one had seen or heard from anyone in the Truland camp. No sightings. No mysterious Babblecock posts. Three days after the shooting and Jake was gone. There was only one story, only one question people really wanted answered. *Where was Jake?*

27

Eric Branson was shocked by the shooting at the taco stand. He loved Bobbyberto's. He ate there all the time. Nothing like this had ever happened in Del Mar. There was the occasional stabbing, often the result of a domestic dispute or a drug deal gone bad. But nothing like this.

All the local fire crews were mobilized for crowd control. The more flashing lights, the better. A four-block area around Bobbyberto's was taped off for three days. TV news vans and state and federal law enforcement officials descended on Del Mar. The sheriff called a press conference to announce he was in charge of the "multidiscipline, pan-geographic Truland Task Force." Detectives would pursue every angle and leave no stone "un-overturned," the sheriff promised the reporters.

But the investigation had stalled, as far as Eric could tell. The sheriff didn't mention it in the press conference, but Eric knew the detectives still had not searched Buddy Landau's apartment. The

newly appointed presiding judge of the Superior Court, a disciple of
Judge Judy who once appeared on *Charlie Rose* to discuss the per-
vasive practice of illegal search and seizure, was refusing to grant a
search warrant. There was nothing beyond media reports to suggest
Buddy Landau's involvement in any crime, noted the judge, who
hated the sheriff with a passion. The sheriff was busily looking for a
more sympathetic judge, invoking several subsections of the recently
reinstalled Patriot Act.

At least that was the scuttlebutt. But Eric didn't believe it. The
sheriff's department was not really interested in Buddy Landau, Eric
believed. The one time Brown had deigned to answer Eric's call, his
lack of interest was palpable. "We're all over Mr. Landau," he said.
"Don't you worry about it." But Eric doubted the detective's sincerity.
Back in his high school football days, Eric could always spot when his
teammates were simply going through the motions.

Eric had reached this conclusion: The sheriff believed the Las
Vegas fashion accessory company was behind the Truland threats.
It was the only explanation for the detectives' lackadaisical efforts
to investigate Buddy Landau. The sheriff had a better suspect. And
maybe they weren't really that eager to pursue Klutch. The sheriff was
not known for his vigorous pursuit of alleged organized crime figures
or potential political donors.

Eric was frustrated and angry. It wasn't right that politics might
impede the investigation. He was still the primary investigator on the
biggest case ever to hit Del Mar. In many ways, Buddy Landau was his
case. The sheriff might be letting a bad guy get away, based on nothing more than a theory.

He knew the chief wouldn't be happy, but there was no choice
but to continue the Landau investigation on his own. He felt he owed
it to Jessie, the TV producer. He promised her there would be an
investigation of Buddy Landau. At the very least he could make a few
calls, make sure all the bases were covered.

He started by reviewing the local suspects, anyone with an arson background or SELT connection. Then he called Roger Talbot, the newspaper editor. The media reports described him as a bystander at the shooting. But everybody in Del Mar knew he was friends with Truland. Eric had seen them surfing together. But Talbot didn't return his calls.

Cassandra Moorehead of SELT picked up on the first ring. "Mi amigo, Ricardo!" she said. "So good to hear from you again."

Eric remembered the TV producer's story about SELT, but he still believed the connection between SELT and Landau might nail down motivation, one of the basics of any investigation into a suspect. Moorehead said she already had been interviewed by sheriff's detectives.

"Mucho, mucho rude," she said. "Not nearly as polite as you."

Eric blushed. "Manners are important," he said, by instinct.

"I'm so sorry I haven't seen you on TV yet," Moorehead said. "That must be horribly frustrating for you."

There it was again. He didn't understand why so many people felt his lack of TV time was worthy of pity. He changed the subject. "Do you know this Landau character?"

"He was also a very rude young man. And a very prolific writer of e-mails and blog comments. I gave it all to those nasty detectives."

"Did Landau ever threaten Jake Truland?"

"Not that I know of. You know our bylaws specifically prohibit open hatred of Jake Truland. Page four, subsection three."

"Why was Landau writing?"

"He seemed far more concerned with our interpretation of Mr. Presley's seminal prophecies delivered from the stage of his Hawaiian rebirth concert. Mr. Landau was *muy loco*, if you ask me."

"What exactly did Elvis say from the stage?"

"It was beautiful. You must rent the DVD. I recommend our special Blu-ray edition. He clearly laid out a plan for societal harmony.

And there is also a wonderful bonus edition of *Suspicious Minds*. It is *la spectacular.*"

"And Mr. Landau didn't believe the plan?"

"Mr. Landau supported Jake Truland's fictional account of that era which, shall we say, took a less heavenly perspective."

Eric spent a few more minutes discussing SELT philosophy and Landau's specific obsessions. None of it sounded like motivation for going after Truland, unless the fire was simply a robbery gone bad. But that didn't explain the shooting. Why would Landau take a shot at Truland? It didn't make sense.

There were still too many questions and few answers. Eric knew there was one major piece of the investigation missing—Jake Truland, the one person who could almost certainly answer his questions. Truland was interviewed by detectives after the shooting and then he vanished. Eric wanted his own interview with Truland. He suspected Truland might be back in Del Mar. But he couldn't prove it. He called Truland's agent.

"Hell, I don't know where the fuck he is," the agent said. "No fuckin' idea."

Truland knew the detectives were looking for him. Heck, everybody was looking for him. But Truland was nowhere to be found. Eric was wondering, just like everybody else—*Where was Truland?*

28

Q: *So what does the future hold for Jake Truland?*
A: *William Gibson once wrote about the Tibetan concept of 'tulpa.'*
Q: *Tulpa?*
A: *It roughly translates as 'projected thought form.' According to Gibson, the concept of tulpa means that celebrity has a life of its own. It can survive the death of its subjects.*
Q: *I'm sorry, I—*
A: *I'm going for tulpa. And, by the way, tulpa explains Elvis sightings.*
Q: *OK...Got it...So...did you really have sex with Jackie Conrad backstage at the Oscars?*
—Interview with Jake Truland, Sizzler, *June 2007*

In the cocoon of his rented Lexus, Jake was stuck in traffic, the cliché of LA life. A layer of brown hovered over the downtown skyline, as he worked his way east on I-10. It was a blazing hot morning. A Santa Ana was blowing, adding an extra dose of crazy to the lattes of Southern Californians. All around him, Angelenos were engrossed in their own worlds, fingering their message pads and yelling into their phones, oblivious to anything outside their climate-controlled interiors. He could lose himself in any city in the world, but only in LA did he feel alone.

Jake knew what he had to do. There was no way he could move this story line, not now. Only one option made sense. He had to stay off the grid. Let the vacuum burn itself out. Don't feed the beast. With any luck, a congressman would get caught in a porn video or a starlet would announce a rehab stint and the crews would move on. Already some shows were turning their attention to the compelling story of a young latex-intolerant Vegas hooker who was suing a Hollywood executive for using a potentially deadly condom. (The hooker was demanding that the Las Vegas DA bring attempted murder charges against the executive, citing his penis as the attempted murder weapon.)

Jake needed to disappear. He'd done it before, he could do it again. The mechanics were easy. Fake IDs. Credit cards linked to dummy corporations. He had instant financial freedom. The rest was simple.

Going ghost was the only move. He had to wait for the tide to shift. *Truism #124: If you are afraid of the undertow, stay out of the damn ocean.*

But first he had one chore, one task to complete...one very annoying job.

Jake called ahead and warned the manager on duty that he was on the way. To avoid attention, the meeting was set up in a back room. Jake wasn't eager to mingle and swap tales with civilians, not today.

Jake parked near a loading ramp in the rear of the building, next to the trash cans. The assistant manager ushered him into the designated room, which doubled as a "rec" room, with a foosball table and a few checkerboards strewn across tabletops.

Jake's appointment was already there, his wheelchair parked next to a window with a view of the stucco-covered courtyard. Jake caught a flash of recognition on his face, mixed with the usual level of confusion.

"Hi, Dad," Jake said, holding the old man's hand, making physical contact, something the doctors said helped Robert Livingston to remember. Robert's hand was a bony claw, his head tilted to the side, a week's worth of stubble covering his chin. Damn, the assholes were supposed to shave him every other day. Jake made a mental note to file a complaint.

"Sammie, how ya' doing, kid?" Dad was the only one who called him Sammie.

"Everything OK, Dad?"

"Did you see the Rams game? The Rams tore 'em apart."

Jake wasn't sure if Robert remembered the Rams no longer played in Los Angeles.

"That Roman Gabriel was always one helluva quarterback," Robert said.

Jake moved Robert into the home for aging actors four years ago. Vince liked to call it "Almost Famous Acres." Most of the residents were AFTRA and SAG members who didn't have other options. Actors who made it big didn't need the space; it housed only actors who never made real money or frittered it away on drugs and bad wives. Once a year a group of rich old stars held a benefit screening of a movie in Bel Air to help pay for new bedpans.

The home was in west Palm Springs, in a warehouse district in the middle of nowhere. Jake made the drive at least once a year, but rarely more than once. During his disappeared days, he spent large chunks of time in a nearby Marriot Suites, after Robert started complaining of chest pains. Talking to Robert on the phone was difficult; in person he could at least recognize Jake and follow a conversation.

Jake was more than willing to avoid this trip, but Becky insisted he go.

"He's probably seen the news," she said. "You need to get out there."

"He can barely remember to tie his shoes—"

"He's probably worried—"

"He's worried the cable might go out."

"It's been eighteen months. Just do it, asshole," she said.

All the Almost Famous Acres employees signed NDAs, so Jake knew he was safe. The attendants quickly left him alone with Robert, who hated being called "Bob."

Few people in Hollywood knew about Jake's connection to Robert Livingston, who was always referred to as a "veteran TV actor." As many assumed but few ever verified, Jake Truland was not Jake's real name. His name at birth was Sam Livingston—not, for the record, Tony Rodriguez, as reported by a Mexican biographer. Jake liked to support an oft-repeated story that that he was raised by Mennonites in northern Mexico. A contrarian group insisted he actually grew up in a small Arizona desert town called Bare Hump, about 150 miles from Tucson. Even today, there are Bare Hump residents, who, for a beer, will gladly tell tales of carousing with a teenage Truland.

In fact, he was born and raised in Glendale, as much a product of the LA scene as bad hair bands, porn, and Disneyland. He changed his name when he was seven, a logical step in Glendale, where many of his classmates at Glendale Elementary were auditioning for sitcoms and working after school on their runway technique. When Sam changed his name, Robert's only comment was, "Good move."

Robert Livingston was one of a legion of hardworking tradesman in Los Angeles who earned a living from the industry but never quite made it big. He appeared in a slew of movies, commercials, and television shows, getting up early most mornings to head to one of the studio lots for a long day of shooting. During one stretch, he was on TV at least once a week; an episode of *McCloud* listed him as a "special guest star."

Jake remembered the thrill of watching that *McCloud* and seeing his father's name in bold letters. It was like finding out your dad is quarterback of the Rams. Often people would stop his father on the street. Usually they wouldn't know his name or the part—they simply recognized the face. Those moments always filled Jake with pride.

But, early on, Jake realized Los Angeles—where a typical day might involve running into Jean-Claude Van Damme at Wendy's— was a city of castes, with clear divisions between the sitcom actors and movie stars, the rock stars and the sound technicians. Even as a kid, he lived with a keen sense that Glendale wasn't Bel Air or Malibu, where the real stars lived. "People in Kansas dream of a place like Glendale," Robert liked to say, when they were barbecuing weenies in the backyard. And Jake understood. But in LA's pecking order, Glendale was the place where Wink Martindale lived, not Johnny Carson. The director of the hot TV series lived in Glendale; the show's star lived in Beverly Hills in a Southern-style mansion. "I would be in Bel Air if I had a better agent," more than one resident of Glendale said. When Jake was twelve his best friend, Johnny Martinez, moved away to Santa Monica after his father landed a recurring role on *Bandit,* a part Robert Livingston was up for but didn't get.

As Jake grew older, his father was recognized less and less. Fewer parts came his way, not even the walk-ons that brought in the regular money. He never aged into the father roles; never landed that quirky-character supporting lead. Soon, speaking roles turned into work as an extra, a face in the crowd. By the time Jake was in high school, his father was working part-time selling real estate and his mother spent afternoons "helping out" in the file room of a law firm.

Robert Livingston was still recognized from time to time. But Jake was always acutely aware that his father was no longer the guy who created a commotion in the grocery store.

Jake's relationship with his dad was, at best, complicated. Over the years, as Jake grew more famous, their relationship grew increasingly distant, until Jake's mom died of a heart attack while making cupcakes. The day she died Robert was working late as an extra, earning thirteen dollars an hour on the set of *Death Racer 2020*. She died alone on the kitchen floor. She could have called a neighbor for help, but it was Glendale—she barely knew her neighbors.

Every few years Jake offered to pay to move Robert to a top-flight retirement home, but Dad wanted to be around his friends, where he could swap stories about raucous *MacGyver* shoots and asshole line producers.

But Jake didn't like to see Robert unshaven. It made him wonder what else they were skipping.

"Do you need anything, Dad? You getting all your desserts?"

"Kid, I was on TV, I don't need anything," Robert snapped. "Hell, I go down to Walgreens, cashier remembers me from *Banacek*. I get the discount, no problem."

Jake tried to tell him about the fire and the shooting; tried to make it clear that everything was OK.

"I was in *Towering Inferno*, you know," Robert said.

Jake had heard the stories a thousand times. Dad played "Fireman Number Twelve."

"That Steve McQueen was a real prick," Robert said.

Jake wasn't really in the mood to talk about Steve McQueen's relative prickishness. He tried to get back to current events. "Have you been watching the news?"

"You know I don't watch the news, except for that hottie Lonnie what's her name. I watch her every day at 5:00. Every day."

"Have you seen anything on the news about me, Dad?"

"You? Sammie? You been on the TV?"

Jake decided to drop the topic. He asked Bob about the food and the Almost Famous Aces attendants.

"That nurse, the one you mentioned, she giving you your pills on time?"

"You know how it is," Robert said. "If a guy is a sleazebag in one area, then pretty good shot he is sleazebag all around."

Jake's jaw almost hit the linoleum. Dad was paraphrasing a Truism: "If someone is a sleazebag in one part of their life, there is an excellent chance they are a sleazebag in other parts of their life."

"You sure you haven't seen anything on the news about me?"

"You get your flu shot?" Robert Livingston said.

"Sure, Dad. Right on time." Jake felt the usual twinge of annoyance at the nagging question. For about fifteen years, anything Robert said had annoyed Jake.

"Do you need anything, Dad?"

"What the hell could I need?"

They went on like that for twenty minutes before Jake said he had to go. He made a point of asking the attendant about the shaving schedule before he left. But he was eager to get back on the road, which, as always, triggered a wave of guilt.

29

Buddy Landau was thinking about the mountains. He would get a cabin, somewhere like Utah or Nebraska, and hunker down for a while. That was the new plan. He could shoot a couple of deer and probably have enough meat to eat like a king for weeks, or at least until they nailed that fashion accessory executive. Then he'd be home free.

For days he watched TV news nonstop. He saw the same stories over and over again. Interviews with cops. Discussions with former cops. Stories about Truland and babes. On every show he was "the suspect" and a "person of interest."

"Who is Randolph Martin Landau?" one announcer asked with a serious face.

I'm a three-name dude?!

Every program showed his mug shot from that old arrest and talked about his record. And there were more damn interviews with Elaine, who couldn't seem to shut up. It looked like she'd gotten a new hairdo, and she wore this slinky shirt he'd never seen before. The shirt was low cut and showed off her boobs. Now she was going on and on about how Buddy liked Bruce Willis movies, like that was some sort of crime.

As far as he was concerned, the relationship with Elaine was now officially over. Screw her. This temporary separation was now permanent. That would show her.

Soon he'd make a break for the mountains; that was the plan. The motel room and its nonworking vibrating bed feature were creeping him out. A guy could disappear in the mountains, be his own man. Maybe he'd grow a beard.

But first he needed money. Some real coin. And that meant he'd have to track down that bitch TV producer. She started it all. She owed him. He just wanted what was rightfully his. The mountain cabin would just have to wait. First he needed to see that TV producer and get his money. Then he'd grow the beard.

30

"Dude, are you, like, on the lam?"

Elgin maneuvered the canary yellow PT Cruiser through traffic on the 405. With a short burst of gas he cut into the diamond lane and accelerated, sending Jake's heart racing.

"Let's just say I think it's a good time to get out of LA," Jake said.

"Dude, it's always a good time to get out of LA." Elgin suddenly veered right, shooting a gap in traffic. Five minutes later he pulled to the curb at LAX's commuter terminal and Jake jumped out, towing his perfectly engineered rolling bag with four-wheel action and polymer-lined secret compartment. In the row of limousines and rented cars, nobody even glanced at the Cruiser. With cool efficiency he was ticketed and scanned and admitted back into the cocoon of the terminal.

Jake loved airports—the hard metal seats in the lounges; the businessmen sitting on the floor, huddled around power outlets tethered to various electronic devices; the families on their way to reunions; the smell of Taco Bell and McDonald's mixing with the faint stench of airplane fuel. Airports were modern Babels with smoothie stands and iPod-dispensing vending machines, where people of all races, creeds, and personal hygiene mingled in passive togetherness. In airports, Jake could merge into the never-ending flow of anonymous humanity. People saw him but didn't recognize him. He was just another look-alike in the flotsam.

Long ago he had determined the most effective airport attire was a simple combination of a hoodie and baseball cap. Travelers lost in their own dramas saw only the sweatshirt and the cap. In general, he stuck to the logos of generic Midwest and Central Division teams, which tended toward low-key, deferential fans. He favored losing teams, which were unlikely to inspire high-fiving camaraderie. He could slide through airports in a bubble, just another lone traveler with a poor sense of fashion and questionable sports allegiances.

When he pulled his Salinger, he didn't hide—he simply stayed mobile, always on the go, creating a moving target. At the time, Jake approached disappearing as a career move. He saw the play with total clarity. He knew he was burning out. His Qs were strong, but the tabloids were yawning. The curve of celebrity was inverting, he could sense it. So halfway through an *Attack Zone!!!* segment cohosted by the former stripper turned Republican consultant who wrote *Liberals Should Be Boiled in Hot Oil: A Manifesto for Conservative Revolution*, Jake walked off the set and never returned.

It was his unabashed homage to Salinger, Pynchon, and DeLillo, the greats. He revered their ability to turn good books into personal legend. Their fame grew in direct proportion to their refusal to play the fame game. It was genius.

After six nights of not showing up for *Attack Zone!!!*, Jake's disappearance was page-one news. After three weeks, he issued a statement through Vince: "I am alive. Do not try to follow. I go in search of something that does not exist." And then nothing more. He didn't call Vince. Didn't answer his phone or e-mail. Six weeks after his departure, Farmore News produced a sixty-minute special report on his disappearance. After six months, he was on the cover of *Rolling Stone*.

He made little effort to hide; he simply stayed away from the business. No talk shows. No interviews. No parties. Nothing. He avoided LA and New York, which, to the industry, was akin to falling off the face of the earth. To the industry, he was a ghost.

But he was no recluse. His model was John Lennon, who was a nightly regular on the LA bar scene during his so-called "lost years." In one night of famous drunken debauchery, the Beatle put a woman's panties on his head and danced around a bar packed with fans. That was Lennon's idea of disappearing. Lennon wasn't hiding; he simply wasn't participating. That was Jake's philosophy.

As the months passed, there were reports of drug use and horrible disfigurement from a Jet Ski accident. Periodically, Jake leaked blurry photos of himself in a long beard getting mail out of a box on an empty stretch of Vermont farm road. (Vermont tourism jumped 1.2 percent the next year.) Once a lawyer from Topeka called *Sizzler* and told a lengthy tale about doing acid with Jake Truland in the mountains of Montana (a true story).

It didn't really matter if people spotted him. Sightings only served to fuel the legend. The more common the sightings, the less the panelists on the Farmore News' weekly "Where's Truland?" updates gave them any credence. Reports from an airport in Fargo or a roadside diner in Charlotte were simply thrown in among the random tales that placed him sipping champagne in a bar in Lisbon or running naked through the bonfires at Burning Man.

After two years in this netherworld, Jake sensed a change. People were not recognizing him in the same way. He was becoming a blurred image, out of range of the public's constantly updating radar. He wasn't on TV; ergo he wasn't really a distinct figure anymore.

And yet his legend continued to grow. People liked the fable.

They wanted the mystery, the eccentricity. In the absence of real data the public filled in the blanks using their own imaginations. The enigma was far sexier than the known quantity. When hardcore fans recognized him, they showed restraint, acting as if they were in on his secret. In a store or restaurant, they sidled up to him and whispered, "Don't worry, I won't blow your cover." Usually, at that point, Jake's cover was something like "man buying cough medicine."

Today, in the LAX commuter terminal, he was well positioned. Wearing a Memphis Grizzlies hoodie and Charlotte Panthers cap—the two teams least prone to provoke random conversations, he concluded—he found a corner seat in the near-empty gate adjacent to his actual departure gate. Headphones were in place and he was dialed in to the latest edition of NPR's *Fresh Air*. The author of a widely discussed historical account of World War II was explaining Japanese bayoneting techniques. But Jake's Memphis-Charlotte hoodie ensemble wasn't working.

A man in his thirties wearing jeans and a dark blue sport jacket sat next to him and scanned the terminal in the manner of an air marshal searching for suspected terrorists.

Jake ignored him. He tightened the full-cover Barcelona-edition Bose headphones over his ears and read the *New York Times*—the airport equivalent of a "Do not disturb" sign. He switched from *Fresh Air* to Chet Baker on the iPod.

"We can help you," the man whispered without looking at him.

Jake ignored him. Thanks to Bose's industry-leading decibel reduction system, he saw the man's lips move but heard nothing. He made a point of not taking off the headphones.

The man winked and looked away. He pulled a small gold case from his pocket and removed a business card. Like a drug dealer delivering the goods, he slid a card across the seat.

Jake looked at the card. It read, "Stan Cannon." There was no title, only a company name, "Bell, Todd & Markowitz."

"We can help you," the man repeated.

Jake couldn't stop himself. He took off the headphones and looked at the card. Stan continued to scan the room.

"We are good at crisis," Stan whispered.

"You create crisis?" said Jake, who was thinking of bayoneting Stan Cannon.

"We help extricate our clients. Think of us as paratroopers. We drop in. Clean up the mess. We have worked with some very important people."

"Really? Name one."

"That would be indiscreet." The man reached for a *Wall Street Journal* and opened it in front of his face. "We are nothing if not discreet."

Jake put a note of fear in his voice. "Do you think I am in crisis? Nobody told me. This could be bad."

"We have friends in many places. High places."

Jake sank back into his chair. "Damn. I wish somebody had told me I was in crisis. I can't trust anybody. I might need somebody like you."

The man nodded knowingly, keeping the paper held high. "We can pull some strings. We're great string pullers."

"I could use some string pulling."

"Our messaging will make you weep." Stan was growing more excited. "We are the man on messaging. Ask anybody. We're the messaging experts."

An attendant interrupted with an announcement that Jake's flight was boarding.

"All this sounds really good, Stan," Truland whispered. "I've been looking for a firm to help with my string pulling and messaging management."

"Perhaps we can arrange a meeting. Discreetly."

The PA speaker blasted a second call. "Yes, definitely," Truland said, keeping his voice at a whisper. "I work through a series of blind contacts. I'm sure you're accustomed to the procedures."

Stan nodded vigorously.

"Expect a call, Mr. Cannon. The code word will be"—Jake paused for effect—"pineapple."

Stan pulled out a notepad.

"No, no paper trail," Truland hissed.

Stan discreetly nodded. He understood.

The day went like that. On the plane Jake huddled in a window seat, avoiding eye contact, reading the latest *Esquire*, a special issue dedicated to the history of the clitoris in literature. An overweight woman who smelled of curry sat in the next seat and stared at him the whole trip, a serious breach of celebrity travel etiquette.

In the cab from the Portland airport, the taxi driver tried to divert him to a high-end brothel featuring "only the finest" nineteen-year-old fashion models from upper Mongolia, a notoriously under-rated region for nineteen-year-old fashion model prostitutes, the driver insisted. When Jake refused (although he was intrigued), the driver took the long way to the hotel, not realizing Jake knew his way around the city. Jake felt a sense of relief when he finally checked into the Regal, a three-star hotel dating to 1878, run by a family of German immigrants who would ignore him with zeal.

Rainy Portland was one of his favorite escapes. He could immerse himself in the bookstores and parks and hike around the Columbia River Gorge. And there was Olga, a waitress in the Budapest Stew, a local Hungarian restaurant. She was a tall brunette who liked classic Russian literature and expressed vast amounts of disdain for pop culture. "I don't care who you are," she said whenever he appeared in the restaurant, unannounced, as always. "You have the face of a Bolshevik. I do not trust you."

That night they ate runny goulash and spent hours discussing

Tolstoy's last days and the dangers of an unchecked military establishment. Chain-smoking cigarettes, her accent thick with vodka, Olga mocked the styles and superficial nature of modern writers, whom she compared to the proletariat hacks of her homeland. Then they slipped into the Regal's feathery bed and drank tiny bottles of Stoli from the minibar. Stretched out naked on the bed, side by side, her leg dangling over his, her heavy breasts resting on his chest, she asked him questions about modern history, mocking his ignorance. If he got a question right, describing DeGaulle's role in postwar France to her satisfaction or appropriately condemning the artistic offshoots of the Prague spring, she stroked his cock with love. If he answered wrong she grabbed his balls with enough authority to make him scream in pain. And then they drifted into sleep watching cable TV political shows, which always prompted her to throw pillows at the TV and curse in her native tongue.

31

Using his Swiss Army knife, Eric pried a small piece of blackened imitation wood paneling from the wall of what used to be the Kramer family's "media room." The house was, as the firefighters liked to say, only slightly charred. Damage was contained to the family room, which was littered with a few blackened toys. An overstuffed chair was a heap of ashes, and a layer of dark film covered the red-and-orange shag carpet and the back wall, which was burned through at the roofline. A cluster of toasted power cords lay at the foot of the outlets, held together with a rubber band.

"I was going to get one of those, you know, power strips, but that was another twelve bucks," said nineteen-year-old Ted Kramer, the family's oldest son and home theater consultant.

No mystery here, but Eric still had to do his job. He diligently worked through his checklist, collecting samples and taking photos, while ignoring the stares of his bored colleagues standing around the hallway.

"Come on, Mr. CSI, I think we got a suspect on this one," Tony, the bucket man, yelled, prompting a round of snickers from his fellow firefighters.

Ten more minutes, he told them.

"Make it five, college boy."

Ten minutes later, the ladder truck managed to burn rubber departing the scene. As he walked toward his van, Eric ran into Tim Downey, a twenty-seven-year veteran of the sheriff's department, who was lazily guarding the yellow tape line. Downey had worked everything from traffic to homicide, never rising above the rank of sergeant. Nothing happened at headquarters without Downey knowing about it.

After the usual crime scene pleasantries, Eric asked, "ICIC got anything new on Truland?"

Downey snorted. "The ICIC guys couldn't find their dicks with a flashlight," he said, loudly, not caring who heard him. "They all think they're fuckin' James Bond."

"They say Vegas—"

"They don't have squat."

"Then how come they're ignoring this Landau character?"

"Did you hear me? They don't have squat. They can't find the guy. And all signs point to Vegas, so what the hell."

"Landau ran," Eric said, feeling compelled to defend the investigation.

Downey smirked. "Yeah, so what the fuck? All I'm saying is those really big crime dicks, they just want it to go way bad, really, really bad."

As he headed back to the station, Downey's words gnawed at him. It was worse than he thought. The case was going nowhere. Truland was fading into the black hole of yesterday's news for law enforcement, Eric could tell. The daily sheriff's media briefings were now focused on the case of Judi Bledsoe, third runner-up in *Survivor: Hong Kong*, who was allegedly robbed at gunpoint coming out of Bully's. ICIC had moved on. And they obviously couldn't take a minute to keep him in the loop, as required, another one of those regulations everybody except him seemed to ignore.

As far as he could tell, no one was really taking Buddy Landau seriously as a suspect anymore. *Hollywood Now!* was one of the few media outlets still reporting on Landau. But Eric's conversation with Cassandra Moorehead left him more convinced than ever that Buddy Landau was trouble. True, none of the e-mails and letters Moorehead forwarded included any direct threats. But one reference from three months before the fire gave Eric chills: "I want you to know I am no big fan of Mr. Truland, right now," Landau wrote. "I believe he may have played a role in my current temporary separation from the woman I love. But that does not mean I feel it is appropriate to condemn him for his writings, which are all kinda made up anyway."

The ex-girlfriend, Elaine, who has been all over the news—she may be motive, Eric thought. The simple answers are almost always the right answers to solve cases, the instructors at the academy repeated over and over again.

It was almost dark when Eric made it back to the station house. A light was on in the chief's cubbyhole of an office.

"Branson! Now!"

Chief Donatello was hunched over a stack of papers. Without looking up he waved Eric to a chair. "I heard you caught a big one today."

Eric laughed. "Turns out you can't put twelve plugs into two outlets. Who knew?"

Donatello sat up and took off his wire rim glasses, which he wore only in his office. "I also hear you were taking your time and you were very careful and methodical in your investigation."

"Somebody complained?"

"You know it's buck-fifty happy hour night at McClusky's, right?"

Eric gritted his teeth.

"I'm not saying to do anything but your finest work. But, you know, it wouldn't hurt to make some more friends in the station, if you know what I mean. You've already got this college thing hanging on you."

Eric felt the anger rising. He was tired of having to defend his college degree. Some of the guys in the station could barely read their nameplates.

The chief put up his hands, palms out. "I'm just saying. Could make your life a lot easier."

Eric nodded. And now that he had the chief's attention, maybe it was time for a talk. "There's something else," Eric said.

"Is tomorrow that lemon pepper fish thing?" The chief put his glasses back on and refocused on the stack of papers.

"It's Truland."

"What the hell, kid. That has nothing to do with us."

Eric decided to lay it all out for the chief. One by one he explained his concerns about the case, the multiple suspects and the lack of interest from the sheriff's detectives. The chief listened patiently, sucking on an earpiece of his glasses. Eric finished by sharing his conversation with Downey.

"That all?" the chief said. "You finished?"

"ICIC isn't doing anything."

"Dammit. That's enough." The chief's face turned red. "Enough. I'm tired of this crap."

"There are—"

"No more. I told you, this is all sheriff's department. I told you to make it go away. And now you're in here yapping about protocols and—"

"But—"

"No buts. Look at this pile of shit." The chief pointed to the papers on his desk. "Just look at it. Do you want to add to my pile of shit?"

"No, but—"

"Damn good answer, kid." The chief was practically shouting at him. "Because you have no idea the shit storm you would be whipping up if you continue with this little crusade."

"We still have jurisdiction here." Eric was shocked. He thought the chief would support him. "It's arson. It happened on our turf."

"You're not fuckin' listening to me." The chief was clearly struggling to keep control, a father trying not to kick the crap out of his misbehaving thirteen-year-old son. Eric had never seen him like this.

"Think this through, kid. You think the sheriff is going to appreciate your new information? You think the commissioner is going to give you a fuckin' medal?"

"But what about the congressional—"

"Are you fuckin' deaf?" The chief seemed to realize he'd crossed a line and tried to regain control.

"That's got nothing to do with us. Drop it. That's an order. Move on. Now get the fuck out of here and leave me to my misery."

The chief turned back to his paperwork, dismissing Eric with a wave. "And I want the report on that house fire on my desk at 8:00 a.m., no excuses."

Eric left the chief's office feeling bewildered. This wasn't right. There were people who might be getting away with serious crimes. But the chief was more concerned about paperwork than the investigation. He walked through the squad room and headed to his locker, ignoring the smattering of firefighters who couldn't get the night off for buck-fifty happy hour at McClusky's. As he changed and went to his car, the irritation continued to percolate.

This case wasn't over, he knew it. There were still too many unanswered questions. Action was needed. The detectives were ignoring their duties. Above everything else, he was pestered by one nagging thought; he couldn't get it out of his head. He had no evidence. But he could not shake the feeling that Jake Truland was still in danger, no matter where he was.

32

Once a day, Jake called Vince from Portland. Vince pitched project after project and Jake always said no. No, he didn't want to do an interview with *Sizzler*. No, he didn't want to head back to Los Angeles. No, he didn't want to sit for a two-part special edition of *Cathy!*

Vince was frustrated, Truland could tell. His voice had that little squeak to it.

"What *are* you going to do?"

"Well, I thought I'd go down for some chowder," Jake said. "They make great chowder here."

"Stop it. You can't just ignore this."

"Actually, ignoring it feels pretty good."

After two days in Portland Jake felt like an addict in the early stages of rehab. For two nights, there was Olga. But she grew weary of his pedestrian attitudes toward Tolstoy and left to attend a seminar in Seattle on Nietzsche's influence on feminist theory. Last night he sat in a bar and watched the Trailblazers beat the Lakers, arguing with two forest rangers who insisted Kobe was overrated. He didn't watch the news, ignored the entertainment shows, didn't read the newspapers. In the mornings he ran along the river and felt cleansed.

"You should come to Portland," Jake said. "It doesn't rain nearly as much as they say."

"Come on, Jake, you have to feed the beast, you taught me that." The squeak was turning into a shout. "A couple of days out of the loop and you're a goner, old news, that's what you always said. Now is the time to move."

"It doesn't feel right. We're still running silent, runni—"

"Cut the submarine crap. *Sizzler* came back with fifty grand. They'll submit questions. Guaranteed cover. *Scandal Too-Day* will pay seventy-five, but only if you pose in your underwear."

"That doesn't seem very dignified."

"It's their 'History of Underwear' special report. It's thematic."

"Posing in my underwear? What happened to 'Truland's Tragedy'?"

"It's been replaced by 'What the Hell Ever Happened to Truland'?"

That hurt. "This story has its own life," Jake said. "They don't need me."

"*HN!* is going after the guy in Escondido," Vince said. "The lone gunman thing always plays."

"Don't even reply to *Scandal Too-day*. I'm not going to do it." Silence oozed from the phone. "Look, Vince, if it's the money, don't worry about it. You know I'm taking care of you."

"It's not the money." Vince's voice was suddenly ice-cold. "You have a job here and you're ignoring it. It's not right. These opportunities don't come along too often anymore, if you know what I mean."

Truland knew what he meant. "No. But keep *Sizzler* on the hook. If I decide to do it, they'll pay."

"You're not disappearing again, are you? 'Cause that stunt only works once and you know it. This time, you're not here, it's *adios* and whatever happened to that Jake guy?"

"Let's just say this story line is not working for me right now."

"Look, if it's Urbina, you know I can help you there."

"It's not Teddy. I need a break. A vacation."

"At least let me call Cathy. You're not going to ignore her, are you?"

"No, of course not—"

"Because I've spent far too long kissing that plump bitch's healthy ass for you to just—"

"Don't worry about Cathy. That's not it."

"Well, I'm glad to hear that, because Cathy is one psycho you don't want to piss off."

"Vince, you're not listening to me—"

"Oh, I-I-I see, this is the poor-put-upon-celebrity-whining-about-being-a-celebrity speech. Wait, I'll call Lucy. She loves these." Vince put Jake on speaker. "Lucy, listen to this, Jake is doing the poor-celebrity-needs-a-change speech."

Lucy said, "OK, boss, but mind if I finish my lunch?"

"I'm serious," Jake said, after Vince took him off speaker. "I'm not feeling it. Maybe I'm semiretired. Think of it that way."

"Take a deep breath, Jake. In two days you're going to be busting my chops when you're not in the *Tattler*."

"Maybe, but I'm still not coming back to LA, and I'm still not doing *Sizzler*."

"Fine, but you have to do the VOPs, right? No way around that."

The VOPs, formally known as the Voice of the People Awards, were an annual event recognizing great accomplishments in getting women to vote for vaguely named awards like Best Male Politician. Jake was scheduled to receive a Lifetime Achievement Award.

"Maybe," Jake said.

"Don't be an asshole. It's the Lifetime Achievement Awards. I spent six months working on that for you."

"Becky is on me. Says it's crazy to go."

"They wanted to give it to, what's his name, Zac Efron. But I talked them out of it."

"Zac has done some good work."

"Look, ok, you want to lay low, fine. But the wheels still turn. You can't just not show up for your Lifetime Achievement Award. It's rude."

33

It was the third message of twenty-seven. Jessie almost skipped over it. But she recognized the voice.

You know who this is. I guess a hotshot important person like you doesn't need to answer your phone.

The voice was steady, slow, menacing. It was the voice she suspected Buddy Landau had possessed when they first met. The anger and bitterness bubbled through the words.

You think you can just toy with me? Put me on TV without my permission and nothing will happen? I told you I didn't want to be on TV. Not now. But you didn't listen, and now my life is going down the shitter.

So I got nothing to say to you. But we had a deal. It's time for you to make good. Don't try to call me. I'll call you and when I do you better have some money. That's the deal. You buy what I got. And then I'm done with you. And I'm telling you right now, don't try to screw with me again or you'll regret it.

Click.

34

Becky was, in fact, angry with Jake. Later that night they talked via Babblecock. Jake was stretched out on his hotel bed in Portland; she was rushing around her kitchen in Austin, making dinner for Bob and the kids. Jake smelled fried chicken, thanks to Babblecock Scent's exclusive aroma add-on. CNN was playing in the background on the ancient little TV on the shelf.

"Why the hell haven't they searched the Escondido guy's house?" she asked.

"Any day now. The detective said they're going to go for a different judge."

"Sounds like the sheriff has his thumb up his ass."

"The sheriff would gladly stick his thumb in his ass if it would get him on *Cathy!*"

"This has to be Urbina, Jake. He's not fuckin' around."

Damn, he hated Becky's cut-to-the-chase habit. "I doubt the sheriff is even looking at Urbina. Out of his jurisdiction. Either way, I shouldn't have pushed Teddy. Playing the gerbil card was a little over the line."

"Bullshit, Jake." He could see her banging a pan with some sort of wooden spoon, apparently attempting to clean it. The scent shifted toward burnt almonds, for no apparent reason. "You need to stop this. This is one of those real-shit moments."

"I did six miles on the river trail today," Jake said, moving to change the subject.

"You said you were going to make a clean break. It was your idea."

"This is clean. Portland is smog free."

She wasn't buying it. "You're just being an asshole, Jake. A congressional investigation? That's a clean break?"

"That wasn't me. It was the congressman, Tattinger, Tittiwiller, something like that. I've never even heard of him. He made a play."

"It's Congress, Jake. It's not a fuckin' game."

"Look, I'm doing my part. I'm laying low. I'm turning down gigs."

There was a pause. "So I guess I don't have to fly out for the VOPs," she said.

Jake knew this was coming. Becky was his date for the show. He always preferred Becky to the publicity-hungry actresses salivating for a red carpet photo op. Becky's presence in a stunning gown was always enough to wow the photographers and titillate the gossip columns.

"Actually, I need to do that. Would you mind?"

She turned off the water. "You're crazy," she said. "You know what? You're fuckin' crazy."

"It's a Lifetime Achievement Award. That's a big deal." He'd promised Vince he would stand firm.

"It's the fuckin' VOPs. Who cares?"

"Somewhere around twelve million women between the ages of twenty-seven and forty-eight."

"Somebody out there is trying to kill you, Jake. And you want to do some stupid awards show?"

"I doubt Teddy really wants me dead."

"We could still do the curtain," she said. "We're in, we're out."

Some events set up black curtains at a back entrance, creating a tunnel for the camera-shy celebrities. To Jake, the curtains were a sham.

"I've never done the curtain," Jake said. "I'm not going to start now."

"Jake, this is just stupid."

Her anger surprised him. "It's my job," he said.

"Fuck your job. You don't have control of this one, Jake. You don't even know what the story is anymore."

"I'm in control. The man who says no is always in control. That's a truism, you know."

"Fuck your truism."

"Give me some credit—I've been saying no to some big money."

"Then why say yes to the fuckin' VOPs? Since when are you worried about pissing off some stuffy Hollywood organization?"

Now he was angry. "It has nothing to do with that."

"Then what? You miss it? Already? You jonesing for the red carpet?"

"Vince thinks it's a good idea."

"Screw Vince." She spat the words at the computer screen, yelling at him the way a mother scolds a teenager. "You want to do it. That's it, isn't it? Why don't you just admit it?"

He didn't say anything. She didn't understand, never would.

"No answer, Jake? Nothing? When does this end? Don't you want something more from your life?"

"You mean, white picket fence, two-car garage, Friday night cocktails at the country club?"

"Start small, asshole. Maybe go to a fuckin' supermarket without wondering if you're being followed by a homicidal photographer?"

She was upset. He'd only seen her this way once before, when Bob went missing for a few hours and she was sure he had been in a car accident.

"This isn't a life, Jake. Living in a loser hotel—"

"It's not—"

"Do you ever think it's maybe just, you know, easier to be a prick? That's why you do it? No commitment. No responsibilities. No hassles."

"I'm no psychiatrist. But neither is Dr. Phil." That was a direct quote from the jacket cover of his self-help book, *Your Pain is a Pain,* a *New York Times* best seller for fifty-three weeks.

"Don't try to finger fuck me, Jake. I know you better than that." Becky's language tended to get raunchier the angrier she became.

"Is this where you call me sick and a degenerate?"

"Damn right. It is a fuckin' illness. You know it is. You're going to that awards show just so you can get a buzz. You need the cameras and the fans wanting to blow you."

"Great. Now I bet you're going to bring up my collection of rare Egyptian porn."

"Stop it, Jake. Stop talking to me like I'm some wide-eyed reporter from Toledo. Just take a break for a few days. Don't play this one." Now she was imploring him, practically begging. "The game is changing, Jake. It's a blood sport. You *know* that. *You told me that.* They don't care about you or your story. In two weeks you're going to be old news. There's no ten-year career arcs anymore. They use you up and that's it. It's right from *People* to *Celebrity Fitness Club.* That's not you."

"You're damn right it's not me." Now he was mad. "I prove that wrong every fucking day. Give me some credit."

"You always said there was an exit strategy. That you wouldn't be like your dad, grasping for the star on Hollywood Boulevard. Well, what is it? What's the grand plan?"

"I'm thinking a firing squad on *The Tonight Show*. Maybe with a rose in my teeth. It'll get a seventy-eight share."

She hung up.

35

Jessie spent three days frantically trying to determine if Truland was going to show up for the VOPs. He'd be crazy to attend, but predictability wasn't Jake Truland's game. And if he was going to attend, she knew every show and publication in the city would be trying to get him. She needed a VOP action plan.

The buzz of her big scoop was old news. She needed to score again, follow up with a thundering rebound dunk. The pressure was mounting.

The Special Committee on Crime and Fashion was going to subpoena Truland, according to the rumor mill. But that wasn't much help. A congressional hearing was not a very sexy lead for the ladies in Des Moines. She was still focusing on Landau. Her three-part series "Hot Stalkers from Hell" pulled a thirteen share. She followed with an exclusive interview with SELT leader Cassandra Moorehead, who condemned Landau as "the type of loco yahoo who gives us all a bad name."

She didn't tell anybody about the threatening phone message.

There was no point to dwelling on it. They couldn't air it without proving it was Landau. And there was no reason for anyone in legal to hear Landau make accusations against her about false promises. Meanwhile, Landau had disappeared. Until he showed up or called again, that well was dry.

The VOPs were her immediate concern—just one day away. *Inside News* had paid $100,000 for exclusive backstage rights, but *HN!* countered by renting the parking lot of the In-N-Out Burger next door to the Farmore Theater. Irked by *Inside News'* preemptive strike, corporate was paying for the construction of a two-story platform in the parking lot with three interview areas.

Truland was the big question mark, the unknown that hung over the entire event. If he did show, she doubted Truland could resist some sort of statement. More likely, through some prior agreement, he would saunter over to one or two crews on the red carpet for exclusives. She needed *HN!* to be one of those crews. The ceremonies were scheduled to air live on the Farmore Network, which was intent on surpassing the ratings of this year's People's Picks, Babblecock Trenders, Vox Populi, and People-to-People awards ceremonies. Pop-up ads were appearing on the phones of all Farmore Wireless customers who landed at LAX.

Most celebrity pundits predicted Jake wouldn't show, sixty to forty, according to a poll in that morning's *SizzleFeed*. But Jessie was working a hunch.

She called an all-hands meeting in the conference room for the bunnies, field producers, and camera crews. She laid out a map of the neighborhood around the Farmore Theater.

"This is the street layout." She pointed to various access routes. It was assumed Jake would approach the theater in the usual line of limousines.

"But I don't give a damn about the red carpet," she said. "We want to get him when he is leaving. That's our goal." She was the general calling out the line of attack. "I want camera nests at five spots, including here and here. We know how Truland operates. He'll try to pull a vanishing act."

"What are the terms of engagement?" one of the photogs asked.

That was a good question. She couldn't risk alienating Truland for the long term. "Approach with politeness," she said. "Cameras rolling."

"Are we looking for action?"

This was a code. The photographer was asking if he should try to provoke a reaction from Truland, maybe get him to push away the camera by getting too close and asking a rude question. In the business they called it "a Baldwin." A celebrity angrily pushing away the camera always made for great video.

"Polite and stalk," Jessie said. "Stay in contact."

"We could miss a great shot," said one of the blonde bunnies, with a very unbunny accusatory tone.

Jessie ignored the interruption. "We're going to put chase vehicles here, here, and here." She pointed to different spots on the map. "This is a two-part plan. I'm not just after ten seconds of video. We want to follow and investigate."

Jessie looked around the room. "I want to track this bastard. I want to know where he goes. I want to know his haunts. I want to know who he is fucking."

There was a murmur of excitement in the group. "I want detailed assignment plans from all of you. I want maps of the area. Points of contact. Possible destinations. Let's not screw this up."

Jessie wanted to rally the troops. She needed them ready to charge the walls.

"This is it, guys. The big one. We need to regain control of this story. I'm tired of getting jacked around by this guy."

Jessie knew this was a risky strategy. Jake might retaliate for the aggressive approach, block her out for months. Worse yet, he might not show. It would go badly for her if she committed Farmore resources on a bad hunch. But it was worth the risk.

Back on the bridge, she dialed the head of the VOPs, Barry Fine, the retired producer. He wore ascots and liked to talk about his days "working the streets with Scorsese"—an apparent reference to Fine's role as an assistant producer on Scorsese's *Mean Streets*. His official title was executive director of the Farmore Academy Theater Board, the nonprofit group sponsored by the feminine hygiene company to stage the awards and hand out $30,000 in youth scholarships each year.

"Absolutely, he will be here," Fine said in the booming voice of an actor trying to reach the back row. "It is going to be the most spectacular Voice of the People Awards ever."

Unconvinced, Jessie called everybody related to Truland in her phone book. They all said the same thing.

"As far as I know..."

"Seems like a go..."

"Who knows with that crazy bastard..."

She kept calling and she kept getting the same responses. It was the same old deal with Truland. So she kept calling.

Jessie was shocked when Vince, on the fourth try, answered the phone. She didn't waste much time with small talk.

"Why have you been freezing me out?" There was no point trying to schmooze Vince.

"You're in, baby, always in."

"Come on. You haven't returned my calls in two weeks."

"Hey, you got your story on that creep in Escondido. You're the big hotshot, Scoop. What are you complaining about?"

"Not even a quote. No video. Nothing for two weeks?"

"You have me now and I don't hear any questions."

"The VOPs."

"He is getting the Lifetime Achievement Award. A huge honor. Damn legendary, if you ask me. You can quote me—"

"Is he going to show?"

"My impression is that he has assured the academy he will be on hand to accept this prestigious honor."

"Wonderful. Inspiring words. Real poetry. I'll lead with that."

"Sarcasm is not one of your more pleasant characteristics, Jessie. You should work on that. Perhaps I need to chat with Sharon, let her take me to lunch next week."

Jessie caught the meaning. In the mob, a made man was a "friend of ours." In LA code, it spoke volumes when you "let" somebody take you to lunch.

"All I want is a sit-down on our stage," she said. "Three minutes. I ask him about this legendary honor. Ask him how he is holding up in these troubled times."

"I don't believe Jake is going to be doing interviews."

"But you really don't know, do you?" Jessie would not let Vince push her around. She aimed at his Achilles' heel. "I always forget, you're just the agent."

"Why exactly am I talking to you?"

"Because you know *HN!* will treat him right. Who the hell else would do three parts on Truland working with Ecuadorian orphans?"

"It was a very touching story—"

"Three fuckin' parts, Vince! Tammy even cried on camera. Real tears."

"I don't know what I can tell you. If he's not doing interviews, he's not doing interviews."

"You're telling me Jake Truland is going to walk by 125 microphones? You've got to be kidding. Not even a backstage moment with *Inside News*?"

"Off the record, we're not very happy with *Inside News*. That whole business with Klutch. That was piss-poor journalism."

Jessie's heart soared. "Vince, give me one minute. A walk-by. Two questions. I stick out a mike. He says his thing. He goes home or wherever he goes."

"Why would we do that?"

"See, you're screwing me. Why? What's going on?"

"I think you need to get beyond that anger. You're not going to get anywhere living in the past."

"Agreed. So where do we stand?"

"Maybe I'll swing him by after the awards Tuesday night. Maybe."

Yes! Jessie pumped her fist. She was OK with a maybe. A maybe was a better than a no. In Hollywood, a maybe was gold.

36

The limo hit traffic a mile from the Farmore Theater, a bumper-to-bumper jam of limousines—another Thursday night in Hollywood.

Becky was still mad. Jake tried to explain his position, as he searched for a corkscrew in the limousine's minibar. "I was agreeing with you," he said, as he opened a minibottle of Chardonnay.

She wasn't convinced, he could tell. But he never doubted she would show up. Loyalty was one of her most endearing qualities. "When she was a kid, her sister slept with her boyfriend and wrecked her car, all in one night," her husband, Bob, once told him. "It was bloody, loud, terrible. Bec forgave her something like a day later."

Becky had eventually agreed to accompany him to the VOPs, but she was still peeved, certain he was in danger. Even now, as the limo inched forward in the line of limousines, approaching the crowds and the familiar row of blazing lights, she glowered at him.

"I have a seriously fuckin' bad feeling about this," Becky said, checking each window like the tail gunner of a bomber watching for Nazi fighters.

"You think Urbina is going to make a move on the red carpet? That's crazy. He's not crazy."

"It still doesn't make any sense to do this. It feels like you're trying to milk it."

"We've—"

"This time you're the dickwad playing for a photo op."

"You're not a very fun date, you know that?"

She laughed. "OK, I'm done. Said my piece." She leaned over and kissed him on the cheek in that sisterly manner that always made him feel like a part of the world. She looked stunning in a sweeping purple gown. Not every woman can wear purple.

"Was Bob OK with the trip?" Bringing up another sensitive topic was probably unwise, but he was always fascinated by her home life. Bob trusted his wife. He never held her back from her jaunts with her old friend Jake. But neither Jake nor Becky really believed Bob was completely OK with it.

"Bob is in saint mode," she said. "The kids are starting Little League. He's working with them on their double play moves."

The limo was barely moving. Jake lowered the soundproof window separating them from the driver. In the passenger seat a tall blonde pretty enough to host a game show tensely listened to the mumbling noises on a small walkie-talkie.

"What's the holdup?" Jake asked.

"We're in the queue," she said.

Jake noted the use of "queue," not "line." Using English expressions to boost your international cred was popular these days.

"We're all boggled up," she said. "They say Clive Derringer created quite a stir."

Jake looked at Becky, who shrugged. "Who the hell is Clive Derringer?" he said.

The blonde continued to anxiously scan the battlefield ahead, barely acknowledging the question. "You know, he's the guy who did that song. You know, that song...'The Belly Bop'?"

Jake knew it. It was sort of a modernized take on "the Macarena," with rap lyrics.

"Call ahead," he said. "Tell them I'm leaving if I don't hit the door in seven minutes."

The girl turned around, panicked. "But I'm not sure if we're—"

"Six minutes and fifty seconds."

The blonde suddenly developed a stuttering problem. "But... it's...no one...There's no way we..."

"Six minutes, thirty-five seconds."

"Oh shit." She raised the walkie-talkie. "Break in. Break in. Everybody shut up for one minute. Please shut up. This is T-1, repeat T-1. We gotta get in, now. Repeat, T-1 needs to move."

Jake raised the window. Becky was laughing. "Fuck you, Mr. Truland, your highness." She kicked him in the shin with her pointy Jimmy Choos. "Why do you do that?"

"You have to," he said, rubbing his shin. "They expect it. If you don't use it, you lose it. Truism number 176."

"I have to pee," she said. "See if you can make it in five."

Five minutes later they were stepping out of the limo into a machine gun line of flashes. A wide and noticeably worn red carpet ran down the sidewalk in front of the theater, passing in front of a seemingly endless line of photographers and reporters herded behind a velvet rope. Searchlights shot barrels of white light into the sky. Across the closed-off street, a row of bleachers was packed with fans, many waving signs. "Bambi G. is the da bomb!" "Clive, marry me!!" "Free the Dolphins!"

A collective shriek rose from the bleachers when the crowd

spotted Jake and Becky emerging from the limo. Jake stopped and waved, giving the photographers a moment to adjust.

A hundred yards down the red carpet, a clean-cut man in an orange Tommy Bahama shirt wandered along the rope line with a microphone. Jake recognized him as half of the *Ken and Bobby Show* on KTSS-FM—Ken or Bobby, Jake could never be sure. Ken/Bobby was the master of ceremonies, pointing out celebs to the crowd, provoking squeals at seven-second intervals.

"Ladies and gentleman, the star of *One Family to Love*, right here in the flesh!" Ken/Bobby announced, scurrying to an older woman in an elegant silver gown, which was probably a touch more Oscars than VOPs. "Karen Klein, tell me what a thrill it is to be here." The fans squealed.

Klein, who had appeared on the soap for something like fifty-seven years, apparently thought the perky man in the Tommy Bahama shirt was actually giving her the award. She had already been told she would win Best Villain in a Daytime or Off-Slot Regularly Scheduled Program Shown Before 3:00 p.m. Award.

"Oh dear Ken, thank you so much..."

"Ho, ho...I'm Bobby!" More squeals.

"I just want to thank all the fans out there, who have made all this possible...especially my dear, dear sister, who you all know tragically—"

"That's great! Just great!" Bobby was already ignoring her, looking for the next celebrity moving down the carpet.

Behind the velvet rope, the media soldiers jockeyed for position, straining to see who would emerge from the next limousine. Positions along the red carpet gauntlet were preassigned, tightly controlled, and hotly negotiated. Placards taped to the street marked each assigned slot, and the photographers and reporters were moved into position hours before the event, in an attempt to maintain order and discipline. Piss off the and you would be stuck next to the correspondent for the *Hoboken News Reader*, competing for a chance to interview the associate producer for the *Muppets* movie.

First in line were the entertainment news shows—*Inside News, Hollywood Now!*, and the rest. They would get first crack, when the red carpet walkers were fresh and vibrant, hearing questions for the first time. Next were representatives of *People, Sizzler, US Weekly*, and the other big magazines, usually stringers paid by the hour to cover these events; staff reporters considered red carpet duty beneath their dignity. Next in line were the network news shows, followed by local news, Internet sites, blogs, the photographer pit, and, finally, newspaper reporters. Smart print reporters abandoned their spots early in the evening and huddled behind the TV crews, hoping to pick up stray quotes. Packs of tabloid reporters roamed the rope line, desperately trying to overhear questions and answers fired at the celebrities by respectable reporters.

Becky whispered in his ear. "I used to think this was like some sort of frat party where everybody down the line gets to paddle you."

"It is," Jake whispered back. He smiled broadly and waved to the crowds, who were in top squeal.

The red carpet was backed up with nominees, their families, academy members, their entourages, actors who were not nominated but showed up anyway, their entourages, agents, managers, and assorted hangers on. Each was accompanied by a bitter-looking publicist, who scanned the roped-in hordes, deciding who would be blessed with their client's attention...or, in other cases, which reporter might cut them a break and talk to their washed-up or unknown client. Weeks of tense negotiations had gone into arranging who would stop where. In front of Jake, hip-hop star Mandy Devine was in the middle of telling a crew from *Hot TV* a story about her recent work with a Nigerian dental charity when the producer suddenly pulled the mike away and started waving his arms frantically, hoping to attract the attention of the cowinners of the Best Lesbian Kiss Scene.

By prior arrangement, Jake stayed to the right of the carpet, steering clear of the rope line, ignoring the pleas for a comment.

"Please, Jake!"

"Look over here, Jake!!"

"Jake, just one question!"

The network guys avoided the pleasantries, shouting out fully formed questions.

"Jake, what are your thoughts on the progress of the investigation?"

"Jake, are you dating Missy Bodacious?"

Photographers tried to provoke him, hoping for a gesture or grimace aimed in their direction, which might make a good picture.

"Jake, are you afraid to talk?"

"Jake, is the mob trying to kill you?"

"Jake, Jake, are you high?"

As Jake passed the *Sizzler TV* camera nest, he turned and flashed a peace sign, another favor to Vince. Any acknowledgement would make them happy, Vince said. They promised to use the shot in their promos.

Further down the rope line, a skirmish broke out near the local news cluster. Tangerine Stevens, the pop singer, was responding to the question, "What is your idea of a perfect workout?" when Tom Plaster, the once-promising actor who was never the same after a motorcycle accident, came up from behind and gave her butt a generous two-handed squeeze. Apparently Plaster mistook Tangerine for his ex-girlfriend. She let out a scream and leaped into the interview area, bursting through the velvet rope like a sprinter crossing the finish line.

Becky hooked her arm under Jake's elbow and pulled him forward.

Jake spotted Vince at the end of the carpet, hovering near the ornate entrance of the theater, which was originally called the Moscow Theater and designed to resemble the Russian Kremlin, with tall bulbous spires. Vince gestured toward a large white platform, covered with the VOPs smiling face logo. Jake let out a soft groan. Barry Fine, the academy president, hovered near Vince, dressed in an all-white tuxedo with a red bow tie. The guy made Jake queasy. But he had promised Vince.

Disengaging from Becky, he bounded up the three stairs of the platform, holding both arms aloft, a race champion celebrating his victory. For the first time the fans across the street had a clear view, and the squeals reached new decibel levels. At least 200 photographers surged toward the stage, a roar of camera motors and strobe flashes.

For at least two minutes, Jake did nothing but pose in his tie-less black tuxedo and black shirt as packs of six to seven photographers were positioned in front of him by an academy media rep. The academy rep moved the photographers in and out with the precision of a Japanese field commander. Becky stood next to him for a few shots and then moved away again, out of frame.

Jake glanced to his right. Fine had magically appeared next to him, waving at the crowd with vigor, radiant in his white suit. Jake looked down at Fine, thinking that this might be a good time to blow off a promise to Vince. The sparkle left Fine's smile as the smaller man sensed Jake veering off course. Jake saw the panic rising in the little man's eyes.

Jake made a wide flourish to the crowd, pivoted toward Fine, and planted a long, slow, wet kiss on the top of his bald head, prompting a firestorm of whirring cameras and flashing lights.

37

The smell of grilling hamburgers was driving Jessie crazy. Renting the In-N-Out parking lot for the VOPs was inspired, she had to admit, a flanking maneuver around the *Inside News!* backstage exclusive. Farmore execs personally invited attendees to visit the special *HN!* Lounge in the parking lot before and after the event. While other crews picked up the same old red carpet crap, *HN!* was grabbing exclusive one-on-ones. Plus, thanks to its prime spot, the crew caught video of three different award winners in the In-N-Out drivethrough. But the aroma of double-double cheeseburgers was making Jessie's stomach rumble.

Jessie was originally skeptical of the whole plan—but the Farmore Studios construction crews had really outdone themselves. In two days, they built an opulent tower in the parking lot, a massive one-night demonstration of the show's influence and opulence, sure to make the attendees feel honored to stop in for an interview with Tammy.

The bottom floor was designed as a seventies disco, a dark

meeting area with velvet booths and a spinning mirrored ball. The
dance floor was big enough for a hundred celebs to boogie, if they
chose. In the back, a long-legged Swedish bartender manned a long
black leather bar stocked with twenty-three kinds of tequila. The
main interview area on the second floor was something out of an
Austin Powers movie, a sunken living room with white shag carpet-
ing. Tammy was perched in a white hanging egg chair that seemed to
float midroom. Guests were arranged on a hard bench coated in black
and white mohair.

Heather Bo, the sixteen-year-old costar of Spielberg's new *Indi-
ana Jane* movie, was squirming on the mohair bench, which was
making many of the guests itch. That could be a design flaw, Jessie
noted, except that it seemed to keep them alert during Tammy's slow
moments. "Tell me about the film?" Tammy asked Heather, who
rolled her eyes and scratched her butt through shiny gold pants.

There's no way they would ever use the interview. Tammy knew
it. The crew knew it. Heather knew it. But they recorded everybody,
even minor celebs, on the off chance the subject would one day commit a heinous crime or die a terrible death—or, more likely, say something ridiculous and controversial, preferably with either racist or
sexist overtones—in which case *HN!* would have great video ready
to run.

"Tell her to ask about the Fourth of July," Jessie whispered into
her headset mike.

Tammy was equipped with a list of generic questions for upcom-
ing stories that she was supposed to ask guests. The answers would be
used to fill up features for the next month.

The reply was hissed through the headset. "God, no, she'll freak."

Jessie wasn't sure whether Alan, the director, meant Tammy
would freak or Heather would freak, but her bet was on Tammy.
HN!'s lead anchor always made it clear that she found asking such
questions demeaning of her role as a "*pro-feshen-al* journalist."

"Then ask about her first kiss, dammit. We need something," Jessie said into the headset. Jessie needed to keep Tammy focused and productive.

"Oh, God," Alan said.

Jessie saw Tammy's face turn into a tight knot as she received the suggestion through her earpiece, like maybe she was overdosing on Botox. She held her finger to her ear, feigning trouble hearing.

Heather finished her statement, a denunciation of killing baby seals based on an article she'd read recently in a magazine. Tammy glared at Jessie. Then she leaned in toward Heather, her well-tussled mane emerging from the egg chair. "Fascinating, Heather. I think our audience would love to hear more about these baby seals."

Jessie sighed. It was going to be a long night. And she was starving. The smell of the burgers wafted through the French doors installed by the Farmore crew. If she strained she could make out the salty smell of the French fries boiling in oil.

It was too early in the night for this type of shit from Tammy. And there was still no word from Vince; Truland was already in the theater. This was bullshit. She needed to eat. Lunch was a granola bar, gobbled after she was called away to mediate a dispute with the mohair supplier.

"I'm out for ten," she whispered into the mike.

"What?! Don't you dare—"

The headset was already off. Jessie headed down the stairs. If she worked it right, she could make it to In-N-Out and be back in time for the next interview.

Descending into the dark disco, she almost did a nose dive on the last step. *Jesus, why did they have to make it so dark?* Her eyes slowly adjusted, thrown off by the sparkling disco ball shooting beams of light across the room. She spotted maybe a dozen people in the room, none of them looking very happy.

Jessie sensed tension in the air, and she immediately identified the source. Missy Bodacious was encamped with her entourage, a crew of about twelve ex-Crips. Most were huddled along the bar sampling the tequila. Raoul, the Samoan security guard hired for the occasion, nervously hovered near the door, petting the holster of his Taser.

Missy, dressed in a sort of fishnet blouse, was in the face of a beleaguered production assistant, who was assigned to prevent people like Missy from going upstairs.

"Y'all need whoever you need to tell that I'm out of here," Missy proclaimed, loudly. "Right here. Right now. I got places to go."

"I'm sorry, but you're not on the schedule." The assistant made a big show of studying the papers on his clipboard.

"My man said I was on the schedule. He gets paid good money to put my name on the schedule. Are you saying my man is a liar?"

The assistant held a finger to his earplug, like there was an important incoming message from higher-ups. Jessie knew the headset didn't work; it was just a prop.

There's no way they would use Missy. Wrong demographic. They'd rather go long with Heather Bo. The production assistant shrugged and acted like he was hard of hearing due to the serious dialogue unfolding in his headset.

Missy got the message. "You go ahead and tell whoever and whatever they can kiss my black ass next time they want some of my time. And you can take a smooch, too, you dumbass lackey. There's plenty to go 'round." She turned and stormed toward the exit, her ample ass bouncing a fierce rhythm in Spandex. Her crew gulped down their shots and moved to follow, giving the PA menacing looks as they strode past.

Jessie bolted toward the door, hoping to get out before Missy's parade clogged the exit.

But she was too late. Just as Missy reached the door, a shirtless black man in low-slung jeans bounded up the stairs and crashed through the entrance, closely followed by a swarm of a half-dozen men dressed in stylish business suits.

"Yo, make way for a sure thing V-O-P winner, y'all," announced the rapper known as Li'l Thug, apparently unaware that the winners had been notified in advance.

Known for his entrances, Li'l Thug grabbed his crotch and made one of his trademark leaps. Unfortunately, he was unprepared for the dark cave of the *HN!* disco and made an uncharacteristically poor landing. He tripped over a velvet bench and crashed headfirst into the chest of the already agitated Missy Bodacious, who let out a screech.

"You groping me, muthafucka?" Missy screamed. She slugged Li'l Thug square in the chest, sending him reeling into a mohair recliner.

Missy's entourage jumped to her defense. Li'l Thug's crew reached inside their suit jackets. There were screams of "Muthafucka!" and "Do it, bitch!" Raoul, the Samoan security guard, reached for his Taser.

Shit, I don't have time for this, Jessie muttered. Her stomach was performing backflips. She pushed through the onrushing wave of Li'l Thug's gang, working toward the exit. Infrared cameras positioned around the disco would capture the action. But right now Jessie couldn't care less. She just wanted a double cheese and fries.

38

Buddy Landau sat in a booth eating a double-double, double-cheese, double-bacon wondering how he was going to find the producer for *Hollywood Now!* Coming to LA was a desperate move; Buddy knew it. And desperation leads to mistakes, something he'd learned from reading books about World War II military battles. But he felt like he had no choice. The little motel was turning him psycho. And he was running out of money, fast. He walked down to the gas station, hoping he could get a job around the garage, but the manager recognized him instantly and said he wasn't so sure he wanted a weirdo cult arsonist working for him.

Last night, watching TV in the motel room, Buddy saw the ad for *Hollywood Now!*'s "live, exclusive, one-of-a-kind coverage of the Voice of the People Awards." The lady anchor, the one who talked like she was straight out of some snooty school in New England, said *Hollywood Now!* would be covering the Voice of the People Awards with "the A team." That producer chick, Jessie Dunbar, had to be there, he reasoned.

Buddy regretted making the call to the producer's answering machine. It probably made him sound like a psycho. But he was tired—tired of all the attention, tired of dodging TV crews, tired of wondering if the guy at the Dairy Queen thought he was a "weirdo cult arsonist." All he wanted was some cash and then he'd just disappear.

So he stuffed some of Truland's papers into a backpack and drove to Los Angeles. He got off the freeway at the sign that said "Hollywood tourism sights" and immediately fell into a line of traffic. He saw the Farmore Theater, but the street was closed, so he spent a half hour driving around trying to find a parking space that didn't cost twenty dollars. By the time he made it back to the theater he was hungry, so he went into In-N-Out.

Now that he was here, enjoying the greasy glow of the double-double, he realized he had no idea where to look for the producer in the huge crowd. There were thousands of people and limousines and security guards racing around. How would he possibly find her in this mess?

Buddy took a slurp of his Big Glug and looked across the parking lot. A huge searchlight blasted a barrel of white light into the sky. The light was massive, not one of those tiny jobbers he always saw at supermarkets and Best Buy openings. It swirled in front of a narrow two-story structure in the middle of the In-N-Out parking lot. There was a big sign on the building with a massive photo of Tammy Bandita seductively holding a microphone to her lips. *Hollywood Now! Disco Lounge*, the banner said.

Buddy took a big bite of his double-double. Could be that producer is right over there, Buddy thought.

39

The backstage area of the VOPs was light on salty snacks, Jake noted with a certain amount of disappointment. The buffet arrangement, a long table near the light board, featured salmon-stuffed celery sticks and carrots with honey Dijon glaze, but nothing that would pass for a pretzel.

The VOPs were moving at a feverish pitch, a swirl of big dance numbers and video montages—two-and-a-half hours in and no sign of slowing up. Jake made it to the first commercial break before bolting, along with most of the celebrities in the first three rows. As they streamed up the aisles, their seats were immediately occupied by tuxedo-clad students—seat-fillers, who were paid to make sure the cameras never showed empty seats. Becky stayed in her seat. "I think I'll get a little nap in," she said, leaning her head on the broad shoulder of the young seat-filler next to her.

While the show rolled along, the nominees wandered the theater, cell phones to ears, looking to see who was looking at them. The men's room was jammed with a long line of rich and famous. While he was waiting for a urinal, Jake spotted two guys in J.C. Penney sport jackets hovering near the paper towel dispenser. Jake pegged them immediately for tabloid snitches. They'd spend the whole night going in and out of the bathroom, hoping to hear something they could sell for $50.

Backstage, cliques were forming around the clear separations of the industry's strata. Film actors gathered with film directors to discuss Bono's fund-raiser for Argentina debt relief and "Julian's" latest Manhattan apartment development. The musicians slumped in a dark corner, sneaking cigarettes with the stage crew and mumbling to each other in a secret language. The TV contingent was a huge mob, dozens of perky ensemble casts and assorted crews all slapping each other on the back, old pals from crossover shows and downtime in the studio commissaries. Off in a corner, soap stars congregated around a separate buffet table; nobody who wasn't in a soap talked to the people in soaps.

Jake spent twenty minutes eating strange carrots and chatting with the cast of *Santa Cruz Swells,* a nighttime soap he watched occasionally. The writers were exploring interesting themes of parental obligations and the government's role in universal health care, wrapped around the story of an aging fashion model who had accidently murdered her biracial stepsister with a nail gun.

The Lifetime Achievement Award was scheduled for two-thirds of the way through the show after a commercial break, in an attempt to maintain viewer attention before the big awards. During the break—yet another ad for the latest scientific achievement by the Farmore Academy—Jake moved into position on the side of the massive stage, waving at the nervous-looking stage manager wearing a headset and clutching a clipboard.

Barry Fine appeared beside him, his suit emitting a soft glow.

"Don't forget to thank the academy," he said. "It would be a nice gesture. Not everybody was that eager for you to get this award, you know. I had to pull a few strings."

"Nice suit," Jake said.

Justin Timberlake introduced Fine, praising his influence on boy bands and young artists in general. To generally lackluster applause, Fine walked to the podium with the air of a noble prince. "There is no greater honor than the admiration of the people," he said without preamble, pausing to let the words resonate in the rafters. "No nobler status." Extra-long pause. "No higher calling." He was a Roman senator, addressing the plebes. "We who honor are also honored by the admiration you bestow upon them with this honor. Our honor is their honor."

Fine paused again, scanning the crowd.

"Once a year we at the academy humbly—" Fine bowed his head but chose not to clench his fist to his bosom, Jake noted—"*humbly* bestow one award that we vote on ourselves. But we draw on the spirit and will of the people as we wrestle with our choice, to make sure we honor only those that deserve the one award that honors a lifetime of achievement."

"Yeah, basically anybody who is willing to show up," Jake muttered as he checked his watch.

The applause sign blinked and the seat-fillers roared their approval. Fine introduced a video tribute to Jake's career, a montage of clips and sound bites. There he was on *Conan* slugging the masturbating bear. Cut to Jake smooching with Sissy Verlaine outside the Bar Room. The crowd roared at an old clip from *Meet the Press*, when he said, "The Democrats need to take more acid, watch more sunsets, and date better women."

Standing in the wings of the grand old theater, Truland watched his career pass before his eyes. Good moments. Wearing a tuxedo on *The Price Is Right*. Appearing nude in *Playgirl* to promote a book. The record for most appearances on *Cathy!*

Finally it was over and Fine returned to the microphone. "Without further ado, ladies and gentleman, the Voice of the People Awards Lifetime Achievement Award is proudly presented to Jake Truland."

The spotlight momentarily blinded Jake as he strode onto the stage, offering a hearty wave to the balcony. He felt the cheers of the seat-fillers and the producers and the publicists sweep across him, a familiar blast of warmth, a soothing old friend. When he reached the microphone, the applause was still going strong, spurred by the orchestra's violin-rich rendition of the Rolling Stones' *Satisfaction (I Can't Get No)*. He saw Becky in the second row, smiling and waving. Up in the balcony, Vince stood and applauded, trying to create a groundswell for a standing ovation.

Jake clasped Barry Fine's hand, and the emotion felt genuine. As the applause died down, Jake moved to the microphone and waited for silence.

"Before anything, I want to say something about this man here." Jake turned to Fine, who looked terrified. "Many of you may know Barry Fine for his work with the academy. But when I think of Barry Fine I think of his role as the assistant producer on *Juliet's Silence,* a movie that moved me as a young man."

"The film was nominated for an Academy Award"—best set design, as Jake recalled—"but more importantly, it touched my heart and yours and I want to thank Barry Fine for that."

Fine looked close to tears. He blew kisses to the crowd as he walked offstage.

"I want to thank the academy and I want to thank the people for this," Jake said, holding up the small gold trophy, which featured the figure of a roaring tiger, for no apparent reason.

Looking across the room, Jake forgot his prepared speech. He recognized many of the people in the seats, understood how they had struggled to reach a point in their careers when they would be invited to shows like this. Many were young, wearing a designer name for the first time, loving the moment in the lights. Jake felt honored that they were still interested in him after all these years.

"I want to dedicate this award to my father," he said.

Jake remembered their last meeting, the guilt he felt for running out of the home so quickly.

"He would have wanted one of these," Jake said, knowing few members of the audience would understand, even though some probably knew Robert Livingston.

"He deserved one of these, far more than me. He would have liked it."

He spotted a seat-warmer in the front row yawning, big and wide.

40

Jessie twirled her finger in the air, signaling Tammy to wrap it up. Two minutes was more than enough with Tony DiNocca, who played a minor cop on a minor cop show. Real names were starting to stream out of the theater. She couldn't get backed up with the likes of Tony DiNocca.

Her phone vibrated in her jacket. She almost ignored it. But her heart fluttered when she saw the caller ID.

"Two minutes," Vince said. "In the parking lot. He'll be walking by your...whatever the hell that is...your tower."

"Excellent." Jessie pumped her fist in the air over and over again, drawing stares from the crew and Tammy, who wasn't quite clear on how to interpret the signal.

"You get two questions. Don't ask him about fashion accessories. Don't ask him about the congressional investigation. If you piss him off, you'll never see him again."

"Got it."

"You and the camera. No one else."

"No problem."

The line went dead. Jessie knew she didn't have to say thank you. She was overcome with giddiness. Her knees bounced in a little jig.

She sailed down the stairs and into the dark of the disco, not touching the steps. She scanned the darkness, trying to make out faces, hoping for anyone with a camera. *There!* Ben Jessop was standing in the corner drinking a Fanta. Ben was not her favorite; he was kind of an old fart. But he was a pro. He had spent twenty-seven years shooting LA news, everything from debutantes to serial killings. Her spirits soared. *Perfect!* She raced through the shower of light from the disco ball.

"I'm on break," he said, holding up his Fanta in a defensive posture.

"Not *now*," she said, bouncing up and down in front of him. "Don't pull that crap. Not *now*." But she was smiling, laughing, enveloped in the gooey warmth of adrenaline and success. She was going to score again! *Three pointer at the buzzer!* A tease for a Truland exclusive almost guaranteed a twelve share. *Hell, maybe an eighteen share in metro Houston!*

"Get off your *ass*," she said, ignoring at least three union guidelines. She was breathless, finding it difficult to put together words. "Truland...one minute...out there...two questions..."

The mention of Truland's name seemed to get Ben's attention. And from Jessie's demeanor he seemed to understand the urgency of the situation. He was outside and set up with twenty seconds to spare.

Thank God for Ben, the old pro! Jessie wanted to scream. She nervously bounced a microphone off her thigh, trying not to look conspicuous. She didn't want to attract the attention of the other crews wandering the area.

"Don't forget the mike flag," Ben said, reaching into his bag for the red, white, and blue *HN!* triangle.

"Oh, hell, I'm losing it," she said, genuinely embarrassed. *No mike flag!?* That would have been a newbie mistake.

"Thanks," she said, unhooking the cord to slide the triangle onto the microphone stick.

Across the dark parking lot she saw a swish of motion near the back of the theater. She slapped Ben's thigh, but the camera was already on his shoulder.

She saw three people moving quickly through the parked cars. And then he was there standing in front of her, hand extended.

"Jessie, good to see you," Jake Truland said, smiling broadly.

"Mr. Truland..."

"Call me Jake..."

Behind him, Jessie could see Vince and Becky Hooks in a long, flowing purple dress. Hooks looked annoyed. Vince pointed at his watch and nervously glanced around the parking lot.

"Jake, a quick question..." She knew Ben would be rolling.

God, she hadn't really thought about her questions, in all the excitement. She froze for a split second.

"Tell me, what was the worst thing you lost in the fire?" It just spat out of her. Not even sure where it came from. It was way down on her list of possible questions. She recoiled at the generic sound of it, preparing for a smirk and a rejection.

"Actually, I've been thinking about that a lot..."

Relief swept through her body, making the cold sweat in her armpits tingle.

"This nightmare has brought my emotions to the forefront, made me appreciate all the women I've known and lost, especially the good times I shared there with Jackie Conrad, one of my true loves." He gave it a beat; the editor would like that. "When I saw the flames, I thought of sitting on the deck with Jackie, just the two of us, watching the sunset."

Jessie couldn't believe it. A gift from heaven. What a tease! "Jake Truland Reveals His True Love!" They could get a two-parter out of that alone! God, she loved this guy!

There was another pause. He looked at her. She looked at him. Another question was expected, she realized.

She wasn't sure where to take this. Follow up on Jackie Conrad? Or try for a different topic? Maybe get a day-two hit on another story line?

In that frantic second Jessie was still racing through the possibilities when she heard a guttural scream that closely resembled an ancient Polynesian war cry.

41

Buddy was leaning against the side door of a Suburban, holding his backpack close, trying to figure the right move, when he saw the producer jump down the stairs of the tower. An older guy lugging a camera and tripod followed her. It was dark, but he could see they were all excited, like they were preparing for something, scrambling around, putting a light on the camera, jabbering away.

He couldn't believe his good luck. She was maybe fifteen feet away, just standing there.

Then a rush of people walked by in a big hurry. One of the men walked right up to the producer and shook her hand.

Buddy stood in the dark, watching the scene unfold, like maybe he was on his couch watching a TV show. And then he realized the man was Jake Truland.

"Holy shit." Buddy wasn't sure if he'd said it out loud. He was in a sort of daze, kind of like the time he took that bad X.

Jake Truland was standing right there, in the flesh, sort of casual, talking to the producer. Buddy couldn't believe it. He didn't know whether to rush forward and beg for an autograph or run away as fast as he could.

A bright light burst from the camera, blasting Truland's face and casting a glow in the parking lot. It snapped Buddy back into reality. He hunched down behind a Lexus and looked around to see if he had been spotted.

On the other side of the Lexus, maybe ten feet away, a striking brunette in a purple gown stood patiently, watching Truland talk to the producer. Buddy recognized her. It was Truland's girlfriend, that woman from Texas. She looked great in purple, he thought.

He felt the weight of the backpack. This might be his one chance. He rose up and crept along the side of the Lexus, moving stealthily, watching out for cops.

In a moment he was behind the woman in the purple gown, who hadn't noticed him. Pulling up his courage he said, "Excuse me." He wanted to tap her arm, just to let her know he was there, but instead, he was so excited, he reached out and grabbed her arm. And he realized immediately that maybe he had grabbed her a bit too hard.

The woman in purple looked startled, but she didn't scream. She simply said, "Hey."

Raoul, the Samoan bodyguard, still amped from the confrontation with the Missy Bodacious entourage, instantly recognized the man who grabbed Becky Hooks's arm, thanks to his extensive preassignment briefing—SOP for Farmore Security. Raising the traditional cry of his warrior ancestors, he leaped into action, pulling out his Taser–cattle prod combo unit, the Chestblaster 7300 with special extender arm.

He brushed past the skinny producer and was almost on the perp, ready to deliver 2,000 volts, when the guy whipped a backpack off his shoulder, knocking the Chestblaster 7300 to the pavement and throwing Raoul off balance. Raoul was momentarily shocked to find his hands empty, but he continued his charge. A former linebacker at Riverside Junior College, he bent his knees and lowered his head to deliver a blow, just as the coaches taught him. But the guy bolted suddenly to his left, jerked by the weight of the swinging backpack.

Raoul's outstretched arm hit the perp's chest, a glancing blow. But the contact was still enough to send the guy sprawling, Raoul noted with momentary satisfaction before he hit the Lexus with full force.

Meanwhile, the perp crashed into the woman in the purple gown, who was propelled off her high heels. She hit the pavement hard, making a loud smack on the asphalt.

Dazed by the collision with the Lexus, Raoul heard several people screaming. More shouts came from across the parking lot. He gathered himself and searched for the Chestblaster. But he quickly surmised there was no time to regroup with the proper weaponry. The perp was on the move, taking off broken-field through the parked cars.

Raoul took up the chase and promptly banged his knee against the steel bumper of a Hummer. He let out a wail but kept moving forward, trying to run, dragging his paralyzed right leg. At Riverside J.C., Raoul's coaches often mocked him as the slowest linebacker in history, a bitter memory that returned as he huffed and puffed through the parking lot. He was losing ground, his leg a bolt of pain. Jake Truland, in his black jacket, ran past him in a blur. That's not good, Raoul thought. The bosses don't like when the clients get involved. Even worse when the client is faster than you. But Truland was already well ahead of him, turning the corner into the alley, in full stride.

Jessie watched the action unfold, sitting on the pavement, rubbing her butt. Raoul's initial rush had knocked her into Truland, who'd tried to catch her on the way down.

Startled at first, Jessie saw the unknown man and Becky go

sailing, like bowling pins hit by a nice hook. As the men ran off, there was nothing for her to do but sit and watch the scene play out. It was over in twelve seconds.

Two security guards were already attending to Becky, who seemed dazed but unharmed. A mass of humanity was running toward the alley, a tornado gathering up people as it moved across the parking lot. As Jessie watched, two dozen photographers—including two *HN!* freelancers—appeared from nowhere, their minicams banging against their guts as they tried to catch up to Jake, who had a long head start.

She looked up at Ben, who was studying the dials on his camera.

"Please tell me you got that."

Ben seemed nonplussed. He used a small rag to wipe a smudge off the faceplate of the camera.

"Please, please, tell me you got that."

Ben was ignoring her. He didn't offer to help her up.

"Don't fuck with me, Ben. *Tell me you got that.*"

"Sure, no problem."

"Everything?"

"Yeah, sure, everything." Ben went back to rubbing on his camera.

Jessie's heart soared. For a moment, sitting in the parking lot of the In-N-Out Burger, she understood the concept of "perfect bliss."

"You guys are going to have to pay to clean my camera," Ben said.

42

Roger Talbot missed the VOPs. Instead he watched the latest installment of *My Mother, the Hooker*, TV Land's latest attempt at cutting-edge reality programming. For tonight's episode, the producers sent Mom and her busting-out teenage daughter to Cancun for a little R & R. To help move the plot along, they stocked the mini-bar at the Marriott with a name-brand tequila, both a nice plot catalyst and effective product placement. Not coincidentally, a convention of pipefitters from Detroit was ensconced at the hotel, and the attendees were also pleased to find complimentary tequila waiting for them. And just to guarantee mayhem would ensue, the producers sent Mom and daughter an invitation to the pipefitters' cocktail gala and told them there was a "pimp and ho" costume theme. The VOPs couldn't compete.

Twenty minutes into the show, when video appeared to suggest Mom was fellating the pipefitter's Man of the Year in the Marriott's well-appointed restroom, Katie Couric, anchor for TV Land's fledgling news department, broke in with a special report. The story was a little vague, something about Jake and a scuffle at the VOPs. There had been a chase. But there were no reported injuries. "No suspects in custody," Katie said. It didn't sound like anything big. "The Hollywood area between the 110 and La Brea has been shut down by SWAT teams searching for the suspect," Katie said, using her serious news expression. Roger chuckled. Just another night in LA, he thought, as he waited patiently for the show to resume, so he could find out if Mom would bring her daughter in for a three-way with the pipefitter.

43

Two hours after the chaos at the VOPs, Becky Hooks jogged down the center of a narrow street in West LA, the plop of her Nikes on asphalt the only sound within earshot. It was a dark, moonless night on the side streets of Los Angeles. Behind her the glow of Sunset suggested some far-off battle. But here there was no light except the occasional street lamp. About one out of every three of the streetlights worked; she had counted on her last run.

She liked to run at night, a habit she had formed in Austin, where the blistering heat made it unwise to run during the day. The cool of the evening was the best time to escape, after the kids bedded down for the night. The twinkling of the fireflies and the buzz of the cicadas after a day of steamy, oppressive humidity made running a fantasy experience. The late runs were her quality time, the chance to unwind and disappear into the buzzing night.

Tonight she needed it. When the limo dropped her off at the hotel after the VOPs, she was still too jittery to settle down. More

Jake insanity. No way could she sleep. A terse ten-minute call with Bob didn't help. Saint mode had worn off. The kids were already asleep, and she could tell he didn't want to talk.

"I had to put the kids to sleep so they wouldn't see it on TV," he said.

She didn't know how to defend the craziness. Nothing she could say would make the night's events sound ordinary and logical. It was all too weird.

She wasn't really scared when the guy grabbed her arm; more startled than anything. She instantly recognized him as the guy from Escondido, the stalker. But he didn't seem threatening. She didn't even scream. And then all hell broke loose.

Relief was her only emotion when Jake returned, out of breath, disappointed that he had been unable to find her assailant. She was touched by his caring, the way he shielded her from the cameras and worked with the paramedics, hopping into the ambulance like a doting husband, worried and attentive, holding her hand, urging her to go to the hospital, even though she refused.

But the VOPs were the final straw. In law school she was taught that the more complex a case, the less likely you're hearing the truth. Too many different elements were swirling around Jake, out of his control. All night she was worried about killers in designer suits and wraparound sunglasses. Instead it was an overweight nebbish in a dirty T-shirt coming out of the dark. It had to stop. Tomorrow she would sit down with Jake for a serious talk. This wasn't about his career anymore. It was about obsession and danger, a sickness. Maybe she would arrange an intervention. Lock him in a room with a bunch of reformed reality TV actors.

The running was helping. Half a mile from the hotel, she was already building up a sweat in the warm night. Lucinda Williams blasted in her headphones. She was working hard, picking up speed in the middle of the empty street, the serenity only occasionally interrupted by a siren or an imagined scream from the debauchery taking place in the hills above.

Becky liked these neighborhoods of normalcy in the midst of LA chaos, the family life glowing from the Spanish windows. The streets were slivers designed for a different era in motoring. Both sides were tightly packed with parked cars, barely leaving enough room for one-way traffic. Most of the garages in the tiny houses had long ago been converted into spare bedrooms, making the competition for street parking fierce.

In this slice of the California dream, there were no parks, no ocean views, no hike and bike trails for miles on end. Only pavement and people locked in expensive California bungalows with postage-stamp lawns. But people made the best of it. Fences were painted with sparkles and rainbows, and sculptures adorned small gardens. On this block, homeowners had turned their mailboxes into tributes to different movies. One mailbox was painted with a picture of Snow White and the seven dwarfs. Another was a small diorama of a castle from a *Star Wars* movie.

She stuck to the center of the street, enjoying the quiet and emptiness. Soon she'd have to turn back. Her knee was throbbing from the VOPs skirmish. She really couldn't maintain her normal pace. But the sweat felt good.

Suddenly the street was blasted in white light, like somebody had thrown a switch. How did a car get up on her so fast? Confused, she slowed her stride, not sure what was happening. She looked over her shoulder and was instantly blinded.

She struggled to focus.

The car was coming up fast. Her eyes couldn't adjust to the light. She could barely make out the approaching shape of a huge black truck or SUV that seemed to take up every inch of the narrow road.

And it was coming fast. She held up her arm, in part to shield her eyes, in part to warn the driver.

But the truck didn't slow down. It sped up. Coming faster and faster. It was almost on her.

She bolted forward like a sprinter leaving the blocks. Frantically she looked for escape. But there was barely a gap between the parked cars. Her heart pounded. Maybe she could make it to the next corner.

But the truck was approaching fast. She could feel it. She was running as fast as possible, pumping her arms. But the lights were growing larger, her shadow expanding at her feet.

She spotted an opening.

For a split second, she paused, calculating her options. But there was no time. She cut to the right, aiming for a gap between two parked cars.

In an instant she realized it was too late. She didn't feel the blow, only the sensation of flying, a brief moment of disconnect between earth and gravity.

Book III

44

When Vince called with the news, Jake did all the things he knew he was supposed to do, even though he didn't know why he was doing them. He tried to call Bob, but an irritated woman, probably a relative, picked up the phone. "He can't talk now," she said. He wrote a card to Becky's cousin, whom he had met once, many years ago. "Sorry for your loss," he wrote, not knowing what else to write.

Fifteen minutes after Vince's call, two detectives appeared at his hotel room door. They were from the LAPD special crimes unit, the team best known as the masterminds of the O.J. investigation. "Sorry for your loss," the taller detective said.

The police were calling it a hit and run because they didn't know what else to call it. "We really don't know what it is," the tall, gaunt detective said, searching Jake's face for a reaction.

A retired special effects artist in his seventies found Becky's body when he went out to get his morning paper. The positioning of the body first led him to assume it was a leftover cadaver from a movie set. Becky was crumpled in the sidewalk gutter, wedged in between the curb and a five-year-old Mercedes. A gaping wound was found in her abdomen, which the first officer on the scene believed to be the result of a bayonet. "I think the person who did this might have some involvement with the military," he told the first reporter on the scene, an insomniac staffer for Reuters, who dutifully transmitted the remarks to his desk, which sent out a news flash. Later, the forensics investigator found a dark red stain on the lance of a Don Quixote–themed mailbox nearby. That detail, mercifully, had not made it to the press, although Jake had no doubt one of the detectives interviewing him would probably leak it.

They interviewed him for an hour. Jake told them about Urbina and the fire, but most of their questions focused on the incident at the VOPs, which already seemed long ago to Jake, a hazy memory of a distant world. It was hard to believe that the scared, chubby character running down a Hollywood alley could be connected to this dark hole.

"Why do you think she was out there at that time of night?" the gaunt detective asked.

"She was jogging," Jake said.

"Sometime people dress like they're jogging, but they just, you know, like to dress casual."

Jake felt the ache in his toes, the weight of a lead collar on his shoulders. "She liked to jog."

"In the middle of the night?"

"Sometimes."

"Could it be, maybe, she had another reason for being out there?"

"Like what?"

"I'm sorry to have to say this, but my experience is that people out in the middle of the night are usually up to something. Maybe she was meeting somebody? Mr. Truland, I hate to ask, but did she have a drug problem?"

Jake considered hitting the cop. He could feel the satisfaction of his knuckles hitting the bony face. Instead he said, "Your experience?"

"I gotta ask these questions."

"She jogged. She liked to jog. She was dressed in jogging clothes because she was jogging." Jake could already see at least one news outlet running the "What was she really doing?" angle, backed by comments from an unnamed law enforcement source. "She wasn't jogging to meet her crack dealer. She wasn't meeting terrorist spies. She was just jogging," he repeated quietly, resisting the urge to leap at the detective's throat. He knew it wouldn't make the pain go away.

45

When Jake walked out of the Austin terminal, the blast of humidity was calming, soothing. The sidewalk was steamy hot. It was the type of day when the wildflowers that fill the scrub of the Texas highways die a withering, burning death, overcome like spiders under a magnifying lens. Jake felt his pores open up, almost popping with liberation. Then a group of photographers hovering around the baggage carousels caught sight of him and dashed in his direction, forcing him to sprint to a taxi.

Vince took control of the arrangements, serving as a liaison with Bob and the family. Without consulting Jake, he arranged for three dummy funerals. Fake orders were called in to florists. Funeral home managers were paid to call reporters with false information. Empty limousines left the house at different times to different locations.

Becky's friends and family were taken to a community center in Westlake, a tree-lined neighborhood in west Austin. The room couldn't handle the turnout. A hundred people stood in the court-yard, wilting in the heat, listening to the ceremony on tiny speakers, many quietly weeping. No one leaked the location. There wasn't a single pap in sight. No camera phone video showed up on *TMZ*.

Bob acquiesced to the machinations for the funeral but insisted on hosting the reception at the house.

At 7:00 a.m., police closed off the neighborhood for two blocks in every direction. Side streets were lined with white vans with telescoping antennas. Six helicopters circled overhead.

Jake arrived in a nondescript Yellow Cab, using a back alley. As soon as he walked into the kitchen, he felt like a criminal. The house was packed with her family, coworkers from the law firm, and her vast array of friends from book club, PTA, and the neighborhood. All conversations abruptly stopped when he walked in. Some stared. Others averted their eyes.

In the packed living room he met the same reaction. Laughter and conversation stopped. He sought refuge in what appeared to be some sort of sitting room. There were two comfortable recliners arranged around a fireplace, a small desk, and a wall of bookshelves, covered with photos of Bob and the kids.

Jake heard a commotion in the next room. "I want him out of here!" It was an angry scream, the scream of the badly wounded. "I want him gone."

Bob burst into the room, trailing a group of concerned friends and relatives.

"You..." he pointed at Jake, his finger an accusation. "You...Get out. Leave. Take all the goddamn cameras and those...those *people* out there and just go. Go back to your world."

A tall man with a goatee stepped between them. "Bob, no, he has a right to be here."

"This was her life. Not that. Not some photo op." Bob's voice was a plaintive wail. He wildly grabbed at a small blue and white vase. "Do you see this? Do you? Her daughter made this. This is real. Not you. Not Hollywood, you bastard." Tears streamed down his face.

"Leave. Go on *Cathy!* Do whatever the hell you want. But leave my wife the hell out of it, you fuckin' sick asshole."

Two middle-aged women in black skirts gestured for Jake to stay and moved to comfort Bob, who collapsed into one of the recliners, surrounded by embarrassed friends and relatives. "She's dead... *because...of him.*" The words were sobs, spasms of pain.

Jake moved to leave. The other guests stood in stunned silence, unsure of how to respond to the outbursts.

"Don't you dare talk to him like that." Jake looked over and saw Vince in the doorway, his face flushed with anger. "You have no right to talk to him that way. You...you...you take that back—"

Jake pushed Vince out of the room and through a screen door to a wide-screened porch with rocking chairs. Jake held a firm grip on Vince's arm. "Stop it. Vince, *stop.*"

Jake fell into one of the porch's white rocking chairs. He couldn't feel his legs.

The gangly neighbor who had restrained Bob came through the screen door. "I'm sorry about that," he said in a slow drawl. "He's hurting right now. Maybe saying more than he should."

"He's right. I'll go," Jake said.

"No, please, stay. I think people here...people who knew Becky... they know she would want you here."

No one spoke. The heat blanketed them on the porch. It was growing dark, and the cicadas started their evening rattle.

The tall man held his ground. He stood awkwardly, rocking slightly in dark brown cowboy boots. "You know, she never spoke about you much," he said. "Believe me, we all tried to get her to talk. But she didn't say much. That didn't matter. We could tell that you were important to her. She wasn't frivolous about picking friends."

Jake didn't know what to say. There was an icy pain in his chest, like the painful numbness after eating ice cream too fast.

The screen door slammed and Bob was standing there. Vince

moved to block an attack. The neighbor tensed. But Bob slumped into a rocking chair.

"Can you leave us alone?" Bob said, waving his hand in Vince's direction. Vince paused, then disappeared into the house, along with the tall neighbor.

Jake and Bob sat in silence.

"I always knew she loved you," Bob said. "Always knew there was nothing I could do about it."

"You know it was never like that," Jake whispered.

"I always knew there was something there, something I couldn't mess with. Part of her I was never going to reach. It made me angry, you know. Really pissed me off, sometimes."

"I know."

"But I sucked it up. It...I...And...now..." Bob withdrew back into the chair. "I think of the kids and I say it's all about them. But, dammit...but deep down...I know it's a lie. I don't think about the kids...I think about me, goddamn it. Me. All I can think about is waking up and not seeing her in the morning and how much I miss her."

Bob crumpled, the tears flowing.

Jake felt nauseated, empty. He didn't know what to do, how to respond. He wanted to put his hand on Bob's shoulder but didn't know how. And then Jake crumpled, too. The sobs broke out of him, retching, hard and loud, dry heaves. He almost fell out of chair, gripped by a seizure.

The two men wept, together but alone, their sobs mixing with the cicadas.

"I'm sorry, Bob. I'm so, so sorry."

"It doesn't matter." Bob didn't sound angry, just defeated, deflated.

"I know," Truland said.

Not far away, in an unmarked white van surrounded by a dozen other unmarked white vans, Jessie sat on a folding chair, staring at the blurry images of the two men on the screened porch. In her earphones she heard static and snippets of dialogue and emotion.

"Do you want me to reset, over?" The voice was a whisper on the walkie-talkie.

An engineer, the only other person in the van, looked at her, waiting for direction. She continued to stare at the jumpy images on the streets, using her hands to press the earphones tighter to her ears.

The walkie-talkie crackled again. "Repeat. Do you want me to reset, over? Please advise."

The last three days had left Jessie beaten and worn. She was in charge, leading the team. "You're our girl," Sharon Jones-Jones said. But she felt cold and distant, removed from the scene. A woman was dead. In her whole career, she had never known anyone who had died. Even in her local news days, she had never been the one to knock on the door of the victim's family. From the moment she arrived at the airport and saw the crews scurrying through the terminal, her peers descending on the story, she felt strange, detached. She wanted to cry but couldn't.

Sitting in the rented white van, she heard the distant voices in her headset, picked out of the ether by a Farmore audio specialist using the latest ultrasensitive parabolic, designed by some murky national security agency. The voices were fuzzy, the words difficult to decipher, but she knew what she was hearing. There was no mistaking the wrenching emotions shared by the two damaged men sitting on the porch in the oppressive heat. She heard their sobs, their pain.

"Repeat, do you want me to reset? Are you getting anything, over? Anybody out there?"

The engineer nudged her. "Do you want me to roll on anything of this?"

Jessie squeezed the earphones to her ears, tighter and tighter. It was garbled. Maybe not even usable. The sobs were needles in her ears. She closed her eyes. Tighter she squeezed, until her ears began to hurt.

"No. Cut it," she said to the engineer. And then into the microphone. "Move. Reset. Over."

"Are you sure?" The response was a hiss on the walkie-talkie.

"It's garbled," she said. "Move. Reset."

"But I think this..."

"Reset." It sounded more like a plea than an order. "Reset. Now. Please." She pulled the headphones off and crashed through the van door, not wanting the engineer to see her cry.

46

At the Austin airport, Jake was met curbside by four armed Texas state troopers. They quickly escorted him through an unmarked security entrance and into a small lounge with a leather couch and a flat panel TV. Bottles of water and fruit juice were arranged on a side table. The TV was off. A representative of the airline, a young blonde woman in a tight blue blazer, told him the airline would do "whatever necessary to ensure your comfort."

Vince tried to arrange a private plane, but Austin wasn't Burbank. And Jake couldn't wait. He had to get out of Austin, flee the stinking heat that reminded him of death. He had to leave now, this morning, within the hour, and he wasn't going to wait for a private plane. He'd always flown commercial, even when he disappeared. He wasn't going to stop now.

After forty-five minutes in the lounge, Jake was shown through an electronically wired door with a "Keep out" sign. A phalanx of state troopers led the way down a ramp separated by Plexiglas from the main terminal.

"They're our little security blanket," the prim airline rep said, nodding at the state troopers. "They charge by the hour. You can hire a couple for a party, if you want."

Jake felt like a criminal under an extradition order. He didn't want an armed escort, and he wasn't impressed that state cops hired themselves out as private security guards. He wanted to fade into the comfort of the wide-open space of the terminal; disappear into the takeout line of the Burger King and its unbused plastic tables. Through the PlexiGlas he saw people stirring. Some gawked. Two grungy characters with cameras raced through the terminal, shouting into cell phones.

Ten feet from the gate, the group was halted by the lead trooper, who suddenly raised his fist in the manner of a sergeant halting a jungle patrol in 'Nam. He appeared worried by a new piece of information whispered into his earpiece. He made a circular motion with his fist, a signal the other troopers appeared to understand.

"There's a problem at the gate," the blonde airline rep said. "We need to maintain our position until further notice."

Jake was tempted to jog back into the lounge.

"We're waiting for everyone to board," said the blonde, who appeared a bit rattled. She seemed new to this, part of the latest crop of media-savvy corporate professionals. Waiting for passengers to take their seats was standard operating procedure for celebrity outbound. As soon as the less-fashionable passengers were securely in their seats, belts fastened, he would be whisked into a first class seat, hopefully before too many of the riffraff noticed.

Jake's escorts stood in the hallway, silent, waiting, hands on holsters. The airline rep looked at her designer shoes. Jake felt like his skin was shrink-wrapping to his bones.

The trooper cocked his fist again and made a quick hammer motion. "We're clear," he said. "Move out."

The troopers moved forward briskly, apparently well-drilled

in celebrity plane entrances. On the boarding ramp, two troopers assumed positions blocking any strays from wandering down the gateway. Two other troopers briskly moved down the ramp to the plane, taking defensive positions on either side of the hatch. Jake felt queasy.

He quickly moved to the window seat he knew was his, guided by a stern flight attendant's internationally appropriate, corporate-approved, closed-finger pointing gesture. Jake gratefully sank into the leathery cushions, enveloped by the ergonomically exact headrests. In the next seat a well-groomed man in a blue suit ignored him and continued reading his newspaper. First class etiquette trumped all. Jake relaxed.

Ten minutes after takeoff, a face burst through the curtain that separated first class from coach. A young brunette wearing a blue Versace blouse and running shoes loped up the aisle and crouched next to Truland's row. She leaned toward him, ignoring the man in the blue suit. "Mr. Truland, I hate to disturb you," the brunette said in a whisper. "But I need to ask you a question. I'm from *Sizzler*—"

The unsmiling attendant, a woman in her fifties with hair in a tight bun, moved down the aisle. "Miss, you'll have to return to your seat."

"Just a minute," the woman said, pressing her breasts against the legs of the man in the blue suit, who readjusted his paper and turned away, struggling to maintain his appropriate first-class detachment.

"The seat belt sign is still fastened," the flight attendant said, jamming her knees into the girl's chest.

"Just a—"

"I'll call the air marshal, miss. He uses mace."

The brunette beat a retreat. The stewardess briskly snapped the curtains closed behind her. She bowed toward Jake. "There is no air marshal," she whispered with a wink.

Five minutes later, a man in a rumpled sport jacket poked his head through the curtain and dashed down the aisle. "Jake, remember me? Bermuda? The golf tournament?"

Jake ignored him. He was from one of the lesser tabloids, he couldn't recall which. The man in the blue suit, tapping on his Blackberry, raised his index finger a notch, an almost imperceptible signal to the flight attendant, who instantly appeared by his side.

The reporter sensed his time was short. "Please. Just this. Are you going to testify in front of the Titweiller committee?"

The attendant with the tight bun moved forward and flicked her hips, sending the reporter sprawling. Before scurrying back to steerage, he tossed a piece of paper in Jake's lap. Jake pushed it into the seat pocket.

Jake closed his eyes, but he couldn't sleep. He read the in-flight magazine, spending thirty seconds on the "Three Days in Darfur" story. A network sitcom on the little TV screen absorbed two minutes. Bored, he unfolded the crumpled piece of paper in the seat pocket. It read, "$20,000. Two questions. We'll be waiting at the gate."

Jake rose to go to the bathroom, stepping past the man in the blue suit, who was now immersed in his laptop. Jake looked back down the aisle toward coach, through a crack in the curtains. Three video cameras poked up from behind head rests like meerkats searching the landscape.

When he emerged from the plane's first-class toilet, he almost knocked over the attendant with the tight bun.

"Hon, can I ask you something?" she said apprehensively, knowing she was violating a subsection of the first class stewardess code. "How did all those *people* find out you were on the plane? We didn't even know until ten minutes before we took off."

"It's standard," Jake said. "Once they know a subject is on the move, they buy tickets for all the flights. They can usually guess the destination. There are not that many flights."

The attendant seemed shocked. "But that's a lot of money."

"Well, that's what they do," Jake said, ready to get back to the warmth of his imitation-leather seat.

She gave Jake a sympathetic look, the same look she offered passengers who were about to miss their connecting flight. "Well, maybe it will all blow over soon, hon," she said.

"Yeah, maybe," he said. But he knew that wasn't going to happen. No way; not now. Now there was blood in the water.

47

Eric Branson nervously tapped the phone with a pen, like maybe if he tapped out the right beat it would speak to him. The station was nearly empty, something about coupons for half-off at Nipples, the new club. Eric had the dining room to himself. He sat hunched over the table, tapping his phone like a teenager about to go out on his first date.

He knew it was wrong. Calling a reporter broke at least five different department rules. But he also knew those rules were broken ten times a day. And she seemed to deserve it.

After all, the dumbass ICIC deputies probably wouldn't even know about Buddy Landau, if not for her. By coming forward, she provided the deputies with a real lead. And she brought the information to him—approached *him*—not the sheriff's detectives, who seemed more worried about their press releases than the investigation. Maybe he owed her one. She'd started it all; that was a fact.

He tapped the phone a few more times.

Heck, in a few minutes everybody would know. What harm could there be? It was her story, after all.

He dialed the number on the card.

The phone rang twice before somebody picked up, a man with an effeminate voice. "Hello, *Hollywood Now*. Speak."

Eric almost hung up but continued on. "Jessie Dunbar, please."

"She's kinda busy, you know. Who may I say is calling?"

"Just say a friend in Del Mar."

"Okeydokey. Friend in Del Mar, it is."

Eric heard a click, and then a commercial came on for the new Farmore reality show, *I Dumped You in High School*.

"Hello, who is this?" She sounded frazzled.

"Jessie, this is Eric Branson, from the Del Mar Fire Department."

He thought he heard a little gasp. Maybe he was imagining it. "Inspector, how are you?"

He was pleased that she remembered his title. "I'm fine. Look, I—"

"I enjoyed our little talk the other day," she said.

"Yeah, so did I—"

"Del Mar looks like a good job."

"Yeah, it's—"

"But you grew up there, right?"

She wouldn't let him get in a word. "Look, I don't know how to say this," he said.

"Then I'd say just go ahead and say it."

"Well, I need to be careful about what I say. And, well...I don't think it's really exactly...and...let's just say there has been a break in the case."

Eric definitely heard a gasp this time. "I understand," she said, sounding kind of out of breath.

"I just don't want you to think—"

"Inspector, what can you tell me?"

"Not much. Except, well, it looks like you were right. There seems to be something pretty funny about Mr. Landau."

"Funny? Funny what way?"

"OK, you didn't get this from me, right?"

"We are off the record, background only."

Eric trusted her. "They finally searched his apartment. They found all sorts of material related to Truland."

The line was silent. Finally she broke in. "Can you tell me anything more? What did they find?"

"I can't be too specific," he said. He wasn't sure how far he wanted to go down this road.

"We're going with a story tonight," she said. "Between you and me, we're going to positively ID him as the guy at the VOPs. You saw our video from the VOPs? We sent it to this lab in Pasadena. Apparently they have some CIA ties and...Anyway, they're really, really good with video. They tweaked it and you can see Buddy pretty clearly."

Eric could hear the excitement in her voice, that passion for her job. Once again she seemed to be a step ahead of him.

"I guess that's going to nail it," he said. "They're already after him."

There was a moment of silence again. "What do you mean, they're already after him?"

"A warrant was issued twenty minutes ago," he said. "They're going to release the news soon. They've already put out the APB."

"What?! Holy shit!" She screamed so loudly, Eric had to pull the phone back from his ear. "Right now? There's a warrant, right now?"

That didn't quite make sense. He wasn't sure how to respond. "They know he had a gun in the apartment, so they're listing him as armed and dangerous—"

"Holy crap! Holy crap!"

"They think he's still in LA..."

"And I'm the only one who knows this? Nobody knows this?"

"As far as I know. They're going to send a press release at 3:00 or so."

"Holy crap! Holy crap! What time is it now? What time is it?"

"About 2:25."

"Holy crap," she repeated. "I gotta go. Thank you so much, Eric. Thank you for the call...And now, I gotta go. I gotta go..."

She hung up. She had called him Eric, he noted.

48

At first, when the fire inspector called, Jessie thought he was going to ask her out on a date. It had been so long, she couldn't be sure of the signs. She didn't make him for a tipster. But as soon as she hung up, all hell broke loose.

Thanks to the feed from *HN!*, Farmore Network News beat the competition by at least eight minutes on news that an arrest warrant had been issued. Plus, for thirteen minutes FNN was the only outlet reporting that Buddy was considered "armed and dangerous."

"I bet *Inside News* is shitting in their pants trying to confirm that," Sharon said, slapping Jessie on the back.

Ten minutes later a helicopter swooshed to a landing in the Farmore Studio's employee parking lot, almost taking out Tammy's new Audi. Jessie rushed out to greet it, followed by a photographer known as Flyboy due to his zeal for using a layout harness to hang out the helicopter door, a move most photographers considered the act of an insane man.

HN! already had two helicopters airborne. It was a long shot that the cops would pounce so soon, but they weren't taking any chances. Once word got out, all the LA news stations would be flying. With an arrest warrant issued and an "armed and dangerous" tag, the cops would go into full court press. Chances are they already had a bead on him before they issued the warrant. If nothing else, they'd get live aerials to illustrate the pursuit for Randolph Martin Landau, aka Buddy. All the newsrooms would put the birds in the air.

Jessie strapped in next to the pilot and pulled on the headset. "Hang on," the pilot said, grabbing a lever to his right. With a rush they jumped into the sky, leaving Jessie's stomach in the parking lot. She fought the impulse to barf, clutching her laptop and bag stuffed with various communications devices.

Soon they leveled out and the ride was exhilarating, racing along the LA skyline. Off in the distance, she could see swarms of helicopters, each at different altitudes, circling and hovering. At 1,000 feet above the freeway under the pounding rotor blades, she embraced the buzz of a big story. She felt like an Army Ranger on a raid, maybe like in *Apocalypse Now*, in a battle copter skimming over the water, Wagner blasting on the loudspeakers.

She quickly established radio contact with Brenda, who was positioned at the assignment desk in the *HN!* studio monitoring the scanners. In every newsroom around the city she knew they were doing the same thing, listening on the various frequencies to the jabber of law enforcement agencies around Los Angeles. You never knew when a dumb cop would let something slip over an open frequency.

"We've got nothing," Brenda said. Jessie could hear the crackling of the scanners in the background. "OC deputies were talking up a pickup truck they saw down in Tustin, but it turned out to be a migrant."

The pilot interrupted. "Where am I going?"

Jessie didn't have an answer. They were almost to Long Beach. She was in charge. She had to make a decision.

"Head to Tustin," she said.

The pilot laughed. "Roger that."

He made a swooping turn to the left, leaving Jessie looking straight down at the freeway below. She heard Flyboy gasp.

When they straightened out, Jessie regrouped her large intestine and tried Brenda again.

"Anything?"

"No, nothing...not even a...Wait, hold on."

Jessie heard the crackling scanner, louder now.

"Hold on..."

Jessie strained to hear above the roar of the helicopter.

"I think we have something," Brenda said, her voice rising. "Wait...yes...I think we've got a runner."

49

Buddy spotted the first helicopter when he crossed under the cluster of freeway overpasses in Orange County known as the Spaghetti Bowl. Normally, a helicopter was no big deal around the freeways, but this one was flying low and fast, patrolling the I-5 like it was late at night and they were using the searchlight to look for some smash-and-grab dude.

Except it was 3:45 in the afternoon. And no smash-and-grab dude was running across the freeway.

Buddy tried to drive straight and stay in his lane while pressing his face against the window, straining to look up at the sky. He didn't want to lower the window. Hanging his head out the window driving down I-5 with a helicopter overhead seemed like a bad idea.

The last four days had been a wired nightmare of paranoia and fear for Buddy. He ran from the VOPs that night with no idea where to go. There was no one to call, no one who would hide him. If his sister wasn't going to talk to him before, she sure as hell wasn't going to embrace him with open arms now. He wanted to run, but he was scared to be seen on the road. Twenty minutes outside LA, in San Bernardino, he paid cash for five days in advance at a run-down motor lodge called the Hotel Kalifornia in an area with the look of a gang war zone. He loaded up on microwave burritos at a nearby gas station convenience store and locked himself in the room to watch TV.

Every minute that passed, he expected the cops to burst through the door. He was sure the stoner at the front desk had recognized him. He kept the chain on the door and refused to let the maid in. He couldn't go to jail. His best friend in high school, Lance Dupree, his partner in shop class, went to jail for sexual assault and never came back. Jail was a death sentence.

"I am so fucked," he said out loud, sitting on the edge of the bed in the well-stained room. How did it all go so wrong? What the hell was happening? He was supposed to collect some money, maybe go on TV and tell his story, and that was it. Now Becky Hooks was dead and the cops were after him, for sure.

"I am so, so very fucked," he said over and over again, as he watched the continuous news reports.

The day after the funeral, things seemed to die down a bit. The head of a Wall Street bank had fled the country with his secretary, a "former exotic dancer," and something like $3.2 billion was missing. That got a lot of coverage. But there were still regular Truland reports. Congressional hearings were coming up, they said. There was talk about "damaging testimony" and "links to Becky Hooks's mysterious death" and "the fashion accessory industry's long history of violence in Hollywood."

Lying on the bed in the Hotel Kalifornia, his stomach grumbling from too many microwave burritos and Dr. Peppers, Buddy started to feel some hope. Maybe they would arrest someone in the fashion accessory business. Maybe it would all blow over, he thought. During reruns of *Wheel of Fortune* the local station broke in to show live helicopter coverage of a black limousine driving down the 405, which they identified as Truland's car under the big headline, "Truland goes home." Buddy laughed and cheered when the limousine pulled through the gate of a Beverly Hills mansion and four girls in bikinis jumped out and held up a sign for TeenTitties.com.

But after three days in the Hotel Kalifornia, Buddy decided it was time to move. The room was creeping him out. He had spent an hour trying to figure out if the shag carpet was red or orange. Blue-white fuzz was starting to grow on the bathroom sink. Besides, he was running out of burritos.

A little before noon, the posted checkout time, he sneaked out the door and walked to his truck with his one duffel bag, momentarily blinded by the sunlight. He'd decided on Alaska. From what he'd heard, Alaska was the kind of place a guy could disappear.

By the time he hit the freeway he was feeling kind of better. All these people around and nobody could give a damn about one more beatup pickup truck. It was a nice day for a drive, blue sky with puffy clouds. The sunny skies reminded him of days playing football with his friends in junior high, back when he was the stud of flag football.

And then he spotted the damn helicopter going back and forth across the freeway like a bee looking for some honey.

Buddy pushed the rattling truck as fast as it would go, sailing past cars in the slow lanes. Some drivers gave him the finger as he whizzed past.

Buddy checked the rearview mirror. There was a cop back there; he could see the lights a few cars back. Evasive tactics were necessary, he knew from watching a zillion Bruce Willis movies. He saw an opening and yanked the steering wheel to the right. The truck's old suspension groaned. He hit the off-ramp going sixty-five and made a quick right turn onto a small side street. He pushed the gas and made another fast right turn onto a winding residential road. After three blocks he made another last-minute right and found himself back on a broad avenue lined with shopping centers.

He checked the rearview mirror. Now there were two cop cars back there, lights flashing. But they weren't gaining on him. He sped up; they sped up. He slowed down; they slowed down.

Buddy felt sweat dripping from his nose. This was crazy. He pounded the steering wheel over and over again until he thought maybe he'd broken his hand, the pain was so fierce. Sweat dribbled into his eyes, stinging. *Shiiiittt!!!!!!* He screamed as loud and as long as he could, until his throat hurt as much as his hand.

Where could he go? How he could get away? He knew he couldn't stop. He couldn't go to jail. He didn't have the constitution for jail life. He knew that. He'd watched every season of *Oz* on DVD. He knew.

Maybe if he made a quick turn, he could duck into a driveway or something, maybe stash the truck. Maybe a semi would pull out and block the cops. He'd seen that happen in a movie. But, oh shit, he wasn't going to stop, no way.

So he hit the gas, causing the truck to lurch forward. He looked at the rearview mirror. The cops sped up, their lights flashing.

And then he heard a helicopter. He tried to look up, but he couldn't see anything. So he lowered the window and craned his head out, not caring. The blast of fresh air felt good, blowing his hair back.

But what he saw almost made him lose control. He momentarily let go of the wheel as he craned to get a better view. The truck swerved left, bouncing into the center divider.

The sky was full of helicopters. Not just one or two, but a dozen. They were in front of him, behind him, and circling all around, all at different heights. He grabbed the wheel and fought for control.

"I am so fucked," he said out loud.

He jammed the accelerator to the floor. Going faster felt good, like maybe he was going somewhere; the wind rushed through the open window. Going faster made him concentrate, made him feel something good would happen. He saw the shadows of the helicopters moving across the pavement around him, following him. Where the hell did they all come from? He didn't know there were that many helicopters in LA.

Buddy turned on the radio. He heard a deep voice.

"The suspect is considered armed and dangerous. He was first spotted in the Tustin area..."

Buddy punched the scan button.

"Randolph Martin Landau is wanted for questioning in the mysterious fire that destroyed author and celebrity Jake Truland's beachfront home..."

I'm soooo fucked.

Buddy punched scan again.

"The suspect was just seen leaning out the window of his late-model Toyota pickup truck, apparently cursing at overhead news teams..."

He punched the radio again, this time harder.

"I tried to talk sense to him, but, you know he just wouldn't listen..."

Goddamn, it was Elaine!! Now? She was on the radio. Now?!

A man's voice interrupted her. "If you're just joining us, we're live with Elaine Starkovsky, who was once engaged to Truland suspect Randolph Martin Landau... "

That bitch! Engaged?! Buddy slapped at the radio, hitting it over and over, trying to turn it off. "We were never engaged. That's a fucking lie!" he yelled at the radio.

He had to go faster. Going faster was the only plan. He ignored red lights. At big intersections, police cars parked across the road, their lights flashing, blocking traffic. He had to go faster.

The speedometer crept up to eighty. The truck felt like it was going to rattle apart. He barreled through intersection after intersection, huge crossings with eight lanes in every direction circled by massive shopping centers.

At every intersection Buddy prepared for the cops to open fire. But nobody got in his way, none of the cops moved to stop him. The cops would probably try to throw a row of spikes across the road to flatten his tires, Buddy knew from TV shows, so he turned every mile or so, just to keep them guessing.

His shirt was soaked through with sweat. How did it get to this point? Where did he go wrong? Maybe they'd listen to him, he thought. Maybe if he stopped they'd see it was just a big misunderstanding. *Hell, they're not going to listen me! I'm a Three Name Dude!*

He had to get away from the surface streets. Hitting the gas, he veered onto the ramp for the 405. He was heading north again. That was the direction to Alaska, he remembered.

He stuck his head out the window again, hoping maybe the helicopters were a mirage. But they were still there. Behind him a row of police cars followed in some sort of formation, like World War II bombers on a run, their lights flashing.

He hunched back into his seat, both hands on the wheel. Why didn't they try to stop him? How come nobody was shooting out his tires? Or trying to ram him? Why wasn't there a blockade or something? He slowed down; the formation slowed down. He sped up; the formation sped up.

The 405 was practically empty. For a moment the lanes in front seemed kinda dreamy, like maybe he was in a *Twilight Zone* episode. He had never seen the 405 with no traffic. He realized it was the first time he could remember driving more than thirty mph on the 405. To his right, people in cars were honking at him and giving him thumbs up as he passed. Many were talking into cell phones and waving frantically. On overpasses, rows of people jumped up and down, cheering like Raiders fans after a touchdown.

He had to go forward. There was only one way to go. Yet even as he gazed toward the horizon, straight ahead, he knew he wouldn't see Alaska. This was it. There was no escaping. The gas gauge was approaching empty. As he accepted that fact, the panic seemed to slip out of him. His energy fizzled away like air from a balloon. There was no point anymore. He knew then he would have to stop.

Going fast didn't seem to matter anymore. He slowed to forty mph and aimed for the next off-ramp, using his turn signal, out of habit. He was always proud of his good driving habits. At the end of the off-ramp he came to a complete stop at the four-way stop, giving it a full legal five-second stop.

He was on yet another wide avenue, eight lanes wide, with shopping centers on both sides offering Target, Walmart, and Best Buy. He would have to stop soon. The gas light was flashing. There was no choice anymore. It was over.

Strangely, he felt no panic, only calm. It was just the way it had to be. It was over. He rolled along at forty mph for a few blocks, soaking in the last moments. Maybe the food will be OK in prison, he thought.

There was another big intersection ahead. He slowed to thirty. Maybe he'd pull in over there, at the Diapers R Us superstore...

He looked to his left.

A huge pickup truck with a shimmering chrome crash rack was barreling straight toward him, ignoring the red light at the intersection. It appeared to be moving in slow motion. Buddy could read the Hemy ornament on the grill. It was the biggest pickup truck he'd ever seen. Buddy was going thirty, but it was like he was barely moving.

And in that moment he was able to calculate that the big truck, without a doubt, was going to broadside him. In that instant, he thought, "Damn, I wish I had one of those neck collars, like the NAS-CAR guys."

50

Breaking all sorts of laws, Jessie's pilot set the chopper down behind an abandoned Kmart, a block from the intersection. "I'll them I had rotor trouble," the pilot shouted as she unbuckled.

Hunched over, Jessie jogged away from the roaring blades, Flyboy right behind her, hauling his HD camera. They hustled across the Diapers R Us parking lot to the big four-corner intersection, which was cordoned off by police cars from every jurisdiction in the surrounding area, the cars arranged in odd and arbitrary angles, their lights flashing.

When she hit the street Jessie stopped dead in her tracks, shocked by what she saw. The biggest pickup truck she'd ever seen was parked silently in the middle of the intersection. There was not a scratch on the monster truck nor its shiny chrome bumpers. Twenty feet away the Toyota pickup was a heap of metal, the driver side crumpled like used aluminum foil. Jessie could see the shape of a man sitting upright in the cab, his head tilted over at a crazy, rag-doll angle, blood covering his face. His eyes were open, staring to the distance. Two firefighters gingerly pulled at the collapsed door, clearly in no rush.

To her left, a crowd raced toward two officers, who were leading a burly man with a dark beard to a squad car. The man's hands were tied behind his back with a plastic cord. He was wearing jeans and a tattered Aerosmith T-shirt and appeared to be bleeding from a small cut above his left eye.

Jessie yelled to Flyboy and joined the crowd swarming around the two officers and their prisoner. Several reporters were shouting questions, all at once.

"Is that him?"

"Is that the guy from the truck?"

"Is that Landau?"

"Hell, I'm not Landau!" the burly prisoner bellowed, just as the cops were trying to push his head into the backseat of the patrol car. The man rose to his full height, putting him a foot above everybody around him. "I'm the guy who T-boned the rat fuck."

The mass surged forward, everyone shouting questions.

"Why'd you do it?"

"What happened?"

"What kind of truck is that?"

"I think y'all can pretty much see what happened," the man said, cocking his shoulder to the hulk of the Toyota, where firefighters were using the jaws of life on the driver's door. "Somebody had to step up and stop this thing. And I guess that somebody was me."

A woman Jessie recognized as the weekend anchor for one of the local stations shouted, "How does it feel to be a hero?"

"Heck, I ain't no hero. I'm just a guy doing his civic duty."

The two officers, who had seemed eager to get the truck driver into the squad car, shrugged and decided not to press the issue, allowing the man to have his moment in the sun.

Jessie glanced at the Toyota, where Buddy's body was a broken scarecrow. "So you did it on purpose?" she yelled. "Is that right? You did it on purpose?"

The burly man looked nervously at the two officers, who appeared interested in his response.

"Hey, I live right on down the road there. I was just watching the guy on TV and thought I'd come down with my truck and see what was what," he said, smiling into the half-dozen cameras arrayed around him, his scraggily beard wiggling. "What happened just happened."

"How did it feel when you hit that intersection?" the local news anchor asked.

"Gosh, I guess I was a little scared. But I ain't sorry. He mighta gone off and hurt somebody."

The cops were getting jittery, and Jessie could tell the impromptu news conference was about to end. Everyone was back to yelling questions at the same time. Finally one voice broke through. "Tell us why you did it! Why'd you come down here with your truck?"

The man offered another broad smile to the cameras, showing off his unusually white teeth. "Well, let's just say it didn't seem right that he was on TV and I wasn't."

51

Eric Branson stood in the back of the sheriff department's new press auditorium, listening to the sheriff address the assembled reporters. The room resembled an exclusive private screening room, with rows of plush leather commander chairs facing the stage, which was framed with massive high-definition 3D TV monitors. Every chair was occupied; rows of cameras lined the stairs on either side of the room.

The sheriff had billed the press briefing as "The Truland Affair: Case Closed." Eric wasn't invited, but he decided to go anyway. He still felt like it was his case. Five minutes after he arrived, the lights dimmed and a spotlight caught the sheriff crossing the stage, the light glinting off his medals.

The press conference was a multimedia presentation. Video was shown of the chase, set to the throbbing pulse of the latest Boom Beat single. Next, the monitors displayed a large chart with a timeline of "Randolph Martin Landau's movements." When the sheriff finished his review, a table rose from a trapdoor on the right side of the stage. It was covered with Truland paraphernalia taken from Landau's house and a few tattered remains from his truck, including a dirty old gray sweatshirt with bloodstains. At one point, the sheriff held up the sweatshirt and pointed to the bloodstains, sparking an audible purring from the photographers.

After an appropriately dramatic pause, the sheriff returned to the podium. "There is one more piece of evidence," he said. Pausing for effect, he strode back to the table and pulled away a blanket with the flair of a headlining Vegas magician. On the table was a hunting rifle with a battered scope. "We found this in Randolph Martin Landau's truck." The sheriff held the rifle aloft with two hands, in the same way that the Dallas policeman held up Lee Harvey Oswald's gun.

Eric watched the presentation with a mix of awe and disgust. This wasn't detective work or justice, it was theater. He thought he would feel a sense of satisfaction. Instead he was confused and angry. This shouldn't be the end of the investigation. The sheriff was breaking all sorts of protocols. Landau seemed like the real deal, but there were too many loose ends. What about Truland's Vegas connections? If that angle was dead, then why was the House Special Committee on Crime and Fashion going ahead with its hearings? Landau's death didn't prove anything. This was more about TV than an analysis of evidence.

When it was over and the reporters were almost all gone, Detective Brown strode over and slapped Eric on the back like they were old buddies. "What do you know, fireman, we got our man."

"The case is closed?"

"Did you try the calamari?" The detective was eying the buffet table.

"The release said the case is closed. Is it?"

"Didn't you get the DVD?" the detective asked.

Nothing about this felt right to Eric. "Landau is dead," Eric said. "That doesn't mean he's guilty."

"Sure it does."

"But what about—"

"Look, kid, the evidence is all there. Give it a rest. Have a cheese puff."

"Procedure calls for—"

"We're kinda busy to worry about procedure. Maybe you've seen we got this new Lindsay Bowman case dumped on us?" The talk show host had slapped a parking valet outside the Four Seasons and then driven off in a Porsche that didn't belong to her.

"But you still need to—"

"Listen, lighten up, fireman. You did some good work on this. I am sure the sheriff appreciates it." The detective walked off without another word, heading for the calamari.

52

In the living room of his house in the Del Mar hills, Roger watched the chase and subsequent press conference unfold on TV with the sound turned off. He didn't need to hear the shrill play-by-play of the announcers; he didn't care about their commentary and the speculation. The swirl of aerial shots, the gleeful crowds, the foreboding phalanx of Kevlar-clad police—it was all too familiar, a bad movie repeating itself. For Roger, the chases always revived the macabre spectacle of a few years ago, when a guy running from the cops stopped his truck on the 405 overpass and blew his brains out, live for the 5:00 p.m. newscasts.

At one point, Roger counted thirteen channels airing the Buddy Landau chase. It went on and on, preempting game shows, infomercials, and reports of the breakdown in nuclear arms talks in Iran. When it was over, Channel 2 lingered on a closeup of the rusty pickup truck and the body slumped over the steering wheel.

Roger grabbed his cell phone from the coffee table, found Jake's number on the speed dial, and punched the send button. Only a handful of people knew the number. It was the one Becky used. Again there was no answer—only the strange, troubling message with no words, the screeching, nightmarish chords of a twisted punk song that Roger vaguely recognized.

At first Roger was angry that Jake wasn't returning his calls. But soon the anger burned out. He understood, in a way. Jake would see his silence as a favor, shielding Roger from the paparazzi. It was beyond Jake to comprehend that Roger wanted to be there, wanted to help, wanted to share the pain. That's what friends do. Jake would never get that.

Throughout the days of coverage there were only glimpses of Jake—or at least people who looked like Jake—jittery video of someone jumping into a car; shots of a mysterious figure eating a burger at a roadside stand in Reno. *Inside News* reported that Truland was in Fiji, "mourning in the ancient way of Polynesians."

The new answering message had appeared two days ago. Even in the realm of Truland, it was disturbing, unsettling. Every time Roger heard the message it sent shivers down his spine.

The song was nothing more than a cacophonous madhouse of shrieking guitars and rhythmless sound effects. Underneath the blast of noise someone maniacally screamed the same words over and over again: *"Hello, Dad? I'm in jail. Daaadddd, I'm in jail. Ha! Ha! Ha!"*

Over and over again, the maniacal laugh.

"Ha! Ha! Ha! Dad? I'm in jail, Dad. Daaadddd! Jail. Jail. Jail. Ha ha ha ha!!"

53

Jake Truland walked into the Burger Boy in Baker at 3:00 a.m., prepared for the worst. For days he'd survived on fast food, using drive-through windows. The possibility of a momentary stare of recognition from a pimply-faced kid working the window was preferable to the gawks and shouted questions that greeted him at every restaurant, every 7-Eleven, every Ralph's. He'd rather live in a cave than face one more blue-haired Bible thumper who wanted to ease his pain. But he was hungry, tired of the road, and he wanted to sit in a lighted room and eat unwrapped food.

In the vast wasteland of east California, Baker, "the Gateway to Death Valley," was a familiar oasis, a desolate high desert truck stop with a zest for self-promotion. Baker was home to "the world's tallest thermometer." Dozens of times over the years Jake had stopped at the Burger Boy—a classic diner with a long counter and chrome booths—on the way to or from Las Vegas, grateful for the glow of the giant thermometer. The fries were OK, and the waitresses treated everyone with equal disdain. Once, when he asked for more water, a broad-shouldered gal leaned into him and said, "Darling, I don't care if you're Frankie Valli's love child, I'll get you some water when I get around to it." No one ever bothered him at Burger Boy. Usually, at worst, he'd rate a few curious glances from the truck drivers, degenerate gamblers, bikers, and bleary-eyed families motoring their station wagons across the desert.

Not tonight. As soon as he entered the double glass doors, he knew that his Brewers cap and four-day growth weren't working. The entire diner stopped, as if someone had shouted "Cut!" No voices, no clanking of the silverware. He felt everyone looking at him, staring. The hostess, a broad woman with tattoos covering her sunburned and wrinkled arms, grabbed a menu and pointed him toward a back room. When he slid into his booth, he looked around and saw six different flip phones open simultaneously, glowing in their owner's hands. Others were furiously thumbing various handheld devices. The waitress was back in fifteen seconds with water and a menu, a Burger Boy record.

He ordered a burger and fries without looking at the menu and buried himself in the *Herald*. The headline on the front of the local section made him sink further into the diner's vinyl booth: "Truland Sought in Companion's Death." He quickly scanned the story. There was no new information, no new sources. The third graph contained the peg for the headline: "Authorities are seeking to further question Truland, who disappeared after Becky Hooks' funeral. Truland has not been completely ruled out as a suspect in Hooks' mysterious death, a law enforcement source confirms." They didn't say he was actually a suspect, only that he "had not been completely ruled out." Further down, the article said, "Insiders say Truland and Hooks were arguing recently over Truland's career choices." The reporter was good. The essence of the story was completely wrong, yet each detail was properly attributed and there was nothing that would warrant a correction. He admired the craft.

Jake had known this was coming. In the absence of breaking news on a big story, a vacuum forms, sucking in any rumor or gossip that fills the void. He knew the "wanted" story wouldn't gain any traction. It was a cheap gambit. The reporter ran with the leak from the cops, hoping it might force Jake to reply. In a day the reporter would move on to a new angle, a new headline.

The dull rhythms of the dreary article bore into his brain stem, making his eyes heavy. He was tired, beat, more exhausted than he'd ever felt in his life. Maybe he should call Bob, make him understand the story was one-day bullshit. But what would be the point?

In many ways, it didn't make any difference. Whatever happened, he knew the truth. He couldn't escape it, couldn't hide, couldn't make it go away. Becky's death *was* his fault. He knew that in his heart. He had killed the one person he loved. She had entered his world without greed or malice or an agenda. And she died because of his world, his inability to protect her. There was no investigation that would change things; no conviction would twist the reality. The cops talking to the *Herald* were right, even if they didn't know it. He'd done it, killed her as surely as if he was driving the SUV himself.

After the funeral, all he'd wanted to do was leave the world. He turned off his mobile and bought a disposable phone at a 7-Eleven— what the druggies called a burner—and gave the number to Vince and no one else. He drove and drove until he couldn't keep his eyes open anymore. At 3:00 a.m. he checked in to a Comfort King in St. George, a small Mormon enclave in Utah, across the border from Nevada, using one of his fake corporate credit cards. He warily watched the clerk for any sign of recognition. But the fresh-faced kid was all polite Mormon efficiency, quickly moving through the card key routine, the model of professional discretion, ready to serve any bleary-eyed traveler along I-15 in the middle of nowhere, lured by the promise of a room for $39.95, including free HBO.

During the days, Jake walked in the desert, letting the sun bake him, enjoying the sweat. He forced himself up long rocky trails at noon, eager for the pain. He hiked until he was afraid that he had walked too far and wouldn't be able to walk back. And then he walked some more.

The heat and sweat didn't change anything. He remained a fixture of the cable shows and blogs and Babblecock and phone zaps. Three days after the funeral all the cable shows continued to report on him, almost ignoring a story about a blonde cheerleader in Wisconsin who was held as a sex slave for two years by a former Muslim cleric. That should have been at least worthy of three nights of live reports. Instead, they stayed on him.

Jake had never seen it like this. A few years ago, after a rumor hit the London tabloids that he was the father of Princess Brianna of Luxembourg's illegitimate child, twenty-seven news vans and eight helicopters followed him up Sunset Boulevard on his way to a movie. But that wasn't like this. Becky had been right, so right. Schadenfreude had morphed into something different, something he didn't recognize. They weren't letting it go. They weren't moving on to the next story.

On the fourth day, the paps found the Comfort King. Maybe the bright-eyed desk clerk finally decided to make a call. It didn't matter. He knew the motel was burned when a photographer popped out of the dumpster in the parking lot. An hour later he spotted a white van in the alley behind the hotel.

He sneaked down the back stairs of the Comfort King and headed west on the I-15, with no destination in mind. He thought of Portland, hanging out at the Budapest Stew for a few nights, talking beat poets with Olga. But he couldn't bring that down on her; it wasn't fair. Instead he was at the Burger Boy in Baker.

He looked around the diner. In a nearby booth, two kids were pointing toy cameras at him, pushing the shutter buttons over and over again.

He ate his burger and leaped out of the booth, leaving $20 for the waitress. Back on the open road, heading west, he rolled down the window and enjoyed the hot desert air. And then he spotted the white van behind him. His stomach cramped. They were persistent, he'd give them that.

He pulled off I-15 at Zzyzx Road, the last road on any list of roads, and drove into the dark of the high desert. The van dutifully followed. After three miles he turned off his lights and turned down a dirt road. The van went past on the main road, continuing into the desert. The crew would probably figure out their mistake in ten or twenty miles, Jake figured.

For ten minutes he parked in the emptiness. The desert filled the car, the smell of sand and dirt, the rustle of a cactus moved by a subtle wind. In the distance, a coyote howled.

Thirty minutes later he stopped for gas in Barstow. Jake spotted the clerk behind the bulletproof glass excitedly talking on his cell phone, like maybe he was calling the cops to report a robbery. Ten minutes later, heading through the open desert, Jake thought he picked up a tail, a black Suburban maintaining a steady distance behind him. He sped up but couldn't tell if it was a pap or just another traveler headed home on the lonely highway. For miles he nervously checked his rearview; the SUV was always there.

He finally called Vince. "You gotta come back," Vince said. "You can't run anymore."

"Do they really know where I am?"

"They don't know squat. Dandy Andy's blog has you in Paris. It doesn't matter."

"I have a tail."

"There's been some video. But, you know, it's Bigfoot. Nobody believes it. They got video of you snorkeling in Key West. You're not in Key West, are you?"

Jake didn't bother to respond.

"Jake, kiddo, this isn't going away. There's no new story line here. Disappearing is just going to make it worse. The cops are not going to like getting played."

Driving down the long highway, empty except for his car and the SUV, Jake knew Vince was right. There was nowhere to hide. They would find him. They had tracked him into the wilderness of Utah. The hunters were not going to give up the scent.

He had to go back. He knew that now, as his car lumbered through the desolate mountain passes. He had to face the judge and jury. Accept his punishment. It was the right thing to do. He had to take the consequences for what he had done. They weren't going to let the story slip away, not this time. Avoiding questions would only fuel the rumors. They'd pick at Becky's corpse until they found something new. He had to go back. There was no choice.

54

"Shut the door."

Jessie moved into Sharon Jones-Jones's office cautiously, wary of traps. In her mind, she raced through the events of the last few days, looking for mistakes. What could she have done wrong to warrant a closed-door meeting? Sharon didn't look up from her computer. Jessie warily lowered herself into the black and chrome chair.

"You're getting promoted."

Jessie wasn't sure if she had heard the older woman right.

"It's straight from upstairs. Lots of people upstairs like your work on Truland. Congratulations."

"What, I...what am I getting promoted to?"

"Executive senior producer. You'll get new cards."

Jessie had many questions, but Sharon didn't appear eager to elaborate. Jessie tried to work through the politics. Sharon said it was "straight from upstairs." That couldn't have made Sharon happy. And why was somebody upstairs eager to promote her?

Sharon flipped down her laptop. "They want you to head up the new Truland Investigative Team."

"The Truland Investi—"

Sharon held up her hand. "Don't. Don't call it TIT. Let's just say the guy who came up with it doesn't have much of a sense of humor. It's going cross-platform. The Web. Print. Even the network guys."

That surprised Jessie. She knew the "network guys" viewed *HN!* as diseased pond water. Reading her mind, Sharon said, "FNN is going to send a producer. I don't think they've committed to airing anything. It's just a show of force."

"And I'm the executive senior producer?"

"Yes, you are, congratulations."

Jessie couldn't tell if Sharon was making fun of her. "I thought the Truland string had pretty much run out? I hear he's probably not even going to show for the congressional hearing."

"Nevertheless, ol' Jakey is still big news. The big dick-swingers upstairs conducted a few surveys."

"Our numbers show—"

"Their numbers trump our numbers. That's the way it is."

Jessie wasn't pleased to hear that Truland was still on top of the agenda. She was sick of the story, ready to move on. She didn't want to be asked about the VOPs night again; didn't want to have to update the crowd at Starbucks. At night, she remembered Landau's body in the squashed truck, his head wobbling at that strange right angle. And she remembered the two men sitting on the veranda in Austin.

Jessie was ready, eager, to go back to stories about heiresses behaving badly.

"Don't count pennies on this one," Sharon said. "Spend what you need to spend."

Jessie recognized a trap. Sharon wasn't giving her a budget number, so she could always fry Jessie down the road for over-spending. Sharon was giving her enough rope to hang herself.

"Oh, and they want you to do Titweiller," Sharon said. "You fly out tomorrow."

"Titweiller? The guy heading up the congressional committee? Since when do we do politicians? He's...he's...bald."

"No, he's not bald. Practically bald. More thinning at the edges. Think of it as your first big assignment, Miss Executive Senior Producer."

Jessie left the office in a daze. As she walked through the newsroom, Brenda and Freddie vectored to intercept her, looking for signs.

"You look like you've seen a ghost," Brenda said.

"Oh no, don't tell me," Freddie said. "Something bad."

That Freddie, he was always ready to pounce. "Worse, I've been promoted," she said. She walked them through the basics of her talk with Sharon Jones-Jones.

"Upstairs? That sounds like the girl has friends in high places." He slid a half-step closer to Jessie.

Brenda, as always, was more practical. "What do they want from you? You can't beat a dead horse."

Jessie glared at her.

"Sorry, maybe not the best choice—"

But it was a good question. "Let's keep all the crews on stakeout," Jessie said. "I'll approve the overtime. And I want somebody on Vince. No more pussy-footing. I want somebody on him 24/7."

Brenda raised her hand. "Remember I told you about my friend's friend at the bank? He thinks he can run credit card info and come up with likely connections and aliases and...and, well, anyway, he has a program. He'll run it, but it'll cost five grand and it's a crapshoot."

Jessie thought about it. They already had contacts at a few financial institutions, guys who would look for credit card purchases. Everybody did. Truland was always too smart to leave that kind of obvious trail. But Brenda's friend had a "program."

"OK, do it."

"Like I said, it's a crapshoot."

"No problem. Give it a shot. We're still at DEFCON Five."

"What can I do?" Freddie purred like a friendly kitty.

"We know he's back in LA. He's been spotted twice. He's got to be somewhere. Work it."

"*Ja-voh, mein* executive senior producer."

Jessie didn't laugh.

55

The hotel's loading dock smelled of stale urine and rotting fruit. Jake stood near the steel door, trying to find some fresh air while avoiding the security camera bolted to one of the cement pillars that bordered the loading dock.

Elgin was late. Jake had already spent ten minutes waiting in the dank back lot of the Holiday Inn, increasing the chance of being spotted by a maid getting off work or a busboy heading out for a joint. It was 2:00 a.m., but he still had to keep an eye out.

Vince was wrong about coming back, at least in one sense. It hadn't made a difference, not a bit. The daily coverage was unrelenting, while the investigation into Becky's death showed no sign of real progress. The LA cops were only interested in "eliminating" him as a suspect and pinning the crime on the dead suspect, Buddy Landau. He agreed to a follow-up interview, but the detectives continued to ask questions about Becky's "lifestyle," refusing to believe she wasn't a crack addict jogging to a late-night score.

If anything, returning to LA simply bought him a little time. In essence, he doubled back on the hunters, showing up where he was least expected. It threw the crews off the scent. Reports of sightings in Oklahoma and Texas followed a logical trail. Suddenly an LA sighting was the weird one, the report no one believed.

Elgin was his lifeline. With Elgin he could travel almost unnoticed. Jake's week-old beard, ragged hair, and tattered Brewers cap worked well with Elgin's wardrobe of heavy metal T-shirts. Together they looked like two unemployed Venice rock 'n' roll bums, as common as flies, unseen and easily ignored by the people with jobs and careers.

The sound of smashing glass in the dark startled him. He was ready to bolt. A set of headlights turned the corner, splashing white light across the cinder block wall. He ducked back into the shadows.

The car was almost on him when he recognized the rounded hood of Elgin's yellow PT Cruiser. "Dude, I thought you meant the Holiday Inn in Hermosa," Elgin said. "Nobody stays at this Holiday Inn."

They drove toward Santa Monica, the I-10 empty at this time of night. Elgin was not in a talkative mood.

"Vince told me to tell you something," he said after a few minutes of silence.

"What's that?"

"One word."

"Only one word?"

"One word."

"You didn't tell him where I am, did you?"

"Hell no, fuck Uncle Vince."

"OK. You know I appreciate that."

"You ready for the word?"

"OK."

"Cathy."

"Cathy? That was his one word?"

"Is it some kind of code?" Elgin asked, confused.

Vince won't let it go, Jake muttered. At first Vince was fixated on *One-on-One with Daniel Strayhorn*, FNN's nightly talk show. Strayhorn was something like 86 years old—"an institution in broadcasting," FNN constantly reminded viewers.

"Presidents go to him when they get caught getting a blow job," Vince said. "It'll be the full hour. He'll throw you nothing but softballs. It's the perfect way to get back. Real classy."

But Jake couldn't imagine sitting across from the suspender-wearing moron. Five years ago, in an interview to promote *Truisms*, Strayhorn was thrown off his game when Truland recited Truism # 342: *Successful talk show hosts are the worst talk show hosts.* Apparently Strayhorn's staff had not given him an index card for that one. Strayhorn spent an uncomfortable few seconds shuffling through his cards before asking, "Tell me, Jake, why all the mystery?"

Jake literally felt a little bile rise in his throat at the thought of talking to Strayhorn.

So Vince switched gears and was now obsessed with the idea of a special blockbuster episode of *Cathy!*

"She'll get on all fours and bark like a dog for you," Vince said.

"I'm not—"

"I'm talking literally, Vince. Her producer said she would get on the stage and bark like a dog, just for you. Whatever it takes."

Jake shivered at the thought. Elgin asked for an explanation of the one-word message, but Jake wanted to change the subject. "How's the gig with the radio station?" he said.

Elgin visibly tensed. "Well, it seems that myself and the management of the Pagan Gods of Rock have come to a kinda, you know, parting of the ways."

"I'm sorry to hear it."

"Not me, man. Radio is screwy. Last week they fired all the DJs, all except that Kid Mike guy. Like, how can you have a radio station with no DJs?"

"So they're not backing your events?"

"Well, kinda...I mean, well, no. It was really just what ya might call a misunderstanding. See, they thought I was going to, like, fuck my ethics. And, it turns out, I was not going to fuck my ethics."

"I thought Vince was buddies with the GM?"

"Nah, the GM said he barely knew Vince. Dude, Vince had to practically beg him to put you on—"

Elgin looked embarrassed. "I mean, not that he had to beg him... But, you know what I mean, he was just pissed."

Jake understood.

Elgin parked down the street from an all-night taco stand across from the Venice beach. They bought squid burritos with extra guacamole, a pint of refried beans, and four beers. They sat on the edge of a stone wall bordering the beach and ate their burritos, watching the moonlight reflect off the white foam of the waves. Round glows of bonfires burned up and down the coast. Elgin talked about why he loved to skateboard. Jake tried to explain why bodysurfing is better than surfing. After an hour, they walked back to the car through the dark corridors of palm trees.

A few feet from the Cruiser, two men in matching dark sport jackets and blue polo shirts emerged from the bushes.

Elgin jumped in front of him. "Dudes, he's not doing any interviews," he shouted.

One of the men—his jacket looked like Armani, but Jake wasn't sure—placed a hand on Elgin's chest and shoved him against the car door. Elgin struggled to get away, but the man's straight arm held him in place.

Jake leaped forward, swinging low, catching Elgin's assailant below the right kidney. His momentum carried both across the hood of the Cruiser.

Jake raised his hand to swing again, but somebody grabbed him

from behind, pinning his arms. Jake struggled, but he couldn't budge
the grip. The two thugs hauled him down the sidewalk, his feet barely
touching the pavement. A door opened in the back of a long black
limousine. He landed face first on plush leather.

Jake rose, braced for a fight. The bigger of the two thugs slid onto
the leather next to him, slapped his iron bar of an arm across Jake's
chest, and pulled the door closed.

"Jake, calm down. Take a breath."

Ted Urbina sat across from him. Jake instinctively tried to leap at
him, but the Armani beefcake held firm.

"Come on, Jake, I need to talk to you."

A tall, thin man with a pointy nose sat next to Urbina. Jake recognized Dick Borovsky, the private investigator. He was holding a
highball.

"Don't look at me that way," Borovsky said. "Technically I don't
have a client anymore. Client privilege doesn't apply."

Jake didn't know what Borovsky was talking about. He knew
Borovsky by reputation, but they had never met.

"In fact," Borovsky said, "you were never actually my client, so
there is no violation here, vis-à-vis ethics."

Urbina sat back in the leather seat; Armani loosened his grip. "I
just want to talk, Jake," Urbina said. "Just talk."

"Fuck you." Jake rubbed his sore wrist. "You want to tell me how
sorry you are?" Jake felt all the anger and resentment of the last two
weeks rising in him. "You want to tell me how you're just a hardworking marketing executive hawking belts and purses, is that it?"

"Look, Jake, I'm trying to be respectful. I stayed away. I felt no
need to address the hysteria."

Jake hated this man in his wide-lapelled black sport jacket. A
platinum watch fob dangled from the jacket, a remnant of Klutch's
failed attempts to make watch fobs the season's must-have accessory.

Jake couldn't recall why he ever worked with the man, why he would inhabit the world of the thugs and marketers.

"I understand you're angry," Urbina said. "You lost somebody special. I got that. I'm sensitive to that. But I'm going to tell you something and you need to hear it."

"The gerbil story was too good for you, Teddy. I'm thinking more little boys. Maybe the cover of *Sizzler*. Maybe a special issue."

"Jake, I don't give a damn. I'm going to say this and you're going to listen." Urbina leaned forward. "I'm telling you, honest, straight up. Look into my eyes." Jake couldn't help but look at the man. His eyes reminded him of a diseased rodent.

"Jake, I did not have anything to do with the fire at your house. Period. End of story."

"What about Becky, you shit?"

"Jake, that wasn't us."

"Maybe one of your friends wanted to send a message? Maybe Dick here?"

"Jake, I'm trying to be patient. You don't know one iota of what's really going on here." Urbina pointed at him with three fingers, Paulie Walnuts–style. "You're just acting stupid. This isn't the smart guy I used to know. I can help you, but not when you're like this."

"I don't believe you, douche bag."

"And I don't give a shit what you believe. I'm just telling you. I'm not denying we were angry. The corporate guys don't like losing a moneymaker."

"And now you don't want me to testify before Congress, right? That's what this is all about, right?"

"Ha." Urbina imitated a laugh. "You want to go testify, go ahead. Talk Titweiller's ear off. I don't give a rat's ass. What are you gonna say? You're going to testify that the evil Klutch organized press junkets? Fuck you."

"Maybe they'll look into your friend Dick here while they're at it. Maybe they won't agree with all his assessments, *vis-à-vis ethics*."

That roused Borovsky off the highball. "Watch your mouth, celebrity boy. Your Q ratings aren't that hot."

Urbina ignored Borovsky. "Jake, I am not saying we are blameless here."

Jake lunged again, only to be instantly bounced back into his seat.

"I'm just saying," Urbina continued, "that thing in the taco stand. Well, that was regrettable. I'm not saying this or that, but it is possible one of my colleagues perhaps suggested an inappropriate method of communication."

"You fuck, then you admit—"

"Jake, shut up and listen."

Jake struggled against his restrainer.

"You want to testify? I don't give a damn. Get it out of your system. It'll be good for you, maybe get you back to your old self."

"How about I tell the committee I think you burned down my house and killed Becky?" Said out loud, the words tasted bitter in Jake's mouth.

"Don't be stupid, Jake. You can't back that up. You'll look deranged. Hell, Jake, you think the corporate guys care if you go on TV? Research shows the Klutch brand will explode with a little *Goodfellas* vibe. The lookie-lous alone will boost the casino take by two percent. Two percent is not bad."

"Maybe I tell the world you're a small-time pimp with a degree from Northwestern."

"OK, Jake, enough. Testify. Fine. All I'm saying? Be careful. Remember, this whole thing is about you. It exists because of you. Not me, you stupid-ass motherfucker. So fuck you. Be very fuckin' careful."

Jake felt his stomach cramping again, the pain he'd felt for weeks. He didn't need this curly-haired hack to tell him that.

Urbina sat back in the limo's leather. "So we're done. You want to talk like reasonable men, like men who understand the marketplace, you give me a call. Now get the hell of my car."

Urbina pounded on the window and the door instantly opened. One of Urbina's men grabbed Jake's arm and pulled him out of the car. On the sidewalk, they pushed him toward the Cruiser, where an agitated Elgin was already behind the steering wheel.

The long limo silently pulled up alongside. The rear window slid down. "Get a clue, Jake," Urbina shouted. "Get back to business. Stop fucking around." The window slid up and the limo drove off.

56

In the fitting room of Marvin G. & Sons, Congressman J.J. Titweiller wrestled with uncertainty. He leaned toward the mirror, trying a different angle. The dark blue suit really hugged his shoulders. In the right light, he practically looked broad-shouldered, and no one had ever described him as broad-shouldered before, ever. He admired himself in the mirror. The snooty-talking poof with the measuring tape around his neck said it was Italian. That might look bad to the folks back home, but there was no denying his shoulders looked darn statesmanlike.

The guy with the measuring tape treated him like the king of England, once he mentioned the Speaker had sent him over *perssonallly*. As soon as J.J. mentioned that, the snooty priss was all, "An honor, sir," and "How can I serve you, sir?" The man was dressed in some kind of English suit, with tails, like a butler. "Please tell me all you can about this occasion for which you desire the perfect suit."

So J.J. gave him the whole story about the committee hearing, leaving out the state secrets, of course.

"Ah, the committee room. A color dilemma."

The blue suit looked righteous good, J.J. had to admit. But he could barely raise his arms above his waist, the dang thing was so tight. How could he gesture if he couldn't raise his arms? His gestures were some of his most effective weapons. He could gesture with authority, with power. He'd studied some of the real pros. Kennedy was a pansy with all that squeezed-thumb crapola. He watched tapes of Nixon and Teddy Roosevelt. Damn, those guys could gesture.

Aides nervously stood around J.J. as he admired himself in the mirror.

"Sir, we have a full roster of expected witnesses,"

said a senior aide, a tough broad J.J. suspected was a lesbo. "You will see a nice cross-section. The *Attack Zone* host is confirmed," she said, reading from her phone. "So is the UN ambassador to the world fashion industry."

"Did you find somebody from the scientific community?" J.J. asked. "We gotta have an egghead."

"We were thinking of Dr. Shumarian from MIT."

"What is that? An Indian name? You gotta be shittin'—"

The aide quickly interrupted. "There is Dr. Randolph from the University of Ireland—"

"Make it so," J.J. said. He often quoted Jean-Luc Picard, which always helped with the nerd vote.

J.J. refocused on his image in the mirror. He gave the hairline a peak and patted the little sprouts working forward. The boys at the national headquarters lab said the process was a combination of plugs and "nanotechnology"—microscopic hairpieces that actually expanded and retracted based on commands generated from a mainframe of some sort. The technicians said that if the process was monitored carefully, he would always look like he was in need of a good trim. The results were amazing; he looked ten years younger. Turns out the formula was developed for the astronauts, some project he'd voted to approve eight years ago as a freshman and didn't even know it.

This special subcommittee on crime and fashion deal was the best idea he'd ever come up with. A real old-school play. The staff guys loved it. They worked the corridors and did some focus group testing, and the idea rang like a winner. "Truland's Q ratings are through the roof," said one guy with a mustache, whom J.J. didn't recognize. "The Destrovsky test shows people are really unhappy with the fashion accessory business." The taco stand shooting was like some sort of cherry-coated icing on the cake.

Then Alberto came to see him.

Alberto was the Speaker's henchman, or at least that's what everybody called him in the halls. J.J. wasn't even sure if he had a title other than "henchman," or if he was really even on the Speaker's staff.

Alberto explained it all. Told him the Speaker was going to back the subcommittee and install him, J.J. Titweiller, as the chairman. J.J. was perfect for the job, Alberto said, with what J.J. thought was a wee bit of a smirk. "You're practically unknown," Alberto said. "Outside South Carolina you don't poll worth a damn."

That sounded kinda insulting, but Alberto said it was a plus. "Your negatives are low. It's a blank slate. And respondents who characterized themselves as only vaguely familiar with your name said they see you as a man of integrity."

Alberto paused and looked J.J. in the eye. J.J. didn't know what to say.

Alberto continued, "Anyway, the people see you as a man of integrity. It fits with your law and order profile. And we believe Mr. Truland will practically guarantee exposure."

The last few days had been a whirlwind. The Speaker's staff sent over consultants and marketing "gurus" and demographic researchers. Yesterday afternoon, a swishy "makeup artist" showed up without an appointment and said the Speaker wanted him to cancel his afternoon schedule so he could do a "consultation."

J.J. wasn't keen on the idea, but he had to admit the guy was darn good. For an hour the "artist," Pat, forced J.J. to sit without moving while he tested different "magic elixirs" on his face. The guy seemed like a real pro. "Don't you worry," Pat said as he left, squeezing J.J.'s bicep. "I'll be there on your big day."

Then came more hair scientists, the voice coach, and the interviews with the media. The Speaker's office arranged for only the big names, even a one-on-one via satellite with Cathy. Then there was that cute young thang from *The Buzz,* who kept asking him questions like, "Who is your favorite celebrity?" and "Boxers or briefs?" like those were appropriate questions for a statesman. But he worked through it (Jimmy Stewart, boxers). Dealing with the dedicated guys and gals of the media was one of his strengths, he liked to think.

Looking at himself in the mirror, J.J. swelled with pride. He knew he wasn't a handsome man or even a popular man. In college, all the fraternities had ignored him, and the girls thought he was kind of weird. He knew that. But he could always talk and he could always gesture, and important people saw something in him they liked. And then he found himself a right smart-looking girl in Janny, already with her Realtor's license, even though she was only out of junior college for two years. After eight years working at a small insurance firm, he ran for Congress and won on his second try, thanks to help from the good ol' patriots of the local car dealers association. Three times he'd been re-elected, practically unopposed the last time out. Nothing to be ashamed about, nothing indeed.

The butch aide interrupted his contemplation. "But, sir, there is a problem," she said tentatively.

"I don't want to hear about no problems."

"It's Truland, sir."

"What about him?"

"Well, sir, it seems that he has disappeared."

"Disappeared?"

"Yes, sir, as in no longer easily locatable."

"Hell, we're subpoenaing his ass, right?"

"Yes, sir, that was the plan. But apparently he has a history of this sort of behavior."

"But we are going to be able to get him, right?" J.J. was growing agitated. His photo op with the Girl Scout Leaders of America was scheduled in fifteen minutes.

"I think so, sir."

"Think so?"

"Yes, sir, most probably. As soon as we can find him I think the subpoena will definitely do the trick. We just have to find him."

"Find him?

"Yes, sir."

"Don't we have drones and robots for that sorta thing? Why the hell did I just appropriate $3 billion for some sci-fi project if we can't use it when I need it?"

"Yes, sir. Good point, sir. But the courts tend to frown on using that particular technology to find an American on American soil."

J.J. sneered, which was almost as imposing as his bark. "Honey, are you purposely trying to piss me off?"

That shut her up. J.J. returned his attention to the mirror. The suit's price tag said $2,499. That's more than J.J. had ever spent on a suit in his life. But the Speaker had said not to worry about it, not to worry about a thing. There was no doubt he looked fine, damn fine. His red, white, and blue tie was going to look spiffy with this suit. He looked...maybe, yes—hell, why not come out with it—maybe even... *presidential.*

57

Roger Talbot felt himself nodding off in the Del Mar city council chamber room, as the council droned on and on about a one cent increase in trash rates. His eyelids grew heavy. His pen started to slip from his hand. Ted Sizemore, representative of District 3A, the coast zone where house prices averaged $5.4 million, said something about the need to consider the "poor and underprivileged." Roger's head started to roll. It would feel so good to lay his head on his folded arms and go to sleep, a long comfortable sleep.

He caught the eye of Assistant City Planner Dan Godfrey, who wagged a finger at him in the manner of a scolding teacher. Roger put a finger to his head and pulled the trigger. If the Council had heeded his forceful editorials and included a cappuccino machine in the recently renovated Council chambers, then they would have enjoyed a more attentive audience, Roger reasoned.

Tonight the chamber was practically empty. Three hours into the meeting, only four people were in the room—three he recognized as students working on a class project, and Sy Walcott, who sat stiffly in

the back taking notes, scowling occasionally. The TV camera opera-
tors had fled hours ago, putting the videocast system on autopilot.

Roger's cell phone vibrated against his leg. He pulled it out of
his pocket and waved it at Godfrey, letting him know, "*See, I have
an important call and I get to leave, neener neener, neener.*" He bolted
toward the door, even though he didn't recognize the number.

But Roger instantly recognized the voice on the phone. "I need
to see you," Jake Truland said.

When Roger drove up to his house, Jake was sitting on the front
porch, wearing a Packers hoodie and tattered jeans. He had the look
of a paranoid meth addict, nervously glancing from side to side.

Roger pushed him toward the back deck and settled him into
an Adirondack lounge chair. He brought cold beers. Jake said little.
A fog settled amid the pine trees, obscuring any view except the gray
wetness enshrouding the hillside.

Jake looked beyond tired. His face was gaunt and haggard, the
four-day growth no longer a fashion accessory. The blank glaze
reminded Roger of Camp Pendleton Marines coming back from battle. Jake's voice was dry and flat. The famed twinkle in his eye was gone.

"You know I wanted to be there," Roger said. "You know that."

"Becky would have hated it. She wouldn't have wanted you there."

"Still, you should have called. That's what friends do, Jake."

"I get it." Jake slumped into the lounge chair. "It was my time to
be the piñata. I deserved it. I had to take my licks."

Roger tried to understand his friend's torment. There couldn't be
anything worse than believing you caused the death of someone you
loved. He remembered the news story of a woman who fled with her
son to Colorado after a bitter divorce. In the thin air of Colorado the
boy suffered an asthma attack and died. The mother never recovered
from her guilt. She eventually put a shotgun in her mouth.

Roger wanted to change the subject.

"Jake, you can stay here as long as you want."

"No." The answer was a snap. "No, sorry, thanks, but..." Jake's voice trailed off. Roger waited quietly. They watched the fog roll through the pine trees.

Jake broke the silence. "I won't bring this to you. I promise. Once they're on you, they won't let up. You won't be able to get rid of them."

"I can handle—"

"It's different now. Becky said that. She was right."

"Jake, there—"

"It was a game. It's not a game anymore. They—"

"Look, Jake, you're tired. There's no—"

"There is. There is a point. I want you to understand. I need you to understand."

"Drop it, Jake. You're tired. We'll—"

"No, now. I need to do it now."

"Jake, whatever you have to say. You need to hear this. Becky wasn't your fault."

Jake ignored him. "I never told anybody this. Not really. But I always thought I would be a huge failure if I wasn't world famous by the age of thirty. It sounds fucked up even saying it now."

Jake wasn't looking at Roger. He was talking to himself, lecturing himself.

"A little famous wasn't going to cut it," Jake said. "Most people get tired of the attention. They can't handle the feeling that everybody wants something from them. That feeling...that *pressure*, gnaws at them. The fans always want something. They always want to be *inside*. But I didn't care. Never bothered me a bit. It made me feel close to people, you know, connected."

The conversation was making Roger feel increasingly uncomfortable. They were venturing into dark places. The ups and downs, the detachment—Roger recognized the signs of someone approaching clinical depression. He wasn't sure how to adequately play the role of therapist for his friend.

"Jake, Becky was a big girl. She made her own choices."

Jake didn't seem to be listening. "A photographer jumped out of a trash dumpster in Utah. Did I tell you that? A trash dumpster."

Strange lights reflected off the fog. Roger heard a woodpecker banging away on a far-off pine. He braced against the cold of the starless night.

"Jake, don't go to the congressional hearing."

"They subpoenaed me."

"You have a choice. Get a lawyer and—"

Jake raised his arm with the flourish of a Shakespearean actor. "My performance is expected."

"Stop it, Jake."

"I need to stop running," Jake said. He sat upright. For the first time Roger saw a glimpse of Jake's old energy. He told Roger about his encounter with Teddy Urbina.

"You, of all people, should understand that I need to go," Jake said.

"I know it's a charade. It's kabuki theater. And you know that."

Jake didn't respond. He sat back in his Adirondack chair. "Before I go, I want to do an interview."

"But...what?"

"An interview."

"With whom?"

"I want to give it to you. Right here. Right now."

"I don't want to interview you, Jake."

Jake moved forward in his chair. "I want to do it. It will be exclusive. I want you to have—"

"I won't run it."

"It could help the—"

"I'm not—"

"I don't care what you do with it." Jake was angry now.

"Jake, I don't want to interview you."

"I insist."

Roger shook his head. How could he make Jake understand that friendship wasn't about giving exclusives or working an angle? He didn't want anything from his friend. He didn't need anything from that world. Becky was right—he didn't have the gene. Selling a few extra papers meant nothing to him.

Jake would never understand. But Roger didn't want to argue with the shaken, wounded man before him. Jake had the look of a warrior who wasn't sure he could win another battle. So Roger went to fetch his recorder.

58

The regal, 140-year-old congressional committee room was packed, standing room only. The Special Committee on Crime and Fashion was usually assigned to a small room that resembled a large coat closet in the back of the building. But today the Speaker had reassigned the committee to the Rayburn Hall, the main room.

Jake entered through a side door and paused to soak up the scene. Congressional aides, security guards, photographers, and harried interns filled the aisles, pushing and shoving for position. A small drone toting a camera floated overhead. In each wing of the room reporters and photographers were packed ten deep, roped off in rectangular sections that resembled hastily constructed jury boxes.

When he was spotted in the doorway, a cheer went up in the back of the room, which was reserved for members of the public. Many of them had spent two days waiting in line for seats. Now they stood and applauded. Some held up homemade signs: "I'll always be Tru!" and "Tell it like it is, Jake." One proclaimed, "Eat Me!" Some wore SELT T-shirts. Congressional security guards tried to grab the signs.

But people ignored them, passing around the placards in a game of keep away, infuriating the guards.

"Order, ladies and gentleman. Order!" Congressman Titweiller pounded his gavel with authority. He sat on the dais a foot above his ten colleagues, resting on what appeared to be a wooden throne. His gavel appeared oversized, a few clicks bigger than a typical gavel, Jake guessed.

"Order!" *Bang.* "Order!"

Elgin stood by Jake's side, wearing a navy blue suit and wrap-around aviator glasses, his hair pulled back in a tight ponytail. Periodically, he put a finger to an iPod earpiece stuck in his right ear, as if he was receiving important security communications. The congressional security office had offered Jake a federal guard detail, but he'd refused.

"Order!" *Bang! Bang!* "Order!"

Elgin moved forward, trying to clear a path. A round bowling ball of a man in a gray suit cut him off. Before Jake could pull away, the man grabbed his hand and started pumping.

"Jake, Bob Diamond, associate committee whip and head of the Arizona Democratic Central Committee." With a firm grip on Jake's hand, Diamond pulled him closer so he could whisper in his ear. "Don't you worry about a thing," he said. "I'll make sure no one roughs you up. I got some pull here." The man winked and then offered a broad smile to a photographer who magically appeared three feet away.

Elgin gave Congressman Diamond a karate chop across the forearm. Diamond yelped and released his grip but maintained a broad smile. Elgin brushed him aside and cleared a lane, shoving Diamond back into his fresh-faced entourage. Jake took a seat behind a broad desk facing the panel. Elgin assumed a position in a seat behind him, looking nervously from side to side, occasionally tapping his ear bud.

Bang! Titweiller called the committee meeting to order. "The Special Committee to Investigate Crime and Fashion is now in session." Titweiller talked like he was addressing Rome's Senate. "Due to the extraordinary circumstances of today's hearing, I move that we waive the readings and proceed directly to the matter at hand. Do I hear a second?"

A voice piped in from far off. "Seconded."

"And so moved. Objections? Fine, let's move on."

Titweiller took off his glasses and ran his hand through his thinning hair.

"Now, before we go any further, I would like to make a brief statement." Titweiller gathered himself and sat up straight. He looked over at a man wearing a headset who gave the congressman a thumbs-up. "This committee has been mocked by some in the liberal media, and I just want to say this." He raised his finger skyward, a strong gesture. "We are in a crisis in this country, ladies and gentleman. And I don't use that word lightly. Our fundamental institutions are assaulted on all sides by subversion, indecency, and corruption. And nowhere is that more true than the fashion accessory industry, which affects so many of our loved ones in so many ways. The families of this great nation have a right to know these institutions are pure and free from corruption. And I vow to fight for America's families until my last breath. Thank you."

The room was silent.

Titweiller put his glasses back on. "OK then, moving forward."

The congressman read from a paper. "Let the record note that our witness today is Mr. Jake Truland, who comes before us of his own volition and has been duly sworn in. Mr. Truland is...uh, Mr. Truland, how shall I list your profession?"

"Unemployed."

"Uh, all right, let the record note that Mr. Truland is unemployed..."

"Mr. Chairman!" From the far end of the dais, Congressman Bob Diamond's voice cut off Titweiller, demanding attention. "Mr.

Chairman! I must protest the tone and the implications of your questioning. With all due respect, I do not believe it is appropriate for you to be badgering the witness in this manner." Diamond flashed his teeth to the crowd.

Bang! "Badgering? I ain't even asked him a question yet!" Titweiller's frontal lobe pulsated in various shades of crimson.

But Bob Diamond was not deterred. "Mr. Chairman, I am appalled at your treatment of this witness. And I would like the record to show that there were true patriots on this panel who did not sit idly by during this persecution so reminiscent of Berlin in 1936."

Titweiller rolled his eyes. "So noted." Titweiller turned back to Jake. "Now if we may continue. I understand you have a statement, Mr. Truland?"

"No, thank you."

A murmur went through the room. The members of the panel looked at each other and then at Titweiller, who appeared confused. He turned back toward two young staffers sitting behind him, each clutching mounds of paper. They both shrugged. He turned back toward the audience. "I'm sorry, Mr. Truland, I was under the impression that there had been some discussion about you making a statement."

"You were mistaken, Congressman." Truland kept his hands folded tightly on the table, the picture of attention and helpfulness.

Titweiller again looked around, straining to make the turn in his tight suit jacket. His aides nervously shuffled papers. Titweiller turned back toward Jake. "Perhaps I misstated myself." Titweiller was nothing if not persistent. "This might be a perfect opportunity to express yourself, to give your perspective on the matters at hand, if you so choose."

"Actually, I do have something to say." Jake leaned into the microphone.

Titweiller appeared relieved.

"I want to correct a false impression about my role in these committee hearings. No matter what anybody might have read or seen on TV, I am here only because I was ordered to appear."

A murmur moved through the audience, prompting more gaveling from Titweiller. *Bang! Bang! Bang!*

"Be that it as it may, Mr. Truland, we are here today dealing with important matters."

"If you say so, Congressman."

One of the staffers sitting behind Titweiller jumped forward and slid a sheet of paper in front of him. The congressman gave it a quick glance.

"Mr. Truland, let's get down to the nitty-gritty, shall we? Did you not in fact work for Klutch Enterprises under the terms of a personal services contract? And, sir, there is no point in denying it. I have a copy of the contract right here." He waved a piece of paper at him.

"Yes, yes I did. A three-year deal, with a fourth-year option. Escalator clause. No health benefits."

"And what exactly did you do for Klutch?"

"I worked for the marketing department."

"I see. Now, in your role with the marketing department were you aware of a program known within the organization as the...let's see here...Tassel Initiative?"

"I am familiar with it."

"I got that right? It was called the Tassel Initiative?"

"That's right."

"Now, let me get this straight. I understand the Tassel Initiative was a calculated campaign to increase the sales of these special kinda tassels..."—Titweiller made a show of shuffling his papers, looking for information—"by—and I quote—'convincing celebrities and women of note to wear Klutch tassels and'—excuse my vulgarity—'various nipple ornaments.'"

"It was an extensive assortment. Klutch was using a manufacturer in Mongolia."

"And what was your role in this *initiative?*" Titweiller made the word sound like a pseudonym for *dog shit.*

"Your Honor, perhaps you saw Jackie Conrad's photo on the cover of *Sizzler?*"

"I am sure I did not."

"Millions of people did see it, Congressman."

"And so you are saying your efforts were successful?"

"My understanding is that sales of nipple jewelry increased thirteen percent for the quarter."

"You must be very proud." Titweiller's smirk resonated through the hall. Another aide popped up with a paper and placed it in front of him.

"Now, Mr. Truland, were you also involved in, or do you have knowledge of, a scheme to send prominent American actors and actresses to Pakistan to promote..."—Titweiller squinted through his bifocals to read the paper—"something called the Li'l Thug Turban?"

"Yes, I was involved in that."

"Pakistan? And, son, what in God's green earth is the Li'l Thug Turban?"

"I believe it was an attempt to create a new hat craze."

"And was that successful?"

"No. It turns out that turban material made women itch. But we did generate a fourteen-minute special report on *Hollywood Now!*"

"Fascinating, Mr. Truland, fascinating. Now, since you're being all forthcoming and all, maybe you can tell us about the operations of one of Klutch Enterprises' key holdings, the Harlot casino?" Titweiller switched course and zoomed in.

"Well, I think the slots may be rigged. And I think they bring in pigeon eggs from Malaysia for the buffet. But that may just be rumor."

The crowd erupted in laughter. Truland was not laughing. Neither was Titweiller.

"I see." Titweiller removed his glasses with a flourish. "Mr. Truland, perhaps it would be helpful to the committee if you would be so kind to explain exactly—and I mean, exactly—what it is you did for the Harlot?"

"I was basically a consultant on press manipulation."

"Press manipulation? That does sound ominous. What exactly did you do in your role as a consultant?"

"Planted stories. Maybe called *Sizzler* when a starlet got too drunk. Maybe arranged for a photographer to show up at the spa. That type of thing. I was essentially a media pimp."

Somebody in the back of the room let out a shout. "Let's hear it for the pimps!" Several whoops went up from the public rows.

The gavel came down. *Bang! Bang! Bang!* Titweiller was getting a workout.

"In your role, as you say, as a media *pimmppp*," he drew out the word, allowing his disgust to show, "Mr. Truland, in fact, were you not complicitly involved in propagating the evils of the fashion accessory business?" Titweiller waved a piece of paper menacingly.

"It's over there, Congressman."

"Excuse me?"

"The feed camera. It's right there." Jake pointed to a camera pod to his right. "I believe you were looking for the primary feed camera. It's right there, the one with the red light."

Giggles could be heard from the gallery. *Bang! Bang!*

Titweiller was all smiles. "For the record, I have no idea what Mr. Truland is talking about. And besides, this is my best side."

Silence in the crowd.

"Congressman, I would also like to say, for the record, that I like the suit. Although, I must say Number Two Estée Lauder blush really doesn't work in these lights. I believe you are getting bad advice from your makeup consultant."

Offstage, there was a loud shriek. Laughter burst from the crowd. *Bang!* A small crease developed in Titweiller's broad smile.

"That's all well and good, Mr. Truland." Titweiller's eyes were dull and hard. "But shall we cut to the chase?" Titweiller paused for effect. "Did not you or one of your representatives in fact express concerns to a news program called *Inside News* that the fashion accessory industry may have been involved with the fire that burned down your house?"

"Yes, I believe that is right."

"And the subsequent shooting at the taco stand?"

"Yes, I believe that was in the news, too."

The murmur in the crowd turned into a rumble.

"Do you, in fact, believe some aspect of the fashion accessory business was involved in the crime?"

Jake considered his answer for moment. "The fashion accessory business? No, I have no evidence to that effect."

The crowd rumbled. Titweiller pounded his gavel. Once again he turned to the aides for help. But no papers came forward.

"Then, why sir, would you tell this *Inside News* that something stinks in the handbag business?" Titweiller glared into the lens of the feed camera.

Jake took a deep breath. He hadn't planned this moment. Hadn't prepared for it. But he'd known it was coming. At a certain point, there was no turning back.

"What do you really want to know, Congressman?"

"Mr. Truland, I want to know why you told this news program that something stinks in the handbag business."

"It's not complicated. I hoped coverage might spur more investigation on the part of the San Diego County sheriff's department. But, in all honesty, it was really just a cheap publicity stunt."

Bang! Titweiller was straining for control. Now he was addressing Jake as a hostile witness. "Mr. Truland, that is a peculiar choice of words. A publicity stunt, is that right?"

"Sure. I was trying to change the story line. Generate more coverage. Move the story."

Bang! Bang! Bang! Titweiller was perspiring visibly.

Jake looked around the room. People were leaning forward, eager for his next words. In the press area, dozens of handheld recorders were pointed at him. All he felt was emptiness. He had nothing to offer them. He was revolted by their interest, physically ill. They weren't the circus, he realized, *he* was; the juggler in the center ring.

Titweiller waved his right arm back and forth in a strange tomahawk-like gesture. "Move the story? My, that does sound callous and manipulative."

"It's a fairly simple process. Let's say, I wanted to change the story line now. I could start by talking about how many of your colleagues have taken campaign contributions from Klutch."

Truland looked straight at Congressman Bob Diamond, who shrank into his high-back leather chair.

The murmur of the crowd rose an octave.

Bang! "Very clever, Mr. Truland. But we are here to talk about your behavior." From his minithrone, Titweiller smirked at him, smug in his victory. "Mr. Truland, I must say I'm dismayed by the activities you describe. Very dismayed."

Jake turned back to his accuser. He felt tired, very tired. "Congressman, I'm not defending my activities. What I did, my line of work...I thought it was fun and there was no harm. I was wrong. It has repercussions. There's fallout." He felt himself sag in front of the microphone. "People have died. I have to come to grips with that."

The room was dead silent. No papers rustled. Nobody coughed.

Jake gathered himself. "But I can say this as a fact. That's no longer my world, Congressman. I quit. I have nothing to do with it."

"You mean you are no longer employed by Klutch?"

"I mean I'm done. I'm saying right now that I will no longer participate in that world. It's my past."

Mobile phones clicked open around the room. Reporters feverishly scribbled notes and checked their recorders.

"Mr. Truland, haven't you pulled this particular *stunt* before?" Titweiller's smile was gone. "Why exactly should we believe anything you say, at this point?"

"Yes, Your Honor, you're right. That's true. But I don't care if you believe me. I'm out of it." He turned to the press section. Many of the photographers lowered their cameras, shocked at the sudden attention.

"I'm done," he said to the group elbowing for position behind the thick rope. "You can chase me; I won't run. You can talk to me, but you will be bored. I no longer have anything to say." He turned back to the dais. "Gentlemen—and I say gentlemen because I see there are no women on this panel—I tell you now that I am not going to write any more books. I'm not doing any more talk shows. I'm no longer going to take money for interviews. No more deals with the tabloids. No more fake news. That's it."

The room exploded into a cacophony of gasps and whispered conversations. *Bang! Bang! Bang!* "Mr. Truland, if you have something to say, you are free to hold a press conference. You had your chance. Now you are here to answer our questions. I will not stand for any more of this speechifying."

"Mr. Chairman, I'm here because you told me to be here." Now Jake glared back at the smug politician. "And you're here because they're here," Jake said, gesturing at the packed media gallery. "This has nothing to with the fashion accessory business. It has nothing to do with me. It's all about getting you on TV." Jake pointed directly at Titweiller. "Maybe you think it's good for your career, but I'm guessing it makes you horny to think of all these people watching you."

A smattering of applause could be heard from the back of the room. Strands of hair stuck to the sweat on Titweiller's forehead. "That's enough. Enough." *Bang! Bang!* "This committee will not be insulted in this way. Mr. Truland."

"Congressman, you have asked for my statement and this is it.

This committee is not here to investigate the machine. You're part of it. People sit at home and watch video of teenage actresses walking to their cars. Investigate that. News organizations send photographers to stake out the homes of realty TV stars. Investigate that. But leave me out of it. I'm done. That's not my world anymore. It's your world."

"Mr. Truland, I will cite you for contempt. Do not push me any further. I will slap down on you with the vengeance of the Lord." Titweiller caught himself and tried to regain composure, stroking his hair and tugging at the lapel of his suit jacket. "Do not provoke me any further, sir."

"Congressman, I've testified as you've ordered. I've tried to explain. I had a disease. I think I'm cured. Congressman, you should see somebody for it."

Bang! Bang!

"Give the bastard hell, Jake!" somebody shouted from the back of the room. The crowd cheered. Security waded into the seats. Two members of the committee stood up and slid out a side door.

Bang! Bang! "That's enough, Mr. Truland. This committee is here for one reason and one reason only. We are here to find the truth, sir. The truth! And if you are not here to aid us in this endeavor...this thing to help American families...then why don't you...you should just..."

"Congressman, you wouldn't know truth if it bit you on the ass. That's the truth. If you're here for the truth, tell them to turn off the cameras. Go ahead. Clear the room of reporters. Tell them, no more pictures. Do it, Congressman."

The gavel came down over and over again. "Mr. Truland, our friends in the media have a right to be here."

"Congressman, you close hearings to the public all the time. This would be a great time to do it. Go ahead, tell them to turn off the cameras. Conduct your investigation."

Titweiller was clearly in a quandary. People in the back of the room were on their feet, waiting for his response. "Mr. Truland, you will not dictate to this committee."

"Mr. Chairman, do it. Go ahead. Look over there and tell them to turn off the cameras. You have the power. Tell them to turn them off."

Somebody shouted from the back of the room, "Yeah, turn them off." Another joined in. "Turn them off." A chant started in the audience. "Turn them off! Turn them off! Turn them off!"

Bang! Bang! Bang!

"Turn them off! Turn them off!"

The chants grew louder, like the wave at a baseball game. "Turn them off! Turn them off!"

Photographers and producers in the roped-off areas nervously glanced at each other. The congressional guards appeared confused. Their training didn't prepare them for this type of behavior. They stood in the crowd, Tasers at the ready, unsure of whom to Taser.

Bang! Bang!

The crowd ignored the gavel. "Turn them off! Turn them off!" A poorly organized conga line formed in the standing room section. It was Mardi Gras.

"Turn them off! Turn them off!"

Bang! Bang! "There will be order in here or I will clear this room. Order!"

Jake couldn't take it anymore. The bile formed in his throat. He stood up and strode toward the side door. Elgin quickly fell in behind him, nervously looking from side to side, his hand stuck in his jacket like he was about to pull a gun from an unseen holster. When the crowd in the back realized he was leaving, they stopped chanting. An eerie quiet settled on the room. Titweiller held his gavel in check, not sure what to do.

59

Jessie started clapping before she realized she was doing it. Her hands came together naturally, slowly at first, and then faster and faster. The photographer next to her started clapping, too. And then everyone around them was clapping. The entire hearing room was applauding, the crowd in the back was standing and whooping like it was a rock concert and they were begging for an encore.

Jessie wanted to shout and yell and jump up and down. She knew Truland was talking about her business, her job, her career. It didn't matter. He had said something that needed to be said, something that made her feel like cheering. And, man, he stuck it to that pompous Titweiller. As the crowd roared, the congressman scurried off the dais, an aberrant thatch of hair sticking straight into the air, a huge rip in the back seam of his suit jacket.

"That was great!" she yelled to no one in particular. But the applause was already starting to die down. Camera crews were packing their gear. Producers and reporters thumbed their handheld devices.

Jessie told her crew to spray the scene and hurried down the aisle, still awash in the buzz. She knew a few shooters would already be searching for Truland's trail. She didn't care. In front of the Capitol she caught a taxi to *Hollywood Now!*'s D.C. bureau, the office space near Dupont Circle the show shared with FNN News. The landscape was a blur. All she could think about was Truland—and the sweaty congressman waddling offstage—and she laughed out loud in the back of the taxi.

FNN investigative reporter Templeton Smith hailed her as soon as she walked through the door. "Helluva show over there," he said.

Jessie gave him the finger and hurried to her temporary cubicle. She didn't want Templeton's condescending old-school banter, not now.

Undaunted, he trailed behind her. "Guess he really told you guys."

Jessie couldn't help herself. She had to let it out. "Temp, it was really fantastic. You should have seen Titweiller squirm. The crowd went crazy—" She caught herself. Templeton would think her enthusiasm unprofessional.

"So what's the angle going to be, scoop? Truland's new hairstyle? Or go straight to the Constitutional issues?"

"Thanks, Temp. Don't you have something to do? There might be three people reading your blog right now."

Sharon Jones-Jones called a minute later. "Ol' Jake does have a flair for drama," she said. "Needless to say, cut all the happy horseshit and stick to 'Truland quits again.' We're not going to let him get away with it this time."

Jessie wasn't surprised. She never doubted which story line would make air. They wouldn't air Truland's condemnation or launch roundtable panels to discuss the "disease." They wouldn't show close-ups of Titweiller looking like a scared rat. She knew that. But it didn't diminish the feeling of exhilaration, the glow of the moment; not today, not now.

For the first time in a long time, Jessie felt like she was part of something big, something important. Truland had called them out, broken the code. Sharon would probably insist on calling Truland's behavior a "bizarre rant." It didn't matter. Jessie felt like she had witnessed history. She was there. She knew the truth.

60

Q: *What keeps you up at night?*
JT: *I worry that people will find out I'm a fake.*
Q: *What do you mean? A fake?*
JT: *I'm a fake. I know it. I'm not really good at anything.*
I didn't go to college. I've never run a business. I'm always
worried people will wake up one day and say, hey, that guy's
really just an idiot.
Q: *Idiots don't get to be rich and famous.*
JT: *Lots of idiots are rich and a lot more are famous. It's a*
whole different game to get famous and stay famous.
                                        —From "The Lost Interview"

When he was in elementary school, Jake's classmates often talked about their dreams, tales of nightmares and vague sexual conquests. But Jake never dreamed. At best he would occasionally wake up and remember a few random images. But there were never story lines or elaborate adventures, the vivid id run amok chronicled by his peers. To him, sleep was always a black hole, emptiness, a TV with no pictures or volume. Jake's sleep was a lonely trip.

But this morning he dreamt in high-def. In his dream he jogged on a wide sandy beach, against a backdrop of slow-curling waves of warm clear water and sunny skies with only an occasional puffy white cloud on the horizon. In the afternoon of his dream he lounged in a hammock that hung in a *palapa* restaurant where Bill Clinton tended bar. Mick Jagger manned the towel stand—it was a weird dream. Becky was there, playing Frisbee on the sand. In the water Tammy Bandita wrestled a giant octopus, kept afloat only by her mammoth breasts. Gunboats with missile launchers cruised through the waves, firing on unidentified strangers on Jet Skis. A Madonna song came on the radio, and everyone in the bar started dancing, including Clinton, who grabbed a waitress and tangoed across the sandy floor of the *palapa* bar...

A long banging on the door woke Jake up, reminding him of a banging on his door on a morning that now seemed long, long ago. Squeezing his eyes closed, he tried to recapture his dream, the joyous feeling. Instead he heard Vince pounding on the door. He pulled the covers up to his chin and scrunched his head into the soft pillow.

The banging on the door stopped for a minute. Peace. And then it started up again, louder, more insistent.

The day after the committee meeting, he had rented this tiny house on the hill overlooking the beach in north Del Mar, using one of the latest corporate accounts set up by Vince. He paid in advance for two months, $16,000. It had only two bedrooms, and it hadn't been redecorated since 1978, but there was a sliver of a deck surrounded by tall eucalyptus trees. And in minutes he could be in the waves.

He put on a fluffy new white bathrobe and plodded down the stairs. As soon as the deadbolt turned, Vince pushed through the door, knocking Jake back.

"I don't like to be summoned, Jake. I'm not some damn flunky."
He strode into the kitchen and started fussing with the coffeemaker.
"And then you won't even open the fucking door? What the hell,
Jake?"

Vince rushed around the kitchen, opening and closing cabinets
looking for coffee and filters. Jake pointed to the cabinet that held
the coffee. Vince ignored him. He continued to open and slam the
cabinets. Finally he spotted the coffee.

"So this is where you're going to hide out, Jake? Del Mar? Not
very original."

"I'm not hiding out." Jake stood in the doorway of the kitchen,
his bathrobe hanging loose. "Anybody wants to find me, here I am."

Vince poured coffee and water into the machine and punched
the button and glared at it. Satisfied the machine was engaged, he
walked into the tiny living room and started pacing back and forth.

"That was quite a show you put on the other day, Jake. Thanks for
the heads-up on that. I really appreciate it."

"There was nothing to tell you. I didn't really know what I was
going to say." He pointed at a chair. Vince ignored him. The coffee
machine spat and churned. Jake smelled the first whiff of boiling
water hitting the Guatemalan. Vince must have chugged a couple of
lattes on the drive down. He was amped.

"So what's the play here?" Vince said.

"There is no play."

"Another disappearance? Is that it? Take a break. Dramatic
return. Crowd cheers? That's what you're thinking? 'Cause, if you
had bothered to ask me, I'd say that's a pretty damn bad idea. You
can't keep pulling this disappearance shit."

"Not disappear. Quit. Retire. I don't need the money and I don't
need the...other stuff. Not anymore."

"Bullshit. This is not a job you can quit."

"The thought of going on TV makes me sick to my stomach."

Jake wasn't exaggerating. For days he had been swept with waves of nausea, which were now gone.

"Then take some fucking Maalox." Vince stopped pacing and pointed his finger at Jake. "You...you of all people...know that's crap. You'll be itchy for a camera in a week, a month tops."

"Maybe, but I doubt it." Jake really wanted to grab a cup of coffee, but he owed Vince his attention. This is why he'd called him down here, to have this conversation. And Vince didn't seem to need any more coffee. He was sweating from his brow, even though the room was chilly, cooled by the morning breeze off the ocean.

Vince continued to pace, moving from window to couch to chair and back again. "You think this will all stop because you say so? Now Titweiller wants to investigate the shoe business. You really stirred up a shit storm with that prick."

"Anybody else wants to talk to me, I'm right here."

"So *Sizzler* knocks on that door, you'll just invite 'em in for a cup of joe? That's crazy talk. You're the one who always said you've got to keep it out of their reach. Give 'em too much and they won't care anymore."

"That's the whole point. No more exclusives. Once they realize I'll talk to anybody, they'll move on."

"Ladee-fuckin-da, Jake. More bullshit. Where are you going to go? You're famous. Famous doesn't rub off, Jake. Isn't that a fuckin' Truism? Hell, I can piss on the counter at 7-Eleven and it wouldn't make the paper. But you can't go to a Taco Bell without getting on *Inside News*."

"That's something I'm going to have to deal with. That's my problem."

"And what about me, Jake? You think this is all about you, don't you? You always have. I'm part of this business, too, you know? Did you ever consider that maybe I'm not ready to retire?"

Vince's anger surprised Jake. He didn't expect the hostility. "You'll get set up. You know that."

"And so twenty years gets me a nice pat on the back and a gold watch, is that it?" Vince finally stopped pacing and plopped into a chair. "Is that really what we're talking about here?" He bounced back up. "Well, I gotta tell you, Jake, I'm tired of getting jacked around like this."

Vince was acting like he was on something more than coffee, Jake realized.

"After all these years, just kiss off ol' Vince and float off into the sunset. That's it?"

"It's my choice. You know I appreciate what you've—"

"Yeah, right, *appreciate* it. A few bonuses. A couple of nice checks. You don't know what I've gone through for you, Jake." Vince's white Ralph Lauren shirt was soaked in sweat. His voice rose an octave, growing into a screech. "You don't know half of the crap I've put up with because of you." Tears were forming in his eyes as he spoke. "You think people were banging down the door for the latest Truland exclusive? I've been making that happen." Vince pounded his chest. "Me. Not you, me."

"Well, I had a little to do with it." Jake smiled, hoping to lighten the mood.

"Don't even try that crap with me, Jake." Vince fell back into the chair. "This is the last straw." He bounced up again. Vince couldn't stay still. The coffee machine buzzed; Jake ignored it.

"Let me explain the facts of life to you, Jake. You were dyin'. Nobody fuckin' cared. Maybe you didn't realize it, but I did."

"Vince, calm down. Have some coffee. Take a seat. Let's talk."

"You think my phone was ringing for you? Hell, no. I was pulling stories out of my ass for you."

Vince paced frantically, waving his arms wildly, almost hysterical. There was no point in trying to answer.

"Few more weeks, and I think you would have been in real trouble. Big trouble. It would have been *Battle of the Network Stars* for you, buddy."

"Come on, Vince, let's—"

"You go on TV and make your grand announcements without even thinking about me. Not even considering what I've done for you."

"I should have listened to Becky after the fire. I should have quit right then. She told me the fire was a sign."

"Hell, Jake, that fire was a blessing. It was the best thing that ever happened to you. Are you fuckin' serious? The fire was a gold mine. Sure, things got out of control. But I mean, if you were looking at it as business, you couldn't have asked for a better story."

Now Jake was growing angry. "What's that supposed to mean?" Jake said. "The fire started—"

"I'm just saying you were hurting and that fire came at a good time."

That's asinine, Jake thought. But there was something else. Something Vince said triggered a memory, but he couldn't place it. A piece didn't fit. And then Truland remembered.

"You sent Elgin to pick me up," Jake said.

"What, you—"

"That day. The day of the fire."

"Hell yes, just part of the service. You're fuckin' welcome."

"You sent me to Tijuana."

"What? Stop trying to change the subject—"

"You said you were buddies with the station manager. But Elgin said the GM barely knew you."

Vince stopped pacing. He looked at the curtains. "That's right, Jake. I got you that gig. You're going to bust my balls about a radio spot?"

Jake's mind raced through the data. "Christ, you set it all up. You weren't doing a favor for Elgin. You wanted me out of the house."

"I don't know what you're talking about, Jake. We're here to talk about how you're screwing up."

It all became very clear to Jake. "You started the fire."

Vince went back to pacing. "Oh, come on, Jake. Get over it. You don't know what you're talking about."

Jake sagged against the wall. He'd been wrong about everything. "Don't lie to me anymore," he said.

"Bullshit. This is what you think? Why would I do that?"

Jake could tell he was lying. And Vince knew it. He stopped pacing.

"OK, you happy?" Vince looked back at Jake, showing only anger. "So what if I set the fire?" He started pacing again. "Maybe that was the best damn career move for you. It was genius. You were dying. *Dying.* That fire put you back in the A-block. It was the type of move you would have appreciated back in the day."

Jake couldn't believe what he was hearing. He clicked through the elements of the new reality. He saw the anger in Vince's face. And then he thought about the worst and began to panic. "What about Becky, Vince? Was that you? Was that you, too?"

Jake surged forward, slowed by the fluffy robe. All he wanted to do was kill this man in front of him. He crashed into Vince's chest. They slid across the coffee table and hurtled into the overstuffed chair. Jake rolled off, landing on his back. His elbow slapped against the stone floor. He struggled to get up, all the frustration and rage of the last few weeks coming to the surface.

Vince stood over him. He was holding a gun.

"Is that what you think, Jake?" There were tears in his eyes. His hand with the gun shook violently. "After all these years, you think I'm that kind of guy? You don't know crap about me, Jake. You don't even know where I live, you asshole."

Jake's head swirled. How could he have been so wrong about so much? "It was you all along. You did this. You ran her down. Why? What kind of—"

"No, Jake, absolutely not—"

"You left her in the fuckin' gutter to die, you fuck."

"Jake, I'm telling you. I had nothing to do with Becky." Now he was pleading with Jake, begging, his voice a mournful whine. "I loved her as much as you did. Do you hear that, Jake? I loved her. What the fuck would you know about that?"

"What about Landau? You just let the cops think he did it all this time? Or did you set that up, too?"

Vince pulled back. "I don't know what the hell that guy was into. Things just got out of control. That's all. He brought all that shit on himself."

Jake rose to his feet, keeping an eye on the gun. "So it's everybody else's fault. You just burned down my house and then what happened just happened? That's it?"

"I was doing my job."

Jake moved a step forward. "OK, Vince, then what's with the gun? Huh? You just decided to bring a gun to our meeting?"

"Back the fuck off." Vince pointed the gun at Jake's chest. "I'm not going to go to jail for you. You can be damn sure about that. I have no doubt you'd turn me in, you cold fuck. After all I've done for you. You'd probably call the cops. Send me to jail. Me. Well, screw you, Jake."

Jake took a step forward, almost tripping over the end table. He pointed at the gun. "What were you planning, Vince? You have a plan you want to share with me?"

Vince stepped back, waving the gun at him. It was a snub-nosed revolver, the type carried by detectives on old TV shows.

"You were talking about quitting. I came down here to talk some sense into you."

"With a gun? What the fuck, Vince. What happened to you?"

"What's happening to *meee*?" Vince's voice was a shrill whine. Whatever was in him had been building for a long time. "Maybe it's my turn for a little recognition here. Now it's my turn."

"Put down the gun and let's talk about this."

"I said it's my turn. *My turn!* Don't you think I wanted my name in the paper? Think maybe I wanted to be on TV every once in a while? When do I get credit? When does somebody say, 'Hey, isn't that Vince Trello?' Don't you think I wanted some of that? Maybe I wanted to wave at the crowd?"

The gun flopped back and forth.

"You won't even stay at my house. What am I, diseased? Not good enough for the great Truland?"

"Vince, stop it." Jake couldn't believe what he was hearing; he couldn't connect the data. He knew there was a vein of truth in Vince's rant. How had he let this happen?

"You can't just walk away. Doesn't work that way. It was your choice, buddy. You wanted it. And I made it happen. Me."

"You're right." Jake meant it. He'd known for months. The house...Landau...Becky...It was all his fault. But it didn't change anything. He wanted Vince to calm down and stop waving the gun.

"So maybe it's time for a little change in the management structure," Vince said. "How about that?" Vince was glaring at him, his eyes wild. "No more, Jake says this and Jake says that."

Jake eyed the distance to the front door. He could probably make it in a few strides, even in the bathrobe. But he wasn't ready to test Vince's resolve. "What are you thinking, Vince?"

"There's only one way to quit. You know that. You pull a Morrison. That's how you get out. Anything else is just a break in the action."

"That's crazy, Vince. Even Morrison didn't pull a Morrison."

"You'll be bigger than ever. Hell, you'll be back on the cover of *Rolling Stone*. I can do that for you, buddy. Me, little ol' me. I can make that happen." Vince was rambling, pacing feverishly. "And I'm sure as hell not going to jail. That's not going to happen."

Jake guessed Vince already knew what he was going to do. He

was simply getting up the nerve to act. Jake looked for an opportunity. Vince waved the gun and continued to circle away.

"Hell, you're just talent, big boy, and talent can always be replaced. Maybe that's a fucking Truism, right? By the way, have I ever told you how much I hate those fuckin' Truisms?"

Jake slowly moved around the coffee table, trying to close the space between them.

"Play this one right, Jake, you'll be bigger than Elvis. Think of that. I can make it happen. Hell, play it right you'll get lead obit, *New York Times*, man. That's pretty damn classy."

"Vince, you can't—"

"I learned at the feet of the fuckin' master. Now I become the master. Maybe I get the beach house..."

Vince turned toward the window. Jake charged.

Jake was quick, but not quick enough. Vince twitched to his left. Jake caught him on the shoulder of the arm holding the gun.

There was an explosion in Jake's face. Gunpowder singed his nose. It felt like his eyebrows were on fire. And then he felt a stabbing pain in his shoulder.

Jake fell to the floor, the room blurring. Pain flashed through his body. And then there was a dullness, a fog. He saw nothing but gray and black. The pain turned into a throbbing beat. He felt like he was floating in a pool. He tried to move, but his arms didn't work. For a moment, he couldn't remember where he was. He slid back into the dream—Mick at the towel bar, Clinton pouring drinks...Becky playing Frisbee on the beach.

The dream ended. Vince stood over him, a crazy glint in his eye. "I guess it's time to call the *Times*, Jake."

61

The beach was covered in a deep mist, one of those spooky, frosty mornings. Dozens of sandpipers in tight formation scurried across the flat wet sand. Seagulls slid over the top of the choppy gray water. The beach was empty; it was too early for the joggers and treasure hunters with their metal detectors.

Sy Walcott yanked on the leash of the mutt Theresa insisted on calling "Pooksie," dragging the dog across the sand. The stumpy-legged Corgi's real name was Edward, which was damn prissy but still better than "Pooksie," by Sy's standards. Sy gave Edward another sharp tug. He didn't like the dog much. The mutt chewed on his handmade Italian loafers and periodically took a dump in his sock drawer. But walking the dog was the one chore he allowed Theresa to assign him. He viewed the walks as an opportunity to exercise his civil disobedience against the local dog poop patrol.

Sy pulled the zipper up on his calfskin bombardier jacket, the pure chinchilla collar blocking out the damp air. Nervously he looked up and down the beach. Civil disobedience was great, but this morning he didn't feel like running into any of his neighbors, who would certainly want to discuss the proper boundaries of the designated dog-shitting areas.

Sy and Edward fell into a rhythm—walk five yards, yank, walk five yards, yank. Occasionally Edward went airborne if Sy yanked a bit too hard. They were almost to Dog Beach, the designated poop ground, when Sy spotted someone in the distance. Damn.

"Heel, dumbass."

Who the hell would be out on the beach at this time of morning? From this distance he couldn't tell if it was a man or woman. Sy would never admit it to Theresa, but he really couldn't see that well anymore, especially over long distances. The figure was only a blur.

He gave Edward another yank.

The figure was definitely a man, Sy decided as they moved closer. Might be a lifeguard; maybe not. He didn't look like a surfer; Sy didn't see a board. The man was on his knees, hunched over on the sand, like he was working on something, maybe digging a hole.

Suddenly the man stood up and ran toward the water.

At that moment Edward stopped short, dug his paws into the sand, and strained toward an appetizing cluster of kelp, almost pulling Sy over. "Get moving, you little piece of shit," Sy said. But Edward wouldn't budge. His little legs wedged like concrete pillars in the sand. Sy used both hands and began dragging the dog, who fought against his efforts with every fiber of his stout frame, his paws leaving deep furrows in the wet sand.

When Sy turned back the man was gone. The beach was empty again. He moved forward cautiously. Edward dutifully trotted by his side, no longer interested in seaweed.

When they reached the spot where he'd seen the man, Sy saw a small mound in the sand. Sy looked out to the water, but he didn't see anybody in the choppy surf. He looked down the beach. He was alone.

What the hell, he thought. He gave Edward a tug and trudged through the deep sand. Bending over, cursing his fading eyesight, he inspected the mound. It was a tidy pile of clothes. A yellow silk Tommy Bahama shirt was folded neatly on top of jeans and sandals. On the top of the pile was a white business-size envelope.

Sy looked up and down the beach. Edward sniffed at the pile of clothes. They were definitely alone. He picked up the envelope and read the address. It said simply, "To My Fans."

62

Roger was driving north on the Coast Highway when his mobile rang.

"I'm sorry to bother you on a Wednesday, boss," Jane said, sounding more nervous than usual. She knew better than to call on a Wednesday, unless there was a big problem.

"It's the sheriff's PR people, and normally I wouldn't think twice about it, you know, I can definitely deal with flacks and—"

Roger cut her off. "Jane, no problem, what's up?"

"OK, OK, sorry, you know how I get. I just want to make sure I'm handling it, you know, in the right way for a newspaper—"

"Jane."

"OK, right, well, the thing is the sheriff's people said he is going to have a press conference, I mean, a presser. And they said it's about Jake Truland."

"Jane, it's OK, the fire is your story. I appreciate the call, but you can handle it."

"But *that's* the thing. They said it wasn't about the fire. They said it had to do with Truland, and that's it. And, you know, they made it sound kind of ominous. They said it was going to be big news. Stan said you were going to want to know about it. And, you know, he didn't seem even a bit worried that I might be insulted by that, like maybe it was my story and I was a real reporter and I could make up my own—"

"Jane."

"Right. So Stan also said the sheriff was going to be making a statement, personally, like I would be all impressed by that. But, see, it sounded important. And I know you don't like to talk about it, but, well, we all know you actually know Truland and, well...I thought you'd want to know."

"OK, when is it?"

"10:00."

Roger looked at his watch. 9:45. Stan wasn't doing him any favors. He could just make it to the sheriff's command center in time, if he ran a few red lights. Jake had called two days ago and said he was going to be in town, but he hadn't heard from him since.

"And, boss, this is probably going to sound kind of silly. Maybe not real evidence or anything. But I tuned into the scanner frequencies for the TV stations and they're all going crazy about it. I just saw two satellite trucks drive through town. Big ones."

Roger made it to the command center in twelve minutes and grabbed a seat in the back. Jane was right. The room was packed. Rows of cameras made it almost impossible to see the podium. Even the cable network reporters were there, hovering in the back, satellite phones glued to their ears. An FNN anchor was reporting live from a rickety two-by-two plywood platform in the back of the room.

The sheriff strode onto the stage in full dress uniform, his gold epaulets bouncing on his shoulders. He scanned the room, giving the photographers a chance to focus. The pool photographer gave him a thumbs up.

"Ladies and gentleman, I have a brief announcement, and then I will entertain a few questions."

The sheriff was using a teleprompter, working from a script. Roger took out his pad.

"Yesterday morning at approximately oh-six-hundred hours, the sheriff's department received information about the possible disappearance of a man from the beach in Del Mar, north of the 22nd Street lifeguard station. I was contacted soon after the discovery and left a meeting of top-level law enforcement officials convened in La Costa to personally lead the investigation. Subsequent investigation by a team of my detectives revealed that the individual in question was Samuel Tiberius Livingston, aka Jake Truland."

Roger's head shot up when the sheriff read Truland's real name.

"Detectives from major crimes and homicide soon confirmed that Mr. Truland was, in fact, missing. At that point we opened a criminal investigation. And, ladies and gentleman, I must stress that these detectives are among the finest in the country." The sheriff turned and pointed to five men in brown uniforms standing stiffly at attention to the side of the stage. The sheriff paused, perhaps waiting for applause.

"After reviewing the evidence and consulting firsthand with the detectives, I've agreed to reclassify the case, with the unanimous assent of all the detectives."

The sheriff paused again.

"We believe that on October 16th, Mr. Jake Truland, aka Samuel Tiberius Livingston, took his own life."

There was an audible gasp in the room. Several producers bolted toward the exit, their cell phones already to their ears. The FNN reporter on the platform said, "Holy shit" loud enough for everyone in the room to hear. Roger felt his notebook slide out of his hand.

The sheriff held up his hand to ask for quiet.

"We believe the cause of death is self-inflicted drowning.

Evidence gathered at the scene indicates that Mr. Truland, a strong swimmer, swam west, perpendicular to the beach, knowing he would not return." The sheriff glared into the lens of the pool camera. "All evidence suggests this was no round-trip for Jake Truland."

Several reporters in the audience shouted for the sheriff's attention. Hands shot up around the room.

The sheriff again held up his hand and asked for quiet.

"I must stress that the investigation is open and ongoing. We have not recovered a body. Detectives will continue to investigate leads as they emerge. But this case will no longer be treated as homicide, short of compelling evidence to the contrary. I will now entertain a few questions."

Reporters launched a barrage of questions. The sheriff ignored their shouts and frantically waving hands and pointed to a balding man in the front row, the reporter for the San Diego daily newspaper, a well-known sheriff toady.

"Sheriff, why are you so sure it's suicide?"

"Well, I am not at liberty to discuss specific evidence, Dave, you know that. But I will say we have discovered a note that we believe was written by Mr. Truland. There was also a witness on the beach who saw a man fitting Jake Truland's description heading toward the water."

Another barrage of shouted questions.

"Who is the witness?"

"What did the note say?"

"Was Jackie Conrad in the area?"

The sheriff raised his hands and asked for quiet again. He pointed to a blonde woman in the second row.

"Why do you think Truland committed suicide?" she asked.

The sheriff was ready for this one. "It is known from our investigation that Mr. Truland was despondent over the recent death of one Rebecca Hooks. This was referenced in the note."

Roger couldn't believe what he was hearing. This was *Twilight Zone* material. All around him, reporters were busily scribbling into notebooks. Producers whispered into cell phones. They were all so excited. One producer was bouncing up and down on her toes, unable to contain her exhilaration. But this was crazy. Who could believe this? Jake commit suicide? That's insane, nonsensical.

"Sheriff! Sheriff!" It was the reporter from FNN, standing tall on his platform. "Just to clarify, you say you have not found a body? How can you be sure this is not just a hoax? Another Truland stunt?"

"Fred, as I have already stated, we have compelling evidence, irrefutable evidence..."

Roger couldn't take this anymore. He interrupted the sheriff, shouting as loud as he could. "Sheriff! This is crazy. Jake Truland wouldn't kill himself."

"Mr. Talbot, as I have explained, we believe he was despondent—"

"Has it occurred to you that this so-called disappearance may be associated with the Vegas group?"

The sheriff nervously glanced at his PR team. "As Mr. Truland clarified in his recent testimony before Congress, there is no verifiable link between any elements of the fashion accessory industry and this case. None whatsoever."

Roger felt faint. He wanted to shout that this was a nuthouse. That there was no way any of this was true. He tried to ask another question, but the sheriff pointed to a young girl on the other side of the room, an out-of-town TV reporter Roger didn't recognize.

"Can you spell your name for the camera, please?"

Roger tried shouting. "Have you even interviewed Ted Urbina about this case? Sheriff! Sheriff!"

The sheriff pointed to another TV reporter in the front row.

"Sheriff, what can you tell us about this witness?"

"Only that he is a respected member of the beach community

and he is absolutely confident that he saw a man fitting Truland's description entering the water at the time in question."

The sheriff turned to the cameras and paused for effect. "He was seen going into the cold water, and he never came out."

Another reporter attracted the sheriff's attention.

"Any truth to the rumor that you're running for mayor?" the reporter asked.

The sheriff laughed heartily, perhaps a bit too heartily. "Next question."

Roger tried shouting louder. "Sheriff, do you really expect people to believe this load of—"

But no one heard him amid the commotion of reporters and producers barking questions. Trying to get a better vantage point, a TV photographer from an LA station elbowed past a photographer from Orange County. The OC photographer shoved back, knocking over his tripod. The LA photog threw a punch. In the cramped space, the frightened herd of reporters tried to shift away from the fracas. One reporter screamed.

"No further questions," the sheriff said, striding offstage with a wave to the cameras.

63

"He swam to his death? You're shittin' me!"

Jessie always admired Sharon Jones-Jones's gift for getting to the point. To be honest, Jessie didn't know what to think. She was still struggling to wrap her mind around the idea that the man who had dominated her existence for the last three months was dead. Three bodies in three months. It felt like somebody had punched her in the stomach.

"That's what the cops are saying," Jessie said. "Suspected death by self-inflicted drowning."

"Doesn't it all sound a tad...*theatrical*?" Sharon said. She sat behind her chrome desk, an array of printouts of wire reports in front of her.

"Cops say they have evidence. Clothes on the beach. Footprints in the sand. They have a witness; a civilian saw him walk into the water."

"But, come on—"

"I know. I know. But they say they found a note. They think a body will probably wash up in a couple of days, depending on the currents."

"It's gotta be a sham. Another Truland prank."

Jessie was still working through all the data. This didn't feel like a stunt. Her every instinct said this was the real deal, even if it didn't make any sense.

"I don't know," Jessie said. "The cops were dead serious about it."

"I never thought he'd have the cojones for suicide." Sharon paused, apparently contemplating Jake's cojones. "I always thought of him as more of a car accident kind of guy, a sports car sailing off a cliff, that sort of thing," she said. "Maybe Morrison in a bathtub, something like that. But suicide? Really? I never saw him as that...*deep*."

Jessie remembered that night in Austin after Becky's funeral, the two men in anguish sitting on the porch. But she couldn't mention that. Instead she said, "We really don't know. But they're not treating it like a murder or a missing person."

"What about the Klutch angle?" Sharon said. "Maybe they rubbed him out. Seems fairly likely. Who the hell knows what he was into?"

Jessie was surprised her boss actually used the phrase "rubbed him out." For a moment she yearned for her old days in news.

"Maybe," Jessie said, trying to be patient with Sharon. "But the cops don't think so. They don't have any evidence of a hit. And they say the pros never, ever act this way. They run from publicity. The last thing they would do is stage this kind of scene."

"Still...it seems like those characters—"

"Then you get back to the note. The cops wouldn't have said anything about it if they thought it was a fake."

"Can we get a copy?"

Jessie resisted the urge to roll her eyes. "We're working on it."

"But who do we trust on this? This is Truland, for God's sake."

"Look, these cops aren't bullshitters. I talked to the FBI, not those county yahoos."

"The feds? Why the FBI?"

"They came up with a statute that if he swam out far enough, he was in international waters. So the FBI is handling all media. The sheriff is plenty pissed off about that."

"How do you want to play it?" Sharon asked.

This was the question Jessie had been wrestling with for an hour. She knew it was coming. And right now she still didn't have an answer.

"Do you want to go with the grand mystery?" Sharon asked. "Is he alive or is he dead? Maybe reports of a strange liaison?"

"No...I...I..." She tried to stall. "The suicide is a difficult twist."

"The thing I don't get is, *why* would he do it?" Sharon said. "His Qs weren't that bad."

Jessie felt her blood draining to her feet. Everything was ratings to Sharon. She thought again of that night in Austin. "It was Becky Hooks," Jessie said. "It was eating him up."

"Seriously, you're not buying that crap, are you?"

"Yeah, I am. I mean—"

"You think that heartless bastard did—"

"Yes, maybe..." Jessie needed to make a decision. This had to stop. This cold woman in front of her wanted a plan of action. That was Jessie's job. She didn't work all these years to get out of the Bunny Patch only to freeze up on a big story. She needed to trust her instincts.

"I think we should go with a tribute," Jessie said.

"What?"

"I'm thinking tribute," Jessie said again. "Long shots of the beach. Weeping kids with flowers. Fans holding candles. Influence on society. The full collectible-special-edition treatment."

"Sounds kind of dorky." The older producer's smirk was dull and hard.

"We'll lead a day of mourning. America bows its head."

"That's...risky."

"We'll be out in front on it. Everybody going with the mystery will look silly. They'll have to follow us. We'll own the tribute."

Sharon was contemplating the idea. "The tribute treatment? For Truland? Really?"

Jessie went in for the kill. "We'll assemble testimonials. Maybe track down Jagger. Clinton. Get a few tears from old girlfriends. Hey, maybe you'd like to say a few words."

"Well, normally, that would be ridiculous."

Bingo. Truland christened as an immortal meant Sharon had banged a big one. She was likin' that idea. Jessie could tell she was already envisioning herself walking behind the casket in a slinky black outfit, a slight twinkle shining through the tears as the Marine band played.

By the time Jessie left Sharon's office they had mapped out a fifteen-minute special report. Back on the bridge, Jessie gave Freddie and Brenda quick, precise instructions. Brenda scurried off to look for tape. Freddie rolled to a computer terminal and began banging out copy. They needed to get something to edit within two hours, if they wanted to make the 2:00 p.m. feed. Jessie sat in front of her terminal and tried to organize her thoughts. She'd have to send a note to marketing. They'd want to get a promo up in the next hour.

"What kind of music do you want?" Freddie yelled.

Good question. She thought for a second.

"Techno depressing?" Freddie offered.

"No, something theatrical. Crying from the mountaintops. Soaring above the clouds."

"Got it." Freddie went back to his keyboard.

She'd have to clear extra satellite time. And get a note to the New York and Washington, DC, office, letting them know the plan—maybe get some preliminary copy to Tammy, so she could coordinate with wardrobe. Social media would need to be briefed. And she'd better write an e-mail to network, letting them know the plan. Lists raced through her mind. She'd have to bring in somebody from

Farmore Publications; they were going to want to get something on the newsstand by Friday.

A graphics assistant jogged up. "Got a title for me?" she said.

Jessie was thinking maybe something simple and elegant, something that captured the emotion of the day.

"Let's call it 'The Last Truism,'" she said.

64

Eric Branson drove to Del Mar's main drag and parked in a fire lane, ignoring department regulations for parking in fire zones during non–work-related activities. He wanted answers. For weeks he'd felt adrift. The Truland case projected him into a strange, mystifying world, an amoral place where two minutes on TV seemed more important than facts. Now, it turned out, that strange world was really his world—no separation, just a continuation, each section feeding on the other.

The sheriff's press conference was the final straw. There was no reason to make the announcement. Who'd ever heard of holding a press conference to announce a suspected self-inflicted drowning? They didn't even have a body. It was a sham. And yet everyone seemed to be going along. The newspapers were running long obituaries. The TV shows were interviewing Truland's ex-girlfriends. And maybe that was to be expected. But it shouldn't affect an investigation. There was no reason to close the case. The chief had told him to leave it alone, but he couldn't do that. It was still his case, dammit.

Walking in to Bully's, he stood in the doorway blinking in the dark for several seconds, trying to adjust to the pitch-black room. The reporter Roger Talbot was sitting at the bar, engaged in a lively conversation with a man with a long gray ponytail, dressed in an old Army surplus camo jacket.

The reporter spotted Eric and quickly turned back to his beer. Eric strode over and sat on the next stool. He ordered a beer.

"I need to talk to you."

Talbot looked at him warily. "You're not a cop, but I know you."

Eric introduced himself. He put his card on the table. "I want to talk about Truland."

"You're pretty far down the investigation totem pole, aren't you, Inspector?"

"I just went to see the sheriff."

That got Talbot's attention. "And why would you do that?"

"I thought he might give me some straight answers."

"I'm guessing you were sadly disappointed."

"He wouldn't—"

The man in the camo jacket leaned forward. "This preppy Nazi bothering you, Rog? 'Cause I'd be all too happy to kick his ass outta—"

"No, it's fine." Talbot turned his attention back to Eric. "So you went to see the sheriff? I went to see the sheriff, too. You probably had the same conversation I did."

"Sharks?"

"Yeah, sharks. Suddenly the sheriff is an expert on shark habits."

"And what do you think of the sheriff's theory?" Eric asked.

"I think it doesn't matter what I think. The sheriff's popularity has never been higher. Focus groups say he's part Giuliani, part Churchill. The PR staff is very proud."

"What does that have to do with anything?"

Talbot offered a smirk. "How long have you been with the department?"

Eric felt his anger bubbling again. He couldn't believe he was getting the same pat answers. "You were his friend. How could you put up with this?"

"You're getting a little beyond yourself now, aren't you, Inspector?"

Eric regretted the accusatory tone, but the journalist was so calm. "You don't believe any of this, do you?

"I don't know what to believe," Talbot said.

"Sharks?"

"Stranger things have happened."

"You knew him. There must be more. Tell me what I don't know. Tell me why I should believe any of this."

Talbot didn't answer right away. He looked at his beer. "I saw him before the hearing. He said some things. He felt guilty. Could he have done something? Maybe."

"But there should be an investigation. Doesn't it bother you that nobody is asking questions?"

"Lot's of people are asking questions. Asking questions doesn't change anything.'

"I don't believe that."

"It's not like you're the only one who thinks something's not right. The *Herald* ran a column about the shoddy investigation. The tabloids are all over conspiracy theories. Nobody cares. The story line is set. It's history now."

"Then you should do more stories."

Talbot was doing a lousy job of hiding his exasperation. "It won't make any difference. If he is dead, everything fits. People like it when things fit, and they get upset when they don't."

"But you're a journalist—don't you want the truth?"

Roger sighed. "OK, let me try something on you. Oliver Stone, you know, the director?"

Eric shook his head.

"*Platoon*? *Born on the Fourth of July*?"

"Oh, yeah..."

"Never mind. Anyway, Oliver Stone used to talk about the idea of alternative myths. You rearrange a few facts from history and you suddenly have new history, a new myth. Take a few facts about the Kennedy assassination out of context and the conspiracy theory makes sense. A new myth."

"That sounds like BS."

"Exactly, everybody thought Stone was a dick. They didn't want to hear it. No one wants the alternative myth. They love the myths they get."

"I still don't—"

"OK, one more film reference. You a fan of *The Man Who Shot Liberty Valance*?"

"I'm not sure ..."

"Geez, kid, get a TV. Anyway, there's a famous line: 'When the legend becomes fact, print the legend.'"

"I still don't see—"

"Jake loved that line. Quoted it all the time. You get it?"

Eric didn't get it, not really. He always believed direct action produced direct results. And there was a right and a wrong.

Talbot looked resigned, defeated. "Look, Eric. Jake was my friend. That's right. And he's gone. None of this crap"—he waved an arm a little drunkenly —"none of this crap means anything. If he's gone, then he's gone. And nothing we do will change that."

"How can you say that?"

"No matter what happened, I know a part of him wanted to be gone. That night, I could tell he wanted out, one way or another."

"But somebody could be getting away with murder. Or maybe he is out there. Don't you wonder if he is alive?"

"If he is out there, he doesn't want to be found. He made a choice. There's no going back on a Morrison."

Eric didn't know what that meant. "And you're OK with the fairy tales?"

"People like fairy tales."

"What about Truland? You think he'd be happy with this?"

Talbot snorted again. "I may not know much, but I can say this for sure—no doubt about it—if Jake is gone, I think he would have been damn happy with the way he went out."

"Come on."

Talbot smiled. "No doubt. Don't even question it. He would have loved it."

Eric wasn't sure about that. But he didn't have an answer, didn't have a better explanation. Instead, he drank beer. He, Roger, and the man in the camo jacket discussed the Chargers, surfing, and Del Mar politics. They argued over the merits of the high-post screen offense and the relative merits of twin-fin boards. And after a few minutes they all raised a toast to the late Jake Truland.

EPILOGUE
(Eighteen Months Later)

ANN ARBOR, Michigan (FNS)—A retired schoolteacher told authorities here that she saw presumed dead celebrity Jake Truland eating carne asada tacos last week in a local restaurant.

"I didn't want to bother him or nothing, 'cause he seemed to be enjoying his tacos," said Rhonda Hawthorne, who said she saw Truland drive away in a Ford pickup truck with a bumper sticker that read, "Vote Pink."

Hawthorne's tale is the latest in a series of unconfirmed sightings of Truland, who authorities say swam to his death off a California beach 18 months ago. From Portugal to Thailand, ordinary citizens say they have seen Truland, although none of the reports has been confirmed....

Crews scurried around the set of the *Cathy!* show, dodging the familiar white leather chair and fake palm trees. "More fill spot in the back!" a lighting technician yelled. Two grips struggled to pull thick cables across the stage. A young girl in jeans and a Raiders T-shirt waved a disc over her head, apparently signaling someone in the director's booth.

Eric Branson squirmed under the lights, tugging at the tight collar of his new Brooks Brothers dress shirt. The collar itched and his jacket was too tight. He had wanted to wear the Armani, which fit like a glove, but that was vetoed. Now he felt like he'd rip a seam if he raised his hand above his elbow.

The girl in the Raiders T-shirt ran over to him. "Let me get this on you," she said, pulling a small microphone out of her pocket. She tried to clip the microphone onto his silk tie, but she couldn't get the cables to hang straight.

"I know the drill," he said with a smile. He took the microphone, working the clip onto his lapel, looping the cables through the back post.

"Right, of course, sorry." The girl blushed and handed him the transmitter pack. He tucked it onto his belt.

Eric spotted Cathy Donoho offstage, her golden helmet of hair shimmering in the near darkness. Three attendants surrounded her, examining and preening. One tugged at the hem of her chartreuse pantsuit, which hugged in the right places, creating what Eric had read was the "perfect hourglass figure, the image of stern, professional womanhood who stands for herself and her unabashed ability to humble the strongest of men."

Cathy caught Eric's eye and offered a small wave. They'd met at an event a few weeks ago, Eric couldn't remember which one. He waved back.

"Ten minutes!" someone shouted.

Eric sat in one of three white chairs arranged on the stage, carefully positioned around the host's famed overstuffed white leather chair. He was starting to wonder about the identity of the other guests when Sy Walcott strode on to the stage. He wore some sort of white linen suit and a white collarless shirt, providing a stark contrast to his deep bronze tan.

"Branson, right?" Walcott stuck out his hand as the girl in the Raiders shirt tried to affix his microphone.

Eric shook his hand, wincing at Walcott's grip.

"Did you read my book?" Walcott barked.

"Sorry, it's on my list," Eric said. Walcott's *Finding Truland* was number six on the best-seller list. One reviewer called it, "As much a soliloquy on the state of California beach politics as a mystery, revealing the secrets of Jake Truland's strange death." Eric's interest level was zero.

"Well, then, keep your mouth shut," Walcott said, brushing aside the attendant trying to put on his microphone. "This show is about my book. The only reason I'm doing this shit is to sell the book."

Eric was about to reply when his mobile rang. He pulled the slim blue phone out of his pocket and checked the ID. It was Jessie.

"Don't forget to talk directly to Cathy," she said.

Eric thought it was cute that she never said hello. No, "How you doing?" Or, "It's me." She always launched into whatever she wanted to say.

"And don't use too many big gestures. It freaks her out and she won't ask you any more questions."

"Got it."

"And don't get all Boy Scout with her. Tell her how you really feel. No one cares about your moral dilemmas. Tell her the story, you know, the one about the kid on the beach."

"Yeah, sure, that one." He loved her attention to detail, the way she was always working through the angles.

"And make sure to smile at the audience. But don't smile too much at Cathy. That freaks her out, too. Oh, and don't forget to turn off your phone."

"Got it. Love you."

"Yeah, right," she said and the line went dead.

It was Jessie's idea to do *Cathy!* Over the months he'd turned down dozens of offers for Truland tributes, investigative panels, and various conventions. The fascination with Truland only seemed to grow after his disappearance. Sightings were frequent. A fisherman in Costa Rica. A waitress in a sardine restaurant in Portugal. Two months ago a British woman vacationing on the Indian Ocean island of Mauritius reported she spent three hours playing Ping-Pong with a man she believed to be Truland. After each story, Eric received calls to appear and comment, which he always refused. But Jessie said he'd be a moron to refuse *Cathy!* And he'd learned to trust her instincts.

After days of agonizing, Eric had called Jessie two weeks after Truland's disappearance. She seemed happy to hear from him. "I don't want to talk business," he said right off. "I just want to, you know, talk." And for ten minutes they talked about the weather, their high schools, and their work; he told her about a fire started by a cat; she told him about new video of a TV sitcom star beating a cat.

"Did you see our tribute on Truland last week?" she asked.

"No, I, uh, I don't really watch TV that much." He wasn't going to lie.

"You're so cute," she said, but not in a mocking way. "You should take a look. It wasn't bad. I kept out all the bullshit. I think maybe it actually captured something about him."

That night he found the segment on the Internet. She was right. He was no judge, but it seemed more sincere, less sensational than all those other Truland stories. Eric had been shocked when the local CBS affiliate showed an unedited, blurry night vision sex tape of Truland and a married actress.

Jessie laughed when he expressed his outrage. "They outbid us by $1.2 million," she said. "They way overspent."

For their first date, Eric drove to Los Angeles and met her at the gate of the Farmore lot at 7:00 p.m., after she got off work. He took her to a place called Barney's Beanery. He had read about it in a magazine, which described it as "a casual hangout for LA's hip set." She giggled when they pulled up.

"This is supposed to be a happening spot," he said.

She patiently explained that Barney's was a tourist spot and hadn't been regarded as "hip" for 20 years. He was embarrassed and apologized and offered to take her somewhere else, but she smiled and said not to worry about it. They spent the night eating chili and drinking beer, trying to explain their lives to each other above the roar of the Friday night tourist crowd.

From the start, there was something about her that made him feel alive and engaged. Jessie grew up only a few miles to the north, but it was like she was a rare and exotic creature from a far-off land. And she was wicked smart, in tune to everything happening around her. She knew everybody and something about everything.

At first he was intimidated, but she seemed so genuinely interested in his work, fascinated by his world. She asked him about his family and his future, stuff no girl had ever asked him before. Without prodding, he told her about his parents' divorce, his sense of abandonment.

Occasionally they talked about Truland. Surprised by her emotions, he was gratified to find her genuinely upset by the story. He didn't profess to understand her world, but he recognized the passion, the same passion he had noticed that first day, when she drove down to Del Mar to tip him about Buddy Landau.

One night, three months after their first date, he was surfing the 15th Street break in Del Mar. Jessie sat on the deck of the Fire Pit working on her laptop, even though it was her day off. The sun was almost past the horizon, creating a palette of orange and red across the sky—the type of sunset that inspires surfer poetry. Sitting on his board between sets, he looked back at the beach and watched Jessie sitting on the deck typing away. This is it, this is what it feels like to be in love, he thought.

Fifteen minutes later on the deck of the Fire Pit, still dripping wet and covered in the ocean's salty grime, he popped the question, getting down on one knee. "I don't have a ring and I don't make much

money, but I would like you to be my wife," he said. Jessie looked
shocked at first, and then she leaped into his arms, ignoring the salt-
water stink. Everyone on the deck applauded.

When Jessie first brought up the idea of a career in TV news, he
resisted. He'd never even taken a journalism class and didn't enjoy
public speaking. But he was tired of the politics at the fire department. The chief had told him his future was limited—that was the
exact word he used, "limited." Jessie insisted he was "a natural" for TV
news, and she was so sure about it.

"Look, all you need to do is read and look sincere," she said, "and
frankly, Eric, you're the only actual sincere person I know."

"But I don't know anything about news."

She laughed at that. Then he mentioned that Vince Trello once
told him the same thing—that he should be on TV. She immediately
picked up her mobile and called Trello, right then and there. The next
day Trello called back and volunteered to represent him as his agent.
Three weeks later he was anchoring the weekend news in Yuma.

In the beginning, he didn't like the job. He wrestled with the
scrolling words on the teleprompter and never knew quite how to
sit or what to do with his hands. But the network sent in an anchor
trainer from Omaha who taught him to tuck the tail of his jacket
under his butt and to hold the script like it was a hot memo from the
news desk. Soon, reading the prompter was a breeze and he learned
to stare into the camera, no matter what happened, just as he was
coached. In his rented apartment, he practiced shifting his gaze from
one camera to the next, teaching himself to slowly turn his shoulders
at just the right speed. The consultant gave him exercises to work on
his facial expressions in front of the mirror, shifting from "earnest" to
"concerned" and back to "earnest."

As he grew more comfortable, he started to like the job. The hours
weren't bad and the bulk of his day was spent at the computer, reading up on the big stories. All his coworkers were bright and upbeat,

unlike the snide firefighters, who were always ready with a cynical comment. And he was dealing with the important issues of the day, touching people directly in a way he had never imagined in his old job. Outside the station, people approached him and told him how much they liked the newscasts. They always smiled, happy to see him.

After Eric had spent six months in Yuma, Teddy Urbina took over as CEO of the FNN affiliates group, and an anchor spot opened up in Los Angeles. Eric started at a salary of $750,000 a year, plus the use of a leased Mercedes-Benz and a $50,000 wardrobe allowance. "It's the best I could do," a dejected Vince told him. "But don't worry, two good books and you'll trigger an escalator clause that gets you over 900 grand, no worries." And that's exactly what happened.

Eric liked his coanchor, Sandra Cisneros, a real pro, a former Miss South Dakota with a master's degree from Northwestern. She took her job seriously. They clicked on the air. She could make him laugh at just the right moments, and he was more than happy to let her take the lead on big stories. By their second ratings book, the numbers were up 6.2 percent and he'd been featured in *Los Angeles* magazine as one of the city's "most eligible bachelors." He was going to refuse the magazine, since he was engaged, but Jessie said, "Don't be a dope."

Cathy walked out from behind the curtain, her entourage trailing after her. The audience squealed. She stopped and waved both arms above her head like a gymnast who just nailed the big landing. The crowd squealed some more. Eric couldn't find a single man in the crowd. It was ten minutes before airtime. Cathy strode onstage and went directly to Branson, ignoring Walcott. The middle chair remained empty.

"Mr. Branson, good to see you again. You've been hard to nail down, you little rascal."

Eric shook her hand and tried to keep his smiling to a minimum, per Jessie's instruction.

"That was quite a coup for K-News to snatch you up. You have a real flair, a certain charisma." Cathy's two assistants vigorously nodded their agreement.

Eric felt himself blushing, his reaction whenever someone complimented him.

"Three minutes!"

"Gotta go, Eric." Cathy used both hands to grasp his right hand. "Don't think of this as a TV show. Think of it as a spiritual event." And then she strode offstage, raising both arms overhead again as she disappeared into the wing, eliciting squeals.

"Hey, that's right, you're one of them now," Walcott said.

"I guess you could say that."

"Why the hell would you want to do something like that?"

Eric smiled and shrugged, the way the consultants told him to shrug whenever fans tried to engage him in embarrassing conversation.

Sitting on the stage of *Cathy!*, he didn't feel any nervousness, not anymore. He was comfortable in the light, enjoyed the anticipation of the adrenaline burst of the camera's red light. It was the same as the moments before the big game, the anticipation and readiness.

As he reviewed Jessie's last-minute instructions in his head, a bouncing butterball of a woman bounded onto the stage.

"*Buenos días*," Cassandra Moorehead said. "I am *mucho* sorry *para* my tardiness. You would not believe how difficult it is to get a jet fueled in Barbados on short notice." The girl in the Raiders shirt trotted over to put a microphone on the former CEO and director of innovation services for SELT.

"You're late," Walcott said.

She ignored him and fixed on Eric. "Why *hellooo* there, sweetie," she said. "I do believe we have met before."

Eric extended his hand and reintroduced himself. "No need, sweetie, I most definitely recall our tête-à-tête. Don't you like the sound of that? Tête-à-tête? The French play a very important role in culture, you know." Cassandra plopped into her seat. The PA scrambled to attach the transmitter.

Eric was surprised to see her. "I thought SELT was no longer in operation?" he said.

"Old news, *mi amigo*. Old news." She fished into a huge black bag with oversized Gucci tags and produced a business card. "Allow me to introduce the CEO and chief strategist for the Organization for Keeping Alive Truland's Legacy and Legend."

"KATLL?"

Cassandra blanched. "We don't use that name, Mr. Branson. We prefer O-KAT. Don't you like the ring of that? We are a serious organization dedicated to preserving literary work and the video records of our times."

"The video records of our times?"

"Yes, yes, I'm sure you saw our announcement in *Variety* last week. We just raised $4.3 million to buy the complete works of Jerry Springer. It was quite a coup. We're building a museum in Baton Rouge."

That got Walcott's attention. "$4.3 mill? How the hell did you do that?"

Cassandra looked at Walcott with a measure of disdain. "We have 1.2 million active members and annual EBITIDA revenues of $7.8 million per annum. No problemo." She turned back to Eric. "And how are you? I do so enjoy your news program. Why have you not called me for an interview, young man?"

A voice blasted from the overhead speakers. "One minute!"

"Oh dear," Cassandra said, patting at her face with a small makeup pad.

"Let's just stick to the book, OK guys?" Walcott said, swiping imaginary lint off of his white jacket.

The show opened with Cathy's familiar jaunty music, the most downloaded song in iTunes history. The crowd stood and squealed. A show staffer beat a snare drum on the side of the stage. Applause signs blinked at a seizure-inducing rate. By the time Cathy walked onstage, arms raised overhead in triumph, the audience was in some sort of tribal trance. As Cathy went through her usual intro, they squealed in rhythm, captivated by her voice.

And then Cathy lowered her head and there was silence, total silence. The lights dimmed. Cathy remained hunched over.

"He touched all our lives." Her voice was a whisper. "He reached out to us and we reached out to him, creating a bond of souls." The audience bowed their heads as one. "Today we salute the man, the myth...the legend that touched all our hearts."

A two-story-tall picture of Truland walking the red carpet appeared on a screen behind her. The studio went dark, and a montage of scenes from Truland's life splashed across the screens arrayed around the stage. Members of the audience began weeping.

When the lights shot back on, Cathy appeared in the overstuffed white chair, as if by magic. Eric was still blinking, trying to adjust to the bright lights. Cathy leaned toward him. The crowd hushed.

"Eric Branson. Investigator. Now TV journalist. Tell us how Jake Truland touched you."

Eric was thrown off. This was not the question he was told Cathy would ask. But he remembered his TV news training and repeated the question while he organized his thoughts.

"How did he touch me? I'd say he was the most unusual man I'd ever met. I've never seen anyone so committed to his craft."

"Unusual." Cathy seemed to savor the word and roll it over in her hands. "So true. So true. It must be hard for you to talk about this for the first time...here...exclusively...now."

Eric didn't hear a question, but he knew it was his turn to talk. "I understand there is a lot of interest. But I never thought it was my place to talk about it," he said.

Cathy leaned even closer, her hot breath on his face smelling vaguely of some Indonesian spice. "Now tell me, do you think he is out there somewhere, mocking us, creating a whole new world of Truisms?"

Eric knew this question was coming, Jessie had warned him. "I believe there should be a complete and thorough investigation, and that has never been done," Eric said. "But to answer your question, I really don't know."

Cathy nodded vigorously. The studio was dead silent.

"That's hogwash," Walcott said. "The guy is deader than a doornail."

Cathy remained focused on Eric, her eyes searching for his soul.

"And what should we make of these tortured, proud people who say they see Truland?"

"I think people see what they want to see."

The crowd sighed as one.

Eric smiled, but not too much, not wanting to spook Cathy. Sometimes it's best to keep the answers short, the consultants told him. So he didn't elaborate. He didn't mention his doubts. He didn't speculate about the stories, the tall tales and myths that surrounded Truland. And he didn't tell her about that one time, late one afternoon, when he was surfing in a secluded spot under the cliffs in Orange County and he spotted a lone figure bodysurfing in the distance, one man by himself riding the last waves of the day. That was one story Eric would keep to himself.

"I thought we were going to talk about my book?" Sy Walcott said.

Roger Talbot put a dollar in loose change into the rack and pulled out the latest edition of the *Gazette*. He still enjoyed the feeling of pulling a newspaper from the rusty, broken contraption, the satisfaction of holding the paper in his hand, an experience no Web site could ever re-create. The paper looked good. In a breach of *Gazette* policy, he'd put his column on page one. His picture was new, a nice shot—chin in hand, looking visionary. In a *Gazette* exclusive, Roger broke the news of possible illegalities in the approval process for the new sewage plant, the journalistic equivalent of lighting a bag of shit in front of the city council.

When he opened the door to the office, the answering machine light was blinking furiously, warming his heart. As soon as he sat down, the phone rang again. Caller ID said it was Dan Godfrey, the assistant planner.

"You might want to avoid City Hall for a couple of hours," Dan said.

"I'm always open to discourse—"

"Yeah, well, there is a lot of discoursing going on around here this morning."

Roger laughed, enjoying the spoils. "I'm happy to hear they're reading the paper." Sandy came in through the front door carrying a bundle of letters and a small box. "Got your mail again," she whispered and tippy-toed out the door.

"That's not all," Dan said. "It sounds like they're going to cancel the whole project, thanks to one pain-in-the-ass local drunk."

"You're kidding."

"Excuse me, the actual term was 'cock-sucking pain in the ass local drunk,' if we want to be precise."

"I can't believe they're that spooked. You sure they have the votes?"

"I'd say unanimous. Oh, and they also want to call for a federal investigation of your taxes. They all agreed on that, too."

Godfrey hung up. For the next twenty minutes Roger enjoyed the moment and ignored the phone's blinking light. He went through his e-mail, firing back at a few of his more vitriolic opponents, accepting the congratulations of a few fans. He thumbed through the snail mail—nothing but the usual business.

The box Sandy delivered rested on the side of his desk. It was four-by-four, wrapped in a thick brown paper and clear tape. The address was neatly printed, his name in block letters with "Esq." at the end—Roger Talbot, Esq. He turned it over and examined each side. There was no return address. The faded postmark, barely legible, said Figueira da Foz; the stamps honored a queen Roger didn't recognize.

He turned to the computer and looked up Figueira da Foz. It was a small resort city on the north coast of Portugal, best known for its sardine festivals. The city was also the site of a famous annual celebration honoring St. John, where believers hit each other on the head with plastic hammers, signifying the holy christening, Roger learned.

Roger gave the box a shake. He studied the postmark for a bit longer. He admired the neat lettering; the use of "Esq." He set it on the desk and opened some bills. And then he picked up the box again and re-examined the markings. But there was nothing else, no other clues, just the ornate stamps and the postmark from Figueira da Foz.

For an hour the box sat on his desk. Roger tried to ignore it. He worked on a follow-up column, answered more e-mails. He looked at the clock and was surprised to find it was past noon. The message light continued to blink.

He gathered up his wallet, keys, and the box and headed to his car. He tossed the box on the passenger seat and drove up the coast. After an hour he pulled off the road at a tiny Mexican restaurant known for its ceviche. He brought the box into the restaurant, setting it on the wood patio table while he picked through the jalapeños in his seafood.

Heading down the coast, the box was back on the passenger seat, riding shotgun.

In Del Mar, he pulled down the beach road. He parked and trudged through the thick sand, carrying the box. On the edge of a mound he plopped down on the wet sand, feeling the dampness through his Dockers, the box by his side. The sun was low in the sky, already moving behind the clouds. A storm was on the way. A few dedicated surfers splashed around in the choppy waves. Roger felt the chill.

For ten minutes, he watched the surfers and braced against the wind. His mind wandered across the ocean. And then he gathered up the box and headed back to the car. On the sidewalk he passed a big metal drum of a trash can. Without breaking stride he tossed the box in the trash and kept on walking.